# The Depth of Beauty

## A SINNER'S GROVE HISTORICAL NOVEL

### A.B. MICHAELS

Red Trumpet Press
P. O. Box 171162
Boise, ID 83716
www.redtrumpetpress.com

Design by Tara Mayberry
www.TeaberryCreative.com

*For those who came to this country despite the hardships,*
*determined to make their lives—and America—better.*
*And for those already here who welcomed them.*

OTHER BOOKS
BY A.B. MICHAELS

*The Art of Love*
*Sinner's Grove*
*The Lair*
*The Promise*

# ACKNOWLEDGMENTS

G reat big thank you's to my editor, Rachel Daven Skinner, and my cover and interior book designer, Tara Mayberry, for their expertise, creativity and above all, patience as they once again helped me turn the story in my head into a tangible and entertaining read.

And to Mike, my gratitude and love are boundless.

# HISTORICAL NOTE

---

T*he Depth of Beauty* is a work of fiction, but includes many historically documented characters, places, and events. Donaldina Cameron, for example, was indeed the director of the Presbyterian Mission house in Chinatown during the early twentieth century. Although reportedly condescending, she was nevertheless a fierce champion for Chinese girls and women who were exploited by their countrymen and others during that time.

The many Chinese customs depicted in the book are based on research, as is the intense discrimination levied upon the Chinese community as a whole. It's a testament to the courage and fortitude of the Chinese immigrants in America that they not only withstood the censure of those in power, but settled and raised generations of families that have become an integral part of American society today.

Finally, there really was an outbreak of Bubonic Plague in San Francisco between 1900 and 1904. Although its victims were mercifully small in number, the "Black Death" was in truth a gruesome experience, primarily because experts hadn't yet figured out the agent of the disease (fleas) nor its cure (antibiotics). The legacy of this chapter of California history remains today: every year several cases of the plague crop up in the San Francisco Bay Area, usually traced to squirrels whose ancestors caught the fleas around the time of another plague outbreak that occurred just after the Great Earthquake of 1906.

For more information about the Chinese community in San Francisco during this period, or the Plague of 1900, check out the following books:

*Unbound Feet: A Social History of Chinese Women in San Francisco* by Judy Yung

*Chinese San Francisco 1850-1943: A Trans-Pacific Community* by Yong Chen

*The Barbary Plague: The Black Death in Victorian San Francisco* by Marilyn Chase

# CONTENTS

## PART ONE
## 1903–1904

*Everything has its beauty, but not everyone sees it.*

CONFUCIUS

# CHAPTER ONE

*San Francisco, California*
*May 7, 1903*

In some circles, the very definition of tragedy can be found in the poor execution of a cream sauce.

"This simply will not do, Chef. The mornay screams ginger when it should be whispering nutmeg. And did you think to slip that cardamom by me? It conspires with the gruyere to completely overwhelm the shrimp. Whatever were you thinking? You will have to start again."

William Firestone watched from the doorway as his mother waved her hand over the offending pile of cream puffs. Chef Bertrand, normally an imposing figure in the estate's kitchen, looked at Will in supplication. Couldn't he do something?

Will shrugged. "You know how it is, Bertrand. Mother's palate rules the day."

The portly, French-trained chef turned again to his patron. "But madam, I have already had the filling inserted into the pastry. They—"

"Well, you will just have to unfill them. Or, no, better yet, you must create a new batch, of both the puffs and the sauce. I insist."

The sight of the huge man caving in deference to Will's tiny whirlwind of a mother made Will grin. Not even the city's finest creator of haute cuisine could withstand the imposing will of his little ol' ma. He had an idea to ameliorate the situation. "Tell you what. Box up the offending creatures and I will take them downtown later this afternoon. I'm sure I can give them away, and those with slightly less discerning tastes will shout your praises to the rooftops."

The chef looked at the pile with a frown. "But—"

"No buts, Chef. Willy has an excellent idea. Waste not, want not." Josephine Firestone patted Will on the shoulder (she couldn't reach his cheek) before sailing out of the kitchen.

Raising his eyebrows to signal *Accept it, that's just the way she is*, Will followed his mother out the door. He turned back briefly and gestured to the doomed appetizers. "I'll be leaving right after lunch, so if you'd be so kind…" He left the chef shaking his head, sighing in resignation.

"You will be coming to tonight's festivities, won't you, dear?" Will's mother made her request in a tone that presumed there'd be only one answer to her question. "Kit will be there, of course."

"Wouldn't miss it," Will replied, knowing his mother wouldn't catch his double meaning. No, he wouldn't miss it. Wouldn't miss this forgettable gathering, or the one next week, or the one after that. Not unless he was traveling, which he sincerely hoped he would be, soon. That was pretty much the only acceptable excuse—that, or a near-death illness—when it came to his parents' never-ending social agenda. Both he and his younger sister, Kit, had learned long ago the requirements of keeping the family peace. But Jamie, their youngest sibling, had found his own solution to the problem. Instead of attending a local college or even the Firestone alma mater of Cornell, as Will had, he'd opted for the relatively new University of Southern California. Jamie's occasional visits home were cause for celebration, and the bounder could do whatever he pleased. Smart young man.

"...and I was saying that Beatrice is such a lovely young lady. Buster Wainwright seems to think so, anyway. He's been paying quite a bit of attention lately, or so I've heard. Clarence and Dinah will have no trouble marrying her off to the highest bidder, I can tell you that."

Will realized he had completely tuned out his mother's ramblings. "What were you saying, Mother?"

Josephine looked up at him. He recognized that speculative gleam in her eye. "I was saying how gorgeous Beatrice Marshall is and that she'll be at tonight's party with her parents."

"My cup runneth over." Beatrice Marshall was a pretty young woman, in a San Francisco Brahmin kind of way. Blond and blue-eyed, like he was, her skin was the pale shade of those who avoid the outdoors as much as possible. She had a figure that, judging by her mother, would probably run to "Rubenesque" over time. For now her breasts appeared high and full, her waist small, and her hips flared to an appealing degree. Ah, but how much of that was her and how much belonged to the magicians in the City of Paris lingerie department?

"And who knows what a mild spring night might conjure up for two young people thrown together by chance?" his mother went on.

Will snorted. "Beatrice coming to the party tonight is about as serendipitous as the tides rolling in and out. I'm on to your game." Experience had taught Will that when his mother threw out accolades such as "she's such a lovely young lady," it was short-hand for "she has a pedigree worthy of the Firestone name."

"I'm sure I don't know what you're talking about." His mother grinned at him, completely unrepentant. Her smile lit up her face with such beauty that Will was convinced it wasn't her pedigree (which was formidable) but her *joie de vivre* that had captured his father's heart. "Just be there," she said crisply with another tap on his shoulder before turning down a long hallway and leaving him behind.

Will gave his mother's retreating back a mock salute. With a quick glance at his pocket watch, he headed in the opposite direction, to his father's study. The two men met weekly. Edward Firestone relied heavily on Will's business acumen to keep the family fortune intact and growing; the older man's interests tended more toward political power brokering. In that regard Will's parents were perfectly suited for one another: his father loved putting movers and shakers together, and his mother loved entertaining them. Given his family's social status, Will con-sidered such engagements a necessary evil. But sometimes he wondered: was it possible to inflict death by boredom? He loved his parents, so he put up with their requests, but it was getting more and more difficult to do.

———————⚜———————

After reviewing some investment projections with his father, Will left his parents' mansion in Pacific Heights, drove his Winton down the hill, and headed toward the Montgomery Street offices of Pacific Global Shipping, the new venture he'd started with August Wolff as part of their company, Wolfstone Enterprises. Gus and his fiancée, Lia Starling, were away on what Gus had termed a "working sabbatical" until their November wedding. Will was at the helm of Pacific Global during their absence.

Chinatown, which occupied several blocks in the heart of downtown San Francisco, stood between the tonier residential areas of the city and the financial district, where he worked. Many people found the neighborhood an inconvenient eyesore, but today Will was glad to head through it. He had to pick up some custom-made shirts, and what better place to drop off the box of leftovers Bertrand had made up for him?

It didn't matter what time of day or night, Chinatown was always teeming with people, the vast majority of them Oriental men. Dressed in their traditional black padded jackets with stand-up collars, wide-legged pants, and bowler hats, wearing soft slippers and sporting long pigtails, they looked like they had all been stamped from the same eerie mold. It was difficult to tell one from another.

Will had gotten to know a few of the more influential members of the immigrant community, however. Back in March, he and Gus had brainstormed about marketing their new shipping company to the Chinese, who were discriminated against to a sickening degree by the rest of the city's commercial elite. As a businessman, Will had never understood such behavior. A Chinaman's money was just as green as anybody else's. Why not get him to part with some of it by offering a decent service—in this case passage for him and his goods—for a reasonable price? To lay the groundwork for a marketing proposal he could sell to Pacific Global's board of directors, he'd been gathering numbers on the potential extent of the market. By and large Will had found the Chinese to be intelligent, shrewd, and more than able to hold their own in a business setting, even if they were, to coin a phrase he'd read in the paper recently, "inscrutable."

He parked in front of Suen Lok Choy's Haberdashery on Washington Street. It was located in a rough clapboard building with a precarious-looking balcony hanging over the front door. On one side stood a noodle shop that Will had never tried; on the other, a Chinese apothecary who seemed to sell an abundance of dried and withered plants.

Suen, who looked to be in his forties, was an excellent tailor. On a colleague's recommendation, Will had ordered a suit from the man. The suit fit perfectly, so today he was picking up several shirts he'd had customized to fit his tall, wiry frame. He figured Suen could also help him unload the box of leftover food, since they all seemed to be thick as thieves in this part of town. No sense having it go to waste, and there were no doubt plenty of immigrants who would love a sample of what the rest of the city ate. He figured it would put a good taste in their mouth for Pacific Global, and smiled at the pun.

"Mr. Firestone, it is pleasure to see you this fine day. How is your family?"

"Doing well, Suen, thank you." Will hefted the box onto the long service counter. He noticed with some chagrin that the bottom of the box looked damp and the smell was less than appetizing. "I was wondering if some of your people might like some food we had prepared at our home earlier today. There was...extra... and I thought I'd bring some of it to share."

"You are more than kind, Mr. Firestone." Suen opened the box and Will was appalled to see that the cheesy sauce had soaked through and seeped out of most of the cream puffs, leaving them limp and soggy. The shrimp looked like little pink lumps of a creature that had died not once but twice.

"Oh," Will said, for once at a loss for words.

Suen's reaction had been to squint and purse his lips at the offensive offering, but he quickly pasted on a smile and closed the lid back up. "No, it is fine. They look...delicious...much like our dim sum. You know dim sum, Mr. Firestone? Very tasty bites. Little plates."

Will shook his head. "No, I've never tried it. I'm sure it's delicious. Well..."

Suen took pity on him and changed the subject as he moved the box out of the way. He then reached under the counter and pulled out a package wrapped in brown paper and tied with string. "And your suit, Mr. Firestone? You still like?"

"Yes. Yes, you did a masterful job. I've gotten many compliments on it. I'm thinking I might want to order another one…in dark gray this time."

The tailor smiled, squinting again, this time with delight. "I would be most honored to create another suit for you, which will go well with your new shirts. I have your measurements already and it would be no problem. It will be ready for you in three days' time."

*He knows I'm just trying to make up for handing him a box of crap. If he can make another sale, why not?* Will smiled back. These Chinese were odd people, but they understood business, and he liked that. A lot.

He spent some time selecting a lightweight woolen fabric for the suit, took his package of shirts, and left the still-grinning Suen waving to him in the doorway. Instead of driving off, he waited a few moments in his car. A perverse part of him wanted to see what Suen would do with the cream puffs. In less than five minutes he heard a door in the alley open and shut. He waited a beat, then sauntered over to the alley entrance. Halfway down the narrow cobbled lane was a heap of garbage that had just been crowned with a box whose bottom was dark with souring mornay sauce. He watched, fascinated, as two rats scurried over to examine the contents of their latest treasure chest. They crawled into the half-opened box and quickly emerged, each with a flattened cream puff in their mouth. They looked quite happy with their discovery.

He returned to his car and headed to his office, the image of the rats stuck in his mind. An odd feeling percolated through him, and it was several minutes before he was able to identify it as shame. Had someone done to him what he had just done to his tailor, he would have been insulted, with good reason.

When it came right down to it, who were these foreigners? According to most of the papers, virtually all Chinese were disgusting, immoral heathens, living filthy lives in even filthier conditions. They were a blight on civil society and should all go back to China where they belonged.

But it didn't add up. Suen was a talented, honest tradesman. His shop was always clean, and he was more than "civilized." Was he so different from the rest of his countrymen?

Will faced the truth: he really knew nothing about these strange people. If he was going to do business with them, he'd better start educating himself…and he knew just the person to help him do it.

# CHAPTER TWO

*Mandy's Journal*
*May 13, 1903*

I think if someone ever asks me what I remember most about the day my pa died, I will have to say the way hot turned so quickly into cold. It began with an awful, sickly heat that mixed with the damp of the bay to create a glue that clung to my body and made me want to peel my shirtwaist off in front of God and everybody, just to feel cool again. I was rocking Sarah's baby Bridget on Sarah's front porch, hoping the meager shade and gentle to and fro would keep Little Bit from fussing too long before she drifted off to sleep. I remember seeing the rider barreling down the street, out of a shimmering dream, it seemed. And he was calling my name, of all things, as he headed right toward where I sat.

"Mandy! Mandy! You gotta come quick—it's your pa!" It was Jacob Turner, sweet on me since forever, shouting at me.

"Hush now, Jacob," I told him. You'll wake the baby." Only he didn't hush, but pulled sharply on the reins, causing Old Buck, who was already heaving, to rear up so he wouldn't gallop right up onto the steps.

Sarah came out from putting her twin boys down for their nap and asked what all the fuss was about. Jacob told her, "They been fellin' trees up in Sinner's Grove and one clipped Mandy's pa. He's hurt bad and he's askin' for her. Foreman says I'm to bring her straight away."

And right that second, the heat left me, and in its place came a wave of cold that traveled down my spine to settle into the core of me, icy and mean.

The next little while was a blur, riding behind Jacob on Old Buck back up the hill. We got to the building site, where the tall trees had been cut here and there to make room for the tiny houses that Mr. Wolff wanted built. Pa was lying in the back of a wagon near the office, flat on his back, and nothing moved except his head. And there wasn't any blood but a scratch on his chin, and I remember thinking, *it's not so bad.*

But it was bad, and Pa drew me down to him with just his eyes and he whispered, "My Mandy girl, I've got to leave you."

And I cried, "No, Pa—then I'm all alone. You can't leave me."

But he shook his head just a little and said, "That's the way it is, little girl. I got to go. I get to be with your sweet mama. But it ain't your time, so you gotta be strong. You remember to do what's right always and use that book learnin' you love so much to be what you want to be and do what you want to do. You keep writin' them stories about all the people and the funny things they do. You keep going. Promise me that, Mandy girl."

And the tears were runnin' down my cheeks like a flood and I wondered if there would be creases in my face, like the river carves a canyon, from so many tears.

They laid my daddy to rest two days later. They dug a grave next to my mama, and the village of Little Eden all turned out in their Sunday clothes, even though it was only Thursday. And they sang lots of hymns, but I only remember "Be Thou My Vision" and "Amazing Grace" because those had been my pa's favorites.

The heat wave ended, they told me, and that made sense because I stayed cold all through that time. My only desire was to go back to the little mud-brick house that Pa and I had lived in just on the outside of town, but Sarah and her husband Dell said no, I was too young to live by myself. It's not safe for someone who looks like you, Dell said, to be alone and unprotected. Sarah told me I was a darn good mother's helper, that I had a way with babies and little ones—Bridget and the boys loved me so much. So I could stay with them for a year or two, until I was old enough to get married and live with my man.

But I don't think Dell really wants me stayin' with them. It's just a feelin' I get. So I'm not sure what to do about it all. Right now, I wish I could just sleep for a week, and maybe when I wake up, the sadness will have found a nice comfortable chair in the back of my mind and leave me be.

# CHAPTER THREE

———————•⊷∘⊶•———————

"You're a sport to come with me, Kit." Will glanced at his sister, Katherine, who was sitting next to him on the buckboard. "I'm not looking forward to this."

Several days after their parents' last soirée, Will got the word about the accident up at The Grove. He and Kit had left early that morning for Little Eden, taking the ferry from the city across San Francisco Bay to Sausalito, then booking seats on the North Shore Railroad to Point Reyes Station. From there they'd rented a horse and wagon and were now approaching the village. Kit, as usual, looked like the perfect San Francisco socialite, despite the dusty travel conditions.

"I'm sad to say I had nothing better to do," she replied. "I swear, I ought to get married just to have something to do with my time."

"God, don't do that," Will said with mock horror. "That would give Mother twice the time to think about leg-shackling me."

Kit smiled. "You're right. Plus she'd only switch to 'baby watch' with me anyway. We can't escape it, you know. Ugh, parents."

Will's own grin died as he thought about what had led them here. "At least we have them."

"The accident wasn't your fault," Kit reminded him.

"Yes, but it happened on my watch, and now there's a little girl who's lost her daddy. What on earth am I supposed to say to her? To his wife? 'Sorry my crew killed the man of the house'? Seems rather inadequate."

"Yes, well I'm sure you're going to compensate them handily for their loss."

Will looked at her. "You really think that's going to make a damn bit of difference to them at this point?"

Kit shook her head, the honey-colored curls beneath her wide-brimmed hat swinging slightly. "No, but it will make you feel better knowing they won't end up in the poorhouse because of something you think you could have prevented…even though you couldn't have." She poked him gently on the shoulder. "Not even you, Mr. Fix-it."

Will said nothing as they rode slowly along Little Eden's main street. The community was set along the shore of Creation Bay, much smaller than San Francisco's natural harbor, but still teeming with oysters, sardines, and other seafood to satisfy the gastronomical whims of the city's restaurant patrons. It was a place for fishermen, shopkeepers, and good country folk to live and work.

They passed a number of tidy storefronts along with the bulwarks of civic virtue: a combination city hall and jail, a lending library, and a small white church. Naturally, more than one saloon was also open for business.

A few modest houses populated the far end of the street. On the front porch of one such house, a tall, thin girl stood holding a baby in her arms. She had large eyes and she watched them intently as they rode past. *She's way too young to be a mother,* he thought crossly. *What are they, cradle robbers in this town?* He paused, recognizing his pique for what it was—a defensive maneuver. Perhaps Kit would help him keep his frustration in check.

At the end of Little Eden proper, they turned onto a road that began to wind its way up the hill overlooking the village. The trees began to change from coastal oaks and smooth-skinned manzanita to Bishop pine and spruce. Finally the majestic redwoods that had drawn his business partner to the site came into view. Will could smell the sea and the evergreens. He could feel the snap in the air, as if God were saying *Stand up! Take notice! I have made few things more beautiful than this!* It felt so pristine compared to the manmade city, which made the worker's death all the more incomprehensible. How could bad things happen in such a lovely place?

The road led to the property Gus had purchased the previous year. Will glanced at his sister. "They call this place Sinner's Grove."

She shot him a devilish look. "Do tell the story behind that one."

"I don't know the details, but supposedly it involves a Catholic monk, a local girl, and some fun and frolic. Oh, and a little magic, they say."

"Hmm, I've heard with the right person, the act can be quite magical," she said wistfully.

"I'm going to cover my tender ears, sister dear. You're not supposed to even be thinking such things."

Kit busied herself smoothing her skirt. "Have I told you how glad I am that our mother can't read minds?"

Will pulled the wagon up to the small, hastily-built cabin that housed The Grove's construction office. "I wouldn't be too sure about that…but thank you for trying to distract me with such an appalling idea."

August Wolff had embarked on an ambitious, complicated project with The Grove. It consisted of a spectacular Arts and Crafts-style mansion for Gus and Lia, which would break ground once the Wolffs returned from their travels. Designed by the well-known Greene Brothers, it was destined to become a showplace of modern, comfortable living that melded perfectly with bold design. In addition, the land would encompass a year-round retreat at which artists of every style and medium could create to their hearts' content. The whole endeavor would cost hundreds of thousands of dollars, which fortunately wasn't a problem for its owners. Will had gladly volunteered to oversee the clearing of the land in preparation for construction. Now, however, he was sorry he'd botched the job.

"I'm glad you could make it so quickly." The project foreman walked up as Will settled the horses. A stocky, middle-aged man, he extended his hand in greeting.

Will hopped down and shook the man's hand. "Abe, this is my sister, Katherine Firestone. Kit, I'd like you to meet Abrahan Castro, the project foreman for The Grove."

"It's a pleasure to meet you, Mr. Castro." Kit rewarded him with one of her smiles.

Abe doffed his cap in deference. "Ma'am." He helped her down from the buggy then addressed his words to Will. "I'm having Dell bring Mandy up here in a little while. She's been staying with him and Sarah, helping Sarah mind the kids, and he wants a word with you privately before you leave."

That sounded odd. "Is there some reason why Mandy and her mother aren't staying at their own home?"

"That's a sad story," Abe said. "Come on inside and I'll put some tea on for you. Fill you in."

After they were settled, Abe continued. "There ain't no mother, for starters. Not since Mandy was five years old, poor little thing. It was just her and her dad. I'll tell you what, that Mose was one hard worker. Worked his tailbone off for that little gal. Two, three jobs sometimes. He had it in his mind that she'd go to finishing school some day and get herself married off to some fine young man." Abe chuckled. "When you meet Mandy, you'll see the folly in that. She got a mind of her own, that one. Says she wants to be a writer and tell stories about the people she meets."

Abe paused, worrying the brim of his cap. "I wouldn't put it past her, you know? There's something special about that gal.

You'll see. But now she's got nobody left in these parts, and that's a damn shame—pardon my French, ma'am."

"How did the accident happen?" Kit asked.

Abe shrugged his shoulders. "I think sometimes Fate just slaps you down. Mose was on clean-up while we was fellin' a few of the big trees. We followed the rules, if that's what you're wonderin'. Odie and Vern blew the whistle to let everybody know she was comin' down. But she had a big hefty branch you couldn't see from every angle and that's what caught Mose. Broke his neck. He didn't last long."

"Are you sure you followed all the safety precautions?" Will asked. "Because if you didn't..."

Abe looked Will straight in the eye. "As sure as I am of sittin' here with you, I know we did everything by the book. You can't predict what's going to happen in this world. No sir, you can't. Sometimes shit—pardon, ma'am—bad things happen. Or maybe it's just God's way, and who can fathom that?"

There was a knock on the door. "Come on in," Abe said.

The door opened and Dell Butler, a man who appeared to be in his mid to late twenties, stood there with the same young girl Will had noticed on the front porch earlier. He was relieved to know it wasn't her own baby she'd been holding. Because up close she looked even younger than before.

She was tall for a girl and almost skinny—gawky came to mind—with long auburn hair tied back in a braid. She wore a blue gingham dress with a white collar. It had a hem that didn't quite match. Will suspected it might have been taken from something else—a flour sack, maybe?—to lengthen the outfit. She wore white socks and old-fashioned black button shoes. In most respects she presented as a poor, awkward girl just barely out of the schoolroom.

Except for her face. It was perfectly oval with flawless skin. Her cheeks had a rosy tint to them, her lips were full, and her neck was graceful. But her eyes were the most arresting of all. They were dark and shaped like almonds, tilted up at the corners, framed by thick eyebrows that drew one's eyes toward hers. Her expression was intense; wary; knowing, but in no way cynical. Almost otherworldly. She unnerved him and he felt small for being distracted from the tragedy she was suffering through. He glanced at his sister and saw that she too was mesmerized.

"Miss Mandy, this here is Mr. Will Firestone and his sister, Miss Katherine Firestone. And they are here to see to your welfare, on account of they represent the owner, Mr. August Wolff, who owns the land your daddy died on."

"I know," Mandy said in a small, clear voice. "Dell told me. I am very pleased to meet you."

The girl had poise, he'd give her that. "How old are you, Miss Culpepper?" Will asked.

"I just turned fifteen in March, sir," she replied. "And how old might you be?"

Abe Castro looked abashed. "Now, Mandy girl, that's not a polite thing to be asking."

She looked puzzled. "Why, it must be polite, Mr. Castro, because Mr. Firestone asked it of me and he is a polite gentleman, isn't he? Aren't you, Mr. Firestone?"

Will fought hard to keep a neutral expression. This girl was a pip. "I try to be, Miss Culpepper. And to answer your question, I am twenty-seven." He looked at the others and shrugged. She had him dead to rights.

Mandy looked from one to the other but settled those enigmatic eyes on Will. "I know you and your sister are kind people who want me to have a roof over my head, and I thank you for that. But I have my own roof and I don't need another one."

"Do you mean you want to stay with Mr. and Mrs. Butler?" Kit asked.

"No, ma'am. Dell here is a good man and he wants to stay that way, and I respect him for it. I'm talking about my own house, the house my pa and me lived in for as long as I can remember."

Will shot a look at Dell, who was fidgeting like mad. *He looks like his union suit's about three sizes too small. What's his story?*

"Ah, you reckon we can talk without Mandy bein' here?" Dell asked. "I got somethin' I need to say."

Everyone looked embarrassed until Mandy spoke up. "I would like to see the spot where my pa got hit by the tree, if that's all right with you, Mr. Castro."

"You sure you want to do that, little gal?"

"Yes sir, I do." The look on the girl's face was calm, assured. She didn't look like she was going to melt any time soon. Will, on the other hand, wanted to weep for the girl who remained so composed in the face of such unbearable sadness.

Dell wasted no time after Castro and Mandy left the cabin. "I can't have her in my house," he blurted out.

Will bristled. The nerve of this man. He probably wanted money. "Look, Mr. Butler, if it's about money, I can assure you—"

"It ain't about the money, it's about the girl," he said. "Look at her, won't you? She's like a temptress—"

Kit looked at the man as if he'd gone insane. "What in the blazes are you talking about? Are you saying she's...she's..."

"... made advances toward you?" Will finished Kit's question with a dose of incredulity to match his sibling's.

"Hell, no," Dell said. "Mandy would never do such a thing. It's not in her nature. But...but I fear it may be in mine." The young man glanced at Kit, shame reddening his face. "Look, I'm a God-fearin' man. I got a pretty little wife and three good kids. But I'm human. And the Good Book says we got to keep ourselves away from temptation whenever we can. We got to put up guardrails against the Devil. I'm not sayin' Mandy's the Devil, I never would. But I'm sayin' you can't spend too much time with her and not see how doggone beautiful she is."

"For God's sake, she's just a child." Will's tone was sharper than he intended. "She's not even grown up yet."

"Exactly," Dell said. "So it'll be even worse once she gets there. She's been such a help for Sarah and the kids, and I hate like hell to lose her, but I gotta look out for me and my family."

The three of them sat there for several awkward minutes. Kit regarded Dell with a thoughtful expression. "Does your wife know you feel this way, Mr. Butler?"

"No, ma'am, she does not. She would probably kill me if she did. But Mandy does. You heard her. We've never said a word about it, but she just knows. It's spooky."

"Well, I admire you," Kit said. "You're doing what you think is best for your family, even though it's a difficult decision to make."

"So what do you intend to do about it?" Will posed the question even though he already knew the answer. Dell, like everybody else in this situation, knew that Will was responsible for what had happened to Mandy's father, and would therefore be responsible for what happened to her. The problem was, Will had no idea what to do. Which is why he was shocked by what Kit said next.

"Don't you worry, Mr. Butler. I will take responsibility for Mandy. As her new guardian, I will personally see to it that she's well taken care of. Isn't that right, Will?"

The look Kit shot him gave Will no recourse but to agree. "Uh, yes. Yes, of course."

His sister beamed. "Well, gentlemen, let's get down to details."

---

"You're daft, you know that?" Will reproached Kit the moment they returned to their buggy for the long trip home. Kit had gracefully answered every one of Mandy's concerns and assured the group that she and her brother would be back to collect the girl and her belongings in three days' time. "What the hell do you know about parenting a child?"

"First of all, Mandy's hardly a child. She's obviously able to take care of herself, for the most part. She's intelligent, she's pretty, and by all accounts she is kind. Did you hear how worried she was about who would take care of her chickens? I mean, honestly, her *chickens*!"

Will wondered briefly if Kit had any idea where her morning eggs came from. "If she's such a paragon of virtue, why on earth would she need you?"

"To help her maintain that virtue, of course. She needs someone who will take her under their wing and gently guide her into womanhood."

"You mean, *you* need someone to give you an excuse to do something other than shop your life away."

Rather than take offense, Kit nodded. "I can't argue with you there. But it's more than that. That girl has already been through more tragedy than you or I have ever dreamed of. Yet did you see her buckle or whine or curry our favor as a way out of her predicament? I didn't. In fact, she was most decidedly *against* the idea of leaving her little house. In case you've forgotten, dear brother, we're Firestones. And everyone knows the Firestones have deep pockets."

"Not everyone, apparently."

"Yes, and isn't that refreshing?" Kit had a militant gleam in her eye and her voice hummed with intensity. "That Mr. Butler is a smart young man. He knows the value of loyalty and fidelity, and he wants to keep them intact at all costs."

Kit wasn't just talking platitudes. Will remembered all too well how badly she'd been treated a few years back by a man she'd considered the love of her life. Obviously she hadn't forgotten that painful episode. Having never been stung like that, Will found it hard to fathom. "All right. You want to be a good little citizen and practice your mothering skills. But did you stop to think what our dear mother might have to say about it? I don't imagine this is what she had in mind when it comes to wanting grandchildren."

Kit hesitated, which was a bad sign because it meant she was about to spring something else on him. No matter what the activity—a shopping trip, night on the town, or new love interest—Will's sister was both methodical and purposeful. He swallowed, waiting for her next move.

She began innocently enough. "Honestly, can you imagine our mother graciously accepting little Mandy in her midst? That poor girl would be flattened by Josephine in three minutes flat." She glanced at her brother. "And it would be so nice to be out from under that termagant for a while. You know how exhausting she can be…so I thought perhaps you might take us in for a while. Your place is certainly big enough. You won't even know we're around."

*I knew it.* "Kit," he said, taking his sister's hand in both of his. "This little girl is not a plaything or an excuse to get you out of a less than desirable situation. People don't just go plucking children out of one situation and putting them in another willy-nilly. I am willing to compensate her financially, but she would be better off staying in familiar surroundings, even if it isn't with the Butlers."

Kit's eyes blazed. "Do you actually believe a girl like that will be better off in a backwater like Little Eden, when I can give her opportunities she never ever dreamed of…that her father *did* dream of? Are you that much of a mossback?"

Will stared back at her. Was he too set in his ways? First the Chinese, now this little orphan girl. Fate was intruding on his comfort zone, and in this case, at least, he wasn't happy about it. He desperately searched for some middle ground.

"You know we're going to have to track down one of her relatives, don't you? She can't stay with you...with us...indefinitely."

Kit lifted her chin slightly and smiled, no doubt savoring her little victory. Then she fussed with her dress, a sure sign she was digging in for the long haul. "We will see about that," she said.

Will almost laughed; his dear sister would be appalled to know how much like their mother she truly was. He made a mental note to begin tracking down Mandy's nearest kin, knowing it wouldn't otherwise get done. In the meantime, Kit could have her way. "You may invade my home on one condition," he said. "You take complete charge of the little sapling and keep yourself out of trouble in the bargain."

Kit sent Will a jaunty salute. "Aye aye, captain."

"Talk about treacherous waters," he murmured, giving the horses a sharp slap of the reins.

# CHAPTER FOUR

Mandy's Journal
June 4, 1903

Dear Pa,

I hope you don't mind, but I am going to pretend that I am writing you a letter, as if you were on a journey to see Mama and I was telling you about the goings-on at home so that you wouldn't be quite as homesick from so far away. I like thinking about the situation, and about you, that way.

You would be amazed at the turn my life has taken. I cannot believe that I have left Little Eden behind and am now living in San Francisco, in a fancy neighborhood called Russian Hill. I have my own room, overlooking a small backyard garden. Honestly, my room is bigger than our entire house was, Pa. The walls are painted yellow and the covering on the bed is made of silk, so very soft with colorful flowers embroidered on it. I still wrap myself up in Mama's quilt, but I wish I could wear the new bedspread, it is so lovely!

Best of all, there is a little desk in the corner, made of the most beautiful cherry wood. Miss Kit told me it is called a "secretary" and she showed me how it folds down to make a writing area with cubbyholes for paper and ink. She showed me how to lock it and even gave me the key. I never needed a key before. I'm not sure where I should keep it.

Miss Kit, whose real name is Katherine Firestone, is my guardian now. We live in the home of her brother, Mr. William Firestone. You may have met him once or twice. He is overseeing the building at Sinner's Grove. Do you remember him? He is a little taller than you, and thinner, with light wavy hair and the bluest eyes, like a summer sky. But it's hard to see them because he wears spectacles, just like Miss Kit does when she reads. Bad eyes must run in the family. By the looks of him, you might think he is a weakling, but I can tell by the way he handles the horses that he is stronger than he looks.

He is also a very smart man. He speaks like a book and he seems to know what he wants from people. I think he usually gets it, too. I will have to stay on my toes to keep up with him. Maybe I will challenge him to a game of Chicken Foot, like we used to play.

I don't know yet what makes Mr. Firestone happy, but I do know he feels terrible about what happened to you, Pa. I can see it in his eyes every time he looks at me. He feels such guilt—as if he knows he should have done something to prevent it, which is silly, because he wasn't even there when it happened. He doesn't know what we know about things like that.

Miss Kit is truly the reason I am here. I wanted so very much to stay in our little house, Pa. I miss it so much. Or maybe I miss it because when I lived there I lived with you. Well, I don't know how she knew it, but she reminded me that you always wanted me to go to finishing school, and that living here on Russian Hill would let me do that. In fact, I am already enrolled in the Weems Academy and will start going there next week. I will be practicing all those things you wanted so much for me to learn, Pa: how to sit right and eat right and even dance. Miss Kit said I could learn to speak another language, and the best part is that I will take a class in which we read important books and write what we think about them.

I think Miss Kit is a good person, but she worries about things that seem unimportant to me, like wearing certain clothes or styling her hair a particular way. I think maybe there is a hole in her that she is trying to fill.

Why have things turned out this way, Pa? Is it just chance that a tree fell over on you and took you away from me? Serendipity that I should now be doing the very thing you always wanted me to do? Did God do this? If He did, I think He could have found a less hurtful way to go about it.

The only thing I know right now is that I cannot simply take from these nice people. I will find a job—somehow—and save my money and repay them as soon as I am able. I know that is what you would want me to do, and it feels right that I should do it.

I love you, Pa. Give Mama a big kiss and a hug for me and tell her I love her, too. I miss you both so very much. I am trying not to cry about it, but it is hard.

# CHAPTER FIVE

"My life has become a renegade corset that's beginning to crush the life out of me," Kit complained to Will. "I'm sure I've passed eighteen inches and I'm about to pass out."

Will held back a smile as he sipped his black coffee. Leave it to his sister to explain her latest conundrum in terms of fashion. "What's got you in a bind this time, Kit?" They were having breakfast in the sunroom overlooking the garden. The fog was light this morning; it would probably burn off by noon. Fleming, Will's major domo, had just left to drop off Kit's ward at the Weems Academy. It was the girl's second week at school. "Wait. Let me guess. Mandy refuses to wear the dresses you've selected for her."

"If only it were that simple," Kit said. "No, she's perfectly agreeable to looking the part of a proper young lady as befits the ward of a Firestone. But she insists that she must work, part-time at least, to help defray costs."

"That is ridiculous." Will took another sip and went back to the morning's headlines. "Massive Clean-Up Program Finally

Underway in Chinatown—Rodents in the Crosshairs" dominated above the fold. "I know, we can get her a job catching rats."

Kit glared at him. "That is not funny. I'm telling you, Mandy feels very strongly about this. She has mentioned it often, and I am afraid if we don't accommodate her in some fashion, she will simply go about doing it on her own."

"I'll take it under advisement," Will said. "If that's all that's bothering you, then by all means, let your laces out."

"I would if I could. But our dear old mama is truly putting the squeeze on me. She insists I move back home and that I board 'the little waif,' as she calls her, with some servant or tradesman's family."

"That is not going to happen," Will said without hesitation. "That girl is much too intelligent to spend her life cleaning bathrooms or stitching garments." He peered at Kit. "You told Mother as much, I hope."

She sent him a self-satisfied grin. "Ah, so you have come to see the situation from the proper perspective."

"After a fashion." He put down his paper. "But don't forget what I told you. Mandy belongs with her own family, not stuck with ours. I've already engaged a private detective to look into the matter."

"Says you." Kit wiped her lips primly with a napkin, then rose from the table, swishing her skirts. She ignored his remark about the detective. "Either you must find Mandy something that enables her to feel her worth, or I will."

"I'll look into it." Will removed his eyeglasses and wiped the lenses on the hem of the table cloth, sending a prayer of thanks that he was no longer subject to his mother's censure about such an "uncouth act." He put the spectacles back on and noticed Kit looking at him with skepticism. "No, truly, I will," he assured her. "In the meantime, try not to push Mother's nose out of joint with this guardianship business. No need to stir up trouble."

"Heaven forbid I should do anything to upset the hornet's nest." Kit put a hand on her stomach and inhaled deeply. Will chuckled and she shot him another glare. "I'd like to see *you* wear one of these," she challenged before leaving the room.

"Heaven forbid," Will answered jovially, and finished his coffee before heading downtown.

---

"I say to you, if there is a living embodiment of the saying 'killing with kindness,' Dr. Blue is it." Cheung ti Chu, a prominent member of the Chinese Consolidated Benevolent Society, known around the city as the Six Companies, waved his chopsticks at Will for emphasis. They were having lunch in a dim sum shop on Jackson Street.

"Come on, it can't be that bad." Will was distracted by the next cart the waiter had wheeled over for their perusal. Shortly after his debacle with the cream puffs, he'd made a point to get to know the real Chinatown, starting with its food. He kicked himself for not trying their cuisine earlier. It was delicious.

"You like more?" the waiter asked.

"Afraid so." Will pointed to a small plate with two objects on it. "What are those?"

"*Ha gow* with prawn."

"Prawn dumplings? Excellent, I haven't tried those yet. Oh, and I'll have a couple of the *char siu bao* as well."

The waiter plopped two sticky pork buns on the table and, waved away by Cheung, rolled the cart over to the next diner.

Cheung grinned and pointed to the plates stacking up on Will's side of the table. "Keep that up and you will look like Buddha." He took a sip of hot green tea and grew serious. "For your information, the so-called clean-up campaign *is* that bad—and for what? To eradicate a plague that does not exist."

Will stopped eating and looked squarely at his colleague. "You know it exists, Cheung. Trying to cover it up cost Governor Gage his re-election. And poking your head in the sand isn't going to make it go away. Besides, what's wrong with a little 'Chinatown Beautification Project'? I'd think your people would welcome it."

"Oh, you think so? Finish up, my friend. I will take you on a little tour and you can see for yourself."

Will had met Cheung months before but had only recently put in the effort required to build a working friendship with men like him who could educate Will about the Chinese culture. Cheung was low-hanging fruit in that regard: the son of a wealthy Chinese family, he spoke nearly perfect English and had been educated in the United States for the express purpose of improving the immigrant bridge between East and West. He was in his mid-forties, with a high forehead and a slight paunch, and although he hadn't mentioned a wife, the man never complained about lack of female companionship—and that was something, considering the astronomically high ratio of Chinese men to women in Chinatown. There was a certain arrogance to him, as if he full well understood the unique role he played within the two cultures. But he was likable, for all that, and had the power to launch or sink Will and Gus's shipping venture, at least in terms of the Chinese market.

The two men finished their meal and set out on foot toward Washington Street by way of Dupont, the area's main thoroughfare. Capitalism, Will noticed, was thriving here. The bustling street was crowded with storefronts: laundries and tailor shops and dry goods stores and bakeries. Cheung stopped briefly at a jewelry store to pick up a small package and they continued on.

From their awnings or the rims of overhanging balconies, butchers hung slabs of fresh beef alongside haunches of smoked pork, ready to be sliced for the next customer. A young boy sat on a stool outside a shop plucking a duck's feathers, soon to hang with other carcasses on display. Fishmongers offered barrels of live crab, sea bass, and the catch of the day, while grocers hawked fresh squash, eggplant, cabbage, and melon. Bins filled with sinister looking roots stood next to containers of equally mysterious grasses and herbs. Will thought he recognized the ginger, but he doubted if even Chef Bertrand would know what to do with the rest of them. He wondered which of them he had already eaten without even knowing it. He couldn't even identify the smells. They assaulted him: sweet, smoky, earthy. The pungent aromas were shadowy and musky. They were *foreign*.

Taller than most of the people he passed, Will noticed that many of the Chinese looked at him with distrust in their eyes. He felt like odd man out in his western-style suit and collar-length hair. It was an unsettling sensation. The thought crossed his mind: *this must be what the Chinese feel like when they aren't in Chinatown.*

Cheung didn't seem to notice Will's discomfort. "How do you like Fung Hai? He hasn't been an interpreter long, but I believe he has the knack for it."

"Yes, he's quite good," Will said. "Thank you for recommending him. He knows Chinatown inside and out, it seems. He's particularly fond of the Mission House."

"Well, I give him high marks for putting up with the Angry Angel. Miss Cameron is a very attractive woman and does good work, but she can be a viper and that does not sit well with some in my community. She is going to get hurt one of these days. Mark my words."

Will was about to respond when the two of them, having reached the corner of Dupont and Washington, heard angry shouts coming from the area in front of Suen Lok Choy's tailor shop. Suen and his next-door neighbors were huddled together talking in rapid-fire Cantonese and gesturing to a team of three burly white workers who had arrived in a wagon carrying a large industrial pump. Ignoring the Chinese men's chatter, the workers dragged a long hose attached to the pump and set it up at the entrance to Suen's store. One of the men tightened a nozzle at the end of the hose.

"I could not have timed it better," Cheung said with grim satisfaction in his voice. "You are about to witness what you barbarians consider a 'beautification' project."

He walked up to Suen and the other distraught shopkeepers, talking to them in reassuring tones. They stood by while the white workers turned on the pump and aimed the hose into the shop. The sound was deafening, but the smell was worse, as if one had fallen into a giant vat of vinegar.

"What are they doing?" Will shouted over the din.

"Spraying carbolic acid to kill the rats," Cheung explained. "Charming, isn't it? But that is just the beginning. Come back in a few hours and you will likely see a pot of sulfur cooking inside. After that they will sprinkle chlorinated lime. One cannot even breathe the air when that happens."

Suen hurried over to Will. "Mr. Firestone, I am so sorry. I did not know they or you were coming today! Your suit ready, but it is inside and…"

"Don't worry about it, Suen. I can stop by later to pick it up."

Suen turned to the Six Companies representative with a look akin to panic.

"He is trying to tell you the suit is ruined," Cheung said. "As is most of the merchandise in his shop. The vapors soak into the fabric and despite many washings, you will still be able to smell it. I cannot imagine you relish reeking of rotten eggs."

"And this is happening in other places?" Will asked.

"All over Chinatown. Can you see why my people are up in arms about it? It's not enough that you squeeze us into fifteen blocks and tell us we cannot expand, despite our population growth. You tell us we cannot work at jobs that pay enough to improve our conditions. You pass a flurry of laws that treat us like dirt. But even dirt has a certain dignity about it. Now you are treating us like vermin to be exterminated."

Will recalled the rodents who had gorged themselves on his mother's spoiled cream puffs. The pests existed, there was no getting around it. He'd recently met Rupert Blue, the head quarantine officer in San Francisco, at one of his parents' fundraisers. According to Blue, it was a veritable war.

For the past three years, rumors of bubonic plague—the Black Death—had swirled around the city. Federal quarantine officers had diagnosed the plague in several Chinese patients and ordered quarantines of the entire community, forbidding the immigrants to leave Chinatown or any non-Chinese to come in. Those restrictions had caused untold hardship for both groups. Chinatown power brokers, like the Chinese consul general and the Six Companies, had formed an uneasy alliance with the city and state governments to fight the restrictions and dispel the plague rumors. Both sides were motivated: the Chinese thought the plague a convenient excuse to run them out of the country, and the whites, well, it boiled down to money. Shipping was the lifeblood of San Francisco's economy. If the world thought there was plague similar to the recent Hong Kong epidemic, commerce between California and the rest of the world would grind to a halt. The enemy, in this case, wasn't so much the plague-bearing rats as the quarantine officers who wanted to wage a full out eradication campaign against the pestilence. It looked like the feds were winning this round.

"I know Rupert Blue," Will said. "Maybe he can do something to lessen the impact on businesses around here."

"I doubt it. In fact, from what I've heard, it's going to get worse before it gets better." Cheung waved his hand dismissively.

"Never mind. There is someone I want you to meet before we part company."

They cut through Waverly Place onto Clay, where Cheung stopped in front of a small, well-maintained apartment house. He rang one of several bells denoting the different addresses. In a few minutes a teenage girl answered, dressed in a plain, traditional Chinese outfit of high collared tunic and pants. A much smaller child, a girl who looked to be about four or five, clung to the older girl's pant leg. Cheung leaned in and whispered something into the older girl's ear, touching her familiarly on the shoulder. She looked embarrassed and turned to go back inside. A few moments later she came back shaking her head, speaking in low tones. "Nonsense," Cheung said. He turned to Will. "Wu Jade says her mistress, the widow Tam Shee Low, is too indisposed to meet anyone today." He pushed open the door. "But she'll see us."

As they walked up the stairs, Cheung explained who they were visiting. "Tam Shee has only been here a few months. Her husband owned a lumberyard and was able to bring her, their daughter Sai-fon, and Wu Jade from China under the merchant exclusion. But he died in a mill accident a month ago, so she's on her own, poor little thing."

Wu Jade opened the door to the apartment and stood to the side, holding on to the hand of the little girl as Will and Cheung filed past. Glancing back as he entered the small parlor, Will noticed the older girl was stone-faced, but the little one smiled at him. He turned back and instantly forgot both girls, because he came face to face with one of the most exotic creatures he had ever seen.

Tam Shee Low sat on an upholstered chair by the far window, with a large piece of fabric on her lap, part of which was ensnared by an embroidery hoop. The light had caught her face in just the right perspective to highlight her alabaster skin, soulful dark eyes, and perfectly shaped lips. Her ebony hair was coiled partially on top of her head, but a long skein of it trailed across one shoulder and down the front of her silk jacket. She was petite and quite young—couldn't have been much older than Kit—which meant she must have been married *very* young to have a five-year-old running around. Along one wall there was a simple table which looked like a kind of altar. A small painting of a man in his early forties—her husband? Her father?—was surrounded by candles and small dishes with bits of food on them. On the wall next to the table a small photograph of a proud-looking young man had been tacked up as if it were waiting for a proper frame.

Cheung bowed, oblivious to the shocked and embarrassed look the widow was sending him. He spoke to her in Cantonese, hopefully apologizing for the intrusion. She was obviously not expecting company, nor did she desire it.

Tam Shee glanced up at Will and her look spoke volumes. As bad as it was to be caught unawares by Cheung, it was apparently mortifying to be caught by a stranger, and a westerner to boot.

Cheung finally noted her reaction and spoke to her again in her language. The only words Will understood were "Will Firestone."

"I told her you were a friend to the Chinese here in the Big City, and that she needn't be afraid of you," Cheung relayed.

*By all means, don't be afraid of me,* Will found himself think-ing. *Let me get to know you better.* He shoved his wayward thoughts aside and executed a small bow. "I am very pleased to meet you, Tam Shee."

"Her English is not good," Cheung said. "I have taught her some, but she is very traditional, very proper—the ideal woman in my culture."

*In mine, too,* Will thought.

Cheung reached into his pocket and pulled out a small pack-age, which he handed to Tam Shee. She proceeded to unwrap it and pulled out a long chain of delicate jade beads. Will could tell she admired it but knew it would be improper to accept it. She re-wrapped the necklace and offered it back to Cheung, who refused to take it. He spoke with a slight edge to his voice, and she nodded, quietly putting the gift on the table next to her chair. Cheung bowed again and turned to leave, but Will stopped him.

"Ask her what she is sewing," he suggested. "It's very beauti-ful and you should complement her on it."

Cheung nodded. "Good idea." He turned to Tam Shee and spoke rapidly, pointing to her handiwork and gesturing to Will, as if to tell her that both he and Will admired her work. The woman looked at Will with a shy expression and held it up so that he could see it better. She was creating an intricate floral design in the center of what looked to be a small tablecloth. His mother would adore it.

"Ask her if she is creating that for someone special," Will said, "or if she would be willing to part with it."

Cheung translated and Tam Shee looked up at Will in surprise. She answered Cheung in sweet, quiet tones, to which Cheung responded rapidly.

"Tell her I would like to purchase it for my mother."

Cheung translated again and Tam Shee bestowed an incredible smile on Will.

"You're in luck. She's willing to sell. She said she would like three dollars for it, but I told her you would not pay any less than ten." Cheung grinned like a carnival huckster.

"Ten it is." Will couldn't take his eyes off the young woman. "When will it be ready?"

Cheung asked and Tam Shee responded. "Four days' time," he said. He bowed to Tam Shee once more and turned again to leave. "Let's go," he said to Will.

They reached the street and Will brought up a question that had been bothering him. "How is Wu Jade related to the family?"

"Wu Jade is what we call a *mui tsai*, a 'little sister' of sorts."

"Her sister." Will nodded. "That makes more sense. Tam Shee didn't look old enough to be Wu Jade's mother."

"No. She is not a true sister. She is more like a…a servant."

"Ah. Well, it's kind of you to stop by and see them. Tam Shee must be lonely, being new to the country and all, and recently widowed. She could probably use a friend."

"Oh, I intend to be more than that," Cheung said. "I have a wife and children in China and my wife has no interest in moving here. So I am going to make Tam Shee Low my second wife. She is worthy of the honor."

Will could barely hide the shock on his face. He'd heard about polygamy among the Chinese, but since there were so few immigrant women around, he hadn't really thought it an issue. "What...I mean, what about...don't you see other women?"

Cheung scoffed. "I try to stay away from the brothels—too much disease. But I do have relations with a few white women— you would be amazed at how much they enjoy my queue." He smirked, tugging at his long, Manchurian-style braid. "And there is the occasional mui tsai. But taking Tam Shee as my concubine, along with Wu Jade, seems to be quite efficient, don't you agree? I won't even have to leave the house for variety."

Will found it difficult to keep the scorn out of his voice. "Why did you want me to meet her, Cheung? She was obviously embarrassed by our visit."

Cheung looked at him coyly. "Tam Shee is a lotus-foot woman, and once she is mine, she will no longer be accepting visits from other men. I wanted you to see my beautiful prize and know what awaits me behind closed doors."

Will left Cheung at the corner and walked back to his parked car, lost in sober thought. He was between mistresses at the moment, but he'd had several over the years. How many of them were respectable women who had fallen on hard times, like Tam Shee Low? Had he even questioned what had led the women he'd kept to join the world's oldest profession? No, he'd simply taken them at face value, enjoying their delectable bodies and shallow banter for the entertainment and physical release they provided him. He tried consoling himself with the fact that he wasn't married, that he would never cheat on his wife once he did settle down. But in Cheung ti Chu's culture, multiple partners were apparently acceptable. So taking that off the table, how was he any different than Cheung? Considering how attracted they both were to Tam Shee Low, he had no answer, and the fact that he had no answer disturbed him greatly.

---

A week later, Will left his office early to send an all's well cable to Gus. He then stopped at his home on Russian Hill to change for another small dinner party at his parents' estate—"small" in his mother's parlance meaning a mere thirty people.

Thankfully, Beatrice and her parents weren't on the guest list this time around. Bea was a nice enough woman, but at the last soirée he'd run out of things to say fairly quickly and had therefore been obliged to participate in a ridiculous game of charades, orchestrated by Kit. Given his current attitude, he'd probably make a regrettable scene if forced to endure a similar waste of time.

He was in for a pleasant surprise. His father sat on the boards of several prominent companies and knew just about every political player in town. Tonight's guest list included a number of individuals invested in the recent Chinatown clean-up efforts. With his usual sly sense of humor, Edward had invited men on both sides of the issue. Missing, Will observed, were any Chinese.

"This notion of cleaning out the infected areas is a farce," Bill Bunker proclaimed as the gentlemen were enjoying *Romeo y Julieta* cigars and port after dinner. Bunker represented the San Francisco Chamber of Commerce in Washington D.C. He was back in town for an update on the plague situation. A born lobbyist, he enjoyed hobnobbing with the rich and famous on both coasts.

"Oh, so you agree with the Six Companies that the methods are draconian?" Will asked.

"Hell no, I think they're woefully inadequate," Bunker said. "Look, the rest of the country—and the world, for that matter—thinks we had the plague. Thinks we still have it, and that it's lurking beneath the rotting floorboards of Chinatown flophouses, just waiting to bust wide open and cause a pandemic. Half my job is spent fending off threats of quarantine and boycotts by other states and countries. The only way to dispel that notion, thoroughly, is to tear it all down."

"Tear what down?" Dr. Donald Currie was a public health officer and assistant to Rupert Blue in the Marine Hospital Service, run by the federal government. The earnest Dr. Currie was no match for these bullies, but since his boss had ordered the clean-up, he was going to have to take the heat.

"Chinatown. All fifteen filthy blocks of it," Bunker said. He took a moment to puff on his cigar. "Raze it to the ground. Move the Chinks out to Butchertown, south of the city. Make a clean sweep of it and the fears about that cesspool will go away."

"Now, Bill, your worries about our city's economic health wouldn't have anything to do with the prime downtown real estate that Chinatown sits on, would it?" Edward Firestone wasn't a talker (he left that to Will's mother), but when he did speak, he usually hit the target dead on. Will grinned along with the others in the group.

"You laugh, but the numbers don't lie," Bunker persisted. "A thirty-day quarantine for our city would cost us more than taking Chinatown down to the ground, and that's the truth." Bunker pointed his cigar at Currie. "It's just a shame the mayor and the governor caved to you federal meddlers."

"If it's any consolation," Currie said, "we're starting the demolition phase as soon as we begin to rein in the rat population."

"Demolition?" Will asked. "I thought—"

"No, no, I'm sorry. I don't mean what Mr. Bunker is advocating. I meant simply cleaning out the structures that typically house the rodents. Chinatown will be much more attractive once the clean-up occurs, and we should be well on our way to eradicating the cause of the disease."

Bunker threw out a final salvo. "You wanna get rid of the disease, get rid of the coolies," he said.

"And on that charming note, I suggest we rejoin the ladies," Edward Firestone pronounced, rising from his chair.

---

A stimulating evening for a change, Will thought as he drove home later that night. He was beginning to see the "Chinatown problem" from a different perspective. He'd already heard tales about the locals hiding bodies from quarantine officers like Currie so that plague numbers dropped and the scare would be downplayed. That was incredibly dangerous for both the Chinese and the rest of the city's residents. But advocating the complete destruction of Chinatown simply because of the people who lived there? That was downright barbaric. Who were the real villains here? Who were the heroes? It was hard to tell one from the other.

Will's thoughts strayed to Tam Shee, as they had off and on throughout the evening. She was unlike any woman he had ever met. She didn't put her beauty purposefully on display, like so many women of his acquaintance did. Yet it was there for anyone to see, as if she were a priceless marble sculpture come to life.

He had to find a way to get to know her. It would help him understand the Chinese people better, wouldn't it? It was good for business and besides, he needed to counteract the bigotry of men like Bill Bunker, didn't he?

Well, didn't he?

# CHAPTER SIX

Mandy's Journal
June 30, 1903

Dear Pa,

My new life is going well. I attend the Weems Academy each weekday until two in the afternoon, even though it is summer. If we were in Little Eden it would be torture. The sun would be warm and I would want to climb right out of my proper dress, race down to Paradise Beach, and jump right in. But here in the city it is cold and foggy most days, so I don't mind bundling up. Besides, the Weems Academy motto is "Learning Should Never Stop."

Our instructors, Miss Thorpe and Miss Rodham, are two older ladies who have never married. They teach us such rules as how to sit properly with our backs straight and our limbs together, and which forks to use when dining. By the way, they say we should use the word "limbs" instead of "legs" and "dining" instead of "eating." They explained that legs are too "carnal" and eating is something only animals do. I happened to ask during the lesson on eating if we humans weren't animals, too. They said my question was "inappropriate." Miss Thorpe and Miss Rodham use that word a lot with me. For example, they say it is inappropriate for me to refer to you as "pa." The words "father," "papa," "pater," and even "daddy" are much preferred in polite society, they say. That seems wasteful to me: why use a two-syllable word when you can use just one? They remind me somewhat of Beulah and Cathy—do you remember our two oldest hens? The way they would strut about, almost rooster-like, and pick at the corn meal on the ground as if testing to see if it were up to their standards? Sometimes I find it hard not to smile when I make the comparison between them.

Three days a week we study French, and on Tuesdays after class we have a dancing lesson with Mr. Longmire. His name suits him. He is very tall and so slender, I wonder what he eats (I mean, "dines on"). He is very agile on his feet, though, and he delights in the music. "It is transporting," he tells us girls. Being tall, I am often instructed to take the lead with my partner (usually Miss Lucy Stanton), as if I were the male. Honestly, I like being in control. Why should the man always have to take on that role?

You will be happy to know I even wrote a story about it. I call it "Beulah Takes Over." It tells about how the rooster—I am calling him Rodney now, but that may change—gets a severe sore throat and can't crow to wake up the barnyard. So Beulah takes over and does a fine job of it. But when Rodney is all better, he wants his old job back. The problem is, Beulah likes doing what she's been doing and refuses to step down. A major argument among all the barnyard animals takes place, pretty much the men versus the women. And in the end they compromise and divide the job between them, so that Rodney can get more sleep and not get sick, and Beulah can feel useful. I like the way it turns out.

Speaking of males in control, I am frustrated in my search to find part-time employment. Miss Kit has assured me that Mr. Firestone is looking into it for me. She seems to understand that I need to do something productive that I can be paid for so I can help pay at least part of my way. I have decided to give my guardian's brother one more day to come up with something or I will have to confront him about it. Currently he pays no attention to me, as if I didn't exist. But that, I'm afraid, is going to have to change.

# CHAPTER SEVEN

W ill had arranged to pick up Fung Hai, the interpreter Cheung had recommended to him. Fung had been converted to Christianity as a boy back in Guangdong Province. He'd learned to speak English from the missionaries and volunteered to teach it to new residents at the Presbyterian Mission House whenever the need arose. Today the young man was teaching such a class and was running late.

No matter. Will had some questions for the mission's director. He'd met Donaldina Cameron on numerous occasions; she wasn't afraid to mingle with society if it meant garnering more financial support for her cause. Saving poor Chinese girls from the evils of prostitution was her passion. He admired both her boldness and her tenacity.

As predicted, he found her hard at work in her office. She was a "no-nonsense miss" in her mid-thirties who had chosen urban missionary work over a traditional life of marriage and family. Will agreed with Cheung that she was attractive, but she was severe-looking, and her attitude only sharpened that impression.

Her work space was tidy and efficient, like the woman her-self. Papers were stacked in neat piles along with ledgers, an ink-well, several nibs, and a well-thumbed Bible. But something else caught Will's eye: a small pistol lying next to the director's purse. Had she ever used it? In their official capacities, she and Cheung interacted quite a bit; perhaps there was good reason Cheung had called her the "Angry Angel."

Will decided to get right to the point. "What do you know about Tam Shee Low?"

Donaldina looked at him in surprise. "How do you know about her?"

"I met her through Cheung ti Chu, and I must say he was rather pushy about it. He seemed to be showing her off."

"Consider yourself privileged, then. You rarely see lotus-foot women like Tam Shee in public. It's too difficult for them."

"What do you mean, 'too difficult'? Is there something wrong with her?"

"Most definitely. Tell me, did she stand up to greet you?"

Had she? No, she'd remained seated the entire time. "No. And what do you mean by 'lotus-foot'? Cheung used that term as well. I thought it signified a married woman."

"How I wish that were true. Tam Shee has bound feet, Mr. Firestone. Do you know what those are?"

"I've heard of them. I thought perhaps they wrapped cloth around their feet to hide them. I know my feet aren't that thrilling to look at," he joked.

"No, they wouldn't be if at the age of four, your arches had been purposefully broken and your toes forced to curl under until the length of each foot was barely four inches long."

*What the devil?* Will felt his stomach turn over. "Who would do such a barbaric thing?"

Donaldina smiled faintly. "Funny you should use that expression. That's what they call non-Chinese like us."

"I don't understand."

"Why should you? The Chinese probably don't understand it either, but they do it just the same. It's been a tradition for centuries. It's a sign of wealth, beauty, and gentility. When a man sees that a woman is lotus-footed, it tells him she is obedient and likely chaste. She can't easily run away from him, you see. Those are signs of superior quality in a woman. God forbid she should *choose* to have those characteristics. No, they must be imposed upon her as a mere child who can only understand the pain of having her feet systematically broken over time. Tell me, did you notice if Tam Shee had a young girl waiting on her?"

Will was trying to process what he'd just learned. He nodded absently. "Yes. Wu Jade. She looks about fifteen or so. Cheung said she was a kind of servant."

Donaldina snorted. "Hardly. Wu Jade isn't a servant who can change jobs if she wants to. She's a mui tsai. *A slave.* She was probably sold to Tam Shee's family by a poor couple back in China."

"Wait a minute," he said. "Slavery in America was abolished decades ago."

"Not in the Chinese community. They come over here disguised as family members, but they're slaves, all right, and there's nothing we can do about it, short of what we...do about it."

"So you're telling me the girls Fung Hai is teaching right now are ex-slaves?"

"Some of them, and some of them are 'thousand men's wives.' A few of them, sad to say, have been both."

Cheung's parting words flashed across Will's mind. *I won't even have to leave the house for variety.* The presumption of the man was appalling. In that moment, Will resolved to do something about it.

"Cheung seems to think he can easily take Tam Shee Low for a second wife. Is that true?"

"I'm loathe to say it, but he's probably the best she can do at this point. If she returns home, she'll not be allowed to marry again or return to her original family's home. She might in fact be forced to become a concubine of her father-in-law, especially if her husband was the only son. She would likely feel honor-bound to bear a replacement heir for the family. So yes, I would say that if Cheung makes her an offer, she'd do well to accept it."

"But he says he already has a wife and children back in China."

Donaldina merely shrugged.

The wheels were turning in Will's head. "What if she could afford to remain on her own, financially, I mean?"

With something akin to pity, Donaldina turned her gaze on him. "You aren't thinking of taking her as your mistress, are you, Mr. Firestone?"

Will looked at her in shock. "No, of course not!" *Or was he?* He didn't even know where his thoughts were taking him at that point, only that he couldn't let such a lovely woman, a woman who was meant to lead a life of dignity, fall so low. "What I meant was, perhaps she can work, earn a living..."

"She was not raised for work like the rest of us, sir. Walking is no doubt painful for her. She can't go to the market, or stand on her feet in a factory, or scrub clothes. You mentioned embroidery. That's practically all such women can do."

Embroidery. Tam Shee excelled at it. He'd seen her work and it was exemplary. Imagine the number of ladies who would like customized embroidery for their handkerchiefs, their table-cloths, their sheets? A market existed for that kind of thing, he was sure of it.

"I have an idea, Miss Cameron. Hear me out."

---

"I must say, when you decide you wish to do something, you do not waste time," Donaldina remarked an hour later. "I'll pay a visit to Tam Shee Low first thing in the morning. If her work is as exceptional as you say it is, I will offer her the opportunity to become head instructor of the new Chinatown School of Needle Arts. As a lotus-foot woman, she will be looked up to by the other girls. I'll find her a suitable space that doesn't require excessive walking on her part. Perhaps she can even live on the school premises. Hopefully she'll see this as a way out of her dilemma."

Will heard Fung Hai's voice in the hallway and knew the young man would be waiting patiently for him. "And we're agreed you'll present it as a new program of the mission and leave my endowment out of it, correct? Once it's established, we'll attach Pacific Global Shipping's name to it as sponsor, but right now I don't want to irritate Cheung ti Chu any more than necessary."

Donaldina squared her shoulders. "There is also the matter of her mui tsai to be considered. I cannot in good conscience leave Wu Jade vulnerable to the likes of Cheung. He may have already taken advantage of her."

"I tell you what. Present it to Tam Shee that she must give Wu Jade her freedom but that the headmistress position includes an 'assistant.' Wu Jade will most likely want to stay on, but at least she'll have a choice in the matter. Something tells me you excel at convincing these young girls they don't have to put up with men like Cheung."

"You'd be surprised at how difficult it is sometimes." Donaldina pulled a sheet of paper from a stack on her desk. "This is a list of the girls who have either returned to their immoral occupations by choice or been spirited away. Some of them simply cannot buck the traditions of their homeland. They are caught in the trap of filial loyalty and family pride. Others, especially the more experienced prostitutes, are too valuable to their tong masters—their procurers, if you will—to leave the trade. It's a constant struggle."

Unbidden, the thought of Mandy having nowhere to go and being forced into such horrific circumstances caused his gut to clench. He remembered the promise he'd made his sister to find her ward a part-time job.

"One more thing, Miss Cameron," he said.

# CHAPTER EIGHT

*Mandy's Journal*
*July 7, 1903*

Dear Pa,

I am on top of the world! My guardian's brother did something wonderful for me. He got me a job! Miss Kit kept her promise and so did Mr. Firestone, without me having to confront him. He asked around and lo and behold, I am to be the new historian at the Presbyterian Mission House in Chinatown. I will be interviewing the girls who live there and talking to them about where they came from and what their lives are like and why they are at the mission.

You might be wondering how I can do that since I can't speak Chinese. But they have thought of that and are letting me use an interpreter. His name is Fung Hai and he is a very nice young man, maybe four or five years older than me. He learned how to speak English at a mission in China. He is a firm believer in the Lord, Pa, which is nice, but I am already learning that being Chinese and being Christian don't often go together.

It *should* go together, according to Miss Cameron. She is the director of the mission and she is a real firebrand! She believes the Chinese are heathen and their best chance for a place in heaven is to accept Jesus. I have my own thoughts on that, as you know. I can't see how the good Lord is going to bar the door for all those people who just missed hearing about Jesus in their lifetime because they lived out in the countryside or the desert or the jungle and never had a chance to get to know Him. I think God has a plan for them too.

But I think Miss Cameron has more on her mind than just serving up the Lord. She wants to take these girls out of situations that are truly the worst they could possibly be. Why, some of these girls have been slaves. I am not making that up. Slaves! They came to our country not even knowing that we got rid of slavery almost forty years ago. So Miss Cameron steals them away from where they're being held and she brings them to a safe place where they can learn English and learn a trade. She has a new program, called the Chinatown School of Needle Arts, where the girls, these ex-slaves along with some fallen women (they must have been slaves of another sort), are going to learn how to embroider beautiful pictures with thread. It is an admirable thing Miss Cameron is doing.

Miss Kit continues to be so nice to me. She looks after me without smothering me. She says she knows what that feels like from her own mother and she wouldn't wish that on anybody. I want to tell her that she should take a moment to thank the good Lord she even has a mother, even though the woman might be a bit too "mothery" (is that a word?) now and then. I would love to say, "Oh, my mother is so overbearing!"

Her and Mr. Firestone's mother's name is Josephine, and she and their father, Edward, live in another mansion on another hill. I have never met them. I don't think Mrs. Firestone wants to meet me. I think she wonders why her daughter is spending time being a mother when she isn't even married. Really, Miss Kit is more like a big sister to me, but I think her mother has a point. In fact, it is the only sore spot in my new life—other than being away from you and Mama, of course. That is why I am so happy to have a job and be able to repay Miss Kit and her brother in some fashion, for helping me when they have no earthly reason to. And to be able to repay them by doing something I love? That truly makes me the luckiest girl in the world.

# CHAPTER NINE

E vents moved so quickly that Will was convinced he'd made the right decision. Donaldina soon found the right location for the school on Stockton Street. On one side of the building stood a lumberyard, and on the other, a residence for "virtuous young women." *Perfect.*

The building had a storefront on the ground floor, and it was a simple matter to remove non-load-bearing walls upstairs to create a big enough classroom space for the apprentice needle workers. Large windows overlooked a walled garden, the ideal place for Sai-fon to play. The light transmitted by the windows was warm and bright; Tam Shee told Fung she was pleased her students wouldn't have to strain their eyes to make the very small stitches her designs required.

To the left side of the new classroom was a small apartment, where Tam Shee had already moved in with Sai-fon and Wu Jade. Mere steps from the classroom, it offered the perfect solution to the widow's mobility problems.

Tam Shee was steeped in tradition, so it took some cajoling on Donaldina's part before she could "purchase" Wu Jade using Will's endowment funds. The director then turned around and rehired the girl to work as Tam Shee's assistant. Tam Shee was finally won over by the fact that she now had money to pay the "bone tax" that would enable her to ship her dead husband's body back to his homeland. Thankfully, she wasn't eager to accompany her husband's remains; the prospect of staying in San Francisco as an independent woman must have won the day.

Donaldina had a concern, however, which she shared with Will during one of their planning sessions.

"The most difficult part in this entire process will be convincing both Tam Shee and Wu Jade that they are God's children, and as such are no longer subject to the whims of master or man."

Will wasn't thrilled with the director's heavy emphasis on religious conversion (he'd never read the Bible, and the director seemed to thump on it way too much for his taste). Yet, given the population she worked with, he had to admit she made a positive difference in the lives of the immigrant girls who stayed with the program. Whether or not Donaldina converted Tam Shee and Wu Jade to her brand of Christianity wasn't his problem.

*His* problem arrived less than a week after they'd brought Tam Shee into the enterprise. Will was reviewing contracts in his office one afternoon when he heard the sound of a familiar voice from Hansen's domain: "I need to see him *now*."

Cheung ti Chu entered Will's office uninvited, his long black queue quivering in his fury.

"How dare you," he spat out.

Will calmly put down his pen. "How dare I what?"

"You know what. You deliberately took Tam Shee Low and her mui tsai out of my reach."

Will motioned for Cheung to have a seat. "I think you have me mixed up with the Angry Angel."

"Miss Cameron can do many things. But she cannot expand her services without money. The money you funneled to her to start that infernal knitting school."

"It's a school for needle arts, and yes, I confess, I have contributed to that enterprise, at Miss Cameron's request. In fact I was about to make it known that Pacific Global Shipping is a proud sponsor of the school, whose goal is to improve the lot of Chinatown immigrants. Good for business, you know." *All right. I would have made that announcement at some point, just not quite so soon.*

Frustration etched deep lines in Cheung's face. "Well, rescind the money, then."

Will gave the man his best imitation of a horrified citizen. "And deprive those girls of the opportunity to make themselves productive members of society? I wouldn't dream of it. Besides, the more stories about how Chinatown is becoming more 'civilized,' the better it is for all of you."

Cheung sat back in the chair, looking dejected. "She won't take any more presents from me," he grumbled. "And she has come right out and refused my suit. I can't even make headway with her mui tsai."

"Who is no longer a mui tsai, I've been told." Inside Will was careening with joy. Tam Shee had rejected the bastard. Didn't need him and didn't want him. Thank God. He tried to muster a sympathetic look for Cheung, but the man seemed to have his doubts. He stared intently at Will.

"You want her for yourself," he finally said.

*If only* passed through Will's mind. A fleeting thought, a fanciful wish. Not to be examined too closely. To protest too much would be insulting; to agree would be suicidal. Time to split hairs. "I would not do such a thing to you," he said. "I am not that kind of man."

Cheung looked at Will a few moments longer, then rose. "I know that we Chinese will never please you whites as long as we follow our traditions. But they have been our traditions for thousands of years and we will not give them up easily. Your Miss Cameron wants to hurry the process of change, and she does so at her peril."

Will felt the coldness of the man across from him, as if an arctic blast had swept through the room. He looked Cheung squarely in the eye. "Are you trying to warn me of something specific, Cheung? Because if you are, I would prefer it if you didn't mince words."

"There are forces at work," he said cryptically. "I cannot stop them, even if I wanted to." With that, the Chinaman left the office, but the chill remained.

———◦———

Drawn by an unseen force, Will spent several mornings a week working with Fung Hai to refurbish the new school. He could easily have hired workers but chose to handle most of the renovation himself. He remembered kidding his business partner once about working so hard when he could afford to have others do it. *Wouldn't Gus get a kick out of seeing me now.* It was an excuse and he knew it; he simply wanted to learn more about Tam Shee. Hell, he just wanted to be around her. Fortunately, Sai-fon's natural exuberance helped pave the way. Will found that by charming the lively daughter, he could please the mother as well.

"Peppermint," he said one morning, dropping to his haunches and handing a stick of the candy to the little girl. He patted his stomach and smiled. "Good. Sweet."

Fung Hai said something in Cantonese to Tam Shee and she giggled in response. "Sweet," she repeated.

Will learned some words in Cantonese as well: *Ngo zung ji* meant "I like it," or "I like you," depending on what or who you pointed to. And *Ne hou leng* meant "You are very pretty." He pointed to Sai-fon and practiced the latter phrase; when she pointed back at him and repeated it, Tam Shee laughed, and he found himself willing to go to almost any lengths just to hear that effervescent sound again.

At five years old, Sai-fon (which Fung said meant "little phoenix") was a perfectly proportioned miniature of her mother, a true "china doll" who danced and twirled, accepting Fung and Will as if they had always been her devoted courtiers. The little girl soaked up the new language like a sponge and must have been tutoring her mama, because Tam Shee was soon able to understand some basic English words and phrases. Will wished he could say the same of Cantonese; aside from those few expressions, he could decipher little of it.

Still, they began to communicate in the way two people do who care enough to make the effort. With Fung Hai's help they talked about simple things at first, like the weather and Sai-fon's latest adventure. But Will found he wanted to know more about the enigmatic beauty. What made her sad, what brought her joy? What were her hopes and dreams? He most certainly didn't want Fung Hai in on a conversation like that. He redoubled his efforts to learn her language and to teach her his, taking time each day to converse with her.

One such morning toward the end of the renovation, he and Fung Hai were in the midst of painting Tam Shee and Sai-fon's bedroom while Sai-fon played in the garden. Tam Shee had let her daughter pick the color and she'd chosen a pretty shade of lavender from the paint samples Fung had brought. Taking a break, Will came out into the front parlor. Tam Shee was in her usual chair and she paused in her needlework to smile at him.

"You most kind man," she said.

"I am not," he replied, shaking his head.

She looked puzzled. "No. You are."

He paused by the makeshift altar she had set up on the other side of the room, similar to the one in her old apartment. A stick of incense had burned halfway down. Its musky scent enveloped him, reminding him he was in unknown territory.

"Your husband? *Lao…lao gong*?" He patted his heart to convey love. "I am sorry."

To his amazement, she hesitated, took a breath and, pushing against the arms of her chair with both hands, lifted herself up to a standing position. She took mincing steps, swaying back and forth, over to his side.

Will couldn't help but glance at her shoes. She wore tiny satin slippers. The image of what her bare feet must look like caused him to swallow convulsively. He kept his expression neutral, but inside he was thinking *you were tortured*.

She stood next to him, barely reaching his shoulder. Tilting her head slightly, she considered the small painting of her husband. Then she looked up at Will and put her two forefingers together. "Family put together when I three," she said, holding up three fingers. "He twenty…twenty-one." She counted to twenty-one and giggled when she finished

Will held his hands apart. "That is a big difference."

She nodded. "I had luck. He good man." She pointed to another picture on the wall, a wedding photo in which a very young Tam Shee and her groom stared solemnly at the camera. "First day I see him," she explained. "We spend small time together, then he leave, come to Gold Mountain." She shook her head, her expression wistful. "Not long time." She quirked her lips then, a shy attempt at humor. "But long enough to make Sai-fon."

Her words threw Will off balance. He immediately pictured Tam Shee in the act of conceiving a child and mentally berated himself for his brutish instincts. Looking for a distraction, he pointed to another photograph tacked onto the wall, the same one he'd seen before. The young man in the picture looked self-confident and almost cocky. Will felt a twinge of jealousy. "Who is he?"

Tam Shee put her finger lovingly on the image. Will saw that her eyes had misted over. "He my brother, Tam Yong."

"What happened to him?"

She spoke in a voice laced with sorrow. "I do not know. He come to Gold Mountain as paper son. My husband know him. When he bring Sai-fon and me from Canton, Tam Yong disappear. Now with husband gone, I no can find him."

Will was about to ask another question when Sai-fon burst into the room.

"Mama, Mama, come see!"

Tam Shee discreetly wiped her eyes and let her daughter lead her back to her favored chair. Fung Hai appeared in the bedroom doorway and Will saw that the young man was entranced.

"Look at how she walks," Fung murmured, passion infusing his words. "Her lotus feet are beautiful." And it dawned on Will that in some ways, their ideas of beauty would never be reconciled.

---

Later that afternoon, Will found himself gazing out his office window, gathering wool when he should have been attending to business. His assistant, Mr. Thaddeus Hansen, cleared his throat. Loudly.

"I'm sorry, Mr. Hansen. Things on my mind. You were saying?"

"I was saying that the Pinkerton Agency's preliminary report on the whereabouts of Miss Culpepper's relatives is rather disappointing."

"Is it? That's a shame. Well, tell them to keep looking."

"I took the liberty of suggesting they place advertisements in major newspapers across the country. If that's all right with you, sir."

Will gazed at the pile of financial reports awaiting his perusal. "Fine. That's fine. Thank you, Mr. Hansen."

Will leaned back in his chair, the financials forgotten. A perverse part of him hoped they wouldn't find anyone related to Mandy. She was good for Kit; she gave his sister a sense of self-worth, a 'project,' as their mother would say. In her role of guardian, Kit could be something other than a pretty socialite waiting to make an advantageous marriage. The fact that Mandy was an agreeable girl, albeit odd, and smart as a whip, helped matters considerably.

He chuckled at the memory of Mandy approaching him one evening a few weeks back.

"I challenge you to a game of Chicken Foot," she'd said, holding a box of dominoes.

"Chicken Foot, you say? Now where did you learn such a game?"

"From my pa, and I am very good at it."

And she was. She'd taught him the rules of the game, and although he'd picked it up quickly, she had still cleaned him out of his pocket change by shrewdly waiting until he'd gotten ahead before betting on the outcome.

Yes, he was quite satisfied with the status quo in that area of his life.

But Tam Shee was another story. He longed to deepen their friendship. He knew she wouldn't accept gifts, but perhaps he could do something for her, something more than provide mere financial support, which she didn't even know about, and a chance to practice her English.

Then it came to him. The brother. Finding Tam Yong would open up an entirely new dimension to their relationship. He reached for the phone to call the mission and track down Fung Hai.

# CHAPTER TEN

*Mandy's Journal*
*August 5, 1903*

Dear Pa,

I am learning so much, I can scarcely write it all down. Fung Hai is teaching me the rudiments (I like that word. It sounds like "rutabaga") of his language. The Chinese people, at least the ones who live here in Chinatown, speak something called "Cantonese," not Chinese. It is a difficult language and my mouth has trouble making some of the sounds, but little by little I am picking it up.

My job as historian for the Presbyterian Mission House has expanded to something that will surprise you. Miss Cameron, the director, was pleased with the stories I have written all summer long about the girls who now live in the home. I described where they came from and how old they were, and all the hardships they have put up with. Do you know, some of them were snatched right out from under their mamas' noses? One girl had a papa who told her they were going to visit her aunt, but instead he put her on a ship for America! I thank the good Lord every day for giving me a loving papa like you. (Oh, there I am using two syllables. I think the Weems Academy must be rubbing off on me!)

I like all the girls, and the school instructor, Mrs. Tam Shee Low, is beautiful. But Pa, she is deformed. Her feet are very tiny and she can barely walk, so she never goes anywhere or does anything. It makes me sad that someone would have such a terrible disfigurement. And do you know the worst of it? She was tortured, as a little girl, to get that way. I do not understand it.

Her assistant, Wu Jade, is fascinating to me. She and I are almost the same age, and in a lot of ways our lives are similar. She does not seem to have parents and she is a mother's helper just like I was.

But she is so quiet and reserved. I wonder what secrets she is holding inside, close to her heart. My own heart tells me they would make good stories. One of the reasons I want to learn the language is so I can talk with her.

As to my new assignment, Miss Cameron has asked me to be, of all things, a *spy*. She doesn't call it that, but that is just what she wants me to be. She even asked that I not say anything to Miss Kit or Mr. Firestone about it. I haven't decided about that, yet. I don't like to deceive people if I can help it. But this might be an exception to the rule. Because Fung Hai and I now go out into Chinatown and interview girls before they even come to the mission. It is so exciting! But I know that neither my guardian nor Mr. Firestone would like me to be out and about like that, even with Fung Hai along as my companion. They think it is a dangerous place for a girl like me. But that is no reason not to do something you feel is very important, is it?

Their worries might have to do with the plague, and I wish I could tell them it's all right. To become Miss Cameron's spy, I got a shot to protect me from it. You remember reading about the plague, don't you, Pa? How they tried to cover it up and pretend it didn't exist, but finally they had to admit that it did? So they have been cleaning out the city ever since I got here, and I will tell you, the times I have walked around Chinatown, it smells bad. Fung Hai says that is because they are using chemicals to kill the rats. Somehow the rats cause the plague.

A while back, they tried to make everyone in Chinatown get shots to keep the plague from harming them. They called it a special vaccine, and Miss Cameron wanted all her girls at the mission to get one. But everyone fought it because it hurts a lot and no one could tell if it would do more harm than good. One girl was so scared that she jumped out a window and broke both her legs just running from the doctor who wanted to poke her! A judge finally said the Chinese didn't have to have the vaccine, so no one gets the shots now.

That leaves just one medicine, called an antiserum. It is made from something inside horses who got the plague and lived to tell about it. It contains something called antibodies, which are supposed to join forces with antibodies already in my body to fight off the plague bugs, in case I should encounter any. When they described what the shot did, I remembered the stories you told of Abraham Lincoln trying to find a general who would fight. You said George McClelland couldn't do it, nor could Nathaniel Banks, nor a bunch of others. And President Lincoln was practically tearing his hair out trying to find somebody. Then he found

Ulysses S. Grant. And General Grant was willing to fight and get the men to fight with him. So that's how I imagine the Yersin anti-serum works inside my body.

I was lucky to get the antiserum because there isn't much of it. They usually only give it to the doctors and other people who have to be around those poor souls who come down with the dreaded illness. But Miss Cameron insisted, and I have already told you how forceful she is about getting her way.

The shot didn't hurt too bad, thank goodness. The man who gave it to me is a doctor named Thomas Justice. Now ain't—I mean isn't—that a strong name? He answered all my questions about what happens when you get the plague. He never once said, "Oh, you're too young to know about things like that," or, "young women shouldn't learn about such horrors." He described the symptoms and what happens to the body as it tries to defend against the disease. He even admitted they don't know much about how people get the plague, except that it comes from rats, or how to treat it once you get it. "It has to run its course," he said. "All you can do is keep the patient as comfortable as possible so they can fight it off."

Dr. Tom helps the government people out with quarantines, but he also examines the girls that Miss Cameron rescues to make sure they are healthy and free of the diseases men sometimes give to women when they sleep with them. He always makes sure Miss Cameron is in the room when he checks the girls. And the girls tell me he is very nice to them, and gentle, not like the bad men, and he talks to them in a quiet voice so they won't be scared. He was very nice to me, too, and when I asked him if I could try to give a shot myself, he said yes and brought me an orange and showed me how to inject it with some sugar water. I didn't hear the orange squeal, so I think I did it right!

Once when I was in the mission offices writing up a story, I heard Miss Cameron arguing with Dr. Tom. She was saying that you had to believe the whole Bible, word for word, and Dr. Tom was talking softly and you could tell there was a grin in his voice. I don't think he agrees with her all the time. But it takes a strong person to just go along and not want to argue every little point. And maybe that comes from just knowing yourself real well and feeling good about who you are.

I don't think I could be a missionary, Pa, but I do feel good about what I am doing to help Miss Cameron and the immigrant girls. They have voices and I am helping them to be heard.

# CHAPTER ELEVEN

———◦———

"What have you found out?" Will asked Fung Hai as they walked down Sacramento Street toward Dupont. It had been a week and Fung Hai had made some discreet inquiries about Tam Shee Low's brother.

"Tam Yong is the only son. He did not obey his parents and stay in China. Instead he came as the paper son of a rice broker—"

"What do you mean, 'paper son'?"

"Your laws do not let us come here on our own, so we must pretend to be the sons of merchants, who are allowed to come and go." Fung Hai shrugged. "I too am a paper son. It is common."

"What happened to Tam once he got here?"

"He worked in a warehouse for a while, but after that the reports are not certain. Some say he tried farming to the south, others that he became a fisherman along the coast. But in the past few months he has been seen back here in the Big City. He seems to like certain…houses of entertainment…which he visits some time."

"Which ones?"

Fung looked distinctly uncomfortable. "They are...they are not good and respectful places."

Will stopped and looked at the young man. "Fung, I am not a simpering miss who's going to faint at the mention of a whore house. Now spit it out."

"Spit it out?" The young interpreter looked horrified.

Will sighed. "It's an expression. It means 'don't be afraid to tell me what you know.' Come on now. I don't have time to dance around the subject."

Fung paused and took a breath. This was clearly out of his Christian comfort zone. "He visits the Golden Dragon on Cooper Alley, and...and the Flower Garden over on Waverly Place."

"Then let's go," Will said.

Their first stop, the Golden Dragon, was a gambling house. Inside it was dim, the only light provided by gas lanterns set near large gaming tables, several of which were surrounded by Chinese men. All were jostling and squawking to be heard above their cohorts as they placed their bets. When Fung Hai and Will entered, the chattering stopped and most of the gamblers looked up, suspicion in their gaze. Fung Hai waved to them, signaling that he and Will were not the authorities. *Good thing I'm not wearing a uniform*, Will thought. *They'd probably scatter faster than rats from a sulfur pot.*

Around one such table, eight men played a type of dominoes. Each player had four tiles and placed them in pairs, one pair in front of the other. They seemed to be betting against the dealer, who had his own four tiles. Everyone moved so quickly that it was impossible to discern the rules of the game. Will wondered what they'd do if he boldly challenged them all to a game of Chicken Foot.

"They are playing Pai Gow," Fung Hai murmured, pointing to the domino game, "and that game across the room is called Fan Tan." Will wandered over to the latter table, where men huddled over the surface, their faces starkly etched by the shadows. They rapidly placed their money along the outside of a rectangle drawn on the tabletop, whose sides were labeled with the numbers one, two, three and four. The croupier cast a pile of buttons from a metal bowl and began to separate them out by fours with his bamboo wand. He soon had forty-five sets of four, with two buttons left over. Those who had put bets on the side labeled "two" won the round.

Fung asked the man who seemed to be in charge of the establishment about Tam Yong. Did he come in often? What kind of a player was he?

"Yes, I know the man you talking about," the man responded in English. "He good player…sometimes."

"Does he win more than he loses?" Will asked. The manager grinned, shrugging. "Sometime buttons smile on Tam Yong. Sometime not. You like try?"

"Not right now," Will demurred, noting how uneasy Fung was inside a place he no doubt felt the Devil frequented. "Maybe another time. When does Tam come in, usually?"

"It hard to say. You want me tell you next time he come in?" The man grinned again and looked expectant, signifying that sharing such information naturally came with a price.

"You're more than kind," Will said dryly. "But no thanks."

Once outside, both Will and Fung squinted at the sunlit afternoon. "I told you not a good place," Fung reminded him.

"You ever play?" Will wanted to razz the self-righteous young man. "It looks like fun."

"Gambling like that, or Pok Kop Pu—you know that game? Like what you call a lottery—that tear my family apart," Fung said. "My father always looking for sign of good luck and good fortune, but he never find it. Only misery, which he bring to our family. I come to Gold Mountain to help pay for his mistakes. Send money home when I can. So no, I never play those games."

*Well, damn it. Open mouth, insert foot.* He didn't pursue the topic. "Okay, let's head over to the Flower Garden. I assume it's a parlor house? You can wait outside if you want."

"I don't mind going inside Flower Garden," Fung said with a slow smile. "Sometimes find blossoms there."

But there weren't any blossoms, only a handful of young, bored-looking prostitutes sitting around the front parlor of the whorehouse during the afternoon lull, waiting for the next customer to cross the threshold. Will could hear activity in the back of the house: talking, the occasional clang of pots, the hiss of steam. Places like the Flower Garden catered to men who liked a good meal before their amorous activities. At least Tam Shee's brother wasn't frequenting a cheap cathouse.

Several of the girls perked up when they saw Will and Fung, and the bravest one, or maybe she was the next one in the rotation, sashayed up to Will and ran her finger down the front of his jacket. "You like?" she said in a voice that could have belonged to a twelve-year-old.

Sadness tinged with both pity and anger settled on his shoulders. "No, thank you. May I talk to your…supervisor?"

A middle-aged Chinese woman stepped through a doorway where the kitchen sounds had come from. The opening was hung with beads that made a tinkling sound. She was heavily made up and had an austere, almost theatrical look about her; she had probably plied the trade in the past but had worked her way into a management position. She glared at Fung; clearly she knew him. She spit out an invective in Cantonese. Fung shook his head vehemently and pointed to Will, no doubt trying to explain himself and his reason for being there. "She thinks I trying to lure the girls away," Fung Hai said. "She knows I sometimes work for Director Cameron. But I told her we are not here for that reason."

Will couldn't swear to it, but he thought he heard the woman use the words "white girl." Was she talking about Donaldina Cameron or someone else?

The thought struck him like a hard thump on his shoulder.

He'd bet a month's worth of dividends she was talking about Mandy.

"But you have been here before…and not alone." Will looked directly at Fung Hai; the young man's frozen expression told him all he needed to know. He gave Fung a look that said *I'll deal with you in a minute* before turning to the madam. "I'm here to ask about one of your clients, Tam Yong. I understand he comes here on occasion."

"He used to visit one of my girls, but no more. He not well." The old whore looked disgusted. "I have clean house here. Now unless you pay, it time for you to go away too."

Will and Fung left the brothel and paused outside. "What do you mean by taking Mandy to places like this?" Will demanded. "She's just a girl. She should not be exposed to society's gutter trash."

Fung raised his arms in a gesture of frustration. "She have no fear," he said, a trace of desperation in his voice. "She go *anywhere* to talk to girls and hear their story, even places I no like." He raised one hand higher. "She not think of herself up here. She say she the same as they are. She want to help. What can I do? Tell her she cannot go?" He snorted. "I cannot stop her, so I am her body protector."

Mandy thinking she was just like those prostitutes? It was absurd...

He paused. Thought about it. Then had to admit, if fate— and Kit—hadn't stepped in, maybe Mandy *would* have been forced down that road.

Chinatown had too many men and not nearly enough women. Market forces dictated a booming sex-for-hire trade. That made sense. But how many of those poor girls actually chose to make their livings on their backs? And didn't the same thing happen in *his* world, where girls were sometimes forced by circumstances to sell themselves? Couldn't the same thing have happened to her?

The thought of Mandy coerced into plying that ancient trade made him sick to his stomach. Then he realized she'd probably come to the same conclusion he just had. That's why she was bound and determined to help those poor creatures. Respect for his sister's young ward fought with his need to protect the girl. He couldn't be with her constantly, and he certainly couldn't lock her up. That left surrogates like Fung Hai to fill in the breach.

"You'd damn well better protect her," he told Fung. "You do whatever it takes to keep her safe."

# CHAPTER TWELVE

From the time Kit and Mandy had moved into Will's home, Kit had insisted they eat at least one meal together each week. Will was not enthusiastic about the prospect, but his sister felt it would give Mandy a sense of belonging to a family, rather than simply boarding with them. To keep the peace, he'd agreed to share the meal on Wednesdays.

Surprisingly, he found he enjoyed the weekly get-togethers. Kit was her usual charming, frivolous self; she could turn a day at the dressmaker into a noteworthy event. Mandy was full of funny stories about her teachers and classmates at the Weems Academy. She seemed adept at describing the essence of a character, often comparing their attributes to either domestic or wild animals. Will decided not to ask which animal she fancied him to be.

The young girl took her job as the Mission House historian to heart and shared some of the more fascinating—and heart-breaking—stories she'd written down. He noticed she never went into detail about how and *where* she heard the stories, but

Fung seemed to have taken Will's admonition to heart, so he didn't press her on the matter.

It crossed Will's mind that Mandy might be a missionary in the making. He shuddered slightly at the prospect. The world could only handle so many "Angry Angels" like Donaldina Cameron.

Kit enjoyed the mealtime camaraderie, he knew, but Mandy seemed to love the gatherings most of all. She had never missed one.

Until tonight.

"Where's our intrepid reporter?" he asked Kit as she came down the stairs for dinner.

"I don't know. I assumed she'd come home and was in her room. Did you check?"

Will jogged up the stairs. "Mandy?" he called down the hallway.

No answer.

He checked his pocket watch. Half past six. They were usually seated and waiting to be served at six. A frisson of unease swept through him. "Did she come home at all?"

Kit looked at him, eyes wide with concern. "I...I don't know. I came home around five o'clock, assuming she was already home. I take it you didn't see her either?"

Will shook his head. "Fleming!" he shouted.

John Fleming had been Will's major domo for the past six years, ever since Will returned from University and moved to Russian Hill. A former boxer from Nevada, he'd convinced Will he could out-butler the East Coast's mainline manservants with one hand tied behind his back. And he could. His duties consisted of virtually anything Will needed him to do, from managing the housekeeping staff to sending flowers to Will's latest paramour. These days at the top of his list was making sure Mandy got safely from home to the Weems Academy, over to the Mission House, and back again.

"Yes, sir? Are you ready to dine?"

"No, I'm ready for you to tell me what happened to Mandy."

Fleming looked alarmed. "Has something happened to the poor girl?"

"You tell me. Didn't you bring her home?"

"No, sir. Miss Amanda told me Miss Cameron would be giving her a ride home this afternoon, that I would not be needed."

"And you didn't think to tell me?" Will could feel his temper rising.

"No, sir. You've never given me any reason not to trust Miss Cameron. Should I not have trusted her, then?"

Will shifted his shoulders uneasily. Fleming wasn't the problem here. "No, there's no reason why you shouldn't. Ring up Miss Cameron, will you?"

Before Fleming could do so, the phone rang. It was Miss Cameron herself, calling to tell Will not to panic, but both Amanda and Fung Hai were missing, along with Tam Shee's assistant, Wu Jade. She had a pretty good idea of what had happened, she told Will. Her voice wasn't teary or panicked. It sounded determined. Almost galvanized. "If you would like to come to the mission, the authorities are on their way."

*What the hell was going on?* The idea of Mandy being hurt in any way sent a bolt of fear shooting through him. He immediately regretted not confronting her about her dangerous wanderings around Chinatown with Fung Hai. Being hurt while under his and Kit's watch was not going to happen to her. He wouldn't allow it. Period. "Apparently she and Fung Hai and another girl are missing," he told Kit, reaching for his coat. "Come on, Fleming. We might need you, too."

By the time they reached the Mission House, Donaldina seemed to be in full battle mode; she was already mapping out a strategy with three policemen and a timid-looking Chinese fellow dressed in a western-style suit who looked both nervous and annoyed. "Any later and we would have left without you," she said, as if Will and Kit were there on a lark.

"Any harm comes to Mandy and you're going to be held responsible to the fullest extent possible," Will shot back.

"Understood. I don't think even the Hip Yee Tong would touch her, though. It's Wu Jade and Fung Hai I'm worried about."

"What in the blazes is happening here?" The charming, frivolous Kit was gone, replaced by a take-no-prisoners Amazon. "Just who are we up against?"

"Every girl who comes to our mission or some other port of safety results in one less girl for the brothels, which means less money for the tongs that control the prostitution trade." Donaldina buttoned up her coat and quickly pulled on her gloves as she spoke. "The tongs have resorted to kidnapping mui tsai and even second generation Chinese girls to refill the ranks. We must fight this perfidy with every resource we have. That is why

I persuaded Mr. Lee Chen, here, to join us. He is special assistant to the Chinese consul. Follow me, gentlemen…and lady."

Will gestured to himself, Kit, and Fleming. "Wait, we're not armed." He glanced at Fleming, who discreetly patted his jacket. "Well, Kit and I at least require some form of protection."

"If my hunch is correct, the situation shouldn't result in violence," she explained, heading for the police vehicles parked along the street. "But the officers here will protect us should the need arise." The policemen in question stood in stoic silence.

"I'm not sure about this," Will said to Kit. "Please, would you wait here for us?"

"Not in your life, brother dear." She quickly walked ahead of him. "Wait for me, Miss Cameron."

Will sighed and hopped into the second police vehicle. The convoy headed down Stockton Street.

"That Miss Cameron sure is a piece of work," the officer remarked as he drove. "We're headed right into the belly of the beast."

"Where would that be?" Fleming asked.

"Hip Yee Tong headquarters on Sullivan Alley. They're having some kind of confabulation there tonight. That lady's got her spies everywhere. She knows what's going on." There was a hint of admiration in the man's voice.

Will felt disconnected, like a boat without rudder or sail, dependent on the vagaries of the wind. He didn't like it. Hated it, in fact. To be without power, to be a mere appendage—it was infuriating. He hoped fervently to be able to add something to the expedition.

They arrived at the meeting hall, apparently located on the second floor of a brothel, one of several situated side by side along the alley. Donaldina, her eyes practically breathing fire, exited the Chinese consul's car along with Kit and marched without hesitation up to the front door. She knocked, and in a few moments the door opened. She said in a loud voice, "We are here to see Tang Lin." The guard started to speak and she held up her hand. "I know he is upstairs and if you do not let us through, we have the full power of the city as well as the Chinese government behind us. We will not be denied."

Will felt a flash of pity for the thug; Donaldina was a force to be reckoned with. He seemed to know who she was and turned, ostensibly to go upstairs and ask his boss what he should do. He made the mistake of leaving the door ajar and Donaldina wasted no time entering the building.

Helpless to do anything except follow, they all trooped up the stairs behind her. On the second floor was a large assembly room filled with Chinese men eating dinner, served by several young women. Will scanned their faces and corrected himself; they were girls, not women. Poor innocent girls, all at the mercy of these miscreants.

Seven men sat on the dais; it was obvious the man in the middle was the boss, Tang Lin. Donaldina walked directly up to him and puffed herself up to her full height of about five foot three. All noise related to the banquet ceased.

"Oh my," Kit murmured, looking around at the room full of less than friendly tong members. "This beats an evening of charades any day."

"Tang Lin, you may not realize it, but your procurers may have made a major mistake this evening and I am here to rectify it."

The tong leader, who was surprisingly young—he couldn't have been older than forty—looked at Donaldina with an amused expression. He had obviously dealt with her before.

"And what *major* mistake might I have made, Miss Do-gooder Cameron?" He looked around the room as if she and her entourage had been hired to provide entertainment for the evening.

Donaldina gestured for Will and Kit to come forward. "You may have inadvertently kidnapped the ward of Miss Katherine Firestone, of the San Francisco Firestones," she explained. "She and her brother William are extremely well connected, sir, up to the highest levels of the state house and beyond. I do not think you want to make trouble with them. They have the power to bury you."

Tang Lin kept his smile, but his eyes turned cold. He looked at Will with speculation, but when he turned to Kit, he stopped and regarded her as a male regards an attractive female. It took all of Will's concentration not to reach up, grab the thug by the front of his satin brocade jacket, and give him some stars to look at. Only Kit's cautionary hand on his arm kept him from doing it.

"Amanda is like my little sister and I love her dearly," Kit explained in a soft, gentle voice. "Do you have a sister, Mr. Tang?"

The tong leader continued to look at Kit, and Will could tell the moment Kit won the battle. Even Donaldina was impressed. She pushed their advantage.

"In addition, I am not sure your men—if they happened to make the mistake—were aware that the girl, Wu Jade, who they thought was a mui tsai, is now a free woman. As such she is entitled to all the protection of the U.S. government."

*Now you're stretching it,* Will thought. Still, it sounded good.

Tang Lin sat back in his chair. "And I'm sure there is a special dispensation related to Fung Hai as well?"

Donaldina tipped her head. "Of course. As well as working for Mr. Firestone, Fung Hai is currently on retainer by the Chinese government as part of their consular staff. Isn't that correct, Mr. Lee?" She turned to the hapless consular deputy, who nodded, probably more afraid of Donaldina than the tong at this point.

Donaldina's eyes bore into those of the tong leader. He seemed to be deciding whether or not to believe her. He glanced again at Kit.

"You simply do not want to be walking down this road, Mr. Tang. It will not bode well for your tong as you transition into legitimate commerce…and I know that is your ultimate goal."

Tang Lin paused a moment longer and then smiled benignly. "I am sure we had nothing to do with the disappearance of your friends," he said, "but should we learn who the culprits were, we will pass along your message."

"Thank you. I am sorry to have interrupted your meeting. Good evening." She bowed slightly, which took Will by surprise, and turned to leave, beckoning the rest of them to follow.

Once back on the street, she turned to Kit. "You were brilliant," she said. "Sometimes even I must admit that there are sweeter ways to catch flies."

"Now what?" Fleming asked. Will saw that his major domo was eager to demonstrate his pugilistic skills.

"Now we return to the mission," she said. "The children will be returned there shortly. Mr. Lee, thank you for accompanying us this evening."

Mr. Lee bowed quickly and took off in his official automobile, relief etched all over him. Donaldina and Kit piled into the second police car.

"Wait—how can you be sure?" Will asked. "The man, Mr. Tang, didn't admit to anything."

"Yes, he did. He was the one to mention Fung Hai, I wasn't."

Back at the mission, the police dropped them off. One of the officers asked if Miss Cameron wanted them to wait until the young people came back. "No, that might be a bit inflammatory," she said, "but thank you for the offer."

Will, Kit, and Fleming followed the director inside to her office and had barely started drinking the hot tea she'd offered when they heard car doors slam outside. The four of them raced out to see Mandy and Wu Jade on either side of Fung Hai. He had been beaten and could barely walk.

"Bollocks!" Kit cried, running over to help the young man. "Fleming, help him inside, please." Kit glanced at Mandy and Wu Jade, apparently saw they were all right, and performed her own version of triage by following Fleming and Fung inside. Donaldina opened her arms to Wu Jade, who fell into them gratefully, crying softly.

Mandy and Will stood there, looking at each other. "Are you all right?" he asked carefully.

She nodded slowly.

He nodded back, and on impulse, opened his arms. She paused as if wondering if he really meant it, but only for a second, before rushing up to him and putting her arms around his waist. She rested her cheek on his chest. He patted her back awkwardly before thinking *the hell with it* and closed his arms around her. He felt her let out a deep breath and heaved a sigh of his own.

Mandy was safe...this time. But what about the next? He now knew he couldn't rely on Fung Hai to keep her safe—the poor fellow himself needed protection.

And where was Cheung ti Chu in all this? Weren't the Six Companies supposed to keep order in the house? Had Cheung's cryptic words been a warning after all? Will would get to the bottom of it, come hell or high water.

# CHAPTER THIRTEEN

*Mandy's Journal
August 26, 1903*

I tried to write to Pa tonight, but I couldn't. How do you tell your father, even in heaven, that you were kidnapped, and that your good friend was beaten up before your very eyes? The stories of the girls at the Mission House have now come alive for me. I still shudder, thinking how close Wu Jade came to being taken by them for their nefarious purposes.

What's more, I do not understand why we were suddenly set free. I know my guardian and Mr. Firestone had something to do with it, and Miss Cameron, of course, but as to the details, they won't tell me, other than to say, "It was a misunderstanding." I do not believe that for a moment.

One minute we were all walking down the street, and the next, we were captured by a group of ruffians and taken to a run-down shack in one of the many alleyways in Chinatown. The men immediately began to yell at Fung Hai in Cantonese. I barely understood one word in a hundred. Words like "pigeon" and "pay a price" were all I understood. Then the nightmare began as they began to pummel my dear friend.

I get so very angry just thinking about it. Fung Hai was only doing the job he was hired to do, which is to help me understand the plight of these poor young girls in Chinatown. He didn't deserve what they did to him!

If there is but one positive thing to come out of this misadventure, it must be that Wu Jade came out of her shell enough to fight her captors, and not simply accept her fate. She has had a taste of freedom, and I believe she's beginning to understand that in order to keep it, she must stand up for herself. I am proud of her.

One thing I know for sure: if Fung Hai is willing, then I am willing to continue finding girls who need help and telling their stories to all who will listen.

My only concern is what will happen when Mr. Firestone finally asks me, "What were you doing in that part of Chinatown?" I am still not sure what I will tell him. I now know he is concerned for my welfare, but I am afraid I cannot make the leap from that knowledge to blind obedience. He is neither my father nor my guardian, which I must say I am very glad about.

# CHAPTER FOURTEEN

❦

"Turnabout is fair play, Cheung. You no doubt heard what almost happened to Wu Jade last night. My sister's ward got caught in the crossfire, not to mention Fung Hai. What the hell is going on with this kidnapping business?" Will had stalked into Cheung's office at the Six Companies headquarters in central Chinatown, surprising the representative. Cheung recovered quickly, however, and shrugged.

"Talk to your Congress," he said. "The law says only a few of us can bring our wives over, and forbids us from importing pleasure workers for our men. So what would you suggest? It is a simple matter of supply and demand."

Will recalled his similar thoughts on the subject and felt ashamed. He didn't want to be of the same mind as Cheung on this. He took a different tack. "You told me a while ago that you had children back in China. Do you have any daughters?"

Cheung beamed, pointing to a photograph gracing his desk. "Yes, two of them. And three sons. I am very busy each time I visit home." He winked.

Will examined the family portrait. "They look like lovely young girls. And who is there to protect your daughters from those who might kidnap them...for ransom, say, or for...other purposes?"

Cheung's smile faded; his tone turned defensive. "I employ a bodyguard," he said. "My family is protected."

Will nodded. "And would your guards prevail against a gang of thugs, or perhaps a kidnapping that took place while they, and your daughters, slept?"

Will's litany of hypothetical calamities had its intended effect on Cheung. He could sense the man mentally reviewing his family's safety procedures and calculating how he might improve them. Cheung looked at him with cold eyes. "I know what you are doing," he said.

"Then you know my next question is, 'What are you, Cheung ti Chu, the great representative of your people here in America, doing to protect those who rely on you, many of whom are no different from your own daughters?'"

Cheung had no ready answer. He looked out the window of his office for a moment before speaking. "I often wonder how my people can bear the way they are treated," he admitted, "both by you barbarians and by the worst of our own society. If I could make things perfect for them, I would."

"You can't make things perfect, but you can wield what influence you have to help things along," Will said. "You can confront the tongs—the Tang Lins of Chinatown—and convince them by whatever means you have at your disposal to cease putting your culture in the worst possible light."

"You don't understand," Cheung said. "They are like your Five Points Gang of New York. They are ruthless. And they have their fingers into everything that goes on here, on both sides of the law."

"If that's so, then they are men who understand profit and loss, who understand deal-making, and will act accordingly," Will countered. "But you have to bargain with them from a position of strength."

"Easy for you to say."

"Only slightly harder to do. Ask Donaldina about it." Will rose to go. "Look, you told me you thought things were going to get worse before they get better here in Chinatown. Maybe that's true, but maybe you can do more than simply wring your hands about it." He reached the door and turned, decided to take one last shot. "You know what they say about turtles, don't you?"

Cheung shook his head.

"Even they have to stick their necks out to get ahead." He heard Cheung deliver what sounded like an obscenity and was glad, for once, that he didn't understand the language.

---

"That was probably a waste of time," Will muttered as he left the Six Companies building. Walking down Washington Street, he felt a twinge of guilt for heaping scorn on Cheung when he himself had done nothing to help the situation. It grated that he'd been a mere spectator during the confrontation. How could Donaldina be so sure that Mandy and Fung Hai were no longer in danger?

Tang Lin hadn't seemed cowed by her, or Will, in the least. There was only one way to make sure Tang Lin got the message.

He had to confront the tong leader man to man.

On impulse, he turned onto Stouts Alley, which, once it crossed Jackson, turned into the narrow street that housed the Hip Yee Tong headquarters. He knocked on the brothel's door, which was soon answered by the same guard whom they'd confronted the night before.

After checking with his boss, the bodyguard came back to Will. "You come up now," he ordered.

Will was escorted to a smaller room off the assembly hall they'd been in previously. Tang Lin sat at a round table with three other men. By the looks of the card layout and the chips piled in the center of the table, they were playing Five-Card Stud. *Now that's a game I understand.*

They had just finished a hand, which Tang Lin apparently won, when Will entered the room. Tang collected the pile of chips and proceeded to shuffle the cards, completely unfazed that a "barbarian" had intruded on his inner sanctum.

"Ah, Mr. Firestone. Do you play?" he asked with an indolent smile.

"I do," Will said.

"Leave us," he said to the other men at the table. Within thirty seconds Will and the Tong leader were alone.

"I've come to—"

"I know why you have come. Have a seat. Please."

Will sat down and silently observed the gang leader. He had to admit Tang was a handsome figure—the male equivalent, really, of Tam Shee. His cheekbones were chiseled, his eyes well shaped, and his hair jet black despite the fact that he had to be at least ten years older than Will. He was tall and appeared somewhat muscular. Some women might even consider the man dashing.

Tang completed his shuffle and set the deck aside. "I believe you've come for assurances that your family and friends will remain safe. The...unrest in our community makes you uncomfortable."

"My discomfort is nothing compared to Fung Hai's. He has a broken arm and a fractured jaw."

"That is unfortunate. He seems like a pleasant young man, but a little naive."

"Then why did you sanction the assault...and perhaps more important, why did you assure Miss Cameron that you would back off?"

Tang looked at Will with a lazy expression—one that Will had used many times against business adversaries. "Did I?"

*Ah, negotiations have begun.* Will smiled. "Hence my need for assurances," he said. "But I am curious. You didn't have to placate her. Why did you?"

Tang continued to gaze at Will. "Your sister," he said.

"My sister?"

"Katherine, I believe her name is? She is a most beautiful woman."

Will straightened in his chair, his hackles up. "Yes, she is," he said slowly.

"Is she attached to anyone?"

He couldn't keep the scorn out of his voice. "No. What of it?"

Tang leaned back, his elbows resting on the arms of the chair while his fingertips pressed together. He nodded slowly as if he'd just deciphered a complex puzzle. "I see. So, Tam Shee Low's yellow skin is good enough for you, but my yellow skin isn't good enough for your sister. Is that about right?"

Will stood up abruptly, his temper nearly causing him to grab the tong leader by the throat. "I don't know how invincible you think you are," he spat, "but you have no right to sully the name and reputation of either one of those women. They don't deserve it and I won't tolerate it."

Tang waved Will back into his seat. "How is that English expression—'Do not get your knickers in a twist'? I was merely assessing the situation. I take it you have a high regard for Tam Shee Low, and that is a good thing. I may be in the business of using people, but I do not care for the practice in my private life. It seems as though that is your standard as well. But we get down to business now. I have something you want, and you have something I want."

*Now we're getting to the heart of it.* "If you think you'll protect my family in exchange for my sister's favors, I can assure you, that's not something I can give…even if I wanted to, which of course I don't." Will leaned forward. "Whether you or anyone else passes muster with me is irrelevant. My sister is a force of nature. Whoever she decides to be with will be her choice and no one else's."

Tang's smile spread slowly across his face. "I believe you. But I refer to something else, something your sister said. Do you remember?"

Will shook his head. "I don't remember she said much of anything. It was a rather stressful situation."

"She asked if I had a sister. And in fact I do." He rose from the table and walked over to a small desk across the room. Reaching into a drawer, he pulled out a framed photograph and handed it to Will. It was a picture of a young woman, about the same age as his own brother, Jamie, wearing a pretty, silky-looking dress. She was standing in a garden. Her feet, Will noticed, were of normal size.

"That is Tang Li Mei. She is the daughter of my father's second wife, and is a student in Canton. She wishes desperately to study in the United States."

"So why doesn't she?" Will asked. "You must certainly have the money for it."

Tang inclined his head in agreement. "Unfortunately, money does not buy everything. There are some schools—Cornell University, for example—that require more than just money."

*Ah, we have arrived.* Both Will and his father were Cornell graduates and heavily endowed the institution. Will looked Tang in the eye. "You have done your homework," he said. "I'm to pay for my family's protection with my family's influence, is that it? Tell me, is she bright enough? Is she—"

"She has passed the entrance examination with flying colors, and her knowledge of English is high. She wants to be an architect. She wants to build things." For the first time, Will detected a bit of defensiveness in Tang's voice, but there was also fierce pride. The man wanted this favor. Badly.

"I am sorry. It sounds like your sister well deserves the opportunity, but I cannot participate in what is essentially extortion. I will have to find another way to protect those I care about."

"As well as to find Tam Yong?" Tang asked.

Will narrowed his gaze. "How did you know about that?"

Tang shrugged, the self-confident negotiator once again. "It is a small community, Chinatown. And yet, if someone doesn't want to be found, well, it is difficult for an outsider to find them... without help." He glanced at the deck of cards. "I can see your reluctance to associate my request with the safety of your family, or even with the receipt of information. Many have found such exchanges distasteful, even when they are necessary. But would you consider a challenge in which the winner achieves his goal?" He gestured to the cards.

"You are challenging me to a game of cards?"

"Not a game. Simply one hand. Five-Card Stud. You indicated you know how to play."

"So, I win, you give me the information I need about Tam Yong as well as keep your goons from my loved ones. You win, I get your sister into Cornell."

Tang nodded. "Simple." He slid the deck across the table. "And you may deal the cards."

Will considered his options. As in any business proposition, it paid to have the power brokers on your side. In Chinatown, Tang Lin was one of those brokers. Winning a legitimate bet was a hell of a lot more honorable than paying for protection or forcing someone to help you out of fear. He sensed that Tang Lin felt the same way. In fact, were their circumstances different, Will could see forging a friendship with the man. But that wasn't in the cards. Will smiled slightly at his mental pun. He nodded. "All right, then."

Tang began to slide his poker chips out of the way and paused. "Just to make it interesting, shall we bet, say, five hundred dollars a chip?" He pushed ten chips over to Will's side of the table. "I know you are good for it."

"Agreed," Will said, and reached for the cards. He shuffled several times and asked Tang to cut the deck, then they each put forward an ante. He dealt one card down to each of them, and one card up. Tang's card was high, an eight of diamonds, to Will's seven of clubs. Tang tossed a chip into the center of the table.

Will matched the chip with one of his own. "Third Street," he murmured, dealing another card face up to each of them. Tang drew a jack of diamonds to Will's seven of spades, giving Will a pair. He tossed in a chip, which Tang matched.

"Fourth Street." Tang's next card was a four of diamonds, while Will drew a queen of spades. Again his hand was better. He tossed in another chip.

"It's looking good for you," Tang said, matching the bet.

"Not over 'til it's over," Will replied, dealing the final card as he said, "Fifth Street."

Tang drew a ten of diamonds while Will drew a queen of spades. "Two pair," he said, tossing in two more chips. Tang hesitated. The two men locked eyes. "It's your bet," Will said.

"So it is," Tang said, matching the bet.

"Showdown," Will said. He flipped over his first card to reveal a nine of clubs. Two pair would have to win it. He waited for Tang Lin to show his hand. The tong leader looked at his card. "Ah," he said, and flipped it over.

It was a six of diamonds.

Added to Tang's other diamonds, it formed a flush.

Which was better than two pair.

Will looked at the hand and blinked. For a split second he couldn't believe it. Then the reality set in. He'd lost. Fair and square. And he had to make good on their bet. After a moment he looked over at Tang Lin.

"Didn't see that coming," he said.

The tong leader smiled. "Neither did I. I'll have Li Mei's information sent to your office tomorrow."

Will nodded and rose to leave. "And I'll have a check ready for your messenger."

Tang Lin waved his hand. "Donate it to the mission…and make sure Miss Cameron knows where it came from."

Will chuckled at that. "I must admit, I've had more productive meetings, but none more interesting." He reached over and shook Tang Lin's hand. They were worlds apart in more ways than Will could count, but for that moment, they were two gentlemen conducting business, nothing more.

He headed down the stairs and was almost to the front door when the tong leader called to him from the top landing.

"He used to work for me but became unreliable," he said. "You'll find him in the den beneath the laundry on Spofford Street. Tell them I sent you."

Will knew immediately that he was talking about Tam Yong.

"Thank you," Will called back. "I'll see that your sister is taken care of."

"I know. You would have, even if you had won the hand."

Will started to reply, but the man had already turned to go back inside. "You're right," he murmured. Because he would have.

---

The next day Will called the president of Cornell University, an old friend of the family, and told him to expect a packet of information about a foreign student he very much wanted the school to "take a close look at." That was Firestone-speak for "ease through the enrollment process." Since Will and his father rarely asked for such favors, the administrator knew it was important.

"I look forward to meeting such an outstanding young lady," the academic gushed.

"Me too," Will muttered when he hung up.

After attending to business matters in the morning and stopping by to check on Fung Hai's recuperation at the mission, he headed to Spofford Street via Washington, determined to track down Tam Yong.

At Spofford, Will turned left into an alley crowded with overhanging structures that made the passage nearly as dark as night. Along the narrow walkway, merchants and residents had tossed out refuse that now reeked of damp and decay.

About halfway down the alley, he stopped at a door with the words LAUNDRY painted on it. "Don't be too obvious now," he muttered. After a few moments a man opened the door and Will quickly put his foot over the threshold. His Cantonese sounded atrocious to his ears, but he managed—or so he hoped—to get the names "Tam Yong" and "Tang Lin" out before the man, who resembled a bar bouncer, could slam the door in his face. He must have succeeded because after a brief hesitation, the guard gestured for Will to enter.

They wound their way through a large yet stifling room filled with Chinese workers scrubbing clothes on washer boards leaning into barrels of steaming suds. Tubs of clear water stood nearby, the floor beneath them soaked. Clotheslines were strung up along the entire length of the workspace, and along one wall men were ironing what looked like sheets. At the far end an older man wearing glasses worked a treadle sewing machine with his bare feet. The Cantonese banter stopped as Will and the bouncer walked by; all he could hear was the incessant drip of the wet hanging laundry.

Every week Fleming picks up laundry for the house, he thought. This is what goes on just so I can have clean sheets.

Beyond the sewing station was a narrow hallway leading to a staircase. The man motioned for Will to head down and followed him. As they descended, Will could smell a cloying, almost candy-like scent permeating the tight space.

At the bottom of the stairs, the space widened out again into a hallway with several doors branching off of it. The bouncer pointed to the third door. "Tam Yong," he said.

Will paused to gather his wits. The notion of what he was going to find repulsed him, but even worse was imagining how the truth about her brother was going to affect Tam Shee. He set his jaw and entered the room.

The smell hit him first: that same sweetness, only a hundred times more intense, mixed with the body odor of half a dozen Chinese men reclining on stained horsehair mattresses. The men, of various ages, seemed to be nearly comatose, just sentient enough to continue inhaling from the bamboo stems that jutted from bowls of heated opium placed next to them. Will fought off a gag reflex that coincided with a lump in his throat.

The bouncer pointed to a bed in the corner. A young man lay on it, his dead-looking eyes sunken in his head, his body emaciated. Will walked over to him and leaned down, hoping that if he spoke slowly enough, the youth would understand his English.

"Tam Yong? My name is Will. I am a friend of your sister. Tam Shee Low is looking for you. She wants to see you."

At the mention of his sister's name, the wretch's eyes opened widely, alarm filling them. He feebly shook his head and turned over to face the wall, as if he could make Will go away simply by not looking at him.

Will asked the bouncer how long Tam Yong had been this way before realizing the man probably didn't speak English. Surprisingly, the man answered.

"Nearly three month," he said. "He love the poppy too much. He very sick."

"What will happen to him?"

"Money run out, he have to leave. Find someplace else to die."

*Not going to happen. This I can fix.* He turned to the bouncer. "Will you please tell Tang Lin thank you, and that I will handle the situation from here? And expect someone to come by in the next few days to collect Tam Yong—whether he wants to go or not." The enforcer revealed nothing in his expression except the raise of his eyebrows, which Will took to mean surprise. *We aren't all barbarians*, he wanted to say, but settled for, "I've seen what I need to see. Let's go."

# CHAPTER FIFTEEN

*Mandy's Journal*
*August 28, 1903*

Dear Pa,

I didn't tell you before, but there was an "incident" a couple of days ago that resulted in my friend Fung Hai getting hurt. He is on the mend now, but not yet well enough to take me out from the mission because of it. As I feared, Miss Kit and especially Mr. Firestone have forbidden me to go about on my own. They say it is too dangerous for a young lady like me. But I look at all the people who live in this part of town and they seem to go about their business with no problem at all. It doesn't make much sense.

But to know that Miss Kit and Mr. Firestone care so much about me makes me warm and happy inside, Pa. Everybody needs someone who cares enough about them to say, "No, you cannot do that because you might get hurt and I could not bear for that to happen." I know you and Ma feel that way about me, but it is so very nice when someone hugs you to show you mean a lot to them.

# CHAPTER SIXTEEN

---

When Cheung said things would get worse before they get better, this is probably what he meant, Will thought a week later as he walked past the Mission House on his way to visit Tam Shee.

It wasn't enough to fumigate Chinatown and catch the rats. Dr. Blue, the quarantine officer, had decreed that all the places where rats congregated had to go, too. The dark, damp, garbage-filled places. The places under shoddily-built balconies and rickety porches. The cellars built from chewable wood, and the ramshackle buildings that both people and rats called home. All of them had to go, and demolition crews were everywhere.

He watched as two white laborers with huge pry bars went to work on a sagging wooden balcony overhanging a pastry shop. The rotten boards screamed as they were torn from the rusty nails holding them in place. The crash as the lumber fell onto the street was harsh, the sound raucous. After they'd removed the entire structure, the workers stacked the wood to the side of the building and moved on. It crossed Will's mind that an awful lot of wood was going to waste, but he decided it was too much trouble to cut it all down to fit the school's fireplace.

He found Tam Shee in her usual chair by the fireplace. She smiled at him in greeting, neither surprise nor irritation marring her flawless face. Sai-fon was out in her beloved garden; Will vowed to pick up some bulbs that they could plant together the next time he came. He'd find some lavender varieties that he knew would delight both the little girl and her mother when they bloomed the following spring.

"You are dedicated student," Tam Shee said, but they both knew practicing his Cantonese was incidental to the visit. In fact, they spent most of the time conversing in English.

"I have brought a game that you can play with Sai-fon when the weather turns too cold to play outside," he said. He pulled a low table from across the room over to their sitting area. "It's called Chicken Foot."

Tam Shee laughed, her eyes gleaming. "I need grain to feed this chicken?"

Will grinned as he opened the box of dominoes and began to place them on the table. "No, no food, but, it does not taste very good either." He pretended to bite down on one of the tiles and Tam Shee, giggling, reached out to stop him. "Do not break your pretty teeth."

"You think they are pretty, do you?" He offered her a wide, clownish smile.

"I think you are pretty," she said, then hesitated. "I mean handsome. That is what you call a man, yes?"

Will stopped mid-smile. This was the first time Tam Shee had acknowledged an attraction to him. He didn't quite know what to do with it. Joy and fear warred within him. He was in completely foreign territory.

"Yes, that is what you call a man," he said quietly, and let the moment pass.

Tam Shee must have also realized the line she'd crossed. She too chose to ignore it. "In my country we use these to play Pai Gow. But I am curious about this Chicken Foot."

Will proceeded to show her the simple game of matching tiles and how the three-pronged shape was created that gave the game its name. He shared the strategies he'd learned from Mandy and soon the two of them were ensconced in a friendly competition that lasted until Sai-fon came bounding up the stairs and demanded to learn the game, too.

Sitting with Tam Shee and her daughter in that little parlor, in that space of time, he could let the rest of his busy world go by. He knew that Tam Shee felt the same way. The outside world, their two disparate cultures, faded to abstraction; between them they were just two souls coming together to *be*.

In that and subsequent visits, Will did not mention Tam Yong. He'd directed his man Fleming and some of Fleming's more burly cohorts to collect the sick young man and take him to a private medical facility in the East Bay where they specialized in treating addiction. With Tang Lin's approval, they'd told Tam Yong that the tong leader was behind his rescue and expected him to cooperate long enough to get well…or else.

Will's motives in the matter were admittedly selfish. He wanted to present Tam Shee with a brother who was strong and healthy, not pathetic and near death from his own weaknesses. It would take time, patience, and, as always, money. Josephine would call Tam Yong a "major project." But Will wouldn't dream of telling her about it, because his mother would never countenance such a thing. She'd never be able to picture a child of hers—Jamie, for instance—in such a predicament, and therefore she couldn't relate to anyone else's problem.

Consequently, Will kept his project to himself and quietly pursued his own personal addiction: spending time with Tam Shee.

Some days later as he read the morning *Examiner*, Will's palms began to sweat. The headline read:

## ITALIAN MAN AND MOTHER DIE FROM PLAGUE-INFESTED FIREWOOD

Despite all the rat-killing and clean-up efforts, the "nonexistent" plague was alive, well, and spreading. A railroad man named Pietro Spadafora lived in a nice, clean house in the Latin Quarter just north of Chinatown. Apparently he'd picked up some discarded lumber from the demolition program to heat his home. A few days later, he fell ill with fever, muscle aches, a rebellious stomach, and complete loss of strength; he died shortly afterward. The diagnosis? Bubonic plague. What's worse, his elderly mother caught it too; she lasted barely a day after he did before succumbing to the same disease.

All evidence pointed to the rotting wood left on every street in Chinatown, thanks to Rupert Blue's "beautification" program. Even though no one knew *how* the wood spread the disease, Blue pronounced a solution to the problem: all the debris from the condemned structures was to be covered in powdered lime, a disinfectant. Now it couldn't be used to keep people warm, but at least it wouldn't kill them.

*Thank God*, Will thought as he read the article. *Thank God.* He considered the Mission House and Tam Shee's school. Both were sound structures with stone cellars and no suspect overhangs. At least the inhabitants there would be safe.

# CHAPTER SEVENTEEN

———◦◦◦◦◦◦———

Under Tam Shee's guidance, the Chinatown School of Needle Arts quickly began to thrive. Twenty girls, transfixed by the revered lotus-foot woman, competed to see who could please their headmistress the most. As a result, the work put out by the pupils surpassed most of the handmade offerings for sale elsewhere in the city. As he watched Tam Shee confer confidently with Wu Jade or one of the students, Will felt as if he were witnessing a life-size blossom unfurl. Delicate, yet powerful. And so beautiful it bedazzled him.

The school was making a name for itself within Chinatown and beyond. Classes expanded to include other skills, like sewing, knitting, and quilting. At the same time, despite the stories of occasional plague cases, the image of Chinatown was improving. Now that it was deemed more sanitary and therefore safe, it became *de rigeur* for white women of the city's middle and upper strata to spend an adventurous day in the neighborhood, eating bizarre but flavorful dim sum for lunch, visiting the open air markets, and completing the afternoon by purchasing a lovely set of linens, comforter, scarf, or other article "authentically created by the artisan women of Chinatown."

Kit got in on the act as well, serving as a local tour guide, first for her friends, later for women's groups. Now that Pacific Global's name was attached as sponsor, even Will and Gus's shipping company benefited.

Fung Hai was recovering nicely from his injuries, and there had been no more threats against young prostitutes or slave girls. Will knew he had Tang Lin to thank for that, but Tang Lin wasn't the only tong leader in the city. Still, there seemed to be an uneasy truce in play.

All in all, things were looking up.

---

Summer slipped easily into fall, and Will picked a weekend in late October to take Kit and Mandy across the bay to Little Eden and The Grove. Since the accident in May there had been no other mishaps at the construction site, and he'd gotten word the ground was now prepared for the building that would commence as soon as Gus and Lia returned. Will wanted to take one last look before turning over the reins.

Sitting across from him on the ferry, Kit and Mandy appeared pretty as a picture, dressed similarly in crisp shirtwaists, short woolen jackets, and striped skirts. Each wore a broad-brimmed hat trimmed with matching ribbons and carried a reticule. Kit busied herself with the contents of her purse, but Mandy sat serenely, looking at Will. He found himself staring back and spoke to break the spell. "Are you excited to see your old friends?" he asked.

"I will be happy to see them, but I don't think they'll feel the same way," she replied.

Kit looked up from her task. "Why ever not, Mandy?"

"Because they're going to feel uncomfortable around me, as if I have risen to a station above them," she answered. "It's an awkward thing, to feel that others are better than you."

"That's ridiculous," Will said. "They shouldn't feel that way. You're just the same girl you've always been."

"Do you think so?"

Will snorted to cover the unease he felt. "Of course."

"Have you ever felt inferior to anyone, Mr. Firestone?"

Her question caught him by surprise. He had to think. And once he thought about it, the answer came to him, clear as a bell: no. Not ever. From the time he was old enough to realize he was his father's heir apparent and the apple of his mother's eye, he'd felt completely and thoroughly confident that no one had it better than he. He was so sure of himself, in fact, that he rarely thought of society in terms of strata.

He recalled kidding Gus months ago about learning how to speak the language of the people he, and not Gus, had grown up with: rich, privileged, secure people. He'd been joking, but as he thought back, maybe Gus had seen it differently. He thought about Tam Shee. She must have grown up in a similar fashion. Donaldina said that becoming a lotus-foot woman was a sign of wealth and prestige. She must have expected such marvelous things for her life. Hadn't she sacrificed her very feet to get them? What would he do if his world fell away like hers had?

"Mr. Firestone?"

He realized his mind had drifted. "What? Oh, you asked about feeling inferior. No, I guess I never have."

"You were inferior to me in backgammon," Kit reminded him with a snicker. "I used to win handily nearly every game."

Mandy's smile was fleeting. Disturbing. Her uncanny ability to see into him set him on edge. "Well, I'm sure your old friends won't think such thoughts about you," he said.

"I hope not," she replied, and turned to look out the window.

They rented a buckboard at Point Reyes Station and continued on their way. Thankfully it was a warm afternoon, what the locals called an "Indian summer" day. As they approached the town of Little Eden, Will glanced over at Mandy and was surprised to see her begin what could only be called a transformation. She removed the pins keeping her fashionable straw hat in place and took it off, laying it carefully on a blanket in the back of the wagon. Then she removed the pins that had kept her long auburn hair in a respectable, stylish knot. All the pins went into her purse, which landed near the hat. Finally she took off her jacket and put it with the rest of her things.

"If you don't mind, Mr. Firestone, I'd like to walk from here."

Kit, who didn't quite know what to make of it all, put her hand on Mandy's shoulder. "Are you sure? This is quite—"

"I'm sure," Mandy said, waiting until Will had almost stopped the team before hopping down. "I will be at the Butlers when you return from The Grove." And with that, she took off running, holding her skirts above her fancy boots, scuffing them up in the dirt and the mud of a recent rain, her waist-length hair sailing behind her. At one point she even stopped to scoop up some dirt and sprinkle it on her skirt. As she neared the first houses along the main street, they could hear her calling, "Little Bit! Little Bit!"

*What the blazes?* Will looked over at Kit, who watched Mandy with a smile on her face. "Don't you see? She's doing it for them," she said.

By the time they passed the Butler house, Mandy was standing on the front porch, holding a big, healthy baby in her arms while two little boys clustered around her. He remembered the first time he'd seen her, just like that. He was right. She hadn't changed, not inside anyway.

One of the toddlers tugged at her skirt and Will imagined with a slight grimace that the little tyke's hands were anything but clean. They could see her laughing and then she twirled, to show the children how the skirt fanned out.

"They are drawn to her like bees to honey," Kit said.

"Much like you and members of the opposite sex," Will observed.

Kit scoffed. "Oh, I'd much rather be the bee...then I can sting."

---

Will sipped a glass of wine in front of a fire he'd built up in his library. It was almost always cooler in the city than in western Marin, and tonight was no exception. By the time they'd made it back to Russian Hill, all were in need of some warming up. Kit sat in the chair next to him, gazing into the flames.

As he'd hoped, all was well at The Grove. Gus would be pleased with the preparation and no doubt eager to begin construction once he and Lia returned. But before that happened, Will would be traveling to see them. They were getting married in New York City on Thanksgiving, and Will had promised to be there.

"Thank you very much for taking me along with you today, Mr. Firestone." Mandy appeared in the doorway, self-consciously brushing the dust from her sleeves, her thick hair already escaping the impromptu braid Kit had fixed for her on the way home. She resembled a not-so-little beggar child who had accidentally found herself at the front of the house. She blinked a few times and stifled a yawn.

Kit yawned in response. "It's catching," she joked.

"You're welcome, Mandy," Will said. "I'm curious. In the end, did your friends think you superior to them?"

She tilted her head, considered the question. "Honestly, I'm not sure. Have you ever noticed how most people have to work very hard to be someone they aren't? Today I had to work hard to be the person I am." She yawned again and smiled with a tinge of sadness.

"I think it's time for bed, young lady," Kit called to her. "Church in the morning."

"Yes, ma'am."

"If only Josephine could see you now," Will teased his sister after Mandy had gone upstairs. "You've had your first child for what, five months? And she's already a good little mama's girl. Mother will be impressed when you show up on Thanksgiving."

"Oh, we're not going there for Thanksgiving." Kit fussed with her still spotless skirt. "We're coming to New York with you."

"What? Now wait a minute." Will straightened in his chair.

She spoke in a rush. "It's all arranged. I reached Lia through Mr. Hansen and told her we would be in the vicinity and would she mind if we stopped by and of course she was thrilled to invite us and meet Mandy and I've reserved seats on the same train and you have nothing to worry about, so there." She took a deep breath and waited.

"Let me get this straight. You basically decided to crash the party—something you'd consider beyond gauche if someone did it to you." Will sent her a sharp-eyed look but softened it when he saw traces of the vulnerability she fought so hard to conceal. "Why?"

Kit met his perusal with a flinty gaze of her own. "I just don't have the stomach for sitting through another interrogation as to why I'm caring for Mandy rather than making myself available for an advantageous match." Her beautiful face turned grim. "It is becoming intolerable, and I don't trust myself not to blow up and cause a scene. As much as I sometimes relish the prospect, I will not have Mandy suffer through any aspect of that experience. She does not deserve it." She paused before adding, "Besides, Mother asked what we were 'going to do with the little charity case during the holidays.' She didn't even invite her."

Will bought some time by cleaning his spectacles with the tail of his shirt. Kit was right. Mandy already felt like an outsider; leave it to his mother to rub it in—all within the guise of polite conversation, of course. Her unwillingness to step outside her comfort zone was beginning to get on his nerves.

"You sure you got on the same train—the Overland? Leaving on the sixteenth?"

Kit grinned, leapt up, and gave him a hug. "You are the best older brother in the entire world," she gushed. "I'm going upstairs to let Mandy know what an adventure we have in store."

Will tarried after she left, watching the fire burn its way to embers. In all honesty, he didn't mind the girls coming along. In fact he hoped they'd make the time go faster.

Because for once he wasn't so eager to leave town.

He told himself it was business. 1903 had so far been a very good year. The slight downturn had actually worked to the advantage of Pacific Global Shipping. They'd been able to purchase ships from a few companies spooked by the threat of a city-wide quarantine. Wolfstone Enterprises as well as Will's personal investments in real estate and manufacturing were holding their own and then some. They needed tending, didn't they?

Then there was Tam Yong. He was making progress, but Will wanted to stay in close contact with the recovery center—although he had to admit, Fleming did seem to have that situation under control.

And the school in Chinatown. The students loved their headmistress and business was booming. Will found excuses to visit the school often; it was morally uplifting to be there. He was helping these immigrant girls build better, more independent lives for themselves, wasn't he? And the underlying threat of the tongs could resurface any time, he was sure of it.

But in his heart he knew it was more than that. More than any of that.

Tam Shee made it so much more.

# CHAPTER EIGHTEEN

*Mandy's Journal*
*November 15, 1903*

Dear Pa,

Would you believe, I am finally going to see the world! Well, not the world, exactly, but the United States, at least. Tomorrow Miss Kit and Mr. Firestone are taking me all the way across country to see Mr. Wolff and Miss Starling, who are building Sinner's Grove. They are going to get married and we have been invited to the ceremony. Did you ever think your little girl would get to do such a grand and glorious thing?

We are to travel by train, of course. Over Donner Pass (I hope we don't get stuck there for the winter!), and across Nevada and Wyoming and Nebraska. We will stop in Omaha and change trains for Chicago and then on to New York.

I have repeatedly asked Miss Kit to tell me what the train fare costs, because I will have to add it to the tally of what I owe the Firestones, but she refuses to tell me. She says not to worry about such things, that for once I should simply enjoy my good fortune.

Do you think she's right, Pa? I think sometimes people are lucky and sometimes they aren't, and over a lifetime I guess it all evens out. So maybe it's not such bad advice. I am having a difficult time keeping my excitement inside, anyway.

I wish I could say the same for Mr. Firestone. He travels a lot, so another trip like this doesn't mean the same to him. But I can tell he especially doesn't want to leave because he is thinking about Tam Shee Low, the instructor at the School of Needle Arts.

I have learned to speak enough Cantonese that I can actually talk with Wu Jade. She tells me that Mr. Firestone comes often to visit, even though there is no more work to be done on the school. He sits and talks to Tam Shee quietly after class. He has even taught her to play Chicken Foot, the game I taught him! Wu Jade says they speak their own special language that has no words. She says he is the "emperor of happiness" when he is with her.

You know the saying "to walk in someone else's shoes"? Well, I would not want to walk in Tam Shee Low's shoes for all the tea in China, on account of her broken feet. But to have Mr. Firestone think about me the way he does about her would be something wonderful, I think. Then again, maybe that would be giving me more than my share of luck, so I will keep that between you and me.

# CHAPTER NINETEEN

Will stared out the window, watching field after field recede as the train headed down the track. He had taken the Overland Limited across country more than a dozen times in the past few years. The trip from San Francisco to New York took the better part of a week, and while it was usually a pleasant trip, he wished it could be made in less time. He hoped he'd live to see the day when that happened.

Back in May, a physician named Horatio Jackson and his colleague had driven a Winton just like Will's from San Francisco to New York. Granted, it took sixty-three days and cost eight thousand dollars, but what a hell of an adventure! Despite the cluckings of some old-timers, the automobile was here to stay. Once more miles of road were paved, a trip like that would take no time at all.

Even more fantastic was the idea of air travel. A couple of inventors named Orville and Wilbur Wright were experimenting with gliders and supposedly any day now they'd be testing a motor-driven version on the sand dunes near Kitty Hawk,

North Carolina. One of the brothers was even going to try fly-ing the thing. Imagine that. Per Will's instruction, Mr. Hansen had already begun researching possible investments in those two modes of transportation. Rubber for tires, cement for roads, metal for vehicle fabrication—the potential was there for anyone with guts enough to invest capital wisely. Will had both the cap-ital and the guts.

For now, however, he was resigned to making one more drawn-out trip to the other end of the continent. What made this one unique, thankfully, was experiencing it through Mandy's exuberant eyes. Standing in the Pullman where Kit had secured berths, she'd exclaimed, "Can you imagine sleeping while you climb a mountain or fording a river ten times faster than a boat? It is darn near a miracle."

"No, the real miracle is going to be maintaining my wrin-kle-free wardrobe without employing someone to wield an iron on short notice," Kit said. "By the way, you may have the top bunk, Mandy." Mandy was innocent enough to be thrilled.

They were barely an hour out of Sacramento, chugging their way into the foothills of the Sierra Nevada, when Mandy rushed into the parlor car where Will and Kit were sitting. She had a tall, broad-shouldered man in tow. He looked slightly older than Will, with dark hair and big hands. He resembled a farmer dressed up for town.

"Look who I found!" she cried. Will and Kit looked at each other as if to say *Do you know this person?* Both came up empty. The man looked slightly embarrassed until he spied Kit, at which point his whole demeanor changed. It brought to mind a buck taking stock of a nearby doe. The man looked bewitched and Will rolled his eyes. Yes, his sister was a good-looking woman, but did she have to have such an effect on men? It made for too many awkward moments, like this one. Will rose from his seat.

"I don't think we've had the pleasure of meeting," he said, extending his hand. "Will Firestone. You're obviously a friend of Mandy's."

The man, still gazing at Kit, was slow to respond. Mandy nudged him and he looked at Will. "Oh. Oh, I'm terribly sorry." He shook Will's hand. "Tom Justice, at your service." He immediately turned back to Kit. "And you are?"

"Katherine Firestone. I'm...Mandy's guardian. Will's sister." She waited a moment before holding out her hand. The man took it and held it a beat too long. Funny thing was, Kit seemed as struck by the man as he with her. *Interesting.*

Mandy watched the interaction among all of them and lightly slapped her hand to her forehead. "Silly me. I just realized you all don't know each other. Dr. Tom works with the mission and helps the girls. He—" Will watched as Mandy caught herself; apparently she'd almost spilled the beans about something. "He sees patients at the local hospital, too. Everybody loves him."

Dr. Tom had the grace to look sheepish. "That's hardly the case, Mandy, but I thank you for the compliment. I understand you are all traveling back to New York to attend a wedding."

Kit looked up at him. "Yes. On Thanksgiving Day. And what about you, Mr. Justice?"

Will frowned. Why hadn't she used his professional title?

"Oh, I'm traveling back for the holidays as well. My family has a farm near North Platte. I'll have a long buckboard ride once I get off the train."

"Ah. How…quaint." The condescension in her tone was lost on neither Will nor the good doctor. Apparently it wasn't lost on Mandy either, but she had the courage to call her guardian on it.

"My teachers at the Weems Academy use that word a lot. I have learned it means old-fashioned or out of date—something you say when you don't like something but are too polite to tell the truth. You didn't mean it like that, did you, Miss Kit?"

Will almost laughed at the nearly identical expression of horror that crossed both Kit's and the doctor's faces. They stepped into the breach at the same time.

"Of course not—"

"Oh, I'm sure she didn't—"

It went downhill from there. After a few torturous minutes of awkward banter, Mandy announced that she was going to go back to the coach car where Dr. Tom was sitting "because there seemed to be some popcorn for sale there that I did not see in our dining car." She took one of the courtesy blankets that had been placed on her seat. "It's going to be difficult for Dr. Tom to sleep in those chairs. This might help."

"That's not necessary," the man said in a tight voice. The earlier light in his eyes when he'd first seen Kit had flickered out. "I can manage."

"Best to let Mandy do what she's going to do," Will said. "Otherwise she'll find another way."

Mandy beamed at Will's advice. "I'll be back for supper," she said, took the man's hand, and led him back the way they'd come.

As soon as they were out of sight, Kit leaned back with her hand over her eyes. "I am mortified."

"You should be. *Quaint?* I could have sworn Josephine was sitting right next to me. When did you turn all high and mighty?"

"I don't know. I just…I was flummoxed. I didn't know what to say. He…he kept looking at me."

"As if that has ever made a difference to you before now. And may I add that for you to know he was looking at you meant that you had to be looking at him. 'Moon-eyed' wouldn't be too far off the mark in describing you."

Kit waved her hand as if to swat him. "Oh, stuff it. I…I was surprised, that's all."

"Mm-hmm. Surprised that you've finally met someone who piques your interest."

"I'm not talking to you anymore," Kit said, and turned to look out the window. She remained aloof for the rest of the day.

# CHAPTER TWENTY

*Mandy's Journal*
*November 22, 1903*

Dearest Pa,

It has been quite an adventure riding the train across America these past several days. I can hardly believe I'll be in New York City by this evening. I have gotten to know the people on this "moving hotel" very well. Mr. Johnson, our steward, is a nice man who has a wife and three daughters. They live in Omaha and he only gets to see them a few days a month. He laughs and says that's all right because they all chatter so much they give him a headache and he has to come back to work for some peace and quiet. I don't believe him, but I didn't want to make him feel bad, so I laughed along with him.

Our porter, Mr. Matthews, is in a similar pickle, except that he isn't married. He says it's better that way, but I think it must be extra sad not to have someone to come home to after working someplace else for so long.

Miss Kit has forgiven me for embarrassing her in front of Dr. Tom. I didn't mean to do it, but I couldn't understand what she was saying. They had just met on the train, and at first it seemed like they might take to each other. But then she put up a wall of snootiness and hid behind it. She does that when she is afraid or uncomfortable, but Dr. Tom, who is the nicest man, gave her no cause to do so. I know. I was standing right there.

In any event, she and Dr. Tom did not see each other any more on the trip. You would think that might be unlikely on a train, but there is a wide gap between the people who travel like the Firestones do and the regular everyday people. Dr. Tom is one of those. So I spent time with him each day until he got off the train in North Platte. I watched from the window as his mama and papa ran up and hugged him. One of his brothers—he told me he has two of them—came to the station as well. He is younger than Dr. Tom. I would guess him to be around twenty, about the same age as Fung Hai. Oh, it would be nice to have such a family to come home to.

After Dr. Tom got off the train, I spent more time with Miss Kit and Mr. Firestone. Miss Kit is very proud of herself that she hasn't asked Mr. Matthews once to iron her clothes. Sometimes I think she acts like a spoiled rich lady because she thinks others expect her to be one. Or maybe she just doesn't know that that's not who she really is. It's important to know the kind of person you are inside, I think.

Mr. Firestone and I have played many games of Chicken Foot, and he also taught me to play poker! The game is called Five-Card Stud. I do not know why they call it that, except that it uses five cards. Mr. Firestone said he didn't know either, but he doesn't always share everything he knows.

It seems to me that Mr. Firestone likes to play games and talk to me because it takes his mind off all the other things that fill his brain and heart, such as his many businesses and his love for Tam Shee Low. He has never talked about love, of course, but I believe he has those kinds of feelings for her. Knowing that makes me both sad and happy. Sad because it isn't me he loves (I know that is a silly dream!) and happy because if she fills his heart with joy, what more could I want for him?

# CHAPTER TWENTY-ONE

———◆———◆—◆—◆———◆———

"I am so thrilled you are here, all of you." Amelia Starling hugged each of them when they arrived at Grand Central Station in New York City. Gus stood next to the petite artist, big and protective. Will shook hands with his partner and then encased him in a bear hug. Gus and Lia were two of his favorite people. It was good to see them after six long months.

"You ready to take the plunge?" Will asked.

"Chafing at the bit," Gus replied, snaking his arm around Lia. "This pre-wedding honeymoon plumb wore me out. I need to get back to the real world."

Lia patted him on his broad chest. "If that was tough on you, you'd better rest up. We've got an estate to build." Stepping away from him, she walked over to Mandy and put her arm around the girl, walking with her and talking quietly as they headed to the cars waiting for them.

It was an unusual situation. They would all be staying at the estate of Mr. and Mrs. George Powell II. Mrs. Powell was Lia's sister Emma, and Mr. Powell was Lia's ex-husband. Gus seemed to have no problem with the family dynamics, and once Will met the Powells, he could see why. It was obvious that George and Emma doted on each other and on their children, the oldest of whom was actually Lia's by birth but being raised by Emma and George. Little Georgie Powell III was a rambunctious young man who seemed to have no problem thinking of both "Memma" and "Mamma Lia" as his mothers. Twin baby girls rounded out the family.

"I'm glad you showed up early so we can have a few days to relax before the wedding," Gus commented to Will after dinner. "George has set us up with some possible investors in case we decide to expand Pacific Global at a faster pace. I've met them briefly, even talked a little of their claptrap. You'd be proud."

"They're good, solid men, with equally solid portfolios," George added. "They're anxious to get in on the Asian trade."

Will grinned as he sipped his port. "I like the sound of that. Gus, you always were a fast learner."

After retiring to his room for the night, Will found he couldn't sleep. He tossed and turned for a while, thought about heading downstairs for a drink, then decided that probably wouldn't help. Something Mandy had said to him on the train kept running through his head. They'd been playing Five-Card Stud and she had bet an unusually high number of chips (which were train tokens provided by the steward) on a hand that required a specific suit to win.

"Why are you betting so much?" Will had asked. "You can see I've got three aces." He pointed to her face-up cards: a three, a six, and a jack of clubs. "The chances are pretty low you're going to draw a club, and your hand is worthless without it."

Mandy looked at him with those eyes that saw so much. "When you really want something, shouldn't you be willing to risk just about everything for it?"

"I suppose so," he said.

She grinned. "Well, I want to win."

"All right then." They turned over their final cards and hers was an eight of diamonds. She had lost, and he felt bad for her... until she spoke.

"It's all right," she said. "I would have felt much worse had I never tried." She looked at him intently. "And so would you."

Lying in bed now, Will thought about Tam Shee Low and the high stakes game he was playing with her. What would happen if he proclaimed his feelings for her and she reciprocated them? Could they ever make a go of it? The problems seemed almost insurmountable. He had never invited Tam Shee out, but tried to imagine what would happen if he ever brought her to one of his family's social gatherings. They would find her beautiful, of course. And different. An oddity, perhaps, like a rare, tropical bird. But they would never get to know her, not really, and in the process, she would be miserable. He couldn't do that to her. He wouldn't. A melancholy found its way inside of him that stayed just beneath the surface. And it led to, of all things, a simmering resentment of Mandy.

The girl disturbed him, plain and simple. There was something about her. Dell Butler had thought it sexual, but it wasn't that. It was as if she had some knowledge or power that the rest of the world didn't have, and the funny part was, she didn't gloat about it or misuse it or even admit she had it. Will knew without question that if he ever let her get too close, she'd be able to see right into the heart of him. At this moment he didn't know what his heart contained, and damn it, shouldn't he be the first one to discover it?

# CHAPTER TWENTY-TWO

---

*Mandy's Journal*
*November 26, 1903*

Dear Pa,

Today I got to see the Wolffs get married, and if I am ever lucky enough to be a bride, I would want my wedding to be just like theirs. It wasn't big and fancy at all. Just a man and a woman who love and cherish each other, who promise to make their love last, no matter what. And they make this promise in front of God and the people they care about most in this world, because they want the promise to mean something. The words cover a lot of things that can happen in life, like losing all your money or getting sick...even being tempted to be with someone else. But when you decide to marry, you say, "Yes, I'll commit to you through all the ups and downs." You and Mama stayed true to your vows and I know I will someday, too, if I ever have the chance to make them.

I am torn because although I want to return home, I know I will also miss the people I have met here. Emma is a beautiful lady and the best mother ever, besides Mama. I had so much fun with her twin baby girls! I felt like I was back taking care of Little Bit, only there were two of her! And Georgie—what a firecracker he is! The good news is, I will get to see him when he comes to visit Lia and Gus out west. Because of course I will get to visit Gus and Lia once they're back home, too. I love them both so much already.

Here is one reason why: when we first arrived, as we were walking to the cars that would take us to the Powells' house, Lia took me aside and told me how very sorry she was about what had happened to you, Pa. She said she could tell right away that you would be proud of the kind of person I was turning out to be. I like to think she is right.

And Sandy! He is a friend of Lia's from the days she spent as an art student here in New York City. I am very glad he lives in San Francisco, too. He doesn't talk about it, but I can tell he fancies men instead of women. You told me about men like that once, Pa, and said that God makes all sorts of people in this world to keep life interesting. Remember that? I do think it could be a lonely life if you didn't have someone who shared your feelings. Maybe there is someone waiting back home for him.

Mr. Firestone seemed a bit downhearted during the ceremony. Was he thinking about Tam Shee Low? I hope not. Does it sound bad to say that? I hope his thoughts aren't entirely of her, not if they're going to make him unhappy. How puzzling to care about someone so much that they make you joyful and sad at the same time. I suppose Mr. Firestone and I have that in common.

Aside from Mr. Firestone, only one thing shadowed Lia's wedding day, and that was the absence of her father. He is still living, but they do not get along very well. I am sure there's a tiny hole in Lia's heart because of it. Have I told you lately how very happy I am that you are my pa? Because I am.

# CHAPTER TWENTY-THREE

The holiday season was supposed to be a happy time, wasn't it? Will wasn't feeling the joy. His relationship with Tam Shee seemed to be in a holding pattern, and the gift he wanted so much to give her—her brother—still wasn't ready to be presented. It didn't matter, though, because Tam Shee didn't celebrate Christmas anyway.

Whatever Will lacked in enthusiasm was more than offset by his parents and with good reason. Jamie was home from the University of Southern California, and that gave Josephine every excuse to not only host lavish parties, but expect all of her children to attend them. Never was a woman more truly in her element than Josephine Firestone planning a party.

"After abandoning us for Thanksgiving, *every last one of you,* the least you can do is make an appearance or two," she'd announced to Will when he'd dropped by to greet Jamie. The three of them met in the sunroom overlooking the estate's expansive gardens.

"The old dame means business," Jamie said with a cheeky grin. "How are you, old chap?" They clapped each other on the shoulders.

"Why do you let him get away with it, Mother?" Will was only half joking. "You certainly wouldn't have let me off the hook for impertinence like that."

Josephine reached up and patted Jamie's cheek. "Because he's a love and I don't want to spend our precious time quibbling over details."

Will remembered his charge from Kit that morning. "Good, then you'll have no problem sending an invitation to Mandy for Christmas Eve."

His mother's bright countenance faded just a bit. "Is that really necessary, William? It is a family gathering, after all. Can't you find someplace else for her to go?"

Will was surprised at the anger that surged within him, and barely tamped it down in time to avoid a full-blown tirade. He felt the clamp of his jaw and took a moment to loosen it. "Mandy is considered a part of our family. Kit is her guardian, as you are no doubt painfully aware. I can tell you without hesitation that if Mandy is not invited, then Kit will not attend...and neither will I."

Jamie watched the interchange, a speculative gleam in his eye. "Well, I for one can't wait to meet this mystery child. Do be hospitable, Mummy...for me, at least?"

Josephine heaved a sigh. "If I must. You may tell her she can tag along."

"No," Will insisted, "*you* will send her a note expressly inviting her to share the holiday with us. And when she arrives, you and Father will treat her as one of us, down to a goddamn stocking if you have to."

Josephine frowned. "No need for histrionics, my dear. I shall honor your request." She turned back to Jamie, her face all sunshine and light again. "Now, tell me all about your latest escapade as a Fighting Methodist," she gushed.

---

Josephine was true to her word and an invitation arrived the next day. Kit presented it to Mandy during their weekly dinner together.

"Oh, your mama invited me to your Christmas gathering," Mandy exclaimed, running her finger over the envelope's embossed *F*. "That is so nice of her." She sent Kit a worried look. "What should I bring?"

Will exchanged glances with his sister. Josephine wasn't worthy of this girl.

"Not a darn thing, darling," Kit said. "Just be your sweet self."

Mandy wrinkled her nose. "I don't think I'm sweet. But I promise to be on my best behavior. I wouldn't want to shame either of you."

And of course, she didn't. More importantly, Josephine didn't either.

"So at last I get to meet the charming young girl I've heard so much about," his mother pronounced with just the right touch of gaiety and grace. By the look of the quiet but unmistakable pleasure on Mandy's face, she had succeeded in putting the girl at ease.

Dressed in a proper schoolgirl's outfit, adorned only with a red velvet ribbon in her hair, Mandy played her own part without guile. She was deferential to both of his parents without appearing witless, and she met Jamie's cocky attitude with a similar but innocent jocularity—enough so that after dinner, when Will and his brother found themselves briefly alone at one end of the parlor, Jamie was quick with reckless praise.

"My God, you say she's only fifteen?" he murmured. "She's already quite the looker. And what a sassy little miss. I hope I can last a few more years until she's reached her prime. I expect I'll have to stand in line, though."

Will looked at his brother, disdain radiating from every pore. His voice, however, was deadly calm. "If I ever hear you talk about Mandy with such disrespect again, either within this family or among your friends, I will personally wipe up the floor with you. And then I'll hand you over to Kit, who will make my drubbing look like child's play. Do you understand?"

Jamie, his eyes wide, backed off with both hands raised in surrender. "Sorry, old man. Didn't mean to cause offense."

They spent the rest of the evening in traditional family pursuits. Josephine presented the same needlepoint stockings she'd hung annually for each of her children since they'd come into the world. In them she'd put the usual silly, simple gifts: some shaving soap and tooth powder, a book mark, the requisite lump of coal. She'd come up with a small stocking for Mandy, too, and filled it with peppermints, a small comb and mirror, and a tangerine. Will watched Mandy discreetly wipe a tear as she opened it. Was she remembering past holidays? Maybe Christmas with her father? He wanted to give her a brief hug, but Kit beat him to it. She too had observed the moment.

Afterward they played charades, with Will, Jamie, and their father against the women. Will pulled the book title *Twenty Thousand Leagues under the Sea* and did his best rendition of a puffer fish to win the game. Kit took silly pictures of them all with her Brownie camera.

It was their custom to wait until midnight in order to greet Christmas Day together. Interaction grew quieter, more reflective, broken into one-on-one conversations. At one point, Will noticed, Jamie began to bend Mandy's ear about university life and the career path he'd chosen. She listened, asked questions, offered valid suggestions that he knew Jamie would ponder.

The evening came to an end. Both Josephine and Edward were tired, but happy; it seemed that Mandy had passed muster, at least for the time being. She and Kit had already said their goodbyes and were on their way to his car. Will made to follow, but Jamie pulled him aside. All traces of his cocky attitude were gone. "I truly am sorry about my asinine remarks earlier. I can see now why you hold her in such high regard. I will respect her, and protect her, as you do."

Will nodded, for some reason too charged with emotion to respond other than to squeeze Jamie on the shoulder in solidarity. "Merry Christmas, brother."

"Merry Christmas."

The malaise that had dogged Will the night before carried over into Christmas morning. He chalked it up to a change in routine; he wanted to spend time with Tam Shee, but he knew it would be inappropriate to leave, especially since Kit had no idea where he might be going.

He was feeling a touch of self-pity as well, he realized. He wanted to share what had always been a jolly time of year with someone who understood that tradition. Tam Shee had no such reference.

He wanted to take her out to see the lights and decorations of the city, which were particularly festive around Christmas, but he knew it would be difficult if not impossible for her.

He wanted to take Sai-fon up to the mountains so that she could build a snowman. Hell, he would settle for taking her to the ocean where she could collect pretty shells instead of the sow bugs she was forever bringing up for her mother.

Instead he filed those thoughts away, slapped on a smile, and headed downstairs where he knew Kit and Mandy were waiting. His sister, apparently eager to start her own family traditions, had laid out the plan before they'd retired last night.

"First we'll have a big country breakfast," she said.

"Uh, the staff is off, and since neither of us can cook an egg to save our lives, we'll have to settle for continental," Will argued. "In fact, just coffee's fine for me."

"Oh no, brother dear. Mandy's got it covered. You may not realize it, but she's quite the cook. Half of the goodies coming out of the kitchen in the past few months have been hers."

"Really? She never mentioned it."

Kit gave him a look that said *Did you expect she would?*

Now, as he descended the stairs, he could smell bacon frying and coffee percolating. It was intoxicating. He stuck his head in the kitchen and saw both Mandy and Kit wearing aprons and wielding spoons. Mandy was supervising while Kit poured batter onto a large smoking griddle.

"Is that enough? Is that enough?" For someone as self-confident as his sister, that panicked tone just didn't sound right. By contrast, Mandy's voice was low and calm. She was obviously the one in charge. That didn't seem right either, but he had to admit, the flapjacks and bacon were delicious.

Afterward they relaxed in the back parlor, where Kit and Mandy had decorated a small noble fir. Will had placed his packages there the night before, as had the ladies. He'd never admit it, but he didn't really like opening presents, not for himself, at any rate. He found it embarrassing. Unnecessary, since he could purchase anything he damn well pleased. So instead of anticipation or even a lighthearted sense of fun, he felt only irritation, and a niggling sense of guilt that he should feel that way.

"All right. I'll play Santa's helper," Kit announced. She handed a large box to Mandy, who opened it to reveal a beautiful red wool coat with fox trim and a matching muff. Mandy was struck speechless and could only hug the coat and her guardian.

"Try it on, try it on," Kit said.

"Can we get on with it?" Will asked, sounding peevish, which of course, he was.

"Fine, you old mossback. Open your present." She handed him a small rectangular box. It contained a pince-nez-style pair of eyeglasses. Kit laughed with delight. "Now you'll look like our dear President Roosevelt," she exclaimed.

Will took off his regular spectacles and tried balancing the new pair on his nose. He could tell in an instant he wasn't going to like them. They seemed on the verge of falling off, and he felt ridiculous. "They're wonderful. Thanks, sister mine." He put the glasses back in their box and handed her a present with her name on it.

She opened it quickly to find a stunning diamond necklace with matching ear bobs. Will glanced at it and nodded.

Kit quirked her lips. "Hansen has good taste," she said. "A worthy addition to my collection. Thank you, brother dear."

Mandy walked over and shyly handed Kit her gift. It was a novel entitled *The Circle*, written by Katherine Thurston. "She's an Irish writer and is supposed to be very good," Mandy explained. "It's about a woman who makes great sacrifices to follow her dream. And the writer has the same first name as you."

While Kit was saying thanks, Will pulled another small box from under the tree and handed it to Mandy. "Use it in good health," he said. She sat looking at the box for a moment before carefully opening it. Inside was a nondescript pen set one of his business associates had given him that he'd never opened. It came with different nibs and ink. "You can write in your journal, or even practice calligraphy if you're so inclined."

"Such a thoughtful, creative gift," Kit said drily. "What's left?"

"Just this," Mandy said, carrying a medium-size box over to Will.

"You didn't have to get me anything."

"I know, but I thought you could use it maybe."

He unwrapped the box and opened it. Inside was a stereo-scope, a wooden viewfinder through which one could see two photographs that replicated what the human eye sees, in three dimensions. Along with the contraption were several dual photographs of places like Niagara Falls and the Grand Canyon.

"I thought maybe you could show it to Tam Shee and Sai-fon, since they never go anywhere, and I know you must want to take them places. So now they can at least see what the bigger world is like. I thought—"

Will's eyes bored into hers, telling her to *stop!* But she didn't catch his warning in time. Within seconds of speaking, however, she realized the mistake she'd made. She clapped her hand over her mouth, making it even more obvious.

Kit had heard it all. "What are you talking about? Who is this Tam Shee person? Why can't she go anywhere?"

Mandy kept looking at Will. "I'm so sorry, I didn't know she didn't—"

"*Enough.*" Will took a deep breath and let the poisonous thoughts roiling within him spill out. "Listen, I appreciate the thought, but you're really not part of this family, and giving me things isn't going to make that happen. Has Kit told you we're looking for your real family? I should be hearing from them any day now. I think it best if you don't try to insinuate yourself any-more where you don't belong."

His speech was met with silence. Kit, he knew, was in shock. Mandy looked at him with those mesmerizing eyes and he wanted to turn away, knowing she knew what was inside him. Her next words proved him right.

"To not be close to the ones you love at special times like this is hard. I know. And I know the steep mountain you have to climb." She gestured to the stereoscope. "I just thought maybe that would help you along the way."

She looked around as if she'd lost something. "I...I think I will take my new coat upstairs and try it on, if you don't mind." She picked up the large box and headed out of the parlor. At the doorway she turned around to face them. "Thank you for sharing your family Christmas with me, both of you. I loved it very much. And Mr. Firestone? You needn't worry. I'll be ready to go when the time comes."

Mandy left the room and Will could hear her running down the hall. He wanted to run after her and tell her it was all a mistake, that he didn't know the prick who had said such vile things. But he couldn't move. He imagined a pit filled with the sticky residue of shame, sadness, and regret...and he was sinking in it.

"What in the name of all that's holy did you just do?" Kit had found her voice. "And on Christmas morning, no less?!"

He turned his gaze toward his sister. "Why, I just taught Mandy one of life's most important lessons: how incredibly cruel one human being can be to another, with only a voice for a weapon."

# CHAPTER TWENTY-FOUR

*Mandy's Journal
December 31, 1903*

Dear Pa,

One of the things we always planned on but never got to do was ride the gravity railroad at Chutes at the Beach. Do you remember? But after the past few weeks, I feel as if I have been on one of those roller coasters, and I never want to go on another one!

First the high part: I was invited to spend Christmas Eve with Miss Kit, Mr. Firestone, and their parents. Their younger son, Jamie, was home from college, too.

Mrs. Firestone is a little woman with a big spirit. She was kind, but very curious about me, asking so many questions about our family and my life that Miss Kit finally told her in no uncertain terms to stop badgering me. Honestly, I didn't mind. Sometimes it feels good to have someone notice you and take an interest in what you have to say...maybe good enough that you don't even care why they are doing it.

It is pretty obvious that Mrs. Firestone thinks it "inappropriate" (there is that word again!) that her daughter is my guardian. She wishes Miss Kit would find a nice young man and get married and make babies. I think that is what every good parent wants for their children—that they be happy and find someone to love. So I can't fault her for that. But those two ladies seem to butt heads *a lot*. I am glad I am not constantly in the middle of it.

Mr. Firestone the elder is the perfect example of that saying "Still waters run deep." He doesn't say much, but when he does, he is funny and clever. His sons get their height and slender bodies from him, as well as their light-colored hair. I can tell by his father that Mr. William Firestone will still be a very handsome man even when he gets old.

The low part? That same Mr. Firestone (the younger, not the elder), put all his cards on the table on Christmas morning. I wish I could say we were playing poker, but we weren't. He reminded me that I am not part of the Firestone family and never will be, and that as soon as he can find members of my own family to take me in, I am to go with them.

It was unsettling to hear that. I am not sure I would want to live with strangers again, even if they are my blood kin. Being a burden to others, even if they seem to like you, just doesn't feel good inside. You taught me that, Pa, and you were right.

So I have an idea. I have saved over half of what I've earned from my job at the mission. I don't know if it will be enough to live on, though. I will have to ask Fung Hai about that. Maybe I can find other people who would like me to write for them, and that could make up the difference. As for the Weems Academy, I'm not sure if I will be able to continue attending there. We will have to see. And maybe Miss Cameron will let me live at the mission with the other girls. I could help her out in the mornings and on the weekends. It could work.

But can I just tell you, Pa? The idea of leaving Miss Kit and Mr. Firestone fills me with such sadness—like losing you all over again. These ups and downs are not fun at all.

# CHAPTER TWENTY-FIVE

J anuary started off with its usual pessimism: it was cold, rainy, and miserable. And that suited Will just fine. He'd brushed off Kit's questions regarding Tam Shee and deftly avoided all remaining Firestone social engagements except one: he took Jamie out to a well-known strip club on the Barbary Coast and proceeded to get his little brother safely drunk. Jamie at least had a grand time, although the poor sod paid for it the next day.

Kit was cold to him, and Mandy tried to be where he wasn't. She didn't even attend their Wednesday night dinners, pleading a headache one week and a stomachache the next.

He couldn't even find solace with Tam Shee. Like the fierce-looking dragons the Chinese were so fond of, his attraction to her had imbedded its claws into him and wouldn't let go. He longed for the day when he'd be able to present her with the one gift she couldn't help but accept: the return of her long-lost brother. Tam Yong was making great progress, and Will had tried on several occasions to convince the young man to reunite with his sister. But Tam Yong kept postponing the visit—he was still dealing with the shame of his addiction.

Tam Shee was oblivious to all of it. She never asked for more than he gave. She seemed content with their arrangement, but Will had grown restless.

He wanted something more.

For the hundredth time he asked Tam Shee to take a ride with him. "I will carry you down the stairs. You won't have to walk at all," he told her. "We'll take a ride in my car and you can see all those places you've only heard others like me tell you about."

Tam Shee gave him the same answer as always. "It would not be proper; my place is in the home. Besides," she added with a quirk of her perfect, red lips, "these places you tell me about cannot possibly be as wondrous as you have made them in my mind. I am sure I would be disappointed." She delighted in using the stereoscope, however; Mandy had been right about that.

Tam Shee did agree to one adventure: making her way down to the little garden in back of the school in order to watch Saifon play outside. Will kept his temper well banked as he watched her hobble down the stairs, clutching the banister to help her unsteady gait. He counted it a small victory that she no longer feared his censure when she walked, but she couldn't control his thoughts, which always turned to disgust when he witnessed what others had done to her for no good reason.

Perhaps the most heartening aspect of their relationship—if he could call it that—was the fact that since meeting him, Tam Shee had put off the decision as to whether or not her little girl should suffer her same fate.

*Not as long as I am in her life,* he vowed as he played catch with Sai-fon one afternoon, tossing a small rubber ball painted with a map of the world.

—————

"You wanted to see me, Miss Cameron?" Given a message by Fung Hai one morning in mid-January, Will stopped by the mission director's office on his way to his regular afternoon visit with Tam Shee.

"Yes, thank you, Mr. Firestone. I wanted to talk to you about Mandy."

Will straightened. "What's wrong? Is there a problem?"

Donaldina smiled and shook her head. "No. On the contrary, we all think the world of her. The work she has done for us has been...remarkable...for one so young."

"Then what is it?"

"I might ask you that same question, Mr. Firestone. Mandy has asked me if there might be room for her here at the mission."

"Room? What are you talking about?"

"I mean, she would like to live here, sir." Donaldina's gaze turned sharp. "And I find I need to ask why she would want to leave your household."

The shame Will felt at the way he'd treated Mandy reared its head, and he pushed it down with a lie. "She...feels beholden to us, I believe. That is why she wanted the part-time job, if you recall."

She narrowed her gaze. "Yes, but why now?"

"I don't know. Perhaps she grows tired of rattling around a large house with so few people in it." *Or perhaps the fact that I was an ass and made her feel unwelcome out of sheer spite had something to do with it.*

"Perhaps." Donaldina steepled her fingers. "Here is my problem, sir. I do have room for her, and she knows it. She's well aware of the census as it relates to our capacity. Furthermore, she would be a great asset to our work here at the mission, more so than she is already. I have come to see myself as her mentor of sorts."

"And she's your acolyte, is that it?" Will ignored Donaldina's shocked expression and his own insolent tone. "I know I can speak for my sister when I say the answer is no. Unequivocally no."

The director busied herself straightening the already ship-shape papers on her desk. Will could tell she was swallowing her bile and preparing a prudent response to one of her biggest donors. He wondered where the pistol was that he had seen on an earlier visit.

Finally the director raised her eyes. "I'm not sure what to tell her without making it sound as if we don't want her, Mr. Firestone. Because in fact we do." Her shrewd gaze bore into his. "What so many of us take for granted, Mandy finds elusive. She just wants to belong."

Will left the meeting feeling like the lowest form of life on earth. He went on to the school but stopped in the small shop on the ground floor before heading upstairs. To hear Kit tell it, all women, young and old, liked frippery. He would give something to Mandy as a sort of peace offering.

In one of the cases, he saw a deep red silk shawl with small tassels on either end. It was intricately embroidered along each side in burnished gold thread with a subtle design of flowers and vines. The central motif, found on each end of the scarf, was that of a large forest-green bird expanding its wings. He asked the girl behind the counter if he could look at it more closely. She carefully took it out and draped it along the counter for him to see. It was smooth and delicate to the touch.

"It phoenix," the girl said. "Bird who rise from ashes."

"I'll take it," he said. "I will pick it up when I return from my lesson upstairs." The girl nodded. "Pretty scarf. She like."

Mandy *would* like it, he mused, heading up the back stairway. It fit who she was—a phoenix, rising from the ashes of tragedy. He smirked at his lame attempt at grandiosity. It was a gift, nothing more. He'd give it to her on her birthday. Sometime in March, he thought. That would settle the matter.

Mandy wasn't going anywhere.

# CHAPTER TWENTY-SIX

*Mandy's Journal*
*January 17, 1904*

Dear Pa,

Our household has started out the new year in an uneasy spirit. Miss Kit told me on Christmas Day to pay no heed to what Mr. Firestone said, and she has made her displeasure with him plain as day. Neither of them have brought up my living situation since then. Miss Cameron is also mum on the topic, except to say she is "looking into it." I feel as though I am in a type of limbo.

There has been one bright light. Gus and Lia Wolff have returned from the East Coast and they are here to stay. They are excited to begin building their estate near Little Eden. That will bring plenty of work for the people who live there, and I am glad of that. Until their new house is built, they will live in Gus's mansion on Nob Hill, where he lived before he met Lia. (In case you are wondering, they asked me to call them Gus and Lia instead of Mr. and Mrs. Wolff. I told them I would try, although it still doesn't feel quite right to be so familiar with them. I suppose I will get used to it.) At any rate, they have invited me to visit them any time I have a mind to. I don't even have to call ahead. That is wonderful, isn't it?

Now that the Christmas holiday is over, I am back attending the Weems Academy. And of course I continue to work for the mission. It helps that Fung Hai is completely recovered from his injuries. We pursue our stories several afternoons a week.

We meet the girls in the marketplace while they are shopping for their masters, or in the alleys while they are waiting for men to come and sleep with them. Fung asks them about themselves and when they answer, he translates and I write it down. We tell them we are going to write about them and they seem pleased. As I said, it is flattering when someone cares about your life story as if you matter.

Fung Hai and I don't talk about the mission right away. We visit them maybe twice or three times before we explain the choice they can make. I try not to make it all about accepting the Lord; that should be a private talk between a person and God, and I hate to present it as the price of rescue. In many cases it doesn't matter, however, because the girls decide to stay where they are. It is such a fearful choice to change your life completely. I can vouch for that! But sometimes a girl will find the strength inside herself to break away.

We know none of the tongs like what we are doing, but ever since that night we were taken they haven't bothered us. I do not know why exactly, but I am grateful for it.

I have been all over Chinatown now and I think Miss Kit at least would be upset if she knew, not only because of the danger from the tong, but because the plague is still lurking somewhere— at least that's what Dr. Tom says, and he knows about such things.

He has given me more doses of the anti-plague serum, so I feel safe in that regard.

It's been months since the city started rat hunting and cleaning out all the rat places. Some people call Dr. Blue, the man in charge of cleaning out the rats, the Pied Piper of Chinatown. But now the sickness has spread to places outside and it seems there are so many rats he can't keep up with them. But even if he could, no one seems to know just how the rats cause the disease, or why some people get it and others don't.

That is something we've learned the hard way, isn't it, Pa? You can have a picnic one day with your mama and get caught in the rain and laugh about it. And then she can catch a cold that turns to something worse, something so bad it takes her from you forever. Or your pa can be walking along, just doing his job, when a tree falls on him and breaks his neck and kills him dead. People use reasons like that to prove that God doesn't really love us. Why would He do such horrible things if He did? It is a very good question. But regardless of why something happens, the truth is, you just can't predict *what's* going to happen, or when.

I've thought a lot about this. I think God means for us to be happy while we're alive, even if it's for a short while. And I think one of the ways to be happy is to not concentrate too much on yourself, because when are we ever satisfied with ourselves? I think it's better to think of others and how you can do them a good turn, like Fung Hai and I are trying to do. Then, if you're called to heaven in the next little while, you can feel good about what you did when you had a chance to do it.

# CHAPTER TWENTY-SEVEN

The danger was supposed to be over.

For months on end, the residents of Chinatown had endured Rupert Blue's all-out campaign against the plague-bearing rats. Gone were the rotten porches and overhangs; gone were the rat-infested wooden cellars; gone were the piles of trash that kept rats fat and happy. Rats, thousands upon thousands of them, were trapped, killed, dissected, and checked for plague. Chinatown had never looked so good.

So it came as a surprise when an actor named Chin Lai collapsed with vertigo, fever, and chills before sinking into a coma and dying.

When a farmer,

an old man,

and a housewife on Jackson Street all fell ill and died.

And most of all, when an adorable, vivacious five-year-old girl, playing in a garden next to a rat-infested lumberyard, called to her mama and cried because she felt so dizzy.

On a brisk afternoon in mid-February, Will arrived at the school for his customary visit with Tam Shee. A sign on the shop door read "No School No Shop Now" along with Chinese symbols. That's curious, he thought. Maybe it's a Chinese holiday. The door to the shop was open so he entered and took the stairs in the back up to the classroom. Normally filled with the chatter of twenty young Chinese women, the large space was now silent and forlorn. The entire place felt abandoned.

Will walked down the hall to Tam Shee's apartment. The door was closed, so he knocked, but got no response. He knocked louder. Still nothing. Growing worried, he tried the knob. Thankfully it was unlocked and he stuck his head in. "Tam Shee?" he called.

The front room was empty, but he could hear a noise coming from the bedroom. It sounded like crying. He quickly opened the door and found Tam Shee sitting on the bed, rocking the limp body of Sai-fon in her arms. Her little girl was drenched in sweat, her tiny breaths ragged.

"Oh my God," Will cried. "Tam Shee, what's happened?"

She started to cry out in her native language, her words spilling out so fast that Will couldn't make out what she was saying. "Slow down," he told her gently. "I need to understand you."

She looked up at him, her eyes reddened and tear-filled. Nodding, she tried again. "I don't know. Sai-fon and I were in garden last evening, but she felt sick and we come inside. She did not sleep well and this morning she had fever, so I cancel school to care for her. But she is worse. Look at her." She unwrapped the blanket that held her daughter, and Will could see grotesquely swollen glands on both sides of her small neck.

He realized with horror that because of her lotus feet, Tam Shee was essentially a prisoner of her house. "Sai-fon needs to see a doctor," he said. "Let me take her to him."

"No!" Tam Shee cried. "They will cut her open."

"No they won't, Tam Shee. They'll help her."

"No, they cut her open to see the germs and her soul will never be at peace. I will not let happen. Only Chinese medicine is good for Sai-fon." Her expression was militant, mutinous. She knew her daughter was dying, Will could tell, and she was doing what was best for her little girl's eternal life. How could he deny her that? He watched as Tam Shee gently wiped her daughter's fevered face with a cloth and kissed her forehead tenderly.

Will could feel his adrenaline surging. He needed to be doing *something*. "Let me bring a doctor here, then."

Tam Shee shook her head vehemently. "I no want," she insisted in broken English. "Please. You my one true friend. Stay with me. Please."

Will was ripped in half. He knew he should fetch a doctor, that maybe, *maybe* they could help Sai-fon. But his gut told him Tam Shee was right—they would only take the little girl from her mother's arms, and Tam Shee would never forgive him for that. He couldn't give up this woman who had come to mean so much to him, so he made the only decision he felt he could.

Tam Shee was shivering now, and he gently took Sai-fon from her arms and beckoned her to get beneath the covers of her bed. She did so and he placed her dying daughter in her arms once again. He went around to the other side of the single bed and climbed on, putting his arm around them both.

He thought of her brother and how he should have insisted the young man come to see her and meet his niece, because it would have made her so happy.

He thought of all the places little Sai-fon would never see.

He thought of how one small thing can change a person's world forever.

He thought.

And he waited.

# CHAPTER TWENTY-EIGHT

*Mandy's Journal
February 16, 1904*

*Oh, Pa.* The worst has happened, even though it all started out fine.

Early last Saturday morning I met Fung Hai at the Mission House. It was a good day for field work, so we decided to go to the Clay Street produce market first. A young mui tsai goes there to buy fresh vegetables for her owners every week, and she seemed to be receptive to what we'd been telling her.

Fung Hai and I headed up Stockton Street and when we neared the school, he stopped. He'd noticed Mr. Firestone's car. An expression of disappointment, followed by determination, crossed his face. "I need to ask him something," he said.

I knew that Mr. Firestone hadn't come home last night, but I didn't share that with Fung. I felt as shocked as he did, but there was nothing we could do about it. I put my hand on his arm. "I don't think you should," I said.

Fung wrenched his arm away. "I thought he was different than all the rest," he bit out. "He has brought dishonor to our friendship." He marched up to the school entrance and I followed. Even though Mr. Firestone might wonder what I was doing out so early with Fung, I knew he didn't care, really. And if I could somehow forestall a very awkward scene with Fung and Tam Shee, then I was willing to do it.

A sign on the door said the store was closed, but we entered anyway and headed up the stairs. It was deathly quiet. We knocked on the door to Tam Shee's apartment, but there was no answer. The door was unlocked, so we opened it.

"Hello," I called, in case we might be interrupting something. There was no response, so we entered. No one was in the front parlor, but the bedroom door was ajar. Fung Hai must have had a moment to think about his actions, because he hesitated. I now felt something was terribly wrong, so I quickly opened the door to the bedroom.

It took me only a moment to realize the horror of what I was seeing. "Fung," I said calmly, "Please run and get Dr. Tom Justice for me, and ask him to bring as much anti-plague serum as he can." Fung's eyes grew wide and for a moment he stood there, paralyzed. "Fung," I repeated sharply. "Please go NOW."

By the time Dr. Tom got there, little Sai-fon was dead, and both Tam Shee and Mr. Firestone had fevers. Tam Shee's illness was more advanced. She was agitated and Mr. Firestone was trying to calm her down despite his own weakness. He barely acknowledged that any of us were there. I swore Fung to secrecy and sent him to the marketplace to at least make contact with the girl we had been talking to. He promised he would not say a word to anybody.

Dr. Tom administered the anti-plague serum to Mr. Firestone and Tam Shee, and then motioned for me to join him in the front room.

"This is a mess," he said. "We're going to have to take the child from her, and somehow get them to a quarantine house."

"Let this be the quarantine house," I suggested. "It's already been exposed, it will have to be cleaned out anyway."

The doctor looked around and nodded. "It could work," he said, "but I'll have to get some nurses willing to work in this environment."

"I can do it," I said. "I know I'm not a nurse, but I've tended sick children plenty of times. You said yourself all you can do is keep them comfortable while they fight it off. I can do that. You even taught me how to give the shots."

He pursed his lips. "I don't like it. It's too...irregular."

I was beginning to feel desperate. I knew in my heart that this was the right thing to do, and that I was meant to do it. I tried another tactic. "Look, Dr. Tom. You're a good doctor, and San Francisco needs you. Chinatown needs you. But the man in there belongs to a very rich and powerful family. If it gets out that he got the plague from what everyone will call a Chinese whore, that will look really bad and put Chinatown in a bad, bad light, just when it was starting to turn around. But more than that, everyone's scorn for Mr. Firestone will kill his parents. *Please.* I am begging you to let me care for them. I can pull them through. I know I can."

Dr. Tom looked at me like I was a little bit crazy, and maybe I was, but I was also right. Finally he nodded and told me he'd be back with supplies for me, including more doses of the serum. I told him he had to contact Miss Kit and tell her everything. As my guardian and Mr. Firestone's sister, she had to know what was happening.

Using his gentlest voice, Dr. Tom talked an almost delirious Tam Shee into giving up her little girl. He promised her he would bring her back and I wondered how he could do that, since Sai-fon was gone forever. Sometimes white lies are necessary, I suppose.

For as long as there is breath in me, I do not think I will ever forget the look on Tam Shee's face when little Sai-fon slipped from her fingers. As if all the goodness of the world had melted away.

In two hours' time, Dr. Tom was back, but he was not alone. He had a very agitated Miss Kit with him.

"This…this quack here," she said, pointing to Dr. Tom, "says I cannot stay and take care of my own brother," she fumed. "That is ridiculous. How is Will doing?" Miss Kit's eyes were full of tears and her hands were shaking. She started to walk over to the bed, but Dr. Tom stopped her. He is a big man so he was able to subdue her, even though she is tall. She struggled and looked as though she wanted to kill him, though.

"He is sleeping now," I told her. "Come into the front room and talk to me."

Miss Kit continued to glare at Dr. Tom, but when she finally calmed down, I explained again why it had to be this way. "Your ma and pa may lose their son, so you can't put your own self in harm's way. Imagine if they lost you, too. It would destroy them. Do you see that?"

She nodded tearfully. "But why you?" she cried.

"I am perfect for the job," I said, taking her hands in mine. I felt my throat begin to close up, so I knew I had to get it out fast. "I don't have anybody who's waiting for me, who will grieve for me. But you do. You are needed."

"No, I am useless," she whispered to me. I do not think she wanted Dr. Tom to hear.

"Never say that," I whispered back, and put my arms around her. "You have been a good mama to me." I stepped back, then, because there didn't need to be two of us crying.

"I've got what you need here, Mandy," Dr. Tom said, pointing to several packages. "There's no telephone, so Fung Hai will stay close and be your runner, should you need anything else, all right?"

I nodded and turned back to Miss Kit. She looked at me with fear-driven eyes. "Are you sure, Mandy? We can't lose him...or you. We simply can't."

"I'm not worried about me, and I will do my best for Mr. Firestone," I assured her. "I will not let you down." She stared a moment longer before letting Dr. Tom escort her out of the apartment.

Pa, I imagine what you're thinking right about now. I can almost hear you saying, "What in blazes are you doing?"

But I also think—hope is more like it—that part of you is saying, "You do what's right, Mandy Girl. You do what's right."

# CHAPTER TWENTY-NINE

*Mandy's Journal*
*February 16, 1904 (cont.)*

I wonder about the properties of time. What makes it race by and what makes it stand still? During the time I watched over Mr. Firestone and Tam Shee, I think I was frozen in time. There was just me, and two very sick people, and the waiting.

The first thing I did was separate Mr. Firestone from Tam Shee. At first he didn't want to leave her, but I convinced him that she would be more comfortable in the bed by herself. Reluctantly he moved to the other small bed in the room. He was almost too tall for it, but he immediately curled into a ball and fell into a fitful sleep.

A kettle full of water sat near the ashes in the fireplace. It was still warm, so I filled a bowl with some of it and placed it on Tam Shee's bedside table. There was a roll of what looked like bandages sitting on the table already, but they were too narrow for me to use. Instead I found some cloths from the bathroom and set them near the water.

I knew pretty much from the beginning that Tam Shee wasn't going to make it. She had those things the doctor called buboes under her arms. Those lumps where the plague bacteria gathers before it begins to race throughout the body. My job was to ease her pain as much as possible.

But it was difficult. Whenever I tried to move Tam Shee or even touch her, she would cry out in agony, and that was after I had given her a dose of morphine. Her voice was soft and feeble, but that didn't mean she felt it any less than a lion would have. The pain must have been almost too much for her to bear.

"I am so sorry, Tam Shee," I would murmur. "So sorry." I think I was saying it more for myself than for her.

After a while, I noticed changes in her beautiful white skin. I knew that the germs were causing tiny blood vessels to burst throughout her body. At the end, she looked like a woman from the circus, covered with blue tattoos.

I tried my best to make her comfortable. She was shaking with chills, but when I would cover her, soon, in a spurt of agitation, she would try to kick them off. Her lips were chapped and small sores had developed on them. I put a moistened cloth to her lips to give her some relief.

I won't go into what the body does to expel bacteria from the body. As painful as it was for her, I changed her clothes and the bed linens. No one should leave this world covered in their own filth.

Eventually she lapsed into a deep sleep, a sleep I knew would end in one last breath. I was so intent on watching her that I didn't notice Mr. Firestone behind me.

"Let me be with her," he said, all the sadness of the world caught inside those five words.

I was surprised and alarmed at the same time. What did he mean by that? Surely he didn't mean to be with her in death? I looked over my shoulder and felt happiness surge through me, even though it was the wrong time and place to feel it. But still, Mr. Firestone seemed better! I sent up a small prayer of thanks and stepped aside to prepare another shot of the antiserum for him. He sat there and took it without protest, without even knowing or caring what it meant for him. There would be no more injections for Tam Shee.

I watched as Mr. Firestone tenderly held Tam Shee's hand, and brushed her once-lovely hair from her mottled forehead. He reached down to kiss her on the lips and I gently stopped him. "It is too dangerous," I said.

"Dangerous for who?" he replied, and kissed her anyway. Then he said the strangest thing. "I want to wash her feet. Help me, please."

Shocked, I looked into his eyes and saw the devastation in them. He knew the end was near for her. I am not sure, but I think he wanted to pay her respect by accepting all that she was.

We lifted the blanket from the bottom half of her body. She was still wearing tiny satin shoes. We each pulled one off and saw that her deformed feet were encased in bandages. Slowly we began to unwind the cloths. I thought of mummies in their sarcophagi and shivered. When we were finished, we both took a moment to look at what had defined her as a lotus-foot woman. Her feet didn't look like blossoms at all. They were dragon claws, narrow and pointed and curled grotesquely, as if her toes had begun to sink into the broken arch of her foot. I started to cry and turn away, but Mr. Firestone had a different response. He began to stroke them in the gentlest way. He reached for one of the cloths I had used to keep Tam Shee's fever down and dipped it into the bowl of tepid water on the nightstand that I'd been using. Then he washed her tortured feet carefully, all the while tears streaming down his hollowed cheeks.

You know the Bible, Pa. You know what was going through my mind. It's something else that will stay with me forever.

After several moments he finished his task and dried her feet with another cloth. He reached for the same bandages that we had taken off, but they were soiled and smelled bad, and I remembered the roll of cloth I had seen earlier. I handed it to him and he took one of the clean strips and began to bind her feet again, winding the cloth around and around, encasing the ugliness into something small and dainty and filled with centuries of meaning. He did the same with the other foot and then replaced her tiny satin shoes. Sighing, he pulled the blanket back down again. Oblivious to me, he crawled into the bed and lay behind her, as if they were a tired, old couple spooning after a busy day. This time I didn't convince him to move. I just let him stay.

Because I could see that Tam Shee had breathed her last.

# CHAPTER THIRTY

--◆--------◆◗◆◗◆◗◗------◆--

*Mandy's Journal*
*February 16, 1904 (cont.)*

Leaving Mr. Firestone alone with her, I went to the apartment's front door. "Fung," I called downstairs.

"Yes?"

"Please go and tell Dr. Tom that Tam Shee has passed away, but there is hope for Mr. Firestone. I'll need clean linens and a change of clothes for him…and they'll need to come and remove Tam Shee's body."

Fung relayed the message and soon two hefty men came in dressed in special suits, along with Dr. Tom, and took away Tam Shee. Mr. Firestone tried to protest, but he was so weak by then that it was easy for Dr. Tom to hold him at bay. While I replaced the linens again, Dr. Tom changed Mr. Firestone and put him in the clean bed.

"I think he's getting better," I said, hoping to add one silver lining to the oppressive cloud. "He sounded all right for a while, and I gave him another shot of the antiserum. Maybe all he needs is sleep."

Dr. Tom gave me a look of pity. He took me by the shoulders. "Mandy, how are *you* feeling?"

I smiled, because this was something I knew. "I feel all right, Dr. Tom. I think the serum has worked on me."

"Still, you don't have to keep doing this," he said. "I can try to find someone else to bring in. This may not turn out the way you want it to and I'm afraid that's going to be too hard on you."

I found myself choking up again and tried to swallow the lump in my throat. "I know what I told Miss Kit, but can you keep a secret?"

He nodded solemnly.

"In my heart, Miss Kit and Mr. Firestone *are* my family. They have done right by me and I could no more walk away from this than you could from those *you* love."

Dr. Tom glanced at Mr. Firestone, who was beginning to mumble and move jerkily in the bed. "He weighs a lot more than you do," he said. "I'm not sure you can handle him."

"I can handle him." I said it with slightly more confidence than I felt. "He will listen to me, and if he becomes too agitated, I can calm him down with a bit of morphine. I will be fine."

The physician looked at me a bit longer before sighing, which signaled that I had won. A sense of relief flooded through me. Whatever happened, I was going to stay until the end.

"Remember, call downstairs to Fung Hai like you just did, and we'll bring you whatever you need. Good luck, dear girl."

I believe in luck, but I hate depending on it. And yet that is all I had to count on during the next two days.

I had thought Mr. Firestone was better, but shortly after Dr. Tom left, he began to get much worse. His temperature rose so high that I could not keep up with putting cooling cloths on his forehead before they would warm my hand to the point of uselessness. He wore no shirt and I was so happy to see there were no buboes on his neck or under his arms as there had been with Tam Shee. I was too shy to check his groin area, which was another place that might be filled with germs, and could only hope that none had sprung up down there.

He did show one symptom that I had not seen in Tam Shee, however: tiny bumps appeared all over his slim chest and arms and neck. He began scratching at them and I had to keep stopping him from rubbing his skin raw. I tried putting cold cloths on them to give him some relief.

The bumps looked familiar to me. One of Sarah's twins had the same thing once; I think she called it "hives." I made a note to ask Dr. Tom about that because he had never mentioned those kind of bumps in his description of the disease.

Like Tam Shee, Mr. Firestone began to feel pain—such pain in every part of his body that he writhed and moaned with it. I was afraid to give him a shot of morphine; he was so jumpy I worried I might stick him accidently or the needle would break off inside of him. I felt so powerless, sitting there, watching him fling the covers off and then, almost immediately begin to shiver violently. I would place them over him again, as gently as possible, but he would still wince, and the cycle would begin all over again.

He began to call for water, and I tried to give him some, I really did, but he couldn't raise his head enough to drink, and although I tried to help him, he flung his arm out and knocked the glass over, spilling it on me and all over himself and the bed. I couldn't change the linens without moving him, and moving him by myself was impossible, so I found a towel, and wedged it underneath him. With another towel I dried him off, but every touch was excruciating to him.

I debated the pros and cons of prayer. I know that God answers every petition, but not always with the answer we are looking for. I was too afraid He might think to test me, or perhaps He might feel He needed to teach me a lesson. On the other hand, would He say, in the end, "You didn't ask, so what did you expect me to do?" I was a coward. I feared being responsible for what happened to this man who had come to mean so much to me.

I tried another tactic. The saying, "God helps those who help themselves" came to mind, so I began talking to Mr. Firestone, urging him to fight the germs that were attacking his body.

"You have too much to live for," I said. "Your family needs you." And later, when I was so tired and anxious and afraid, I put my head on his chest and whispered, "I need you. Please don't go."

I must have fallen asleep that way, because when I woke up a little while later, I felt a hand stroking my head and Mr. Firestone, who was still not himself, was mumbling, "Tam Shee. Beautiful Tam Shee."

I didn't mind, because he felt much cooler than before, and if I could bring him some comfort by pretending to be someone else, I would do it a thousand times over.

Shortly after that he fell into a deep sleep, but I could tell it was a good, clean rest. The little bumps had almost gone away and he no longer thrashed about in the bed. I went into the front parlor and built up the fire, which had burned out hours before. Once the flames began their dance, I curled up in the chair that Tam Shee had used, put a small blanket over my shoulders, and promptly fell into a deep sleep of my own.

# CHAPTER THIRTY-ONE

*What is she doing here?* Will's response to seeing Mandy curled up in Tam Shee's chair by the fire filled him with both anger and fear. He remembered the death of Sai-fon—what was it, a few hours ago? He knew it was plague, which meant Mandy would be exposed. But where was Tam Shee? And again he thought, desperately, *Why is Mandy in Tam Shee's chair?*

He must have made a noise of some kind because Mandy's eyes opened and she smiled so beautifully that for a moment he was spellbound. He couldn't remember her ever smiling at him that way. He stared at her so long that her smile faded to a look of puzzlement and then concern.

"Where is she?" he demanded. His voice came out harsh and brittle.

Mandy sat up in the chair and put her long legs back on the floor. She pulled a small blanket around her shoulders and stood up. "I'd better tend the fire," she said.

He stalked over to her and grabbed her arm. "I said where is she, damn it!" She flinched at his words and looked at him with those cursed, almond-shaped eyes, telling him everything he needed to know without saying a word. He dropped her arm and spun around so quickly that he almost lost his balance. He reached out to save his fall and waved Mandy away when she tried to steady him.

"I don't need your help," he growled. "I need to know what happened."

"If you promise to sit down, I'll tell you," she said calmly, gesturing to the sofa.

Reluctantly he did as he was told, tapping his knee impatiently.

"Tam Shee has…gone away," she started. "She—"

"What do you mean, 'gone away'? She can't just leave here. She can't walk, remember? She's not like you or me."

Mandy shook her head. "No, she's not like you or me." She took a breath. "She's dead."

Will stared at her again, trying to process what he'd just heard. Tam Shee couldn't be dead! Just minutes ago he had nodded off while watching her pouring love into her little girl. "But I was just—"

"Tam Shee died of the plague three days ago, along with Saifon. You've been near death yourself. But you're better now, thank the Lord."

She started to walk to the door, but again, he stopped her by touching her arm. "What are you doing here, then?"

She looked pointedly at his hand; he felt ashamed and dropped it. "I checked in on you, that's all."

"Well, you'd better run along, then." He waved his arm. "As you can see, I'm fine." He looked around, bewildered, still clutching the back of a chair for support. Tam Shee was gone, but he was so tired he didn't know how to react. Weakness overtook him. What was it he needed to do? Perhaps sleep.

Mandy looked at him briefly before calling down the stairs. "Fung Hai?"

"Yes?" came the response from below. *What was Fung Hai doing here?*

"Run tell Dr. Tom that Mr. Firestone's over the worst of it. And tell him it's time to clean house." She pulled her red coat off the hook by the door and buttoned it up. Then she paused as if she'd remembered something, and took the coat off, hanging it back on the hook. She stroked the fur collar and patted it gently.

"Someone will be here to help you shortly," she said to Will. "Maybe you should lie down until they get here."

"That's...that's what I was planning." He ran his hands through his hair; it was stiff and matted. "You're no longer needed here."

She didn't answer him. Instead she walked out and closed the door quietly behind her. The click of the lock sounded ominous, like the hammer of a gun being cocked. He lay down on the sofa and closed his eyes.

---

Tam Shee, this was not the way to finally leave your apartment, Will thought with a trace of despair. He stood apart from Donaldina Cameron, Cheung ti Chu, and several members of the School of Needle Arts as the caskets holding the remains of Tam Shee and Sai-fon were loaded onto the S.S. *China* for transport back to their homeland. Mandy had come as well; she stood with Fung Hai and Wu Jade, commiserating with quiet tears.

Tam Yong, devastated to learn of his sister's death, had nevertheless made a sound decision: he was going to accompany his sister and niece back to their village and see that they were buried properly next to Tam Shee's husband. Will had paid the bone tax and given Tam Yong a substantial grubstake so the young man could return to his family with his pride intact. It was the least Will could do.

"I never forget all you do for my family," Tam Yong said, clasping Will's hand. "I learn it you and not Tang Lin who rescue me. You give me life back and I not lose it again."

"See that you don't," Will said, his voice gruff with emotion. Without warning, his eyes welled up. "You...you make sure they are taken care of, all right?"

"I make sure." Tam Yong squeezed Will's hand one more time and turned to board the ship. As he walked away, Donaldina and Cheung took his place.

"We will all miss her," Donaldina said. "She exemplified the very best of Old China."

Will looked at her askance, acid lacing his words. "But the old must make way for the new, isn't that right?"

Rather than take offense, the crusader merely nodded. "It must, despite the difficulty such transitions entail."

He knew she was speaking on multiple levels. In the strictest sense, the school where Tam Shee and Sai-fon died had already undergone a major upheaval: it had been "sanitized" by the authorities. That meant all of the work already completed by the apprentice needle workers had to be burned, along with all of the material and supplies. Everything in Tam Shee's apartment had to be destroyed as well. An investigation into the cause of death brought attention to the lumberyard next door and, under Rupert Blue's direction, all of its wood products were demolished and removed. No trace remained of the plague that had annihilated such beauty.

But the school itself would survive. Donaldina had already tapped Wu Jade to succeed Tam Shee. Apparently she too was a skilled seamstress and possessed quiet leadership skills of her own. Will's reaction to all of it was tinged with bitterness. *The show must go on.*

A student called Donaldina back to the group. Cheung's expression was stoic.

"She's right, you know. As much as I hate to admit it."

"What, about the need for change?"

Cheung nodded. "Don't tell her I said that."

Will managed a grim smile. "My lips are sealed."

Cheung continued to look ahead as he spoke. "I could not have brought her the happiness you did."

Will knew Cheung was talking about Tam Shee now. He hesitated, afraid his emotions would come tumbling out. "I...I'm not so sure about that."

"I am. And what you did for Tam Yong...out of love for her... is an honorable thing. I am proud to call you my friend." Cheung looked at Will then, and bowed slightly before walking away.

Under the guise of a busy work schedule and phantom business trips, Will kept his convalescence from his parents. Time passed and he began to mend, his physical strength improving every day. He found out that although the antiserum had helped him fight off the plague bacteria, his body had reacted poorly to the serum itself. There was even a name for it: serum sickness. Either way, he was damn lucky to be alive.

All well and good.

But the chasm in his mind between *then* and *now* kept widening, until he could barely remember the man he'd been before. In his place was a man now defined by loss.

A series of questions kept demanding answers: What kind of person would he be if the loss continued, if he had no money, no status, and no support system of family and friends? Would he thrive? Would he even survive?

The need to find the answers to those questions began to burn itself into Will's soul, and finally, two weeks after Tam Shee's death, he decided it was time to search for them.

He began to make plans, enlisting the discreet aid of Mr. Hansen to iron out the details. Then fate stepped in to answer one of the obstacles he'd been trying to overcome.

Someone answered the newspaper ad he'd placed asking for relatives of Amanda Marie Culpepper.

# CHAPTER THIRTY-TWO

*Mandy's Journal*
*March 1, 1904*

Dear Pa,

Something is going to happen. Ever since Tam Shee and Sai-fon's deaths, Mr. Firestone has been struggling. Not physically; he is all right in that regard. But his heart is broken and I don't think that's ever happened to him before. I so wish I could help mend it.

But I can't, and neither can Miss Kit, who seems to be having her own secret struggles. She feels bad because she wasn't there to help her brother, and Mr. Firestone feels bad because he couldn't help Tam Shee. How can you feel happy when you feel such things? Each of them is looking for an answer to make themselves happy, and when they find it, it will never be the same for any of us again. I wonder sometimes if it doesn't make more sense to never let yourself become completely content, because it will never last. Your life just has other ideas in mind.

Things are going to change. I feel it, but I don't think I'm ready for whatever's next.

# CHAPTER THIRTY-THREE

The man stood at the front door, card in hand. "Mr. William Firestone? The Reverend Josiah Trent, at your service." He was a preacher, all right. He looked to be in his mid-forties and was dressed in black, which, given his height and body configuration, made him look like the latest incarnation of Ichabod Crane.

Will looked down at the card. It said *Missionary* on it. "May I help you?"

"Yes, I'm here about my cousin, Miss Amanda Marie Culpepper? You or someone in your employ placed an advertisement in *The Indianapolis Star*, which I am responding to. I have been out of the country, but a dear friend of mine, who knew my late cousin Kay Culpepper, saved the paper, knowing that I would be returning soon."

Ah, the ads. It had been so long since the agency had placed them, he'd forgotten about them. He'd just assumed Mandy was alone in the world. It seemed unreal that someone would be answering it now. This man bore checking out. "Come in, uh, Reverend Trent."

He ushered the man into the front parlor and offered him a drink.

"Oh, I do not indulge in spirits," he said primly.

*Strike one for you, mister.* "Yes, well, tea, maybe? I'm sure we can scare something up."

"No thank you, really." He pulled out a sheaf of papers from the bag he had strapped across his front like a mail carrier. "I'm sure you want to check out my bona fides. Here are documents showing my relation to Amanda through her mother. Kay and I were first cousins."

Will glanced at the papers. He'd have his attorney go over them with a fine-tooth comb. "I see. Well, the truth is, Mandy is doing quite well right where she is. She's in school, and—"

"May I ask, sir, if you are married?"

"No. Why do you ask?"

The man pursed his lips and his tone was full of reproach. "It's obvious, Mr. Firestone, isn't it?"

*Okay, the man's judgmental. Strike two.* "Um, no, I haven't a clue what you're talking about."

"May I ask how old you are, sir?"

Will narrowed his gaze. "Twenty-eight. And that is relevant because…?"

The man arched his brows, as if Will were an idiot. "It is manifestly improper for a single young lady to be sharing an abode with a single man without the benefit of marriage. I would think you'd be aware of that fact."

Will ground his teeth. *Remain civil.* "Oh, I see. It's improper for a young girl to live with a grown man…and his *sister?*"

The reverend visibly relaxed. "Oh. Oh, that's much better. At any rate, may I see my young cousin? We have much to discuss."

"I told you, she's in school, and I'm afraid, *Reverend* Trent, that before any decisions are made here, I will be checking on these documents. *Thoroughly*. When I am satisfied as to their legitimacy, I will arrange a meeting between the three of us to discuss changes, if any, in your cousin's living arrangement. Where may I reach you, sir?"

The preacher squinted at Will for several moments. "You seem very proprietary, Mr. Firestone. Perhaps too proprietary."

Will refused to take the bait. "I asked, where may I reach you?"

Reverend Trent rose and headed imperiously toward the door. "I'm staying at the West View Hotel," he said. "If I don't hear from you within a day or two, you can be sure I'll be back. Perhaps with the authorities."

"I am quaking in my boots, Reverend. Until then."

He wandered back to his library. *She has family*, he thought. After all they'd been through, and after the unforgiveable way he'd treated that girl, she now had an alternative. She could leave.

He sensed in his gut the papers would turn out to be legitimate. And Mandy truly was too young to be on her own. But it didn't feel right.

He leaned over to poke the embers in the fireplace. When he straightened, Kit was standing in the doorway.

"I thought I heard you speaking to someone earlier. Anybody I know?"

*No sense putting it off*, he thought. "Not yet, but you will. Come and sit down. I'll fill you in."

"Good," Kit said. "I've got some news to share as well."

"Don't tell me you're getting married," he said, half in jest.

"No, I…" In a move uncharacteristic of her, Kit hesitated, plucked at her skirt, settled herself on the sofa before continuing. "I've applied to the Training School for Nurses on California Street—and I've been accepted!" She ended her pronouncement with a beatific smile.

Will was floored. Kit hadn't mentioned a word about seeking such a major life change. *But then, neither have you.* "My, that's… well, congratulations," he managed. "This calls for a drink." He poured his sister her usual sherry and himself two fingers of Scotch.

"You have no idea what you're missing, Reverend," he muttered, taking a swallow.

"I have a problem, however," Kit continued. "It's a residential program and although I've asked for an exemption because of Mandy, they are not budging. They say they can't make exceptions no matter the circumstances because—" here she mimicked an older matron's pompous voice "—each of our students must demonstrate their full and undivided commitment to their studies." Her voice became serious again. "You see the pickle I'm in. I was thinking maybe you—"

"You know leaving Mandy here with me unchaperoned won't do," he said. "The tongues would lash us all to pieces, especially Mandy, and that's simply not going to happen." He took another fortifying drink. "Besides, I won't be here anyway. So yes, I'd say we're in a pickle."

"What?! What do you mean, you aren't going to be here? Where in blazes are you running off to?"

*How much to tell her?* "I wouldn't call it running off, as much as perhaps 'searching for,'" he said.

Kit looked at him intently, as if she realized she hadn't been paying attention, as if she'd somehow forgotten what he'd been through with Tam Shee. He thought he saw a dash of compassion in her eyes but wouldn't swear to it. "What are you hoping to find?" she asked quietly.

"Ah, that's the question, now, isn't it?" He stared at his glass. "I think perhaps myself." He swallowed the last of the drink.

Silence reigned for a few moments before he heard Kit sigh. He looked up and saw that she wore a tender but melancholy expression.

"Then I suppose I should cancel my acceptance," she said. Although she tried to hide it, he could hear the disappointment in her tone. "Mandy and I will stay here."

Will shook his head and reached for the bottle to pour himself some additional fortitude. "That's not an option either, I'm afraid. You staying here unchaperoned along with Mandy would be nearly as bad as me keeping her by myself. In case you hadn't noticed, there's a double standard when it comes to a woman's reputation."

Kit rolled her eyes. "You don't have to remind me of something I live with every damn day." She rose and paced the room, her skirt swishing briskly. "I'm not sure I can handle begging Mother to take us both in, or what the consequences of her agreement might be." Her eyes, he noticed, had misted with tears, which she hastily wiped away.

That's when he told her about the visitor. Hoping she'd swallow the lie, he said the Reverend Josiah Trent seemed upstanding, and being a man of the cloth, he'd no doubt do right by Kit's ward. And if not, Miss Cameron at the Mission House had once suggested Mandy move in there. Kit was visibly relieved and they discussed how the transition might work.

"I'll have to meet this reverend fellow to make sure," she said, her voice markedly lighter. "But I'm so happy she has options." Kit leaned over and kissed her brother on the cheek. "You always come through, Will. Thank you." With that and a smile, she left for an appointment with her hairdresser.

Not always. Not with Tam Shee.

Alone with his thoughts, Will didn't feel the relief his sister seemed to. No question that having Kit and Mandy under his parents' roof had always been a terrible option. His mother and father were going to be shattered when Will announced his departure; he wouldn't put it past his mother to have found some way to blame Mandy for his actions. From experience he knew how easy it was to lash out at others when you're in pain.

Now that option was off the table, and the choice for Mandy was either the mission or the missionary. He huffed, emptied his glass a second time. Some choice. He couldn't stomach the thought of Mandy turning into another self-righteous, old-before-her-time Christian warrior like Donaldina. She'd no doubt make a good one, what with her ability to size people up and get to the heart of them.

No. She deserved something better. A chance to explore what *she* wants out of life instead of always pleasing everybody else. A chance to see how far her talent would take her.

An idea came to mind. He'd have to follow up on it, of course, but it could be the answer to their problem. He had to explain his plans to his partner and detail what he needed anyway; what was one more request?

He set down his glass, donned his hat and coat, and headed out the door.

———

Will found Gus outdoors, wearing an undershirt and a pair of workmen's trousers, splitting wood near the extensive gardens of his Nob Hill estate. For years Gus had lived there alone, but now he and his bride shared the elaborate, renovated Victorian-style mansion that Will had once dubbed "the monster."

"Ah, the gentlemen farmer back at work," Will commented as he walked down the sweeping stairway.

"Don't knock it 'til you've tried it," Gus said. He brought the ax back down with a harsh *thwack*, splitting the wood neatly in two. Will watched his friend's muscles bunch and relax with the effort. He felt weak by comparison. Ineffectual.

Well, that was going to change. You got a minute?" he asked.

"Of course." Gus set the ax down and pulled on the shirt he'd left on the banister. "Lia's upstairs organizing her sketchbooks. Now that she's settled in and ready to work, she's in a pickle. She captured so much on our trip that she's fretting over what to paint first. It doesn't matter, I told her. It will all be great."

Will felt a tug at the admiration, not to mention affection, contained in Gus's offhand remark. He wanted what Gus had. Not the woman, but the feeling. "That's all right," he said. "I wanted to talk to you alone anyway."

Gus stopped and gazed at Will. "Sounds serious."

"It is."

"Then come inside and tell me about it. Whatever I can do to help, I will."

---

"I think the plague must have addled your brain," Gus said an hour later. They were sitting in Gus's library by the fire. "Are you sure you want to do this?"

"Absolutely sure," Will replied. "We already know one of us can handle the reins of Wolfstone and Pacific Global in the short term, and I trust you to handle my personal investments. That is, if you're willing to."

"Hell, you know I'm willing. That's not the point. The point is, are you going about this for the right reason?"

Will paused a moment, staring into the flames. "My entire life I've had someone available to chop my wood and build my fires. I've learned basic skills here and there, but just on a lark, not because I had to." He looked at Gus. "You had to. You started with nothing and you built something. Many of the Chinese who came here were in the same boat as you. And some of them had resources just like me, only they lost it all. I'm not sure I have it in me to make a go of it starting with nothing. But damn it, I've got to find out." He smiled gamely. "Think of it this way: as a deck-hand for Pacific Steam, I'll get a bead on the competition."

"You're dreamin', boyo. No one's going to hire a Firestone to swab the decks."

"That's why you are now looking at 'Will James, adventurer at large.'" He patted his jacket. "And I've got the papers to prove it."

Gus pursed his lips. "Mr. Hansen's work, no doubt."

Will grinned for the first time in a long time. "No doubt."

"We aren't all cut from the same cloth," Gus said in a last attempt to dissuade him. "You don't have to prove anything to anybody. Look, you've created wealth—"

"Which is immeasurably easier to do when you start from wealth," Will pointed out.

"I wouldn't be so sure of that." Gus leaned back in his chair. "I can't tell you how many men I watched gain a fortune and fritter it away in the course of three months."

"Well, hell, I'm giving myself a lot longer than that," Will quipped. "Who knows how many fortunes I'll lose?" He turned serious once more. "Listen, I'll never know what I can do unless I get out there and challenge myself. I have to prove something to *me*."

"Josephine and Edward are going to go round the bend," Gus cautioned.

"I know. That's the one regret I have about my plan. But if I pass on it for that reason, I'll never know if I used them as an excuse because deep down I didn't think I could cut it. I have to have confidence in myself, and if I lose that, I've lost everything."

"I can't argue with you on that score. What about Kit and Mandy?"

"Kit's headed for nursing school. And Mandy, well…that's why I'm here."

Gus looked at Will and smiled. "We'll have to ask the boss lady," he said. "Let's go find her."

# CHAPTER THIRTY-FOUR

---

*Of course he'd be punctual,* Will groused as he heard the doorbell chime. A week had gone by and he'd set the meeting with Reverend Trent for eleven o'clock. Since Gus and Lia had come early, they were already waiting in the front parlor with Kit and Mandy.

Last night he'd gone over the plan with Kit and she was ecstatic, but she agreed that Mandy's feelings were of paramount importance. Earlier this morning they'd broken the news that the girl's situation was about to change, that she indeed had a relative. However, they told her, she had choices, and when the good reverend arrived she'd hear what they were. He felt confident that all would work out once they sent the preacher man on his way.

It began well enough. Will made the introductions all around and when Mandy met her cousin, everyone could tell right away they were related. They had the same body type, same coloring, same facial structure. Even the eye color was the same. Will told himself that meant nothing.

The reverend spoke first. "I am happy to take Mandy under my wing. I run a successful mission in the south of Australia. We have quite an impressive heathen conversion rate and I'm sure she will like working with the little picaninnies."

Will glanced at Gus and Lia. They looked as appalled as he felt. This man put Donaldina to shame! But it was Mandy who made him proud.

"Do they truly want to embrace the Christian religion?" she asked. "Or do they do it because of the things you do for them? Is it possible to help without forcing them to believe what you do? That way they can come to know the Lord on their own without you backing them into a corner. I try to do that with my job at the Mission House."

*Yes,* Will thought with satisfaction. *That's my girl.*

"Ah, your so-called job at the mission. My guess is you can take whatever approach you like, seeing as how Mr. Firestone pays your wages."

"No he doesn't," Mandy said. "The director, Miss Cameron, does." She looked at Will for confirmation, but he couldn't meet her eyes. *Shit.*

Kit took up the charge. "You've got a lot of nerve, mister."

Trent's eyes and his demeanor turned glacial. "It's *reverend* to you, miss." He turned to Will. "To the extent you checked my bona fides, I checked yours. I have many friends in the mission community and I did some digging. Pacific Global Shipping funds that little sewing school there in Chinatown, and buried in those accounts is a line item explicitly for your direct donation to Mandy's supposed wages. Do you deny it?"

Will couldn't, and the look on Mandy's face was enough to send his insides to hell. She asked him, without words, if what her cousin said was true. He couldn't lie to her, so he said nothing, and watched the light inside of her fade away.

Trent looked at Mandy and his voice was surprisingly gentle. "You may think you work there, my dear, but you're in fact a charity case, just like all the Chinee you purport to help. I guarantee that you will feel useful and appreciated in my care, and you will certainly earn your keep."

"But that won't be necessary, reverend," Lia spoke up. "Mandy is welcome to stay with us, as our ward, and pursue her own path in life here where she is most comfortable."

Everyone paused in awkward silence. Mandy took a deep breath and sent Lia a fleeting look of gratitude. Then she nodded slightly and straightened her shoulders. "That is very kind of you, Mrs. Wolff—I mean Lia," she said. "I sure do appreciate the offer. But seeing as how the Reverend Trent here is my flesh and blood family, I think it's probably best that I go with him." She turned to Kit and hugged her guardian. "You will make the best nurse," she whispered. Then she stood and said to Will, dignity and grace infusing her words, "I thank you so much for all you've done for me these past several months, Mr. Firestone. I felt safe in your care and I am grateful for the opportunity to go to school. I...I will never forget you." She turned to the reverend. "I don't have too much to pack, so if you don't mind waiting, I'll be down shortly." With that she left the room, with one man sporting a self-righteous smile and four adults shell-shocked.

"Wait a minute," Kit said, looking bewildered. "That wasn't..."

Will looked at Gus and Lia, *What the hell just happened?* etched on his face. Gus and Lia exchanged looks and nodded slightly to each other.

"Pardon me," Lia said quietly, and left the room.

"Reverend, let's you and me take a walk," Gus suggested. "I want to hear more about this mission of yours."

In a matter of moments, Will and Kit were left by themselves. He saw tears running down her cheeks. She sent him a look that begged him to *Fix this*. But he didn't know how. He could only sit there wondering like an idiot how it happened that the bottom had just dropped out of his life.

# CHAPTER THIRTY-FIVE

*Mandy's Journal*
*March 9, 1904*

Dear Pa,

When you make a choice, and it's the right one, shouldn't you feel light as mist, lighter than a feather? When I decided to go with Reverend Trent I felt the opposite, like a heavy blanket had been placed on top of me, weighing me down. I tried to imagine the relief on everyone's faces now that I'd no longer be in the way, but in my heart I knew even that wasn't true. Miss Kit would miss me. And Mr. Firestone would too, in his own way. For a while, at least.

The thought of never seeing them again sent a bolt of panic through me, as if I were standing on a rickety bridge, swaying to and fro over a swamp full of hungry crocodiles. For a moment I couldn't breathe. I told myself, *You will get through this. Just like every other time.* But then I thought about saying goodbye to Fung Hai and the girls at the Mission House and the tears I had tried so hard to hold back just burst through and I couldn't stop them.

I was so *angry*. Not at anyone in particular, although I admit I wanted to blame someone. In truth, I wanted to poke my finger at God and say *Stop doing this to me!*

But deep down, I was angry at myself for acting like such a baby about the latest turn my life had taken. Some of the girls I had come to know, like Wu Jade, were all alone in the world. At least I had someone who was willing to take me in. You know me, Pa; being mad isn't something I know how to do very well, so I like to avoid it if I can. Today, though, it seemed impossible to hold it in.

But I had to keep going, didn't I? So I pulled my suitcase out of the closet and hefted it onto the bed. Just then, someone knocked on my door.

"Please go away," I called. I couldn't bear to have Miss Kit hug me in sympathy, or worse yet, have Mr. Firestone pat me on the back for having done the right thing for all of them.

"It's Lia. May I come in for just a bit?"

Suddenly I felt so very tired and sat down on the bed. "Alright."

The door opened and Lia stood there, smiling at me. She is a lovely person; it shines out from inside of her, you know? She is also beautiful to look at. I feel somewhat like a moose next to her, because she is so much smaller. I was glad to be sitting down.

"May I?" she asked, gesturing to the space next to me. I nodded and she hopped up on the bed. "You are lucky to have long legs," she said.

I said nothing, and looked around the room. She waited a moment and reached over to gently take my hand. Just that little movement made me tear up again.

"What do you think about the changes Kit and Will are making in their lives? It's having quite an impact on you."

I searched for the truth within me and found it. "I know they need to do it, to get happy again. That is a good thing. And I know we weren't a real family, but even so, at times it felt like we were. So I will miss that. I will miss them."

"I saw your face when you discovered Miss Cameron and Will had led you to believe you were working on your own when in fact Will was paying your wages."

"It was humiliating," I whispered.

"I can see that, especially coming from one who values her independence as much as you do. Because I am just like you," she said.

I looked at her in disbelief. "How can that be?"

"I left my home in New York to come here for many reasons, but one of them was to finally be my own person, and not be beholden to anyone. Your father was a loving man, but mine was not. As you recall, he didn't come to my wedding. All the time I was growing up, I felt as I suspect you feel right now: like a burden."

I couldn't hide my response. "But…he was your father."

She nodded and I could tell the memory still made her sad. "So you chose the option you thought would make you feel less of a burden, even though I can see in your eyes that's not the choice you wanted to make."

How could she tell that? "What...what choice do you think I wanted to make?"

"The one that lets you be you, whoever that turns out to be. And as I see it, I can provide you with what you need."

"I don't see how," I said. "You have no obligation to me. Neither did the Firestones. They're good people, just like you. But I was taught to do what's right. And it's not right to take charity when you don't absolutely need it, even from those who are willing to give it. I can work and I should work."

"I agree. Which is why I would like to hire you, Miss Culpepper, to be my assistant."

I narrowed my eyes. That sounded a lot like my supposed part-time job with Miss Cameron.

She held up her small hand. "I know, you're thinking, 'Ah, just like the mission.' Well, I can assure you, if I didn't hire you, I would be hiring someone else. Gus will be busy with his and Mr. Firestone's business, especially while Will is away. And I have so many ideas about how The Grove will work that I can't follow through with them all on my own. I need someone. Someone smart and creative and resourceful. Someone I can count on to tell me the truth and be the support I need. Someone who can write well and communicate both on paper and in person what I need them to say. I think you fill all those requirements and I am asking you to take the job."

The wheels started spinning in my head. Could it work? "Would...would it pay enough that I could afford a place to live?"

Lia smiled. "We have a very big house here in town with too many bedrooms, and the home we're building at The Grove will be just as large. So, yes, I think some of your salary could go toward room and board. But Mandy?"

"Yes?"

"People do talk. And since you're still very young, it would be best for the world to think of you as our ward. It will only be for a few years, but it will give you an *entree* into society that you wouldn't have if you were just an employee. We'll have a lot to do together, both here and at The Grove, and I need you to be able to navigate any waters we encounter. Do you understand?"

I looked at my hand clasped in hers. The happiness inside of me began to bubble up and I tried to tamp it down. "What about Reverend Trent?" I asked. "I told him—"

"Don't you worry about him. I'm sure between Gus and Will, they'll make things right with the good reverend."

"Then I say yes," I whispered. And because I was afraid of bursting into tears again, I raised her hand to my cheek and held it there. And she let me.

# CHAPTER THIRTY-SIX

In a monumental case of bad timing, Will was scheduled to report for duty aboard the S.S. *Manchuria* on Mandy's sixteenth birthday. He'd said goodbye to his parents and sister the night before but rose early the morning of his departure to wish Mandy a happy birthday and give her the scarf he'd purchased before Tam Shee's death. He was dressed in seaman's clothes and had his duffel bag stashed by the front door. Fleming was standing by to give him a ride to the docks.

Will found her in the downstairs library, sitting in front of the banked fire and writing in her journal with the pen he'd given her. He sat down on the chair next to her. "Let me guess," he said. "'One hundred and one reasons I can't wait to get rid of Will Firestone'?"

"Not enough pages," she said with a half-smile.

He tried to tell himself he wasn't disappointed. He would miss her, he realized with a start. Deeply.

"But I am glad you're leaving."

He frowned. That was unexpected. He'd only been joking, after all. "Why do you say that?"

She closed her book and looked at him with those mysterious eyes. "Because unless you go, you will never fully understand all that you have right here waiting for you."

"I need to understand who the hell I am," he argued, pointing to his heart.

She replied with a hitch in her voice. "That too."

He remembered the package and handed it to her. "Happy Birthday."

She looked at him with surprise.

"What, you didn't think I'd remember?"

"I didn't think you knew." She looked at the package for a moment before carefully untying the string and placing it on the arm of her chair. Just as carefully she unwrapped the paper.

She'd done the same thing at Christmas. It dawned on him that she'd probably not gotten many gifts at all. Of course she'd treat each one as if it were special, even a goddamn pen. *God, I am a fool.*

She pulled out the scarf and stared at it. "It's beautiful," she said, a touch of awe in her voice.

*No, you are.* The thought skittered by and he let it go, choosing not to pursue it. "It's a phoenix," he explained.

"I know. The mythical bird."

"It symbolizes rebirth. Tom Justice told me what you did, so I guess in a way you did that for me. Brought me back, I mean. And I'm not sure I ever said it, but thank you."

She shook her head. "I had nothing to do with it. You were meant to live." She stood up and put the scarf around her. It set off her auburn hair perfectly. She reached up and kissed him on the cheek. "Thank you, Mr. Will Firestone." Her voice was soft and shaky. "And come back to us." With that she ran out of the room and up the stairs.

Will sat there for a moment, absorbing the quiet of the early morning. He glanced over and saw that Mandy had left her journal. On impulse he picked it up and opened it to the last page she'd written. In her simple scrawl he read the words:

*Once upon a time, a handsome young man set upon a journey to far-off lands. He was in search of a priceless treasure, one that only he could find. It was the key to his own true heart.*

His eyes welled up before he could stop them. *She knows me,* he thought, an odd sensation curling through his veins. *More than anyone else, she knows me.* He pulled himself together, taking off his spectacles and wiping his eyes with his shirt tail.

"Fleming?" he called.

"Yes, sir." His major domo stood in the doorway, the duffel in his hand.

"It's time to go."

## PART TWO
## 1905–1906

*A man is never too old to learn.*

CHINESE PROVERB

# CHAPTER THIRTY-SEVEN

◆━━━━━◆◇◆━━━━━◆

*The Grove*
*Christmas Eve, 1905*

"Georgie, hand me the berry garland, will you, please? I think it will go perfectly in this spot." Mandy reached down from her perch on the ladder in front of a twelve-foot-tall Douglas fir dominating the great room of the Wolffs' new mansion at The Grove. Georgie Powell, Lia's son by her first marriage, stretched on his toes to hand her the decoration but couldn't quite reach. She could sense his frustration.

"I could do that for you, Miss Mandy," Georgie insisted. "You shouldn't be up so high. You might fall down."

Mandy chuckled at the eight-year-old's latest ruse to show how big, strong, and capable he was, even though he was small for a boy his age.

Unbeknownst to him, Gus Wolff, his stepfather, had walked up behind him. In a whoosh, he caught the young boy and swung him up onto his shoulders.

"Whoa!" Georgie yelped in delight.

"Now, step up and show her how it's done, young man." The boy carefully balanced on Gus's broad shoulders and happily strung the garland in place.

"Perfect. Thank you, kind sir." Mandy climbed down the ladder and surveyed their handiwork. The Christmas tree was lovely, made more so by the dozens of silly, handmade ornaments everyone in the blended family had contributed.

Gus's daughter, Annabelle, visiting from southern California, had proved expert at cutting out paper dolls and snowflakes; Georgie loved stringing popcorn, although he seemed to eat every other piece. The two children had worked together, using Lia's paper and paint, to draw angels, snowmen, stars, and reindeer, as well as Santa, which they cut out and hung on all the branches they could reach.

"What do you think, Papa?" Annabelle bounced into the room showing off her head of golden girls through which Lia had strung tiny ropes of glittering glass beads. "Didn't Lia make my hair beautiful?"

Gus, who had let Georgie hop back down onto the floor, cocked his head and rubbed his chin as if rendering judgment. "I do believe you might be the absolute prettiest ten-year-old girl in this entire room," he declared.

"Ha!" Georgie cried. "He's funnin' you, Annabelly—you're the *only* ten-year-old girl in this entire room!"

Annabelle frowned, then grinned and swatted her father's muscular shoulder. "Ho, ho, ho," she said.

After gathering the remains of the decorations, Mandy put the ladder away and tidied up the area around the tree. Like the kids, she was almost giddy with excitement. Spending Christmas last year with Gus and Lia at their Nob Hill estate had been wondrous. Like a fairy tale. Their warmth and generosity had overwhelmed her.

And now here it was, a year later, and the holiday promised to be even better, because it was the first year at The Grove. Mandy wanted it to be perfect.

The Wolffs had invited several friends to help them celebrate, most of whom Mandy had gotten to know during the past year and a half. The famous artist William Keith and his wife, Mary, would be coming, as well as the banker Hunter Mason and his wife, Bertha, who knew everything there was to know about orchids. Thaddeus Hansen and his family would be there, as would Sander de Kalb and his close friend, Roger.

Sandy held a special place in her heart because he specialized in painting the immigrant children of Chinatown and was now branching out into older subjects. She had introduced him to several people, including Fung Hai and Wu Jade, both of whom had posed for him. As one of the first year resident artists, Sandy actually lived at The Grove, and Roger often came to visit.

A few other residents, who had chosen to stay at The Grove rather than visit their families for the holiday, would also be there. Mandy could honestly say there were only two she didn't particularly care for: a young photographer named Peter Raines, and Ethel Steubens, who wasn't really an artist at all but an artist's model, which meant she posed nude so that artists could draw and paint the human form. She was a beautiful woman, but she seemed to be troubled on the inside. Mandy vowed not to let Ethel or Peter Raines spoil what she hoped would be a wonderful evening.

⁂

"I declare, that Mrs. Coats is the best damn cook in the county," Hunter Mason said, patting his substantial stomach. "That mince pie of hers puts all others to shame."

"Don't be getting any ideas, Hunter," Gus warned him with a wink. "Mrs. Coats is a treasure and we have no intention of parting with her."

"She's the secret to our happy marriage," Lia added. "If Gus had to eat my cooking for any length of time, I think he'd be looking for the exit."

Gus raised his wine glass and gazed at his wife. "I'd just live on love, sweetheart. That's all I'd need." His declaration was met with "ahh's" from the women and lighthearted jeers from the men.

"And I'm sure a virile man like you would be eating several times a day." Ethel laughed raucously at her own innuendo. Peter Raines, who often insinuated himself next to Lia, snickered. Thankfully the rest of the group didn't respond; there were children present.

Unfortunately, Ethel often drank too much, as she had this evening. A few of the resident artists looked to Lia, but she merely shook her head. Mandy knew that meant to let it go. Lia would let them know when to take Ethel home.

After dinner they all regrouped in the large gathering room to admire the tree. Gus stood with Lia and their two children.

"Mandy, the lights please," he said. As they'd planned, she turned off the lights, pitching the room in darkness. She could hear murmurs of surprise and curiosity. But then Gus said from the darkness, "Merry Christmas, everyone," and at the same time, the Christmas tree lit up in a blaze of electric lights.

"Oh my!" "Incredible!" "Don't that beat all!" Most in the room had never seen a tree lit by electricity before.

"It's magical!" Annabelle cried. And it was.

———❦———◦◄●►◦———❧———

Hours later, the guests had all retired for the night, either in the cottages or upstairs. Mandy had put Annabelle and Georgie to bed, warning them sternly that Santa would never come if they didn't close their eyes and go to sleep. Georgie vowed he was going to wait up and listen for hoof beats on the roof, and Annabelle poked him and said she'd never forgive him if Santa found out he'd stayed awake. So he promptly closed his eyes, and in a matter of minutes, the two children dropped off into slumber.

Mandy walked downstairs and saw Lia sitting on Gus's lap. He had given her a necklace and she was kissing him passionately, holding the back of his head. After the kiss, she tucked her head into his shoulder and they gazed at the tree. Feeling intrusive, she cleared her throat to give them warning.

Gus looked over his shoulder and smiled. "Thanks for handling the urchins and giving us a little smooching time," he said. "But come and sit down. We'll have a crowd tomorrow morning, so we wanted to share a little Christmas just with you."

Mandy came and sat down next to them; Lia reached over to take her hand. "I hope you know, you are a part of this family," she said. "I feel as though I have both a sister and a daughter in you, Mandy, and that's the truth."

Mandy felt her throat tighten. "This past year and more, it's been more than I ever hoped for. Thank you for taking me in, and I hope I've…earned my keep."

Gus laughed. "I heard from your cousin last week. He says he's doing the work of the Lord and sends his love."

"Uh huh. And I'm sure he's enjoying the new wing of the Mission School as well," Mandy said.

"No doubt," Gus said with a grin.

Lia stood up and knelt by the tree. Looking under the branches, she pulled out a box and handed it to Mandy. "Merry Christmas from us."

"Oh, well, I have yours too." Mandy reached under and brought out two smaller boxes. "You first."

Gus opened the box to reveal a pair of leather work gloves. "Thank you, Mandy girl." He tried them on. "Perfect fit."

"I thought maybe you'd get fewer blisters," she said.

"Yes, fewer blisters would be nice." Lia's slow smile telegraphed a message that only she and Gus shared.

I want to have that someday…and I know who with, Mandy thought. "Your turn," she said to Lia. Her guardian and friend opened her box to find a soft leather pouch with several small compartments in it. "It's for your brushes," Mandy explained. "I thought maybe…"

"I know just what it is, and I thank you. It'll come in very handy. Now it's your turn."

Mandy looked down at the gift. "You shouldn't have. The clothes you bought for me last week were more than enough." She and Lia had gone shopping in the city before meeting Gus in the afternoon. Lia had purchased several items for Mandy, including delicate lingerie and a velvet cocktail dress in the *chinois* style. "You need something special for the Firestones' New Year's party," she'd said. Aside from the scarf Will had given her, she didn't own anything nearly as fine.

She hefted her Christmas present and shook it. "It's heavy." With her usual deliberation, she untied the ribbon, slowly opened the box, and drew out three volumes bound in richly tanned leather: *Aesop's Fables, Bulfinch's Mythology,* and *The Complete Works of William Shakespeare.* "Oh, they're wonderful." She ran her finger along their embossed spines. "I shall cherish them."

Gus was ever practical. "And read them too, I hope."

Lia playfully nudged her husband before turning to Mandy. "Every writer should have a library full of references, and now you're on your way."

"Yes I am, aren't I?" Mandy leaned over and hugged the couple. "I can't thank you enough." She straightened and headed toward the stairs, the books held tightly in her arms. "Merry Christmas," she said.

"Oh, Mandy?" Gus called after her.

"Yes?"

"One more thing. Not a gift, exactly, but maybe. I heard from Will today. He'll be there on New Year's. He's coming home."

# CHAPTER THIRTY-EIGHT

W ill Firestone was going home. As Will James, his travels over the past twenty-one months had taken him to fourteen countries. For the most part he'd avoided the Russian–Japanese hostilities plaguing the Far East, but his time wasn't conflict-free. He'd been in four barroom brawls; been stabbed once, with a faint white scar to remind him of it; lost three sets of spectacles (including the pince-nez pair Kit had given him); and bedded six women, none of whom had given him any souvenirs (thankfully) to remember them by. He'd developed an impressive pair of biceps, and after one particularly liquor-fogged night he'd acquired a tattoo to put on one of them. He was reminded of *that* experience every time he took off his shirt. He was damn lucky he still respected the design in the morning.

Thanks to a dubiously issued mariner's certificate, he'd started as an able-bodied seaman on the S.S. *Manchuria*, a passenger steamship heading for ports east. By the time they'd reached their final destination of Hong Kong, he'd risen to the newly created position of "special third mate" in charge of "ship efficiencies," all by making discreet suggestions regarding pro-ductivity to those above him. He'd parlayed that promotion, along with his by-now passable knowledge of Cantonese, into a brokerage position with an import-export firm based in Kowloon. He'd been given Southeast Asia as his territory and his first six months on the job had netted him ten thousand dollars.

But none of those things came close to topping what Will *really* got out of his journey: the knowledge of who he was—with-out the name, the money, or any of the trappings belonging to William Arthur Reginald Firestone.

He wasn't entirely thrilled with the person he'd uncovered. He was too rigid, for one thing, too judgmental. He found himself a protector of women, even as he used them—with their permis-sion—to satisfy his needs. He thoroughly enjoyed little children (even grubby ones) and old people, but couldn't tolerate men and women who took advantage of the youngest and oldest of a group. As time went on, he became more in tune to the plight of others, but that awareness wasn't always productive, because it drove him to take action based on emotion rather than intellect and logic.

So he compensated by exerting firmer control over his sur-roundings, which was itself a dubious attribute. He would have to work on that. It was a process.

Because the one thing he realized above all else: he preferred being William Arthur Reginald Firestone to being Will James. That's why he was going home.

Once his ship docked and he went through immigration, Will headed straight to Suen Lok Choy's Haberdashery in Chinatown. Since he'd bulked up a bit, he knew Suen would need new measurements to create the updated wardrobe Will had in mind.

The tailor was happy to see him. "Mr. Firestone, sir! It has been long time since we see you."

"I've been traveling, Suen. Visited your home country, too. It is a beautiful place. But I need—"

Suen grinned, pulling a tape measure out from under the counter. "I see you need different size. I measure."

An hour later Will walked out having given Suen an order for three suits, several shirts, three pairs of casual slacks, two sports jackets, and a tuxedo. He paid extra to have the latter ready in three days' time. As usual, his parents would ring in the New Year with a gala celebration. For once, Will was eager to attend.

———•◦⊶•◦⊷•◦•◦⊶———

A social event at Will's parents' home was always a lavish affair, and the party welcoming 1906 was no exception. The theme for the year was *Progress*. Josephine and Edward, with input from Kit, had posters made to look like newspaper headlines depicting various domestic and worldwide events. If one only read the headlines, one would indeed think the world was headed to a better place: "Russian Reforms Underway" and "Sun Yat-sen Works to Free China from Tradition-Bound Manchu Dynasty" graced the walls, along with "Las Vegas: Modern City Rises from the Desert Floor" and "San Francisco Declared Plague-Free." Kit had apparently insisted on adding "Albert Einstein Discovers Theory of Relativity with E = mc2 Formula," even though no one, his mother admitted, had any idea what it meant, only that it was a breakthrough of some kind.

The menu, as ever, was outstanding. Chef Bertrand, having switched from French to Italian cuisine, was still at Josephine's beck and call. She continually kept him hopping as he tried to please her finicky palate, and Will finally understood that Bertrand preferred it that way. As he sampled the *risotto alla piemontese* and the *tortelli di zucca*, Will was confident the more than three hundred guests would have no complaints.

In his new, custom-fit tuxedo, he felt right at home, but with a difference. Now as he surveyed the friends and colleagues he'd known all his life, he couldn't forget that so many of them, including his parents, spent more on the food for a party like this than most people in the world earned in a lifetime. He'd eaten canned stew and moldy bread with swabbies, and fresh-caught eel and rice with Chinese fishermen. He'd dined at ten-course banquets given by trade ministers and the same day watched mothers go without food to feed their hungry children.

In short, he'd glimpsed the other side, and realized he was in a unique position to do some good in the world. The key, he knew, was to help others help themselves. The Chinatown School of Needle Arts—which he had supported during his absence—was a perfect example. He was certain he could get many of the monied men—or their wives—at tonight's soirée to invest in similar enterprises; it was just a matter of pairing the right money with the right investment.

"We're so glad you made it back safe and sound after all your adventures, aren't we Beatrice, dear?" Dinah Marshall brought her daughter into the conversation without losing eye contact with Will.

"Looks like you put on some bulk there, young man." Clarence Marshall had ample bulk of his own, but of the wrong variety. "Eat a lotta rice, did ya?"

"Oh, Father, really." Bea rolled her baby blues at Will as if they shared a private joke about awkward parents. She looked almost the same as she had before he'd left; only the fashion of her gown had changed.

At that moment Will glanced over to see Gus and Lia enter the ballroom. As usual, his business partner made quite an impression. Big, dark and rough-hewn, the man many called a "Klondike King" exuded an air of elemental power and virility. His wife, Lia, was a perfect mate for him. She was petite and striking, but in no way subservient. Will smiled, thinking about the no-holds-barred arguments those two must have, and the fun they no doubt had making up.

But who was the woman standing behind them? Although partially blocked from his view, he could see she was statuesque, with long, gorgeous dark hair, and a siren's body caressed by a dark green gown that allowed no room for the magic of lingerie. As she handed her coat to the attendant, he noticed the dress was designed in a style he'd rarely seen on white women: it featured a stand-up collar in the manner of traditional Chinese dress. And her slender, shapely arms were bare.

Well, not entirely bare. Because the other thing he noticed was a deep red shawl that...looked...familiar.

Oh. My. God. It couldn't be.

But it was.

Will felt an immediate rush of blood to his groin, and a second after that he felt shame wash over him.

"Oh, there's the artist Amelia Starling and her husband," Bea's mother pointed out.

Beatrice turned and looked at the group across the room. "Who's that woman with them?"

"Uh, that's…that's their ward, Amanda Culpepper," Will said.

"She's quite a stunner," Bea's father observed, taking a swallow of his gin and tonic. "What's her story?"

Will bit back a sarcastic retort; the man was hardly interested in her pedigree. "She lost her only parent a few years ago. She recently graduated from the Weems Academy and has been Lia's personal assistant for a while now."

"Damn, looking like that, she'll get snatched up right quick." Clarence's voice held more than a tinge of appreciation.

Bea looked up at Will, a sly expression on her face. "Didn't she live with you a few years ago?"

"Are you implying something? My sister was her guardian while Gus and Lia were overseas, and yes, both she and my sister lived in my house on Russian Hill during that time. If you'll excuse me, I haven't seen them in a while and would like to say hello."

Will was still irritated by Bea and her father's innuendos when he reached Gus and Lia. Lia ran up to him first, laughing like a schoolgirl at her first party. "Oh Will, it's so good to see you!"

Will returned her hug and couldn't help grinning over at Gus. He'd known Lia was a treasure since the first time he'd met her, when she'd been commissioned by his parents to paint a family portrait more than three years earlier. It gave him enormous pleasure to know she'd found passion and happiness with his best friend. Gus raised his eyebrows in the age-old communication between men regarding women: *mystical creatures, but you gotta love 'em anyway.* Will extended his hand to shake Gus's while still holding on to Lia. A waiter passed by and they ordered cocktails.

"It's good to have you back," Gus said.

"And doesn't Mandy look splendid?" Lia said, breaking away and presenting Mandy to him.

Will extended his hand formally, as if he were meeting a banker. "Yes, hello, Mandy. It's nice to see you again. I'm glad you're making good use of that old shawl."

Mandy gazed at him, those dark, almond eyes seeing too much, as always. He saw a familiar hurt in them and wished he could rewind the conversation.

"Welcome back, Mr. Firestone," she replied in an equally formal tone. "I'm glad you made it home safely."

"Oh, I think you're old enough to call him Will, don't you think?" Lia shared a smile all around.

"Will, then." Mandy glanced beyond Will's shoulder. "I see Kit over there and I'd like to say hello, if you don't mind." She turned to Will. "It was nice to see you again."

Once she was out of earshot, Gus said, "Well, what do you think?"

*I think she's spectacular... and I think I shouldn't be thinking that.* "I...uh, think you've done a good job with her," he said carefully. "She seems like a very poised young woman."

Gus sent him a look that said *you aren't fooling me*, but Lia spoke up with a burst of enthusiasm.

"Oh, goodness, yes, she is an incredible person. You know she's a writer, but she's also a natural-born mother. We have Annabelle and Georgie with us for the holidays and they adore her. But it's more than that. She's the confidante of half the artists at The Grove. She puts up with their idiosyncrasies and really listens to them. Plus she's been invaluable to me in putting the program together. I can't say enough about her. She's one in a million."

"I can see that," Will said, keeping his voice neutral. If Lia knew what he was thinking, she'd probably go after him with a pitchfork. Time to change topic. "So you're glad you set up the retreat, then."

Gus sent him a knowing grin. The message this time was *excellent diversionary tactic.*

"It's working out splendidly," Lia said. "Sandy agreed to be in the first group and we picked nine others from different media." She ticked the varieties off on her fingers. "A sculptor, a potter, several painters, a glass blower, and a textile artist. Peter Raines, who's volunteered to help me with various projects, is a photographer."

The waiter returned with their drinks. Will took a pull from his Glenlivet and practically smacked his lips in appreciation. He did love a good Scotch. "And they each have their own place?" he asked.

Gus nodded. "Nothing fancy, just a single bed and bath with a front parlor they can use as studio space if they need to.

I guess you left before we put those up. I've lived in worse, I can tell you that."

"They're larger than our stateroom was." She put her arm around her husband and looked up at him coyly. "Of course, I didn't mind the close quarters."

Gus gave her a squeeze. "Space is overrated."

Letitia MacIntire came up to greet them and was soon joined by Hunter and Bertha Mason. Since Letitia was also one of Lia's patrons, the talk soon turned to the latest trends in art.

"I say, this new breed of art coming out of New York, this emphasis on the seamy side of life, seems quite brutish to me," Letitia pronounced with a sniff. "I'm not at all sure I like it. I much prefer the natural drama inherent to a well-rendered landscape."

"Or the beauty of the human form," Bertha added.

"Really?" Lia said. "I'm intrigued by what Robert Henri is trying to achieve. He calls his work 'art for life's sake.' He tells his students they should make a stir in the world. Doesn't that sound marvelous? I love the concept of trying to find certain truths about the way real people live, no matter how harsh those truths might be."

"Does the way real people live make you uncomfortable, Letty?" Will asked.

She didn't notice his veiled sarcasm. "Well, I just see nothing *heroic* about it, those pictures of laundry flapping in the breeze, or people standing around in a saloon. It seems so utterly banal."

Lia put her arm through Letty's and pointed to Sander de Kalb standing next to his partner, Roger, and chatting with someone near the buffet table. "Come with me, darling. I'd like you to talk to Sandy about his latest series in Chinatown. Mandy has helped him take his work to the next level. I think it will pierce even your black heart."

Letty laughed with gusto and sauntered off with Lia.

"Your wife is an amazing woman," Bertha said to Gus with unabashed approval. "She'll have Letitia setting the trend in 'gritty realism' before the summer's out, I'll wager."

"And you, too, if you're not careful. Come, darling, and feed me." Hunter Mason winked at Gus and Will, and led his wife away.

Will took another swallow of his drink and frowned. "So, Mandy is still spending time in Chinatown?"

Gus watched his wife across the room, a bemused expression on his face. He was obviously as besotted now as he was three years ago when he met her. "Not as much, since we now live primarily out at The Grove." He took a sip of his own drink. "Speaking of which, you need to come out there as soon as you can. We've got something special you ought to see."

Will glanced at him. "Can't you just tell me about it?"

"Nope," Gus said. "Gotta see it to appreciate it."

"All right then, how about next weekend?"

"Sounds good. Plan to spend a few days, would you? I'd like you to get a lay of the land, tell me what you think—you being an efficiency expert and all."

Will grinned. "You heard about that, huh?"

"Mandy and Kit stay in touch."

Will looked over to where the two women were still deep in conversation. "Mandy seems to have made an impression on just about everybody," he murmured.

"Never doubt it," Gus said. "She's special, that one."

"So I've heard." Will finished his drink and suddenly felt like another.

# CHAPTER THIRTY-NINE

He hasn't changed his attitude toward me one bit, Mandy thought with dismay as she headed over to see Katherine Firestone. He doesn't see me as anything but the little girl he practically patted on the head when he left. She didn't know what to expect when Will Firestone came back, only that the idea of seeing him again filled her with a thrilling combination of excitement, trepidation, and joy. All those month he'd been gone, she'd thought of him every day, even written letters which she hadn't had the courage to send. Somewhere along the way she'd accepted the fact that her father was gone, and she rarely pretended to write to him. But she still wrote in her journal, and often it was about Mr. Firestone. She speculated about his life… tried to imagine the places he'd traveled to…worried about his safety…and longed to know if he would ever decide to come home again. When she'd heard of his intended return, her heart had danced a jig in anticipation.

What had she expected—that he'd look at her differently? See her as someone other than the gawky girl who'd been foisted upon him? Yes, she admitted, if only to herself. She wanted him to see her as a woman and not a girl. And a woman who might even interest him. She had hoped the new dress would help him to do that.

Because that is certainly the way she saw him. She dared not look back for fear he, Gus, and Lia would be watching her. But oh, how she wanted to stare at him! It was as if the man, who started out handsome enough, had been sent through a crucible and forged into a sharper, more masculine version of himself. His face was tanned, which made his icy blue eyes stand out more, even behind his ever-present spectacles. His hair was longer, just brushing the collar of his elegant attire. And he seemed bigger and broader, stronger, somehow. Her body responded to him of its own accord. Feeling this way made her extremely uneasy and she wished she could talk to someone about it. But the logical choice, Kit, was his very own sister. And Lia, well, she was afraid Lia might still think of her the way Mr. Firestone apparently did: as nothing more than a schoolgirl, at least when it came to men.

Perhaps Wu Jade would be a good sounding board. She was a woman of the world now, having married Fung Hai last summer. They already had a child on the way. But Wu was so busy, still running the School of Needle Arts, that in truth she didn't have time to listen to Mandy's whining.

Because that's certainly what it was. Why couldn't she be happy with what she had? Lia appreciated her work, and she and Gus and their children were the best substitute family one could hope for.

But for so long now, she'd wondered what it would feel like to have Mr. Firestone touch her, as a man touches a woman. As Gus touched Lia when he thought no one was looking.

It would feel, she imagined, simply *wonderful*.

"You look like you've seen a ghost," Kit said. "Did my prodigal brother say something obnoxious to you?"

Kit's words brought Mandy back to earth. "What? Oh, no. He was perfectly polite. You must be so glad to have him home again." She shifted topics. "How is the new job, Kit? It's been too long since I've seen you."

"Busy. I thought nursing school was time-consuming, but working at the hospital is more than a full-time commitment."

Mandy smiled. "But I'll bet you love every minute of it."

"You know me too well, sister."

Once Mandy had moved in with Gus and Lia, Kit had asked her not to use "Miss" anymore when addressing her. "I've decided it makes me feel decrepit," she'd joked. From then on they truly had become like sisters. After Will's brush with death (an event that even today his parents didn't know about), Kit had shocked everyone by announcing her desire to go to nursing school "and do something with my life." Over time her parents had gotten used to it and now were quite proud of her. Josephine's only concern was that she worked too hard to ever find time for love. At the age of twenty-five, Kit was already "long in the tooth," according to her mother.

But looking at Kit now, Mandy could honestly say her friend had never looked lovelier. There was a vitality about her that actually seemed to hum from within. She was like a sleek jungle cat—elusive and wary, but magnificent to see if you caught a glimpse of her. Kit now spent most of her time in a nurse's uniform, but oh, when she dressed up, as she was tonight, Mandy wondered why men didn't fall at her feet, she was that gorgeous. At one point, Mandy had hoped Kit and Dr. Tom would get to know and care for one another, but ever since the physician had kept Kit from helping her brother during the plague scare, Kit had declared him *persona non grata*. Mandy had tried countless times to reason with her: "He was only trying to protect you." But Kit would have none of it. It was a shame.

Kit and Mandy talked some more and Kit promised to come out to The Grove as soon as she had a free day, but Mandy knew that was unlikely to happen. She finally chanced a look back at Gus and Lia and found the coast was clear: Will had moved on.

Now if only *she* could move on—from her obsession with Will Firestone.

⸻ ⬩◉⬩ ⸻

"Do you really need this position, Edelman? It's causing a pain in my elbow and I'm beginning to get a leg cramp."

Mandy watched from the doorway as Ethel Steubens, naked as the day she was born, lay on a divan on a raised platform at the front of the life drawing class, looking bored and sounding cranky. Her hair was swept up on top of her head, providing a clear view of her graceful neck and large, firm breasts. Her stomach was rounded and her hips flared in an enticing manner. The only covering she wore was a small shawl, draped over the space between her legs. She offered the artists in the room an almost complete view of what many might consider the ideal female human form. Unfortunately, the form had a rather annoying voice attached to it.

Marcus Edelman, who was in charge of posing her for the session, had no sympathy for the model. "You get paid to hold the pose we ask you to hold, Ethie. It's not as though I'm asking you to be a human contortionist."

"You're damn right," she shot back. "I'm not a circus performer. But you try sitting in one position this long and see how you like it. It's not an easy thing to do, let me tell you."

"I'm sure it isn't," Mr. Edelman said. "But it is your job. And by the way," he added, "what have you been eating? I swear your belly's looking like a kangaroo pouch these days."

Ethel quit her pose immediately and sat up, her eyes filling with tears. "It's one thing to instruct me on how to pose," she said. "But I shouldn't have to sit here and listen to insults. I'm through for the day." With that she grabbed her robe and walked imperiously out of the room.

"That was well done," George Winterfeld said. "At least you waited until the end of the session to tee her off this time."

Mandy cleared her throat. "Luncheon's being served in twenty minutes," she announced.

"What's on the menu?" John Clayton Jones asked.

Mr. Jones was a portly young painter whose best work, Mandy noticed, seemed to revolve around still lifes of succulent fruit and sweets. "Your favorite—pork loin and mashed potatoes," she said with a grin. "Mrs. Coats made an extra portion especially for you." The artists in the room joined in the jest and began cleaning up their work areas.

Mandy gazed briefly at the divan placed strategically on the platform and felt a twinge of envy. Ethel, she thought, was fortunate to feel free about her body. For as long as she could remember, Mandy had loved the idea of moving freely. She was perhaps too in tune with the weather, especially during the warmer months. She remembered living in Little Eden down the hill and wanting to cool off by shedding her shirtwaist and long skirt. It would have been scandalous, of course. But oh, how refreshing it would have felt! She still had those moments, and watching Ethel on the platform was one of them.

# CHAPTER FORTY

———————✦———————

After the holiday, Will headed over to the Presbyterian Mission House to pay a visit to its director and see for himself how well both the mission and the Chinatown School of Needle Arts was doing. He found Donaldina hard at work in her office, as usual, but this time she was not alone. Cheung ti Chu was with her.

"I didn't expect to see you here." Will extended his hand. "The Six Companies haven't kicked you out for insubordination yet?" He laced his jest with a grin.

Donaldina, Will noticed, gave Cheung a "look." If he wasn't mistaken it seemed to be filled with…affection.

"Mr. Cheung has not only not been kicked out, but last fall he was elected leader of the Chinese Consolidated Benevolent Association." Donaldina shared the news like a proud spouse would have done. What was going on here?

"Congratulations." Will kept his smile in place. "You no doubt deserve it." He had thought a lot about Cheung during the past year and a half and decided the man deserved a lot of credit for at least trying to bridge the gap between his native culture and that of the west.

"He most certainly does," Donaldina said with enthusiasm. "He—"

"Donaldina, that is not necessary," Cheung said quietly. "Mr. Firestone does not need to hear—"

"But he does." Donaldina's voice was sharp and intense. "Ever since our run-in with the Hip Yee Tong, Mr. Cheung has worked tirelessly to help sway public opinion among the Chinese away from the prostitution trade. He has been in talks with the tongs about shifting their focus, and he has been negotiating with our representatives in Congress to repeal parts of the Chinese Exclusion Act to enable more respectable immigrant women to be able to come here. It's a law of nature that good men need good women or they will go astray."

Will and Cheung glanced at each other.

"None of that now, gentlemen; you know I'm right. As a result of Mr. Cheung's efforts, the number of kidnappings has dropped, and with the help of people like Mandy, we are spreading good news like that to the white community."

Will's mind drifted. Mandy again. He was surprised to feel a fierce pride in the fact she'd continued to help with the mission despite her position with Lia and otherwise advantageous circumstances. But really he shouldn't be surprised at all; that was part of her nature.

"…understands that his people won't be fully accepted among western culture unless and until they abandon their sinful ways."

Donaldina finished praising Cheung. She was in her element; her pretty face looked softer, somehow. She was actually beaming.

Will looked at Cheung, who sent him the same look Gus had sent him about Lia. Something was going on between those two; he could feel it.

And what did he think about it? At one time he'd imagined having a similar relationship with Tam Shee; he'd been enamored of her and little Sai-fon. But over the past several months he'd taken a good hard look at himself and realized his time with the lotus-foot woman had never progressed beyond an idealized fantasy. Their relationship hadn't had roots in the real world or in common interests. Donaldina and Cheung, on the other hand, were very much connected to the here and now. It would be an uphill climb, as Mandy once put it, but maybe the two of them were strong enough to handle it. *Good luck to you both*, he thought, and meant it sincerely.

"I'm glad to hear it," Will said aloud. "I'll certainly do my part to spread the word among my circle. Now tell me how the school is faring."

"You will be impressed," Cheung said. "Little Wu Jade has turned out to be a strong headmistress and a supporter of reform. Many consider her the face of the new China. She has even organized a group of Mission girls to march in the upcoming parade for the Lunar New Year."

"Fung Hai must find it difficult to keep up with her," Will said.

"Oh, he catches her once in a while," Donaldina said coyly. "She will have a baby in late spring."

The three laughed and caught up on other business. Will left the meeting feeling encouraged, not only about the Chinatown School for Needle Arts, but the progress being made within Chinatown as a whole. Perhaps the theme of his parents' New Year's party wasn't so far-fetched after all.

———◦——

Mandy was irritated, and as usual, she didn't like the feeling. It was difficult to push thoughts of Will Firestone out of her mind when Gus and Lia insisted on inviting him over, which they'd done at the New Year's party. As soon as they'd returned to The Grove, Lia had asked Mandy to make sure the surprise for Will was "freshened up" and ready for him.

He had no idea, but Gus and Lia had actually built a cottage just for him. It was larger and more elaborate than the artist bungalows, with stone trim just like the Great House. It had a cozy front parlor, small kitchen and bath, two bedrooms, an office, and a wide porch—perfect for one or two people to live in for a long time if they wanted to.

"Will needs a place to stay as long as he wants and not feel like he's puttin' us out," Gus had explained when construction began. He'd labeled the structure as a "large bungalow" on the plans so that Will wouldn't know it was being built specifically for him.

Mandy had just finished sweeping and was arranging a vase full of winter-blooming daisies when she heard footsteps on the porch. She assumed Lia was showing Will the place, but when she turned, he was standing there by himself.

Taken aback, she stared at him a beat too long before saying, "Oh." She touched her hair reflexively and smoothed her skirt. "Where's Lia?"

Will gave her a half-smile and looked around. "Back at the Great House. She said for me to follow the path and that when I found you, I'd find my surprise."

"Oh, well, I'm not the surprise," Mandy said, feeling herself blush.

Will looked at her a moment before speaking. "I'm not so sure about that."

"No, I mean, this…this cottage is your surprise. Gus and Lia had it built just for you."

Will looked around the room and then back at Mandy. "You're joking."

She waved her arm as if presenting the place. "No. They call it your own 'private getaway.' To come to whenever you want and stay as long as you like."

Will smiled. "It's charming. What do you think of it?"

"I love it," she said. "It reminds me of the little house I had with my father, except it's a bit bigger."

Will continued looking at her, but after a moment he began walking toward her. "May I?" he said, gesturing to move past her.

"Oh, yes, of course." She moved out of the way and Will brushed past her toward the three rooms and bath in the back. He peeked into the office and the second bedroom, and stepped into the master. She followed him to see his reaction.

264 | THE DEPTH OF BEAUTY

The main bedroom was simply furnished, with a large four-poster covered with a soft down comforter. He stopped and gazed at the bed, then looked over his shoulder. "Looks comfortable."

Mandy worried her lower lip. "I wouldn't know. I've never tried it."

He frowned. "I would hope not."

Mandy frowned back at him. "What does that mean? Would you not be willing to sleep in a bed I had slept in?"

He looked surprised for a moment, then shook his head. "Forget it." He walked back past her and out to the front porch. Reluctantly, she followed.

Will leaned his forearms on the railing of the porch. The sleeves of his shirt were rolled halfway up. She remembered his bare arms from the time she'd nursed him. Back then they had been well shaped and pale. Now she could see they were sinewy and tanned beneath the sun-kissed hair that covered them. They looked much stronger than she had ever imagined them. His nails were clean and blunt, and his hands looked like they had been used for something other than flipping the pages of an accounting record.

He noticed her staring. "What are you looking at?"

"Your arms," she said without thinking. "They look so different than they did before you left."

He looked down at them. "Why? What do you mean?"

Mandy shrugged. "They look…well used."

He smiled in understanding. "Yes, I suppose you're right. I used a lot more of my body during my trip. It felt good." He turned around and leaned against the railing, facing Mandy. "So, I've heard you kept busy while I was away."

She eyed him suspiciously. "What did you hear?"

"Oh, that you've become indispensable to Lia, that you've written great stories on behalf of the Mission House, that you've helped Sander de Kalb 'take his art to the next level.'"

He made it sound as if he didn't believe she was capable of such things. "I just try to be useful," she said carefully. "It's the least I can do."

"What's the most you can do?" he asked suddenly.

"What...what do you mean?"

"I mean, what would you do if you weren't doing things for other people; if you could spend time doing just what you wanted to do?"

*I would spend time with you*, she thought wistfully. *I would lie in your arms.* She turned away, feeling the blush creep back up her neck. She looked out over the porch railing into the grove of redwoods. "I...would write stories, I suppose. I mean, more than I do now. I would travel to places and meet people, like you did, and write about them."

Will leaned on the rail next to her, looking out at the same expanse of trees. After a moment he asked, "Would you write about me?"

Oh Lord, had he read her journal? "I might," she hedged.

He turned and looked at her. After a moment she couldn't help herself, she returned his gaze. Her heart started to beat rapidly in her chest. What did he see when he looked at her?

"I wonder what you'd say," he mused.

Her natural inclination was to speak the truth. "I'd say you were a man who was willing to look beneath the surface...to see things from a different perspective than most people, even if it scared you to do it."

He frowned, but the frown turned to puzzlement. His eyes softened and he reached out to lightly touch her cheek with his finger. "What is it about you?" he asked quietly. "This...intuition of yours. It's extraordinary. It's—"

"It's nothing. I don't know anything, really," she said in a rush, knowing she couldn't bear to have him call her some kind of oddity. Because then he would think to avoid her as he had when she lived in his house on Russian Hill. She glanced down at the pendant watch Lia had given her. "Oh. Oh, I'm afraid I must be getting back now." With that she lightly ran down the steps of the cottage and headed back to the Great House.

"Thank you for showing me the cottage," he called after her. "I love it, too."

After she turned the corner onto the main trail, Mandy let out the breath she felt she'd been holding forever. *You expect too much*, she scolded herself. *You need to open the door to your heart and let him leave.*

But oh how hard it was going to be! While it hurt very much to lose someone you love through death, at least you could, when you were ready, accept the fact that they were well and truly gone from this earth. To have the object of your affection still in your life, but just out of reach, was a particularly cruel form of torture. You had to guard against wishful thinking and false hope, and most of all, longing. She could do it, though, couldn't she? *Oh please, Lord, give me strength.*

# CHAPTER FORTY-ONE

———

"Chin Moon, you must hold still or I will never be able to secure the plum blossoms in your hair." Busy helping another young woman, Mandy grinned to hear Wu Jade admonish the fluttery young girl in Cantonese like a sergeant mustering his troops.

Along with the other mission residents, Chin Moon was vibrating with nervous energy. Three months ago, before Miss Cameron had rescued her from a parlor house, could the girl have imagined she'd be marching proudly down Dupont Street in Chinatown's New Year's Parade?

Truth be told, Mandy was nearly jumping out of her skin as well. She had only seen the spectacle once before and then, only from the sidelines. This year, even though she now worked primarily at The Grove, Miss Cameron—or rather, Donaldina, since the woman had given Mandy permission to call her such—had asked her to come into the city and actually be in the parade. The two of them, along with Wu Jade and Fung Hai, would walk along with the girls, making sure they stayed together as an organized, well-behaved group. Chin Moon and another girl had been selected to march in front, holding a banner proclaiming they were part of the Presbyterian Mission House.

Since many of the girls were needle arts students, they'd created traditional costumes in red and yellow silk, representing good luck and wisdom. The flowers adorning their hair symbolized the new lives they'd been blessed with. Although Donaldina privately insisted it was the Lord's work and not chance that had saved them, the director still understood how people learned an awful lot through symbols. She was keen to show the world how lovely the Chinese people could be once they'd been converted from their "heathen" ways.

For Mandy, those so-called heathen ways were fascinating, especially during the Chinese New Year celebration. In the three weeks since the Western New Year, Wu Jade had insisted that both the Mission House and the school be thoroughly cleaned in order to sweep out the old, bad luck and make way for good fortune. To scare off the mythical beast called the *Nian*, she had Fung Hai place red lanterns everywhere, because it was well known the beast didn't like the color red. Together they hung glittering banners for all to see with greetings such as "May You Realize Your Ambition" and "Everlasting Peace Year after Year." Every building in Chinatown was transformed in the same way—colorful, exuberant, and hopeful—so that when Mandy walked down the street, she felt as if the entire community wished her well. This is exactly how each new year should begin, she thought.

The previous year, she'd come to watch the parade with Gus and Lia, and Gus had surprised her with a red envelope containing twenty-five dollars.

"What is this for?" she'd asked.

He'd just grinned, said "When in Rome..." and diverted her attention to a pair of jugglers performing in the street. Later in the day she learned that Chinese parents traditionally give their children money in just that manner. Holding back tears, she had wrapped her arms around Gus and squeezed him tight, thinking of her own pa, and giving thanks that she had come to know such kind people as Gus and Lia Wolff.

This year, Donaldina did the same kind thing for the mission girls, giving them each a dollar in a little red envelope. For Chin Moon and the others, it was likely the first time they'd ever received such a generous gift.

Excitement ran high as the girls began to march in the parade. They were just one of dozens of groups participating in the event. Most were Chinese, representing different benevolent societies, schools, clubs, and temples. The jugglers had returned from last year, along with lithe acrobats who performed the traditional lion dance, driving away evil spirits as they weaved in and out among the spectators lining the parade route. Wild young men with grins on their faces waved their arms and took every opportunity to bang on drums, strike gongs, and crash cymbals just in case the spirits were still lurking about. And in case *that* didn't do the trick, they lit firecrackers every few seconds, filling the air with smoke and even more noise.

This year's dragon was most impressive—nearly two hundred feet long. Holding the brightly colored fabric body on tall poles, several Chinese men manipulated the enormous green serpent as it undulated its way along the street. They moved in such perfect harmony that one could actually imagine the dragon was real—a royal dignitary who had come to bestow a special blessing on Chinatown.

Mixed in with the traditional processions were non-Chinese groups. Mayor Schmitz, his wife, and their two daughters rode by in a carriage, waving to the crowds lining Dupont Street. The Christian Women's Temperance Union marched crisply in formation, holding a banner that read "Agitate—Educate—Legislate." Several jockeys from the soon-to-open Ingleside Racetrack trotted by wearing brightly colored racing silks.

"I'm glad we're not behind them," Fung Hai joked.

The parade was boisterous and joyful. Mandy delighted in being part of it, even though she was disappointed that Gus and Lia were too busy at The Grove to make it this year. Despite her resolve, she found herself thinking about Will and couldn't help but look for him in the crowd. He had probably seen the parade countless times. He no doubt knew the mission girls were marching, but would he care enough to watch them?

Mandy continued to scan both sides of the street until, near the corner of Dupont and Commercial Street, she actually saw him. She couldn't believe her luck. She started to wave, but stopped herself just in time.

He was not alone.

He was standing next to a pretty blond woman, his head tilted down so that he could hear what she was saying over all the noise in the street. The lady was smiling up at him and pushed playfully against his chest. They looked perfectly matched standing there so close together. Mandy's heart contracted. She'd met the woman at the Firestones' New Year's Eve party. What was her name—Beatrice? Bea?

She was so discouraged to see Will with the blond that she didn't notice the first rotten tomatoes being lobbed toward her group. Only when one of them hit Chin Moon, causing the girl to stumble, did she cry out, "Hey!" She quickly scanned the sidelines and saw to her dismay that spoiled fruit was being lobbed at them from both sides. She heard shouts and winced. The angry voices were hurling insults in Cantonese.

"Whores!" they cried, and "Hundred Mens' Wives!"

She was so busy searching for the source of the hatred that she didn't realize the fruit had been replaced with rocks...until one struck her in the head.

---

"What the hell? Bea, wait here!" Will couldn't believe it. One minute he was watching Mandy walk proudly down the street with the mission girls, and the next, objects were flying, people were shouting, and she'd fallen on the ground. Something—a rock?—had struck her on the side of the head. His next and only thought was to get to her.

A dark pandemonium broke loose, made worse by snapping firecrackers and the incessant bashing of drums. No one seemed to know what or who had caused the ruckus. Confusion reigned.

Fung Hai and Wu Jade tried to corral the girls. Some of them had been hit with the rotten fruit, their cheery yellow tops smeared with ugly shades of red and green. A few were crying, still looking to either side of the street in justifiable fear although the pelting had stopped. Two girls had even run from the chaos and disappeared into the crowd.

Donaldina reached Mandy first. She was using her jacket to serve as a pillow when Will ran up. He knelt down and gingerly lifted her head onto his lap. She was just coming around, those large almond eyes blinking as if to clear her head. *Thank God*, Will thought. *Thank God*. She tried to get up, but he stopped her with a gentle push of his hand.

"Not quite yet," he said calmly, although inside he felt like one of those goddamn firecrackers, ready to explode. He could hear distant shouting in both Cantonese and English. Policemen had already moved in, brandishing billy clubs to keep the crowds from spilling onto the parade route. He watched, incredulous, as the group behind the mission girls edged by them on either side like water flowing around a boulder and continued marching on their way.

Mandy gazed up at him. "What are you doing here?" She looked confused, probably couldn't process what had just happened.

He sent her a halfhearted grin. "Making sure you stay out of trouble, but apparently I'm doing a very poor job of it. Listen, can you stand?" She struggled but managed with his help to get back on her feet. He put his arm around her waist to steady her. She felt…warm…and right. He swallowed, looked around for Bea. She was waiting where he had left her. What should he do?

Donaldina came to his rescue. "Our regular clinic is just around the corner. Can you help me get her there?"

"Of course. Just give me a second." He ran back to Bea and explained the situation.

"Oh, the poor thing," Bea said. "I suppose if you're going to consort with such people, misadventures are bound to happen."

*What? Mandy was simply walking in a parade with a group of young Chinese girls. What could be more innocent than that?* He said nothing, however. Because he'd left his car at home, he walked to the nearest side street and flagged down a taxi. "I'll have to pass on dinner," he said, seeing that she got into the cab safely. "I'll call you next week." He noticed her pout just as he turned and jogged back to where Donaldina and Mandy stood.

Ten minutes later, Mandy was seated in a chair, being examined by a young man who Will swore couldn't have been older than eighteen. The door was closed, which agitated Will even more. Donaldina noticed his discomfort.

"I know he looks young," she said, "but Dr. Cotter is doing an internship at Saint Francis Hospital, and he helps Dr. Justice on occasion. Tom says he is a gifted doctor in the making."

"Doesn't he have to go to medical school—no, make that college, first?"

The mission director patted Will's arm. "Come now. I have it on the best authority that Dr. Cotter is twenty-three years old, which makes him not that much younger than you. Still, Imagine how *I* feel." Donaldina heaved a dramatic sigh. "Ah, to be that young and vital again. And he's a rather good-looking gentleman as well."

Will glared at her. "What does that have to do—"

At that moment Cheung ti Chung burst into the clinic, heading straight for Donaldina. "Are you all right? I was nearing the end of the parade route when I heard about the commotion."

"Yes, I'm fine, but Mandy got hit by a rock. Do you know who did this?"

Cheung glanced at Will before answering. "We don't know yet. No doubt it was your typical white hoodlums."

"I don't think so," Will countered. "They attacked from both sides of the street at a point that gave them good cover, which means they know the area well. They were calling out foul names in Cantonese as well as English…and their English was heavily accented."

Cheung paced the floor of the small waiting area, looking as if the weight of the Six Companies was squatting on his shoulders. He shook his head. "I don't see who—"

"Don't you? Who's been hurt the most by Donaldina's work— white people, Cheung? Hardly."

Cheung opened his mouth to argue but shut it quickly.

Donaldina gave voice to everyone's thoughts. "It has to be the tongs getting testy again. I had hoped they'd take heed from your efforts, Cheung, but perhaps the drop in illegal activity only signified a change in tactics." Her chin inched up a notch. "I will pay another visit to Tang Lin. I thought he had agreed to let us be, but if he is behind this, I will make him very, very sorry."

"You will do nothing of the kind," Cheung shot back. "You will stay out of it, Donaldina. Those highbinders would just as soon cut your throat as look at you."

Donaldina's eyes blazed. Will didn't think she'd been checked like that by a man in quite some time. It obviously didn't sit well.

"I will do what I need to do," she said fiercely. "And you will do what *you* need to do, which is to use all the influence at your disposal to rid your beloved Chinatown of these vultures who prey on your people's own children."

Their stand-off was interrupted when the door to the examination room opened. Mandy looked a bit wobbly and pale with a small bandage covering her right temple. The baby-faced Dr. Cotter stood close to her—far too close, in Will's mind. He brushed the image away.

"Miss Culpepper is a brave young woman. Fortunately the blow to her head doesn't seem to have left any lasting damage except perhaps a slight scar, which she'll easily be able to cover." He looked at her face and smiled, then touched her back. *Was that really necessary?* Will set his jaw.

"She'll have a headache and will need to rest for a few days," the doc-in-training continued. "And someone should keep an eye on her in case there's any swelling we need to be made aware of."

"You can stay at the mission tonight," Donaldina offered.

"No, ma'am, that's all right," Mandy assured her. "I made arrangements to stay with Kit."

Cheung smiled and turned to Will. "How fortunate, your sister being a nurse and all."

"If you're sure," Donaldina said.

"She's sure." Will turned to Mandy. "Well then, I'd best get you over there."

"You don't have to," she protested. "My overnight bag is back at the mission. I can—"

"Don't be ridiculous. You're in no condition to do anything but lie down. I'll have Fleming pick up the bag later."

They left Donaldina and Cheung in front of the clinic, still arguing about the best course to take regarding the recalcitrant tongs. The answer wouldn't be easy. The Presbyterian Mission House and other like-minded do-gooders were hell-bent on getting rid of Chinatown's "hundred men's wives." But the hard work of prostitutes, along with gambling and opium dens, continued to be the lifeblood of the Chinese gangs.

Will suppressed a shudder as he hailed another taxi, this one to take them to his sister's place. He told the cabbie to wait while he made sure Kit was home. She wasn't, but she'd left a note on her door telling Mandy to "Come on in—I just found out I have to work late, but help yourself to anything you'd like."

"Oh for God's sake," Will said as he read the note. "Why not invite the neighborhood thieves while you're at it?" He got back into the cab. "Russian Hill, please."

"Why? What's wrong?" Mandy put her hand on his sleeve.

He looked down at her hand and covered it with his. "Nothing. Kit has to work late, so you're coming home with me."

He hadn't figured those eyes of hers could get any bigger, but they did. She shook her head. "I don't think—"

"No, sometimes you don't," he snapped. "You've been running around Chinatown like you owned the place for too long. Kit and I knew from the start you and Fung Hai were trolling for converts. I should have stopped you way back then." He leaned toward her, one of his arms on the back of the seat, trying to convey the seriousness of the situation without scaring her half to death. "Change is coming, Mandy, and some people, bad people, don't like it. They're fighting back. You've gotten caught in the crosshairs twice. That's pushing your luck. You are not to go to Chinatown unchaperoned anymore."

He could sense her anger shimmering beneath the surface, and the exact moment when she mastered it.

"Change is already here," she said in her deceptively quiet voice. "I'm not a little girl anymore, and I don't take orders from you." She looked out the window, dismissing him.

"We'll see what Gus and Lia have to say about it," he muttered. "For now you're staying with me, and tomorrow I'll deliver you back to The Grove."

She turned back to him, her gorgeous eyes on fire. "That's not necessary. I can travel on my own. I do it all the time."

"*Enough*," Will said, and the look on his face discouraged further discussion.

Once they arrived at Will's home, Mandy tried to explain that it wouldn't look right for her to spend the night with him without a chaperone.

"No one saw us, and no one is going to see us tomorrow because we're catching the eight a.m. ferry." He didn't say another word, simply carried her up the stairs to her old bedroom, despite her protests that she was totally fine.

Holding Mandy in his arms seemed to have no effect on Will, but being so close to him caused Mandy's heart to beat faster. Could he feel it? How mortifying if he could! Her head began to throb again and she tried to calm herself. Tried to put them on safer footing. "I'm feeling much better, really. Maybe...maybe we could play Chicken Foot later."

Her suggestion fell flat. "I...I have another engagement this evening. Cook has the night off, but I'll have Fleming check on you periodically. He can rustle up a light dinner for you later. If you need anything, just ring for him...and be ready to leave by seven." With that he turned tail and practically ran out of the room. Mandy would have objected more to his high-handedness, but at that moment she wanted nothing more than to lie down and give in to her emotions.

Spending the night back in her old bedroom filled her with both warm memories and a sweet sadness. The thought that Will might be going out with that Bea woman settled heavily on her.

But Fleming always cheered her up. During Will's time overseas, his butler had filled in over at Gus and Lia's estate, so she had seen him often. Now, however, he was back in his domain. Within the hour he had fetched her overnight bag from the mission. She changed into a comfortable dress and sat down at the little secretary to write in her journal.

Several framed pictures adorned the desk now. They brought her back to a place in her heart she tried not to visit too often, because it reminded her that she was, in the end, an outsider. They were pictures of the family playing parlor games on Christmas Eve. In one she had taken a photo of the entire family: Edward, Josephine, Will, Jamie, and Kit each struck a silly pose. There was one of Kit, Josephine, and Mandy acting out a scene from *Hamlet* of all things, and there was a shot of Will and Jamie on the couch, both obviously cut from the same cloth and yet so different.

But there was also a photo she didn't remember. Kit could be seen in the background but Mandy was the subject. She was smiling with her heart, opening it to the person taking the photo.

The only other person to use the little box camera that night had been Will.

---

"Mr. Firestone? Your table is ready." Sitting at the bar of the Cold Day Restaurant, Will finished his second Glenlivet and gestured to the barkeep to add his drinks to the food tab. He followed the waiter to a booth toward the back of the establishment.

"Will someone be joining you tonight, sir?"

"Nope. On my own this evening, Rick."

"Very good, sir."

Over a meal of grilled steelhead trout and new potatoes, Will pondered the mess he found himself in since he'd returned from overseas. Waiting back at home—sleeping over, for God's sake!—was someone he'd seen for so long as just a girl. Yet the feelings he had for her now were decidedly different. Mandy had matured into a stunning young woman with a flawless face, thick, lustrous hair, and the kind of body any red-blooded male, including him, would kill to devour. The beauty only hinted at when he'd first met her was now openly on display. Worse yet, she had no idea how lovely she was.

The thing of it was, her true beauty radiated from within. Her intuition about people—about him—was uncanny, but it was never expressed in a self-serving way. Will knew scores of young women in his social set who would gleefully take any insights they might have about someone and use it for their own ends. Not Mandy. Her nature was to give, not to take.

He remembered the young family man—Dell Something... Butler, that was it—practically pleading to have them take Mandy away so he could avoid temptation. The man must have been clairvoyant. Or maybe he just saw something...felt something unusual about her.

Because whatever Butler was fighting against back then was out in full force now, and hell-bent on capturing Will. What in blazes was he going to do about it?

He sat up straighter in his chair. Be strong, that's all. Treat her the way she should be treated, as a naive young girl who needed some reining in.

Will was set to spend a fair amount of time at The Grove over the next several weeks to keep an eye on things while Gus and Lia traveled back east to attend the birth of Emma's latest child. The timing couldn't be better. He'd have a word with Gus before his partner left. He'd explain how dangerous Chinatown was getting and how Mandy shouldn't be given such freedom to roam about the city. He'd make sure she stayed safe.

*But what about you?* a little voice said. *How will you keep her safe from you?*

Simple, he thought.

No problem.

Easy as pie.

Really.

He gestured to Rick, who'd been standing by. "One more for the road," he said, tapping his glass.

"Glenlivet it is, sir."

# CHAPTER FORTY-TWO

"**I**'m so happy to have you home again." Lia wrapped her arms around Mandy when she and Will arrived at The Grove the following day. She gently brushed Mandy's hair back to reveal the small bandage. "Are you sure you're going to be all right?"

Mandy returned the embrace. "I told you on the telephone, it's nothing. I was simply in the wrong place at the wrong time. That's all." Mandy sent Will a peevish look. "Contrary to what others may feel."

Hell, he didn't care what Mandy felt about it. It wasn't just *nothing*. "Well, she's right about one thing: She's been in the wrong place and it's not the right time."

"Please don't listen to Will about this. He is blowing the situation well out of proportion. I am in absolutely no danger."

Gus looked from one to the other, but his gazed settled on Will. He looked bemused, damn him. Gus encircled Lia's waist. "I'm glad we're leaving town, darling. I sure wouldn't want to be caught in the middle of this…difference of opinion."

"I wish you two were the only source of discord around here." Lia let out an exasperated breath. "I'm afraid you've arrived just as someone's upset the apple cart. If Emma weren't so close to delivering, I'd think strongly about postponing our trip to New York."

"What's wrong?" Just like that, Mandy's demeanor changed. She obviously cared a great deal about what went on at The Grove.

"Ethel Steubens, of the bountiful breasts and ample thighs, is threatening to quit," Gus explained. "Apparently Marcus Edelman made one too many comments about the lady's growing...uh...midsection."

"Let me guess. Mr. Edelman announced something along the lines of—" Mandy mimicked a gravelly voice "'—What's her beef? I call it like I see it. Fat is fat, and Ethie's turning into a lard pot.'"

"You've got him down perfectly!" Lia said, chuckling. "He said something equally insensitive, which of course set her off in a flood of tears."

"Seems she's been knocked up by someone stationed at the Presidio and is having second thoughts about baring her charms for the oglers."

Lia pursed her lips. "Gus, really. Those in the figure drawing class are not 'oglers'—they simply want to improve their knowledge of the human form by sketching a live model. I took several life drawing classes in art school. There's nothing unsavory about it."

Gus glanced at Will and turned back to his wife with a grin. "If you say so, sweetheart."

"I do say so. But the situation is unsettling. Marcus doesn't care for Ethel, but George is inspired by her and feels his work may suffer. Either way, several artists are up in arms about her possible departure, since they all chipped in at the beginning to supplement her modeling fee. See if you can calm the waters, will you, Mandy? You are so very good at that sort of thing."

"There's a lesson in there somewhere," Will remarked.

"Damn straight," Gus agreed. "How about 'Pay for the service *after* it's rendered, not before.'"

Lia put her arm through her husband's. "We can't all be brilliant tycoons, you know. Some of us have other gifts." She gave Gus a look of pure, unadulterated lust. Will reflexively glanced at Mandy, only to find her staring right back at him. *Damn.*

He cleared his throat. "Gus, I wonder if I might have a little chat with you privately? I'd like to go over a few…business items with you."

Mandy shot Will a look that said she knew perfectly well what he was going to do. She raised her chin. "What an excellent idea. I have something I'd like to talk to Lia about privately as well. *Business,* you know."

"Splendid," Lia said. "Shall we meet back at the Great House for dinner around 5:30? I'd like to make an early night of it since we leave first thing tomorrow."

Gus grabbed his hat. "Done. I want to show Will some of the newer buildings, anyway. I even put in a weight room. On the way back we can stop by your cottage and make sure the liquor cabinet's stocked the way you like it."

"By all means," Will said.

"I'm the reason many of those girls decided to live at the mission." Mandy flattened her hand on her chest to make the point. "I have to do something to help them."

Armed with sun hats and a picnic blanket, she and Lia had walked down to the private cove nestled between The Grove and its neighboring estate, Puerta del Mar. They soaked in the relative warmth of the mid-afternoon sun while Mandy described the parade attack in detail and what it meant to the girls who had marched in the group. They had been publically humiliated and physically threatened. Was it any wonder that two of them had run into the crowd and not returned?

"You interviewed them, yes, and you wrote about them. But you didn't force them to leave their wretched circumstances," Lia said. "They did that on their own, knowing there might be consequences."

"But that's just it. If you had to choose between being pushed off a cliff or being thrown into a nest of vipers, which would you choose?"

Lia looked at Mandy with surprise. "Are you equating living at the mission with being a slave of the tongs?"

"No, but many of those girls are just like me. They find themselves in difficult situations through no fault of their own, and their choices are whittled down to practically nothing. Many who choose the mission don't do it because they've had a spiritual conversion. They just find it more tolerable than being a household slave or worse." Mandy watched the waves crashing against the shoreline, trying to find the right words. "I love Donaldina and all she's done. She is a fearless crusader against so many horrible things.

"But the life she requires of those she rescues is so regimented. Her standards are very strict. The girls work, receive only a basic education, and pray. That's about it. The best that many of them can hope for is to marry a Christian convert that Donaldina has approved of—whether or not he'd be a good match for them. How is that any different than me staying a mother's helper in Little Eden until I grew old enough to marry Jacob Turner? He was sweet on me and everyone assumed I'd marry him."

Lia took Mandy's hand. "But your life took a totally different path, didn't it?"

"Yes, and I'm so very grateful it did. Not because that life would have been so bad, but because I wouldn't have had a chance to determine what *I* really want." She caught Lia's eyes and held them. "I know you understand this."

Lia smiled. "I do. Tell me, what do you have in mind to help these girls?"

"I think the only way any young woman can become who she wants to be is if she can learn and grow freely, like I'm doing. She should go to school."

"Hmm. Are you sure you aren't merely substituting your own philosophy for Donaldina's? Not every girl is like you. In fact, very few are."

Lia had a point. All types of girls came to the mission, each of them unique. "I know not every girl would want this," Mandy admitted. "Many of the girls are happy with the life Donaldina gives them—it is so much better than what they had before. Wu Jade is a perfect example.

"But for some of the girls it's not enough. I can see it in their eyes. I have talked to them. They are hungry to learn more. To be more."

"They can go to the Chinese School, can't they?"

Even though Chinese immigrants had fought in the courts to be admitted to white public schools, they had been shut out under some kind of policy called "separate but equal." But Mandy knew better. The schools for the "colored" races—and that included the Chinese—weren't the same, not by a long shot.

"The fact that it's called the 'Chinese School' says it all, don't you think? The students learn about their heritage, which is fine, but what chance do they have to learn much beyond that? They need an education that will help them in the world, the same education white girls get. There are private schools who will take them, but they cost money."

Lia nodded. "You would know that better than most. As I recall, you still send some of your wages back to Kit for putting you through school."

"Yes, and I would send money to Will except that he won't accept it. I have tried. Kit at least understands that I need to do that for *me*. But my situation proves my case: it takes money to get an education, and it occurred to me that the same people who can afford to sponsor a Chinese girl in school are the same people who purchase fine art. So if you're willing, I'd like to set up a partnership, of sorts, between the Mission House and The Grove."

"I see. And how would you bring the potential sponsors and the girls together?"

"I've thought a lot about that. People, no matter who they are, like to belong, don't they? They like to be part of something. So instead of just trying to match one girl to one sponsor here and there, I want to create a program that sponsors can belong to, and maybe they would invite their friends to join. They could get together and talk about their sponsored girls and have parties, and—"

"Whoa. Wait a minute. First things first. How do you get the word out about this new venture of yours? You don't want to set these poor girls up for disappointment if no one is willing to sponsor them."

"You're right. I thought we could start it off with some kind of fundraiser using the artists at the retreat."

"How so?"

Energized, Mandy stood up and began to pace the beach in front of Lia and gesture as if they were playing a game of charades. "I see setting up a portable stage and studio, perhaps at the mission on a particular day—maybe a day that would draw more people to Chinatown anyway, like a festival—and charging a fee to see the artists at work. Then, at several points during the day, we could put on a series of *tableaux vivants*— living pictures using girls from the school along with the artists themselves as models. We could select pieces the artists are working on, and maybe some classical works."

"Oh my, you don't do anything half way, do you?"

Mandy grinned. "Perhaps in between performances they could demonstrate certain techniques or create something simple that people could purchase. Or maybe they could be sketching one of the girls. They could even display some of their other work for sale, as long as a percentage went to the program. Once the patrons came, they could learn more about the girls and sponsor them. They could develop a relationship with the girls, so they'd have a stake in how their sponsored girl progressed."

"I hate to put a damper on your idea, but what's in it for the artists? When they signed up for The Grove retreat, I didn't require them to put on fundraisers."

"Yes, but you did say they would interact with the public through occasional workshops, and this is a perfect opportunity to do that. This will also give them exposure to possible patrons who perhaps don't have the time or energy to make it all the way out here to The Grove. And it would only be for one day."

Lia stood up, brushed herself off, and gathered up the blanket. "Tell you what. I'd like you to put your ideas in writing—which I know you're very good at. I won't insist that any of the artists participate, but if it looks as good on paper as you make it sound right now, I will give it my blessing. I'll see about spreading the word about the event. It will be up to you to cajole as many of the artists as you can into helping out."

Mandy gave Lia an exuberant squeeze. "I just knew you would understand. I promise, by the time you return from seeing Emma, I will have the entire event organized."

"And while you're at it, see if you can resolve your differences with Will, all right? He seems to be a bit put out by you."

Mandy couldn't mask the frustration in her voice. "He still thinks of me as a little girl who needs protection wherever she goes. He doesn't see that I've grown up."

"I'm not so sure about that," Lia murmured. In a louder voice she added, "But do work your magic on him, won't you? I hate to see him in such a grumpy state."

*I wish I* could *work some magic on him*, Mandy thought with a twinge of despair. *I wish I could.*

# CHAPTER FORTY-THREE

——————♦—————

Two weeks later, Will received a telegram. Apparently, Emma's latest child had decided he or she didn't want to leave such a comfortable womb, so Gus and Lia's trip back east would take longer than expected. Will didn't mind, however. He enjoyed the peace and quiet of The Grove, especially since his mother was once again agitating for him to walk the matrimonial plank.

"Beatrice isn't going to wait around forever," Josephine warned him during his weekly telephone call to her. "I don't see why you have to be way out there in God knows where, when you can be here in the city seeing to both business and pleasure."

"You haven't been to The Grove, Mother, so you don't know just how pleasurable it is," Will countered. "Besides, I'm needed here to keep an eye on things while the Wolffs are away. The estate is huge and includes ten volatile artists. Herding them is no mean feat, you know."

He could hear his mother sniff on the other end of the line. "Perhaps not," she admitted, "but still, you have other obligations. Don't you have a business to run?"

Will smiled. "Several, actually. But they've invented something called a telephone. It's very helpful. Besides, Mr. Hansen is quite capable of handling just about any legwork I might need. Alas, that doesn't include squiring Beatrice Marshall everywhere. She'll just have to make do on her own while I'm away."

"Well, now that Buster Wainwright has left the field—for the life of me I can't fathom what he sees in that skinny little Meredith Scott, aside from her dowry, but to each his own...Will? Will, are you there?"

Will had removed the receiver from his ear while his mother prattled on. He only heard her last sentence, delivered at a much higher volume. "Yes I'm here, Mother. How's Kit, by the way? Still burning the midnight oil?"

Another sniff. "I wouldn't know. She rarely calls, and when I do, she's never home. I swear, I do believe one day she's going to wither away from overwork."

"I doubt you have to worry about that. She's got a pretty good head on her shoulders."

"She's got a *beautiful* head on her shoulders, but it won't stay that way indefinitely, especially if she keeps running herself ragged. I just...I just want you two to be happy, that's all."

The wistfulness in his mother's voice tugged at him. He knew how much she missed having her children around her. Jamie was still off at school, Kit had her career, and Will himself had been gone for nearly two years. She probably figured a marriage, followed by a grandchild, would give her ample projects to fill her time. From the sound of things, it was going to be quite a while before any of her children gave her the distraction she sought.

"We *are* happy, Mater dear, in our own ways. Perhaps you should take up a hobby of some sort. Or convince Father to take you away on a grand tour. You know, keep your mind on something other than the love lives of your wayward children."

A third sniff. "Perhaps I should, my darling boy. I'll think about it. In the meantime, you *will* come to our little get together on Saturday, won't you? I've invited Bea and her parents."

Will snorted, which he supposed was the masculine form of a sniff. Some things never changed, and his mother's penchant for matchmaking was one of them. "I'll think about it. I've got to run now. Ta ta."

Will hung up the phone, donned his jacket and headed out the door toward the Great House. He'd decided that morning that he needed to confer with Mandy before the day was over about...about...

Oh, who the hell was he kidding? Except at occasional meals he'd taken at the Great House dining room along with everyone else, he'd barely seen her since he'd arrived. As far as he could tell, The Grove, under her sole supervision, was running just fine. Apparently she'd even worked her magic regarding the Ethel Steubens dust-up.

He didn't need to confer with Mandy about anything.

He just needed to be with her.

⸺⸺⸺⦿⸺⸺⸺

As Will neared the main trail that led up to the mansion, Sander de Kalb joined him. Sandy was a welcome sight—one of the few Grove artists Will knew or, frankly, even cared to know.

"You attending the demonstration, too?" Sandy asked.

"Don't know a thing about it."

"Should be interesting. Mandy cajoled some doctor into bringing all his props to talk about human anatomy. He arrived late this afternoon. My guess is she wants Ethel to realize how important her contribution is to our work. Mandy's quite clever for her age."

Will zeroed in on the word "doctor." His insides clenched. "Oh? What's the doc's name?"

"Anson, I think. Anson Cotter. I hear he's from a mainline Philadelphia family, slumming it out here on the west coast. Comes from money but wants to make his own way. Sounds like an admirable chap."

*Shit.* "Yep. Sounds like."

They reached the Great House and filed into the library along with several other artists, a few of whom had brought sketchbooks. Chairs had been set up at one end of the room. At the other, a skeleton hung from a portable stand on one side of a lectern, flanked by a life-size illustration of the human body showing its internal parts. Off to the side, the same damn baby doc who had examined Mandy after the rock-throwing incident—wearing a white lab coat, no less—stood conferring with her, their heads together. Only he didn't look quite so young as Will remembered, and neither did Mandy. They looked...compatible. Will exhaled slowly.

"I'm glad to see most of you could make it," Mandy announced when everyone was seated.

She glanced at Will and blinked. Obviously she hadn't expected him to show up. He sent her a nod, which she ignored.

"We're pleased this evening to have with us Dr. Anson Cotter, who is serving an internship at the new Saint Francis Hospital in San Francisco and who assists Dr. Tom Justice in his work with Chinese immigrants. Dr. Cotter has graciously offered to give us all a quick lesson on the musculature of the human form so that you will have a better sense of why the body looks and moves the way it does. And perhaps Ethel won't feel so much like a pretzel during life drawing class." Her light remark evoked a titter from the group. Ethel preened at the attention she drew.

During the next hour Will learned more than he expected to about how the muscles in the body interacted with each other through joints and ligaments in order to create various positions, both active and stationary. After discussing what happens beneath the skin, Cotter asked for a male volunteer to come up and demonstrate how the principles he had just talked about applied to a living person. None of the artists raised their hand, and Will certainly wasn't about to, so the doc said "I guess I'll be the guinea pig." He proceeded to take off not only his coat, but his shirt, leaving his undershirt on but still showing an impressive set of biceps.

"My, my, my," Sandy murmured. "Roger would certainly enjoy this."

Baby doc wasn't a baby at all.

Feeling out of sorts, Will was contemplating an escape when Cotter turned to Mandy, touched her sleeve, and murmured, "May I?"

She was wearing a light blue, body-skimming dress that had some sort of beige lacy thing over it that formed loose-fitting sleeves. Mandy looked a bit embarrassed but nodded, and the bounder proceeded to roll up the lacy sleeve to reveal her perfectly shaped arm. He then extended his much larger arm next to hers.

"In our everyday world, the difference between male and female shape and muscle mass is readily apparent, yet subtle for all that. Thus any exaggeration that's out of proportion on the part of the artist will signal to the viewer that more symbolism or meaning is intended beyond a simple rendition of the human form." He then gently unrolled her sleeve and gave her arm a slight squeeze.

Will wanted to deck him, and would have gladly made a fool of himself except that Ethel Steubens beat him to it. Apparently Marcus Edelman had a sadistic streak. He pinched Ethel's plump arm and said loudly enough for others to hear, "Hey, you got any muscle beneath all that fat, Ethie?"

Ethel showed just how much muscle she had by hauling off and slugging the artist right in the face.

"You're a piece of crap and I'm sick to death of you," she cried.

"Shit!" he yelled, falling backward in his chair and clamping a hand to his nose, which had started to bleed all over the floor.

Mandy came running over, looking at Will for answers. "What happened?"

He shrugged. "He had it coming, I'm afraid. Egged her on one too many times. Ethel probably should have let him have it long before this."

Will helped Edelman up while Mandy stood there, hands on her hips. "I am very disappointed in you, Mr. Edelman. I'd like you to apologize to Ethel." By this time not-so-baby doc had waltzed up with his bag like some kind of holier than thou white knight and politely asked Will to step aside so that he could attend to Edelman's nose.

Will was about to leave when it dawned on him: it was too late for Cotter to get back to the city, which meant he'd be staying over at The Grove.

But where?

Will drew Mandy to the side. "Where is your doctor friend sleeping tonight, Mandy?"

She frowned. "In the Great House, of course. We have plenty of bedrooms there."

Will clamped his jaw to keep from blurting out *Hell no.* "Um, no, he isn't," he said quietly. "He will not be sleeping under the same roof as you."

"Oh, for heaven's sake. Anson is a perfect gentleman. He—"

"Anson, is it? Well, let's hope *Anson* brought a sleeping bag. Because he is not sleeping with you."

Eyes glaring, Mandy put her arms on her hips once again. Leaning into him, she hissed, "I suppose you're going to pull rank and switch places with him?" The moment she said it she froze and stared at him.

He couldn't help but stare back. An image of Mandy lying naked under him seared itself into his brain and he almost staggered with it. And he could tell by her eyes that she was seeing pretty much the same thing. He looked around in a fit of panic and his eyes hit upon Ethel. "There's your answer," he said, pointing to the still agitated model. He walked over to her.

"Ethel, I wonder if you might do us a very big favor and let Dr. Cotter use your cottage this evening while you stay at the Great House. We have to maintain propriety around here and you could help us out a lot."

Ethel looked at Cotter and Mandy, then back at Will. She grinned. "You sure she wants that, Mr. Firestone? Maybe you better ask her."

"Let me put it another way, Ethel. I'm *telling* you to spend the night at the Great House. Understand?"

The model gave him a sly look. "Sure, sure. Keep the merchandise fresh. I get it. I'll go down and get my things." With that she sauntered off.

Will walked back to where Mandy and her doctor beau were standing. Edelman had limped off holding a cloth to his nose. Will decided to take the high road. He extended his hand.

"Good to see you again, Dr. Cotter."

"Mr. Firestone."

Will gestured back to the lectern "When you're finished here, I'll be happy to escort you to where you'll be staying tonight."

Cotter looked at Mandy, perplexed. "Oh. But I thought… well…"

Wearing a complacent expression, Will looked directly at Mandy, daring her to argue about it. Mandy stared back at him and he could see her weighing her options. Finally, expediency won. She turned and smiled at Cotter. "You'll find the cottage to be very comfortable, Anson. And do come back here for breakfast before it's time for you to get back to the city." She reached out and touched his arm. "I'm very sorry about the little altercation at the end, but I think your presentation was most enlightening."

Will watched with irritation as Cotter looked into Mandy's eyes. "Anything I can do to help," he crooned. "Are we still on for next week?"

"Yes. Certainly. I look forward to it." She glanced at Will. "Well, I have some matters to attend to, so I will leave you now. Good night."

"Here, why don't I help you pack up," Will offered. "Wouldn't want you to waste any more of your valuable time."

While they were wrapping up the skeleton and the other materials, Cotter paused. "I heard you survived the plague."

Will looked up sharply. "Who told you that?"

"A little bird—and no, I'm not referring to Mandy. What was it like? Facing death, I mean."

Jesus, he did *not* want to be talking about death with this upstart. "I wouldn't know. I wasn't thinking clearly at the time."

"Well I'm impressed you made it through. I hear it's a damn ugly business."

"That's an understatement," Will said, and left it at that. They finished packing up and Will took a lantern off the porch before leading Cotter down to Ethel's cottage. Dark and quiet had settled over The Grove, but only momentarily, because Cotter started chattering again.

"She's beautiful, isn't she?"

Will didn't bother to ask who. "Yes, she is."

"Ever since I met her, I can't get her out of my mind." He stopped and faced Will. "Listen, I heard your sister was her guardian for a while. You must know Mandy pretty well. Do you think I might have a chance with her?"

*Damn it to hell and back.* "I honestly don't have any idea. Mandy is...her own woman. She makes thoughtful choices about all things."

Cotter's voice took on a desperate quality. "I know this sounds crazy, but I've never felt like this before. I've had other women, sure, but none like her. There's just something about Mandy that I can't explain."

Will looked into the face of a man who was at the very least in lust—an accomplished man who would be an excellent provider and who was by all accounts a decent human being. He couldn't wish for a better mate for her.

He wished the man to perdition.

───────◆───────

Mandy fluffed the pillows and smoothed over the quilt on the little four-poster in the blue guest room. "I think you'll be comfortable here, Ethel. Thank you so much for giving up your cottage for Dr. Cotter."

Ethel set her overnight bag down and looked around the room. "It's real pretty here, Mandy. Thanks for not putting me up in the servants' quarters."

Mandy frowned. "Why would I do that? You aren't a servant. And besides, you're doing *me* a favor."

"Well, I appreciate it anyway." Ethel sat down on a pretty chair upholstered with pale-blue flowers. "I didn't realize how much my feet would swell being knocked up," she said. "It feels good to get off them."

"Oh, I'm so sorry!" Mandy scanned the room and saw a low, decorative chest in the corner. She dragged it over in front of Ethel's chair. "Here, put your feet up on this. That should help." At Ethel's questioning look, she added, "I used to be a mother's helper. Mrs. Butler's feet swelled a lot, too. She was carrying twins."

"God forbid," Ethel said with a sigh. "One is bad enough." She reached out and took Mandy's hand. "Thank you."

"It's nothing."

"I don't mean just for this. I mean for being the kind person you've been to me this whole time. I know I've been a pretty thorny rose in your garden, but you have always stuck up for me and I appreciate it."

"Oh. Well. You're welcome, I guess." She never quite knew what to do with praise, so she busied herself tidying up an already tidy room.

"So, how does it feel to have two young bucks locking horns over you?"

Mandy whipped around. "What? What are you talking about?"

"Honey, I know a thing or two about the opposite sex—" she pointed to her stomach "—obviously. And I can tell when a man's got it bad for a woman. But to have two at once, and such fine specimens, both of them—Lord have mercy."

Ethel's words caused Mandy's skin to flush, the heat working its way up her back and her throat to her face and hairline. "Really, I don't know what—"

"On the one hand you got that sweet young doc danglin'. He looks like he's shopped around a bit and likes what he sees in you. But then you got your Mr. Firestone…" The model pretended to fan herself.

Mandy couldn't help asking the question. "You…you think he's interested in me, too? Are you sure?"

"Sure as I am that I've got a big fat bun in the oven. But that one's tricky. He's like a dog and you're the nice, juicy bone. He's not quite ready to eat you, but he'll be damned if anyone else will take you from him."

The flush that had crept up Mandy's body now crept down again, all the way to her unmentionable parts. "I…I think maybe you misunderstand Mr. Firestone. He still thinks of me as a child."

"Don't kid yourself. I've seen how he watches you when you're not looking. That man is hungry for a woman, not a girl. He knows *exactly* how old you are and what he'd like to do to you. Problem is, he's having a hell of a time squarin' up what he's feeling with what he thinks he should be feeling."

"Do you think so, Ethel? Really?"

"So, I guess you've made your choice," Ethel said with a grin. "Now what are you going to do about it?"

Mandy sat down on the edge of the bed, her shoulders slumped. "Honestly, I don't know what to do at this point. I have told him over and over that I've grown up."

"Yes, but have you shown him? I think steppin' out with the young doc is a good first move. It shows Mr. Firestone that others are interested and he better get moving if he knows what's good for him."

"Oh, I wouldn't want to do anything to hurt Anson—I mean, Dr. Cotter. He has been so nice to me, so kind in coming all the way out here. He even…"

"Even what?"

"He invited me out for…for Saint Valentine's Day."

Ethel clapped her hands. "So much the better! And don't you go thinking he's such a saint, either. That young man has more on his mind than simple kindness. He wants you, and not just for holdin' hands, neither. Watch out you don't get in the family way before it's time, like I did. And here's some more advice: when Mr. Firestone comes to heel and you have to lower the boom on the doc, don't spend more than two minutes worrying about him. He'll get over it. Believe me. They always do." Ethel's slightly bitter tone gave Mandy pause. She reached over to touch the model's hand.

"Did your—" she glanced at Ethel's stomach "—your young man get over you?"

"My young man wasn't so young. He was a sergeant who happened to be married, more fool me. But, I got a plan…which I wanted to talk to you about anyway."

"Tell me," Mandy said.

"I know I've been squawking about leaving for a while now, but I got to follow through." She pointed to her ankles and tapped her belly. "Your doc talked about proportion. Well, this body of mine, for the short run, at least, is headin' way out of proportion. It wouldn't be too long before Marcus heaved me out the door himself, and he'd be right to do it. I haven't exactly delivered my end of the bargain."

"But what will you do?" All the sad stories she'd heard and written about girls set adrift came flooding back. No one deserved to be cast aside. She felt tears welling up.

"No, no, don't worry about me, pet." Ethel leaned over to wipe away a tear from Mandy's cheek. "I'm one of the lucky ones. My family—they're farmers down south of the city—they want me to come home and raise the baby with them." She wiped some tears from her own eyes. "Ah, now look what you've done."

"Are you sure, Ethel? Because maybe…maybe we could find another job for you around here. You know, until you had the baby and all."

"I'm sure, thanks. No, I'm ready to go home. I just feel bad about leaving the folks around here in the lurch. That George sure does love my curves! But I think it's best I sneak out on the afternoon train."

Mandy rose and walked to the door. "There were times I wouldn't have believed this, but I can truly say I'm going to miss you, Ethel. You did keep things lively." She paused before asking what she'd wondered for so very long. "What is it like, baring everything like that?"

"You mean standing naked in front of a whole bunch of men?"

"And women."

"And women. Well, the way I see it is, the human body is a gorgeous piece of work. God got it right. And in a nice piece of art it can bring real meaning to someone's life. Not everyone has the courage to say 'This is me. This is who I am, warts and all, like it or not.' So it's a good thing when someone is willing to help artists learn their craft by doing that."

Mandy nodded. "I wondered." As she reached to pull the door closed, Ethel called out to her.

"And Mandy? There's one more thing. Just between us...I was never ashamed. Whenever I was up there posing, knowing that I was helping to create something beautiful, I felt glorious... and free."

# CHAPTER FORTY-FOUR

Will had just returned to his cottage after dropping off Cotter when the phone rang. It was Mr. Hansen, asking when he'd be back in the city to meet with some disgruntled suppliers as well as sign a passel of documents related to Pacific Global business. He decided to head back the next day and punished himself for thinking uncharitable thoughts about Cotter by joining the man for breakfast back at the Great House. He even offered to accompany the man on his return journey.

"Splendid," Cotter said. "I like having someone to chat with on these long trips. Perhaps we can talk more about your experience with the Chinee. They're a peculiar bunch."

Mandy had joined them for Mrs. Coats's mouth-watering apple pancakes. She frowned at Will's announcement. "So you'll be leaving us, then?"

"I doubt you'll even know I've gone," he said. "You're obviously more than capable of holding down the fort."

"When will you be returning?"

"Three or four days. Five at most. I'm just a phone call away should you need me, which is doubtful."

"Well, you may want to coordinate your return with Mandy since she's coming into the city on the fourteenth." Cotter reached across the table to take Mandy's hand. He smiled at her, even though he was speaking to Will. "We have a date, you see. I'm sure you wouldn't want to leave The Grove totally unattended."

Did Will actually think he'd be able to stomach this maggot all the way back to San Francisco? There was punishment, and then there was *torture*.

Mandy had the decency to avoid Cotter's adoring gaze and make eye contact with Will. "We will work it out." She bestowed one of her spectacular smiles on him, which soothed his outlook, but only slightly.

No matter which way he sliced it, it was going to be an excruciatingly long day.

---

*Courage. Remember what Ethel told you.*

Mandy took a deep breath, waiting for the rest of the artists in the life drawing group to enter the studio. It was a fairly large space, designed for classes and for those who liked to create with others instead of on their own. Several easels with chairs were set up on one side of the room, while on the other, a raised dais was placed to take advantage of the front windows' natural light. On the platform was a small couch; behind that solitary piece of furniture a muted gold drape on a portable stand served as a backdrop. A pot-bellied stove on the other side of the dais provided heat.

Marcus Edelman walked in carrying his palette and satchel of art supplies. He already wore a scowl. George Winterfeld followed. He was a heavyset man in his late forties who seemed to be all business as he bustled about setting up his workspace.

Peter Raines the photographer sauntered in. Mandy had seen him once or twice before in the class. He usually observed from the back of the room, camera in hand. The idea of him taking nude pictures of Ethel had always bothered her. Today of all days she wished he'd skipped the class, but no, there he was.

Several other artists, including Sandy, took their places. Sandy smiled at her and raised his eyebrows, looking around the room. No doubt he and the rest of them were wondering where Ethel was. They were in for a bit of a shock.

Mandy looked out over the group and forged ahead. "Hello everyone. I hope you enjoyed the anatomy lesson the night before last. I have a couple of announcements to make and then you can get started with your session." She explained the new student sponsorship program and how they could help by participating in her fundraiser in Chinatown.

"With the help of the girls in the mission and whichever of you would like to perform, we could put on tableaux vivants of your very own work. I call it 'Living Works in Progress: The Grove Artists Visit Chinatown.'"

Peter Raines raised his hand. "What's in it for us?"

"I'm glad you asked that, Peter." Mandy proceeded to hand out papers labeled with each artist's name. She'd worked all week customizing each person's role in the enterprise and the benefits they'd get out of taking part.

Marcus Edelman scanned his sheet. "So I can offer some of my earlier works for sale?"

"Yes. In between performances, if you're so inclined, you can also create small projects on site for a quick sale or even talk about future commissions with prospective patrons. A small percentage of your sales receipts will go toward the fundraiser, and you'll be able to keep the rest. Think of it as a type of trade show for The Grove artists."

George Winterfeld sniffed. "It sounds rather low rent to me. I didn't sign on to The Grove just to be a carnival performer or worse, a huckster."

Mandy mentally counted to ten before smiling. "But you did sign on to give workshops to the public, and this falls into that category." She zeroed in on the portly painter. "By the way, Mr. Winterfeld, I can assure you, many rather wealthy individuals will attend this event. They are not of the 'low rent' persuasion. You will be making contact with art collectors who may not ever travel out to The Grove, but their money is just as good as anybody else's." Mandy tried to keep her voice from quivering. She wasn't even sure at this point if those kinds of patrons would attend, but confidence must rule the day.

"Sounds like fun to me," Sandy chimed in. "These living art performances are all the rage." He struck a dramatic pose and held it for several seconds, causing the group to laugh.

"I'm not seeing the connection between the Chinese girls and the art," Mr. Edelman said.

"The connection really lies in the patrons," Mandy admitted. "But I think we can use the tableaux to show not only the plight of the girls, but our common humanity. For instance, if we recreated Renoir's *Pink and Blue* or Whistler's *Symphony in White Number One*, using the girls as the subjects, I think the audience would understand what we are trying to achieve, both with the art and with the educational program."

"I'm not sure Lia would approve of this. Aren't we biting the hand that feeds us?" Peter's voice approached a whine. "I mean, more money spent on sending little girls to school means less money spent on our work, right?"

Of course he would be the naysayer. He'd been a bit of a complainer since shortly after he'd arrived at The Grove last fall. The fact that he fawned over Lia at every turn didn't sit well with the other artists, either. Mandy had listened to more than one of them gripe about him.

"Obviously you don't understand very wealthy people," Sander de Kalb pointed out. "If they are moved by the plight of the immigrant girls in Chinatown, they'll look kindly upon a group of artists who share their sentiments. It's much easier to indulge oneself if one thinks it is part of a greater cause."

Mandy threw him a grateful look. "Sandy's right. The event is really beneficial to all of us."

Mr. Winterfeld had begun tapping his very wide foot. "This is all well and good, but where is Ethel? It's my turn to pose her today and I'd like to get started."

All right. It's now or never. "About Ethel—"

"Don't tell me she's pouting again," Mr. Edelman said. "I apologized for the other night. I may have been a little rude…"

"Well, yes, Mr. Edelman, you were quite rude, but that's not why Ethel isn't here. She…well, she's quit and has gone home to her family to await the birth of her child."

The news skittered through the group, who all seemed to voice their opinion on the matter at the same time.

"Well, damn it!" Winterfeld grumbled. "I was in the middle of one of my most intriguing studies…"

"What about the money we paid her up front?"

"Yeah, what about the money!"

"Do we get a refund?"

"No, there won't be a refund, but I believe I've solved the problem by getting you all a replacement model."

"Excellent!" Mr. Edelman said. "Where is she?"

Mandy paused as long as she could, then stepped to the side and lifted her arms. "She's right here…It's me."

The chatterboxes fell silent.

"Are you kidding?" Mr. Edelman asked. He immediately realized how it sounded and amended his tone. "I mean, truly, are you joking with us or are you serious?"

Capturing the artist's gaze and holding it, Mandy nodded. "I am absolutely serious."

Sandy rose from his painting area and walked up to her. "This isn't necessary," he said to her in a gentle voice. "We can find someone else to fill in."

Mandy smiled at him before addressing the room. "Eventually we will find another professional model, but in the meantime this is something I have thought about trying for quite some time." She made sure to look at each artist. "With your permission I would like to give it a go, and if I am horrible at it, you may kick me off the dais. But I think what you all do is important and I would like to be a part of it. What do you say?"

For Peter, all roads led to his mentor. "What does Lia say about it?"

*Time for a tiny little lie of omission.* "Lia finds absolutely nothing wrong with modeling. As she told me, she took several classes with live models in art school and found them to be quite professional and helpful in her work." *Of course she never said I should do it.* Mandy looked around the room. "Well?"

Marcus Edelman looked at Sandy, shrugged, and checked for reactions from the rest of the group. No one kicked up a fuss, thank goodness. Finally George Winterfeld cast the deciding vote. "Well, let's get on with it, then."

On the side of the dais opposite the stove was a tri-paneled privacy screen with a silk robe hanging over the top of it. Mandy stepped behind the screen and began to unbutton her shirtwaist. *If I stop to think, I'll never get through this.* So, doing her best imitation of a woman who had no qualms about standing naked in front of a group of people, she busied herself with removing her blouse, skirt, petticoats, and camisole. It dawned on her that she should have taken her shoes off first and she stifled a nervous giggle, wondering what they would all think if she marched out there with nothing on but her stockings and boots.

Eventually she ran out of things to take off. The air felt cool on her skin and goose bumps rose on her arms. Her nipples contracted and she felt a quick jolt of alarm. What if that wasn't allowed? Donning the thin robe, she carefully stepped out onto the dais. All of the artists were at their easels setting up their work stations except Mr. Winterfeld, who stood by, waiting to put her in the pose he had chosen for the session. "What would you like me to do?" she asked in as calm a voice as she could muster.

The painter, bless him, was a thorough professional. He stood between her and the class. "Take the robe off and set yourself down on the sofa, putting your hand along the back and tilting your head back as if you are languishing at home, waiting for your lover, who is late."

An image of Will formed in her brain without her permission. She told it to go away. She disrobed and sat down as he'd instructed. "Like this?"

Mr. Winterfeld gazed at her for several moments, rubbing his chin. At first Mandy thought he was staring at her for nonprofessional reasons, but she soon realized he was simply deciding how to pose her. He tried several variations—legs on the sofa, back down, legs crossed at the ankle...one leg bent. Per his instruction, Mandy lay on her side and on her stomach, and ultimately sat back in her original position, her hand along the sofa back and her legs slightly bent. Mr. Winterfeld decided that was the pose he liked. "I think I'll put some more wood in the stove," he told her with a wink. "Now hold that position and don't breathe." He then turned to the rest of the class. "Behold, I give you Culpepper in her first-ever pose as an artist's live model." He stepped to the side to show the class.

There was silence at first, then some murmurs. Finally, Sandy broke the tension by clapping loudly so that soon the rest of them joined in. "Brava!" he cried. "Brava!"

Mandy didn't bother stifling her giggle that time. In fact, she laughed out loud. Their silly fanfare not only showed they accepted her, but that she shouldn't take her new job too seriously. And though he probably didn't realize it, Mr. Winterfeld had done Mandy a big favor as well. By calling her "Culpepper," he'd given her a special identity and relationship with the group. Outside these walls she would likely remain "Mandy," but here she was "Culpepper the model."

Two hours later the session was over. As they filed out, several artists complimented her on holding the pose without moving.

"You're a natural," Mr. Edelman said. "I hope I do as well during the tableaux. Good job."

She had put the robe back on and was getting ready to change into her regular clothes when Sandy walked up and gave her a hug. "You are an outstanding example of the human female form," he said. "As both an artist and a connoisseur of beauty, I thank you for sharing your considerable assets with us."

Mandy smiled broadly. "Why thank you, kind sir." She leaned into him. "May I tell you a secret?"

Sandy leaned in as well. "Of course."

"I loved every minute of it."

Sandy laughed delightedly. "Did you, now?"

"Yes, I did. Before she left, Ethel told me she loved modeling because she felt she was contributing to the creation of art. I feel that way when I write, but this…this is something different. It's

physical, you know? It's real. And, I don't know. I felt somehow...
free. Just like Ethel said I would."

"Will you do it again?"

"Yes, in a heartbeat."

"Good. Because I am in charge of posing during our next series."

"I look forward to it," she said.

Later, fully dressed and walking back to the Great House, Mandy couldn't help but grin at nothing in particular. She had faced her trepidation and conquered it. And found it was nothing to worry about.

Yet a voice inside of her kept chirping, *What about Lia? What about Gus?* And more often than either of those...

*What about Will?*

# CHAPTER FORTY-FIVE

*When am I going to learn?* Will stood at the doorway of the clinic in Chinatown where Mandy had been treated following the parade debacle. He was waiting for Kit's date to appear. He really did have to put his foot down about this match-making business.

Per his mother's request, he'd attended his parents' dinner party the night before. Fortunately Kit had also been roped in so he was able to catch up with his sister between polite conversations with Bea. That advantage was short-lived, however. Immediately after dessert, Kit announced she was working a late shift at the hospital and left.

The guests had reconvened in the drawing room for after-dinner drinks, and once more Will forced himself to indulge in small talk with his potential intended. Logic told him he should quit wasting Bea's time, that by continually accepting his mother's attempts to throw them together, he was leading her on. But another part of him kept hoping he'd feel something more, something that would take his mind off another woman who wasn't the supposedly perfect match Bea was, but whom he felt, in his gut, was absolutely right. Once again, the connection with Bea hadn't happened.

Before long, Josephine sailed up to them with a spritely look on her face. He knew that look and it didn't bode well.

"You'll never guess what I've got," his mother said.

Will smiled apologetically to Bea before answering his mother. "No, I never will."

She ignored his retort. "The Chinese consul general gave your father tickets to a private box at the Royal Chinese Theater for tomorrow's performance. I'm sure you and Bea would love to attend." One thing about his mother, Will noticed: she never actually *asked* if you wanted to do anything, she simply assumed you would do it because she wanted you to. That was probably because ninety-nine percent of the time, her strategy worked.

Bea looked at Will with a gleam in her eye. "Oh, that would be delightful, wouldn't it, Will? I've never been."

Josephine looked at Will as if to say *Try getting out of it now, my dear.*

"I guess we'll have to give it a go," he said.

"Oh, there's one more thing. I told Kit you would pick her up, and I'd dearly love it if you'd find a young man to join your group. I'm terribly afraid she's withering on the vine in terms of a social life. Will you see what you can do?"

"Mother, I'm not sure—"

Josephine turned to Bea for support. "Perhaps you know of someone, dear? Someone who might enjoy a night at the theater with a lovely young woman…and you and Will, of course."

Bea glanced at Will before smiling at his mother. She did have a lot of social poise, he'd give her that. "Why of course, Mrs. Firestone. I have someone in mind already who might enjoy such a romp."

"Splendid! I'll leave you two to iron out the details. The program begins at three in the afternoon."

Very quickly, Will realized that Bea had begun to orchestrate the entire outing, from picking up Kit and the date Bea had in mind, to catching a bite to eat at Coppa's Restaurant afterward.

So now he was standing in front of the clinic where Tom Justice lived and worked because Bea had met him at a fundraiser. She had no way of knowing that Kit despised the man. Upon hearing the name, Kit had managed to keep her annoyance to herself, but Will knew that wouldn't last long.

Fate intervened, however. It wasn't Tom who opened the door, but the baby doc, Anson Cotter. He greeted Will like a long-lost buddy, which he probably felt he was after bending Will's ear for hours on the way back from The Grove a few days earlier.

"Will, good to see you, man!"

"Hello, Anson. We're here to pick up Tom."

"No, no, I'm stepping in for him. He had an emergency pop up and asked if I'd like to come along in his place. I hope that's all right?"

*Hell no it's not all right. I've seen more than enough of you this week.* Will swallowed his thoughts and pasted on a smile. "Certainly. Come and meet the ladies. They're in the car."

By the look on Kit's face (relieved) and Bea's (speculative), Cotter was indeed a suitable substitute for the outing. Will drove until he found a closer parking space on Dupont. They walked up Jackson Street to a nondescript door with red calligraphy on it. A flag with similar lettering fluttered from its bracket above the open door; the doorway itself was strung with brightly colored paper lanterns. Several Chinese men were loitering in front of the building. Only because he'd attended a few performances with Cheung did Will know this was in fact the entrance to the well-regarded Royal Chinese Theater.

He showed his pass to the ticket taker and they were allowed to enter a long hallway. On one side a dark-skinned Chinese clerk stood behind a table offering figs, sugarcane, nuts, and other, more mystifying handheld snacks. Bea, Will noticed, was fascinated with the odd assortment, but when he offered to purchase something for her she politely declined.

She leaned in close. "I'm not so sure where those hands have been," she whispered.

They continued to the end of the hallway and up a flight of stairs. Will could hear the muted screech of a Chinese fiddle and the occasional low pulse of a gong.

"This way please, sir," an usher said, motioning for them to take another flight of stairs to the gallery. Once they reached that level, another man, this one dressed in western clothes and no doubt part of the Chinese consulate staff, directed them to one of the private boxes overlooking the theater below.

"I say, this is quite remarkable, isn't it?" Cotter remarked, looking about. "It's so…"

"*Foreign.*" Bea finished his sentence for him and giggled. Kit caught Will's eye and raised her eyebrows.

In some ways, Bea was right. Unlike western theaters, the stage was completely bare, with no scenery and simple red doors on either side for the actors to enter and exit. Instead of sitting in front of the stage, musicians sat at the back. Music was all-important to Chinese theater: the drums, horns, cymbals, and reed pipes would soon enliven whatever tale unfolded on stage—that is, if one could get used to the often dissonant noise they produced.

Will glanced down at the pit, where great numbers of Chinese men were rapidly filling the stark wooden benches in front of the stage. Already the air was filled with the smoke of hundreds of cigarettes. The Chinese did love their tobacco.

Kit surveyed the theater. "How many people does this place hold, I wonder?"

"Upwards of fifteen hundred, I've been told," Will said. "They pack them in."

Bea leaned over the railing of the box and Anson reached his arm out to steady her. "Careful now. Wouldn't want to lose you," he said.

Will watched as she turned around to baby doc and matched his smile. Their eyes held and Will felt a current of ire surge through him. It wasn't jealousy that burned him, however; it was knowing that Cotter, who professed to care so much about Mandy, was flirting with someone else. Mandy didn't deserve such a cavalier attitude on the part of her potential mate. She deserved better. Much better. He pushed the unsettling thought to the back of his mind.

"Where are the women?" Bea asked.

"I understand they have their own private gallery section, which we aren't able to see," Kit said. "Apparently they aren't allowed down in the pit."

Bea shuddered and drew her wrap more securely around her shoulders. "I can see why. It looks quite uncivilized down there."

Will thought better of responding and waited patiently for the performance to begin. Bea would see soon enough just how boisterous Chinese theatergoers could be.

That afternoon's performance was a morality play about an old man with three daughters who makes a deal with the Devil. In exchange for seeing to it that the two older daughters marry well, the Devil demands the third and most beautiful daughter for his bride. When it comes time to hand her over, however, the father refuses, unleashing all sorts of calamity on himself and his family, leaving him poor, sick, and alone in the end. Dr. Faustus had it worse, but not by much.

While the audience didn't laugh at the few comical scenes, nor give applause, they were quite vocal throughout the show. And viewers up front had no qualms about talking with one another, getting up, and walking across the stage to get to the other side, even if it meant winding their way through the actors who went about their business as if the intruders didn't exist.

Unfortunately, this day's performance had a twist that no one could have predicted. Will watched as one man, a tong member by the looks of him, stalked across the stage and started getting into the face of another man, jabbing the fellow's chest. The second man pushed back, causing the first man to stumble and fall, taking one of the actors down with him. The actor got up and kicked the aggressor, which led to others streaming on stage to help their respective champions.

It went downhill from there. Shouts and epithets—thankfully in Cantonese—gave way to shoving, fisticuffs, and worse. Knives came out and the occasional scream of pain added to the cacophony.

At one point Cheung, of all people, got up on stage. Will hadn't realized his friend was attending the theater that afternoon; he'd probably been watching from one of the other private boxes. As the head of the Six Companies, he was obviously hoping he could get the rabble rousers to see reason.

"Settle down!" he implored the crowd in both Cantonese and English. "This is not how we conduct ourselves! We are not animals!"

His words had no effect. In fact, for a moment it looked as though he himself would be attacked. He was quickly ushered from the stage.

"Oh my heavens!" Bea cried as the melee began to expand to the back of the theater.

Cotter looked equally unnerved. "Perhaps we should…"

"Yes, it looks like some people have been hurt," Kit said, rising out of her chair. "Let's go down and see if we can help."

Will clamped his jaw. He'd bet a small fortune Cotter was about to say "get out of here," and Cotter was right. The situation was deteriorating fast.

He rose along with Kit and took her arm. "We are all leaving now, dear sister, and letting the locals deal with this situation. They don't need you butting in."

Kit glared daggers at him. "You are not in charge," she began. "You—"

"He's got a point," Cotter said quickly. "I think we might do more harm than good." He helped Bea out of her chair and the four of them, Kit silently fuming, exited the box.

Probably the last person Will expected to see was standing on the other side of the door. It was Tang Lin, the leader of the Hip Yee Tong, who had let Mandy and her friends go years before. "You are wise to leave," he said quietly, his eyes on Kit the entire time. "Come this way, please."

The leader took Kit's arm and escorted them all down another flight of stairs and out the back of the building. Already they could hear sirens in the distance. Someone must have sent word that another battle of the tongs was about to break out.

"This was not my doing," Tang said to them. "We want to keep the peace, but sometimes the…emotions…of my countrymen become a bit excessive."

Will quirked his lips. "If that's what you want to call it." He extended his hand to the crime lord. "Thank you. Once more I am in your debt."

"No. I remain in yours. My sister as well," Tang said. "Now go, before you are caught in the snare of the authorities. It wouldn't do for a Firestone—" he glanced at Kit "—or two—to be caught slumming in such circumstances."

"This is not slumming," Kit argued. "This—"

"We need to leave, Kit," Will interrupted before turning back to Tang Lin. "Thank you again…and I'm glad it worked out with Tang Li Mei."

Tang Lin nodded and disappeared back into the theater.

"Oh, how deliciously thrilling!" Bea exclaimed as they walked back to the car. "I can't wait to tell Bitsy McFadden; she'll be pea-green with envy."

Bea's excitement at being part of a near-mob didn't abate once they reached the restaurant. Because it was close to the Stock Exchange, Coppa's was a popular lunch spot for financiers like Will. But at night it became the favorite haunt of the North Beach bohemian crowd. No matter what time of day, it was one of the city's best places to "see and be seen," which was no doubt why Bea wanted to dine there.

Baby doc was wide-eyed as they entered the long, narrow dining room, bustling with customers even on a Sunday evening. "Isn't that—"

"—Jack London? Yes, I think it is!" Bea scanned the premises like a seasoned Indian scout. "I wonder where Charmian is. I heard his new bride sticks to him like glue."

Cotter sounded star-struck. "Have you read *Call of the Wild*? It's marvelous."

"Oh no," Bea said, wrinkling her nose. "Much too violent for these tender eyes." She playfully put her hand on Cotter's arm. "But I hear you bloodthirsty types are in luck. He is supposed to be coming out with a companion novel later this year."

Will had made a point to read London's well-known novel because it portrayed life in the Yukon. Gus had corroborated much of London's descriptions, which earned Gus even more respect in Will's eyes. Surviving that godforsaken wilderness was impressive enough, but leaving it a multi-millionaire was something else indeed. None of this did he share with Cotter, however. The last thing he needed was to dissect the vagaries of the wild beast within us all with the good doctor; the man was insufferable enough.

Kit had her priorities straight, bless her, and expressed them with precision and clarity: "I'm starving." She examined the menu and announced she'd have the risotto with beans and salami. She looked at the table next to theirs, which was occupied by several young men who Will guessed were art students. "And if they don't bring me some antipasto soon, I'm going to commandeer theirs." She winked at the young men, who started to drool—and not over their food.

God, he loved his sister.

While they waited to be served, Will gazed at the enormous fresco that covered three of the four walls. Artists and writers had joined forces to create the amazing mural free of charge. A giant lobster lorded over the island of Bohemia, where artists and animals, dancers, musicians, and disembodied heads shared the limelight with voluptuous nudes. A fanciful border of black cats featured the names of local customers along with the greatest thinkers who ever lived. One section was left open for spontaneous writings. On this night, someone had written "Something terrible is going to happen."

"Oh, it already has," Bea said in a too-loud voice when she read it. Naturally she was rewarded with several *What's* and *Do tell's,* which prompted her to regale the listeners with the tale of their near-death escape from an angry Chinese mob.

Will's head was beginning to throb.

"Don't tell me you are even considering it," Kit whispered at one point. "I don't care what Mother wants."

Will knew exactly what she meant. "If I ever weaken, shoot me, will you?"

At last the evening drew to a close and Will dropped off first Kit, then Bea, and finally Cotter, who lived closest to Will's Russian Hill estate. The only silver lining Will could see from the outing was the possibility that perhaps Bea and Cotter might match up. Those hopes were dashed, however, when Cotter asked Will to wait a moment while he ran into his apartment to bring something out.

"I'll just be a minute. You'll be returning to The Grove in the next few days, won't you? I have something for Mandy."

Will looked around for something to punch. Unfortunately, nothing was nearby that wouldn't break his hand in the bargain. On top of everything else, now he was a delivery boy? When Cotter came back out holding a small red box, Will couldn't help himself. "Don't you think whatever that is might be a better fit for Bea?" he asked.

Cotter looked puzzled for a moment, but his face quickly cleared. "Oh. Oh, were you jealous, old man? I'm so sorry. I've got an eye for the ladies, and they usually have an eye for me. But it means nothing, really. Besides, while the cat's away…eh?" He emphasized his point by gently nudging Will in the ribs. It was all Will could do to keep from decking the conceited ass.

Instead, he looked at the man without expression for so long that Cotter started to squirm. And only then did he say, calmly, "If you ever hurt Mandy in any way, you will answer to me. And you may take that to the bank."

He was gratified to know that for once he had left the bounder speechless.

# CHAPTER FORTY-SIX

Will couldn't bring himself to call Mandy and let her know he was returning to The Grove, so he called the housekeeper instead. When he arrived at Point Reyes Station, he was surprised to see the photographer, Peter Raines, waiting for him with a buckboard. It was a beautiful day, quite warm for February, and he'd been looking forward to a ride on horseback to help clear his mind. Ah well.

"There was no need to pick me up." Will dropped his bag into the wagon bed. "But thank you, Mr. Raines."

"Oh, my pleasure, Mr. Firestone. Mrs. Coats told me you'd called. I took the opportunity to shoot some landscape studies on the way, so it was to my benefit as well."

*Of course it was.* It hadn't taken Will long to peg Peter Raines for the sycophant he was. He fawned over Lia to such an extent that Will had even brought his observation up to Gus.

"I agree, he's an annoying young dog," Gus had said. "But Lia reviewed his portfolio when he applied for the retreat and said he had an 'uncanny eye for beauty.' What do I know about such things? So we all put up with him."

They weren't very long into the trip before Peter revealed his true reason for picking up Will. "Um, I felt I should warn you," he began.

"Warn me about what?"

"Well, there've been some goings-on at The Grove, and—"

Will turned to him. "What do you mean 'goings-on'?"

"Ethel Steubens quit, for starters. She apparently took the afternoon train the same day you left."

"That's unfortunate. Did Mr. Edelman finally get to her?"

"Well yes, that may have been part of it. But she was getting too fat to model, anyway."

"Funny how being pregnant does that to a woman. I assume Miss Culpepper is looking for a suitable replacement?"

"Not exactly."

Will narrowed his eyes. "Out with it, Mr. Raines."

"That's just it, Mr. Firestone. That's what I wanted to tell you. About the replacement. Miss Culpepper *is* the replacement."

It took a moment for Raines' statement to sink in. "What?"

"I'm saying Miss Amanda Culpepper is our new life model."

"Oh. You mean she's standing in for Ethel wearing clothes, of course."

Raines slowly shook his head.

"You mean…?"

Raines slowly nodded.

Will didn't say a word. He couldn't. His mind was too filled with images of Mandy lying naked, on a bed, on *his* bed, on a couch, on the floor, on…on a stage in front of people?! *Wait a minute.* "That is not funny."

Raines lifted his hands as if in surrender. Feeling the command, the horses slowed down. "On my mother's grave, I am not joking. She says it's all right with Lia, but I have my doubts. I wouldn't want Lia to be unhappy with us for any reason, thinking that perhaps we coerced Mandy into doing it, which we absolutely did *not*. Nor would I want her to be upset with Mandy. I thought perhaps you could talk to her before Lia returns."

Will managed to mutter an "I'll see what I can do" before he set his jaw and remained silent for the rest of the trip.

*I go away for less than a week and all hell breaks loose.* What was she thinking? She's no more an exhibitionist than the man in the moon…

Or is she, underneath it all? Maybe she's a wanton, just waiting for the right opportunity…

No. That was ridiculous. Knowing Mandy, she probably took the blame for Ethel's departure and felt she'd let the artists down. What could she do on such short notice besides step into the breach? Yes, that was it. He'd put a stop to it and they'd all forget it ever happened.

He felt in his pocket for the small box that Anson had given him to deliver. Another messy business to deal with. But deal with it he would.

"So you'll take care of it?" Raines confirmed as he stopped to let Will off near his cottage.

"I said I would." Will dropped his valise off and headed back up to the Great House on his own. *May as well get it over with.*

"She's gone down to the cove, Mr. Firestone," Mrs. Coats informed him several minutes later. "It bein' such a nice day and all, she decided to soak up some sun."

Will glanced at the sky on his way to the trailhead. It was sunny, yes, but clouds were forming on the horizon. Looked like a storm front could blow their way before nightfall.

The trail to the cove was really nothing more than a narrow deer path that wound its way down the hill from The Grove through an old growth stand of redwoods mixed with bay laurel and pine. At the bottom it opened onto a small, protected beach. Few people knew about it, and fewer still cared enough to hike the steep trail to get to it.

He emerged from the trees to see Mandy standing at the water's edge. She was facing the ocean, so he could only see the back of her. She had taken off her shirtwaist and her skirt, leaving only her chemise and a petticoat. Her feet were bare and her rich, dark red hair flowed down her back.

He swallowed.

She was trying without success to skip rocks into the calm water. Will's own heart skipped. He knew he should respect Mandy's privacy and leave, but his attraction to her kept him rooted to the spot. He watched her arms, those same pale, graceful limbs the baby doc had touched during the presentation. His fists coiled in response.

He couldn't stand it. "I can show you a better way," he called out, walking toward her.

Startled, she turned, and when she saw him, she too froze. She glanced at her clothing sitting on a piece of driftwood, and Will reflexively took off his own jacket.

"Here," he said, beginning to cover her as if she were a child. He paused, looking at the swell of her breasts beneath the filmy material of her undergarment. They were rising and falling with her rapid breaths.

She was anything but a child.

He looked up and lost himself in her almond eyes.

Mandy was the first to break the spell. "What did you mean, a better way?" she asked softly.

He stepped back. "Skipping rocks. Hard to do in the ocean, but it can be done." He looked down at the sand where they stood. "First, find the flattest rock you can. Not too big, about the size of your palm." He picked one up and stood close to her again, reaching for her hand, turning it over, and placing the rock in it. "You hold it like this," he murmured, taking her fingers and wrapping them properly around the stone. He absorbed the feel of his hand touching hers and wanted to hold it properly, as a suitor would, even though he knew he couldn't. He looked around for another rock to demonstrate the throw. "You stand like so, pull your arm back and flick your wrist, so that it spins. See?" He demonstrated and they watched his rock skip four times before disappearing into the water.

Mandy smiled with delight and looked up at him. "I want to do that!" she cried.

"Then give it a whirl," he said.

It took several tries before she was able to skip a rock even twice, but she reacted as if she had just climbed Mount Everest. "I did it!" she crowed.

Will couldn't help but grin at her enthusiasm. "I'll attest to it."

They stayed in companionable silence for a bit longer until Mandy brought them back to reality. "I don't think you came down here to teach me how to skip rocks. Why did you come?"

He had practiced his little speech on the way down the hill. Why was he so loathe to begin it now? Because it had to be done.

"I heard that Ethel Steubens quit and that you've, um, stepped into her place, as it were."

Mandy's voice lost its levity. "Who told you?"

"Peter Raines."

She nodded. "I should have known. He's beyond worried about what Lia might think."

"So, he's correct? You've been displaying yourself in the... altogether?"

She looked at him with the knowing expression of a woman twice her age. "Do you mean, have I been modeling naked?" She squared her shoulders. "The answer is yes."

Something primal escaped him—something he had worked hard to control. "Well, you are damn well not going to do it anymore."

Her eyes grew wide at his aggression, then narrowed. She pulled her arm away and stepped back. He hadn't even realized he'd touched her. "This doesn't concern you."

"It *does* concern me. You are...you were..." He looked around, took off his glasses, and pinched his nose before replacing them.

This was not the way he wanted it to go. "Look, I know you probably feel like you have to help out. You are always helping out. But it's not necessary. We will find someone else. Hire someone else. You are not to engage in that activity any longer."

Mandy placed her hands on her hips, much like she had when she'd scolded Marcus Edelman. "You think I am helping out, and I am. But here's what you don't understand: I *like* it. I enjoy modeling for the artists and helping them to create. It brings me pleasure, do you understand? *It makes me happy.*" She was breathing harder now, as infused with righteousness as he, no doubt. She glared at him. "You have no say in it, *Mr. Firestone*. No say whatsoever."

She marched over to where her clothing lay. As she whipped off his jacket, the red box fell onto the sand. She picked it up. "What's this?"

Will was still getting himself under control and barely registered what she'd said. "It's for you."

He watched her expression change from irritation to joy in a matter of seconds. Another memory intruded: Mandy opening the birthday present he had given her. A silly scarf, but oh, how thrilled she'd been. He watched, horrified, as she opened the package, taut with anticipation and what looked like a fierce, tightly controlled joy.

"Wait—" he said, but it was too late. She had opened it to reveal a small diamond- and ruby-encrusted heart hanging from a delicate chain. She looked up at him, wonder in her eyes. "It's beautiful."

"It's not from me," he said dully. "I saw Anson Cotter in the city and he asked me to give it to you. He'd like you wear it when you go out with him."

He watched the joy slowly seep out of her, replaced by a mask of indifference. "I see. Well, I shall be honored to do so." She looked him directly in the eye—a dare. "Will you put it on me, please?" She handed him the pretty necklace, then turned around, lifting her heavy hair.

He paused in anguish. Her shoulders were slender and smooth and soft-looking. And her neck, so graceful, so lovely. He wanted to kiss it, explore it with his lips and his mouth. He wanted to breathe the essence of her to calm his agitated soul. He wanted to lay her down on the soft sand and touch her neck and her shoulders and her breasts, every part of her until he had his fill of her loveliness.

He wanted all that and more. But he said nothing. Did nothing except what she asked. He put another man's collar on her without a word, and stepped away.

As if they were lovers, or perhaps as if he didn't exist, she began to dress, sitting on the driftwood and pulling on her stockings before stepping into her skirt and buttoning her shirtwaist. She quickly donned her shoes and picked up the blanket she had brought down to the beach. Without looking at him, she headed back up the trail.

"This isn't the end of it," he called out.

"You will do what you do, and so will I," she said before being swallowed by the trees.

He sat on the driftwood for some time after she left. The sky had darkened considerably. Thunder rumbled in the distance. A storm was indeed coming their way, a perfect companion to the turmoil in his heart.

# CHAPTER FORTY-SEVEN

*Mandy's Journal*
*February 13, 1906*

I haven't talked to you in a while like this, Pa, but oh how I wish you were here now and I could cry on your shoulder. Having loved Mama the way you did, I know you would understand my feelings about Will. I feel like I have loved him since I understood what that word means between a man and a woman, possibly even before. I know that he cares for me in return, but I cannot be sure about the character of those feelings. He looks at me sometimes and I sense desire coursing through him, but maybe that is just my own yearning made manifest in him.

Perhaps I should pursue what could be a "bird in the hand." Dr. Cotter professes to care deeply for me, and he's given me a pretty necklace, I suppose as a token of his esteem. I am not quite sure if it is an appropriate gift or not, having never received anything like it before. Anson (that is his first name) has invited me to dine on Valentine's Day, of all days. That must mean something! I will try to be open-minded about his suit.

I know that most women would not feel comfortable talking to their fathers about such things, but I have the advantage of them, don't I? You are no longer here in the flesh, but you are in my heart, and there we have no need of such things as embarrassment or shame—only love.

——◄ ————◂◉▸◂————▸——

Mandy put her pen down and closed her journal. She'd be catching the early train back to San Francisco in the morning and it was time to turn in.

She fingered the dainty necklace that Will had put on her at the cove that afternoon. She could still feel the brush of his fingers on her neck, the warmth of him standing so close behind her. Her body had nearly shimmered at the nearness of him. Why did he affect her so?

Yes, he was handsome. She loved his blond, sinewy strength, loved knowing that while he may *look* the part of a mild-mannered businessman, with his spectacles and his perfectly tailored suits, he was far from that persona in reality.

Perhaps that was her answer. She was drawn to Will Firestone because she *knew* him. Knew he tried to see beyond the surface of things. Knew he would do anything to protect those under his care. Knew his soul wept when he felt he'd failed.

Oh, how fortunate the woman would be who captured his heart.

Mandy feared above all else that it would never be her.

——◄ ————▸◂◉▸◂————▸——

On the morning of Saint Valentine's Day, Mandy sat in Donaldina Cameron's office explaining the details of her idea to help send some of the mission girls to school. Thankfully, the director was all for it.

"The more we can educate the young women of this community, the more likely they will adopt western attitudes and leave behind their heathen traditions," she said. She looked through the ever-present stack of papers on her desk and pulled out a list, which she handed to Mandy. "I've made notes on some of the girls I've been especially worried about. Most of them are quite intelligent. I'd like to see their restless behavior channeled in a more positive direction, or else they may choose to leave the mission altogether."

*Maybe if you didn't constrain them so much, they wouldn't become so restless.* Mandy kept her concerns to herself, saying instead, "Perhaps we can use them in the tableaux vivants."

Since she'd moved to The Grove, Mandy's time at the mission had been sporadic. She scanned the list to see if she recognized any of the names. "Oh, there's Ling Ma and Ah Fen. They'll be good."

"I hope so. I'm still not convinced this fundraising idea of yours will work."

"Neither am I," Mandy admitted. "But I do think it's a good way to bring potential sponsors together with the girls. It will give the mission more exposure outside of Chinatown as well."

Donaldina inclined her head. "Not to mention The Grove. I assume the Wolffs are on board with this? And Mr. Firestone?"

Mandy hesitated. She hadn't mentioned the project to Will yet, nor to Gus. She was hoping that once Lia returned, both of them could convince the men of the venture's worthiness. "Ah, well, Lia approves of the concept in general. When she and Mr. Wolff return, I'll fill them in on all the details, such as where we might hold the event."

She was ready to dive into that topic when they were interrupted by a brief knock on the door. Cheung ti Chu entered, carrying a bouquet of flowers and quickly taking off his bowler hat. He was surprised, even flustered, to see Mandy. He looked at the flowers in his hand as if willing them to disappear.

Donaldina looked equally chagrined but quickly regained her poise. She stood up, walked around her desk, and held out her hand to shake his. "Ah, Mr. Cheung. You are just the person I wanted to see. Miss Culpepper was telling me about an intriguing fundraising project that you will be most interested in. Are those flowers for the girls? How kind of you to remember a western holiday." Without batting an eye, she took the bouquet from him. Mandy couldn't help but notice the subtle message that flowed between them. "I'll just find a vase for them. Why don't you have a seat?"

And that was that. Donaldina quickly returned—without the flowers—and before half an hour had passed, she'd persuaded Mr. Cheung to hold the artists' show, including the tableaux vivants, in the large gathering hall of the Six Companies. Mandy had been in that building—it was a perfect venue, located in the heart of Chinatown.

As if that weren't enough, Donaldina got him to agree to schedule the event during the Qingming Festival in early April. Many westerners would be in Chinatown for the festivities, she explained, giving both the Mission House and The Grove artists even greater exposure.

"The rules you've been passing to thwart the tongs show how serious the Chinese community is about cleaning up its undesirable elements. Over time you'll eliminate the scourge of lawlessness that feeds the 'Tear down Chinatown' crowd. By hosting this event, you'll show the public just how very civilized your community can be." Donaldina's voice was filled with enthusiasm. "It will be a perfect blending of eastern and western culture. I daresay it will go a long way toward helping your people's standing throughout the city."

Mr. Cheung huffed. "I wouldn't go that far. Still, you make good points. The truth is, whether we seek it or not, reform is coming. Do you remember the young student who gave such an impassioned speech about the future of China a few years ago? She is returning and will be holding a women's rally at the Dangui Theater the night of the festival. I have agreed to introduce her. I wanted you to know." Cheung gazed at Donaldina while he played with the rim of his hat.

"Oh, that is marvelous!" Donaldina said. Mandy had never seen her look so radiant. "The steps you've taken to clean up the vice has been the difficult thing, but the right thing, to do. And embracing reform is…well, let me just say I am very proud of you."

Mandy felt as though she were intruding on a private conversation. She had gotten what she came for, so she rose to leave. "Well, I can't thank you enough for your help, Mr. Cheung."

"I am most happy to accommodate you," he replied, even though he was looking at Donaldina and not Mandy. It was clear the man would do just about anything for the director of the mission. When had their relationship changed?

With an "I'll be in touch," Mandy left Donaldina and her most unorthodox suitor alone. *There is someone for everyone*, she thought as she hailed a taxi to the Wolffs' Nob Hill mansion. *And it isn't always whom you planned on.*

---

It took Mandy some time to decide whether or not to wear the necklace Anson had given her. In the end, she put it on. It went well with the rose-colored evening dress she'd chosen, and by displaying it she hoped to avoid a scene or hurt feelings on his part.

Mrs. Coats had traveled from The Grove with Mandy. She'd said it was to check on the skeletal staff of the Nob Hill estate, but Mandy suspected she was acting as chaperone as well—possibly at Will's insistence. Mandy had no proof, of course, but she didn't really mind because she enjoyed the woman's company. It didn't hurt that Mrs. Coats knew how to tame Mandy's thick hair into some semblance of quiet elegance for the evening.

Anson picked her up looking very handsome in a long, tailored, dark gray checked coat with a stiff white shirt, red ascot, and soft gray vest and trousers. He carried a bowler hat and a cane, of all things. She wondered if he had hurt himself and needed it to walk. As she quickly learned, it was all part of the ensemble.

"You look divine," he said as she approached him in the entrance hall of the Wolffs' home. He handed her a small bouquet of red roses. "These don't nearly do you justice."

Mrs. Coats stood to the side, waiting to serve in any capacity—or perhaps taking mental notes to report back to Will. Mandy smiled at the thought, and Anson must have misinterpreted her expression because he stepped much too close to her and whispered in her ear, "My necklace looks lovely on you."

*This is not good*, she thought. Feeling flushed, she stepped away and handed the bouquet to the housekeeper, who was glaring at Anson's impropriety.

"They're beautiful," Mandy said. "The roses, I mean."

"And what time will you be bringing Miss Culpepper home, Dr. Cotter?" Mrs. Coats was all business.

Anson continue to gaze at Mandy. "Late, I hope," he murmured.

"Well I'll be waiting up, no matter the hour," the housekeeper announced. "We're expecting the Wolffs back any time now."

Mandy hid a smile. Her guardians weren't due back for another week at least. It warmed her to know someone was watching out for her, even though she didn't really need it.

At least she didn't think she did.

------◦------

She should have known by the way Anson was dressed that he wanted to impress her. Because impress her he did. He had gotten tickets to a very popular show called *The Geisha* which was playing at the new Tivoli Opera House on Eddy Street. The theater was located inside one of the city's original panorama buildings, a round, three-story structure with dramatic arches and columns. As they waited for the performance to begin, Mandy looked around in wonder.

"I came here once with my guardian, before it was a theater," she said. "We saw an enormous painting of the Grand Canyon—it was two stories tall—and it wrapped around this entire circle. It was amazing."

"So, Will Firestone brought you here?"

"Will Firestone was never my guardian. I was referring to Amelia Starling, the painter. Have you heard of her?"

"Yes, but I thought…well, the way he was talking the other night…"

Mandy instantly went on alert. "What are you talking about, the night of your anatomy presentation?"

"No, I was with Will, his sister, and the woman he's seeing—Miss Marshall—a few evenings ago and you came up in conversation. He told me in no uncertain terms that I was to treat you with the utmost respect, or I'd answer to him. He sounds quite territorial when it comes to you."

Mandy felt her cheeks flush. "He thinks he knows what's best for me."

Anson reached for her hand. "Well, I think he'll soon be distracted elsewhere. To be honest, I think most of the ire directed at me was due to a misunderstanding."

"How so?"

"Oh, the old man started to turn a little green. He seemed to think I was getting a little too friendly with Miss Marshall, which couldn't be further from the truth." He paused and looked into Mandy's eyes. "You have the most gorgeous eyes, did you know that?"

Mandy was saved from having to cover her embarrassment by the orchestra striking up the overture. *The Geisha* was supposed to be a lighthearted musical about an already-engaged British naval officer whose flirtation with a geisha in a Japanese tea house causes all sorts of trouble for the rest of the characters in the story. The proprietor of the tea house, for some odd reason, was Chinese, not Japanese, and much of the second act dealt with mistaken identities and the selling of girls. It was difficult to laugh at such antics when she knew it was happening for real just a few blocks away.

But Mandy couldn't deny it: the real damper of the evening was Anson's news that Will was jealous of him, not over Mandy, but over Beatrice Marshall. Having observed the young doctor on a few occasions now, she could tell he was a man who loved women. He'd no doubt been flirting with Beatrice and maybe, because he was so handsome, she had responded in some way to him. But why on earth would she bother with Anson if she already had Will?

Anson leaned over and murmured in her ear. "You seem quiet. Are you enjoying the show?"

"Yes, very much." She worried her lower lip over the little white lie she'd just told. She'd promised to keep an open mind, hadn't she? Could she live with a man who came in contact with women all the time and who liked to flirt with them? Perhaps she could, if she felt secure enough in his love for her.

But what she'd asked herself a moment ago was the more important question: *If a woman had Will's love, why would she look anywhere else?*

And the fact that she even asked that question was a good indication of where her heart lay, at least in regard to Anson Cotter. She straightened in her chair and tried to focus on the play. It was going to be a long night.

⸎

After the performance, they headed to the Fairmont Hotel for a late supper. Anson insisted she have a glass of wine to help her "loosen up" while he enjoyed two whiskeys in rapid succession. He spent the better part of the meal talking about his background—how his family was on top of the social pecking order in Philadelphia, but he wanted to explore the country a bit before settling back down in that milieu. "A milieu is a person's usual environment," he explained.

"*Je comprends plus que vous savez,*" Mandy responded in perfect French, deriving a smidgeon of satisfaction from the surprised look on his face. It backfired, however. He broke into a wide smile. "You understand more than I think you do, is that right? Oh, you are a delightful little minx." He took her hand across the table, turned it over and planted a kiss in her palm while watching the expression on her face. This was an awkward moment she couldn't hide. She gently pulled her hand away and took a sip of wine to give herself something to do.

"So...you haven't told me why you took up medicine," she said, assuming he would launch back into his life's story. He didn't disappoint.

"I always liked science, and being a physician is an honorable profession—much more interesting than politics, business, or the law, if you ask me. I'm especially enjoying this time with the Chinee and seeing their way of life. From what I've observed, it's no surprise they got hit with the plague."

Mandy frowned. "Why do you say that?"

"Well, their hygiene leaves a lot to be desired, for one thing. Some of the women I treat, well, I know it's indelicate to say so, but they simply smell bad. One older woman had those bound feet and one of them developed an abscess...oh, I'm glad we've eaten...and, well, it was fairly putrid."

Memories assailed Mandy—of a beautiful young mother, dying of a hideous disease while a young man, his heart broken, paid his respects the only way he knew how.

And the answer came to her: Anson was a good man, but even if Will Firestone was out of her reach, she could never settle as long as men of Will's caliber existed. Someday, somewhere, she would find such a man. Or live without one.

"I'm feeling a bit tired," she said, ignoring his last statement. "I really should be getting home."

"What? The night is young. I thought we'd stop by Jimmy's a bit later. It's a great black and tan club on Terrific Street."

Mandy had never heard of it. "Black and tan?"

"Yes, you know. Negroes and whites together. They start playin' their rag time music and you can't help but jitter to it."

"It sounds…fun. But I really must be getting home. I'm leaving for The Grove early in the morning."

Anson, who had ordered a third drink just a few moments before, downed it quickly. "All right then," he said, his voice a bit curt. "I wouldn't want to keep your housekeeper up too late."

He drove his car very slowly, the way a man drives who is aware that he isn't one hundred percent on top of a situation. It was far better than driving too fast, so she set her worries aside. Fortunately he was able to make it up Nob Hill and back to the Wolffs' estate with no mishaps. He walked her to the front door.

"There is something about you, Miss Mandy Culpepper," he said, stepping in close to her. He wrapped his arm around her waist and drew her in for a kiss, but she put both of her elbows up to stop him. "What are you doing?" he asked roughly.

It took her a moment to undo the clasp of the necklace he had given her, but she finally managed to do so and handed the delicate piece of jewelry back to him.

"I am sorry, Anson, but I don't think this is working out between us."

"Wha…what are you talking about? What did I do?"

Mandy shook her head and placed her hand gently on his chest. "You may not be able to see it now, but you and I…we just aren't a good match."

Anson stared at her for a few moments, then nodded. He wasn't as muddle-headed as she thought. "I get it. He's too old for you, you know. And he's probably going to marry Miss Marshall."

*You will not hurt me. You will not.* "I…I don't know what you're talking about."

"Yes you do, but I have news for you." Anson smirked. "Even if Will Firestone doesn't marry that woman, he'll marry someone else who comes from his *milieu*. No matter who he ends up with, he'll always treat you like a child, a child he rescued from the gutter." Anson slowly perused her body in what could only be construed as a sexual way. "And you, my dear, are no child."

*No, I'm not, as a roomful of artists have already discovered,* she wanted to say. She wanted to tell him he was wrong about her feelings for Will, and Will's attitude toward her. But she didn't, because she couldn't. Weariness overtook her.

"You're right, Anson. I'm not a child. I'm old enough to know when a situation isn't right, and this isn't right. Thank you for a lovely evening, however. I wish you great happiness as you finish out your internship here." She turned to go into the mansion, but he reached for her.

"That's it?"

She gazed at his hand on her arm. It was a good, strong hand. It would save lives and accomplish many things. But not with her. She looked up at him and saw what seemed like genuine sadness in his eyes. Or perhaps, like her, he was tired from a long evening, and in his case, three whiskeys.

Before she could respond, the lights of the front entrance came on and Mrs. Coats opened the door.

Mandy smiled at the housekeeper. "I'm back, safe and sound, as you can see. Dr. Cotter was a perfect gentleman." She stood next to her gatekeeper. "Good night, Anson."

After thanking Mrs. Coats for her vigilance, Mandy went up to her suite and quickly got ready for bed. Having decided to write in her journal on The Grove-bound ferry the next day, she lay in her familiar four-poster, missing her favorite quilt, the one her mother had made so many years before, which now graced her bed at The Grove.

Everyone she loved seemed to have someone else. Lia had Gus, Wu Jade had Fung Hai, even Donaldina seemed to have Cheung ti Chu. Worst of all, Will had Beatrice Marshall. Then Mandy remembered: Will's sister Kit had no one, but she didn't complain about it. She was dedicated to her nursing career and it seemed to fulfill her—well, most of the time.

All right then. Maybe the good Lord means for me to be alone. Maybe caring so much for someone else is just a distraction from what I should be doing.

She drew the covers tightly around herself and mentally reviewed all the girls whom she might be able to help through the sponsorship program. After much struggle, images of Will receded to the background, and she surrendered to sleep.

# CHAPTER FORTY-EIGHT

A rmed with her no-nonsense outlook, Mandy returned to The Grove and threw herself into her fundraising project. With the date and the venue set, she was able to secure the commitment of several artists in residence. After reading her initial handouts, a few, including George Winterfeld, even had a change of heart.

"I can see where you're taking this, my dear," he enthused at the first meeting she called. "It's actually quite brilliant."

*Brilliant* wasn't exactly how she'd term it, but Mandy was still happy for Mr. Winterfeld's newfound enthusiasm. She put him and Marcus Edelman at the head of a "hanging committee," a group of artists who would determine which works of art would be depicted in the tableaux vivants. They agreed to limit their selections to six—three well-known paintings and three entirely new works created just for the exhibition by artists from The Grove. By interspersing the old and the new, Mandy hoped potential patrons, as well as the public, would associate The

Grove artists with the masters, even if they didn't precisely know that's what they were doing.

The hanging committee in turn put together a hands-on work group that would create large backdrops resembling the backgrounds of the original paintings. These backdrops would be attached to large frames that would be rolled onto the stage for each exhibit. Gloria Pinyon, a textile artist from The Grove, volunteered to find any props necessary for each tableau, and the glassblower Frieda Mallock stepped up to handle special lighting wherever it was needed.

Once the artworks were chosen, Mandy would select the models for each rendering. Wherever possible, Chinese mission girls would assume the roles of young women in the paintings. Because he was used to working in three dimensions, the sculptor Mason Tanner agreed to choreograph the exhibits. Peter Raines reluctantly agreed to photograph the entire event, and Marcus Edelman said he would be more than happy to act as master of ceremonies and narrator. His job would be to help the audience interpret what they were seeing on stage and connect back to the original work.

During Mandy's first days back, Will was nowhere to be found—not that she was looking for him. It seemed as though he was purposefully staying away. Aside from taking herself to task several times a day for even thinking about the man, she managed to focus on the work at hand, and there was a lot of it. Seeing to everyone's general needs took precedence, followed by her modeling, which had become almost second nature after the first session. In her spare time she ironed out project details such as timelines, scheduling, and publicity. She was hoping that by having it so well organized, she'd hear little opposition from either Gus or Lia when they returned.

Return they did four days later, but when they asked her to join them in the library soon after their arrival, Mandy's intuition told her it had nothing to do with the project—and everything to do with her new avocation.

—

When Mandy entered the library, Will and Gus were standing by the portable liquor trolley. She had to swallow an anger that threatened to burst like a boil. How *dare* Will run to them about her modeling, like a little boy tattling to his parents about a wayward sibling. He had no right—

"Come, sit by me," Lia said, gesturing to the vacant spot next to her on the settee. Once Mandy did so, Lia added, "So, do you know what this is about?"

Mandy glared at Will, who returned her censure impassively. "Oh, I'm sure Will has given you all the details already."

Lia frowned and looked at Will, who shrugged before sitting in one of the wingback chairs facing the ladies. Gus handed his wife a glass of wine, and since Mandy declined his offer of lemonade, he took the other chair.

"Well, actually, no, Will hasn't said a word. I'm referring to what Peter told us when he picked us up at the train station."

Will snorted and took a pull from his drink. "He's a regular town crier, that one."

Mandy's anger was replaced by confusion. Will hadn't told them? Even after he'd implied as much? She thought about it. No, he'd said *this isn't the end of it.* That wasn't the same thing at all. Her anger abated even more.

"This is no doubt a simple misunderstanding," Gus said in his usual straightforward manner. "Raines says you've been posing nude for the life drawing class and that Will gave you permission."

Will put his drink down. "Now wait a minute…"

Not only had Will not tattled on her, but he was being called to task for something he didn't do. That was not right. Mandy raised her hand to halt his speech.

"Peter Raines is half correct, Gus. Yes, since Ethel Steubens left, I have stepped in as the life model. But Will had absolutely no say in the matter. In fact, he expressly asked me to stop doing it and I refused. So please, don't blame him for any of this."

"I don't need you to fight my battles, Mandy," Will said in a tone that implied she wasn't the only one whose anger simmered beneath the surface.

Oh, he was maddening! She had just defended him and here he was being all prickly about it. "I'm terribly sorry, I just thought the *truth* might come in handy. I must be mistaken."

Lia looked between them and suppressed a smile. "I suppose it was too much to hope the two of you would mend your fences while we were away." She turned to her husband, her tone once again serious. "We can at least eliminate the possibility that it was all a mistake. Now, what should we do about it?"

Mandy stood up so that she faced the three people she cared for most in the world. Standing her ground was not going to be easy. "There is nothing to be done about it," she began. "As I tried to explain to Will, I am modeling because I enjoy it. I feel as though I'm part of the creative process, that I am helping these artists improve their craft."

"Yes, but damnation, Mandy, you're naked when you do it!" Gus was never one to mince words.

"But what is wrong with that?" she shot back. "The human body is beautiful—why wouldn't artists want to recreate it? Yet how can they without models who are willing to show them all of it? Lia, you said once that modeling is a worthwhile and useful occupation, and the only scandal attached is in the mind of those who wish to make it so. You said there was nothing unsavory about it. If you truly believe that, then why are you opposed to my doing it?"

Lia took a moment to ponder Mandy's question before looking again at her husband. "She has a point," she said. "I can't be a hypocrite about this. Mandy is a lovely example of the female form, and—"

"Well, so are you, and I'd be damned if I'd let you parade yourself like that."

Lia puckered her brow. "You are lucky that modeling doesn't appeal to me. Because I can assure you: if it did, I would do it—with or without your permission."

Gus raised his hands in mock surrender. "I am indeed the luckiest man on earth."

Lia turned back to Mandy, her voice serious. "But what if word got out beyond The Grove? Are you prepared for what society may say about you?" Mandy knew Lia's was the voice of experience. Years earlier she had put up with horrible public censure for the steps she'd taken to end her first marriage.

Mandy reached for her hand. "The people who know me, know that I am not a wanton. The people who don't know me will believe what they want, regardless of the truth. Like you, I can't live my life according to what other people may or may not think."

Will popped up out of the chair. "Can we get back to the matter at hand? Mandy has unparalleled charms and she shouldn't be showing them off to every Tom, Dick, and Harry."

"That's just it, Will. She isn't displaying herself to just anybody." Lia turned to Mandy for confirmation. "If you're simply posing for our class here, it's a controlled setting with plenty of 'chaperones.' I don't think any of our residents would ever knowingly do anything to hurt Mandy in any way, publically or otherwise. In fact, my guess is, if anyone got frisky with Mandy, they'd be taken to task by the others."

"More like drawn and quartered," Mandy said with a grin. "Believe me, no one in the class thinks of me in unseemly terms when they are working. It's all business." She turned to Will in her enthusiasm. "Come and watch. You'll see."

Will immediately looked at Gus, who smiled slightly and shrugged. Will downed the rest of his drink. "Obviously I cannot stop you, but for the record, I think it's foolhardy in the extreme. Now if you'll excuse me." Then he stalked out.

"I don't think he's comfortable with your newfound profession," Gus remarked with a twitch of his lips. "I wonder why?"

"He is so…judgmental. He still thinks of me as a child. But he has nothing at all to worry about." Mandy sat down again next to Lia. "It's only temporary," she assured her guardians, "but I do enjoy it and would like to finish out the year, if it's all right with you."

Gus and Lia exchanged looks and Lia nodded. "You're going to be eighteen in a month, Mandy; I'd say you're old enough to make your own decisions. Just…try not to egg poor Will on about it, all right? I don't think the poor man's heart can take it."

"Now that we've got that settled, such as it is, what's all this about sending these Chinese girls to school on high society's dime? Lia says you've cooked up quite a project."

With a sigh of relief, Mandy once more put thoughts of Will aside and launched into a spirited recitation of her plan.

⚓

Later that evening, Will sat in the small parlor of his cottage reading Upton Sinclair's *The Jungle*, a book the New York literati had been gushing over. He had put the novel down and taken off his glasses, intending to rest his eyes briefly, when he heard a knock on the door. "Door's open," he said, expecting Gus or Lia.

Mandy stood at the threshold, a box of dominoes and a small bag in hand. Her face held a look of hopeful expectation. "May I come in?"

Caught by surprise, he had no excuse as to why she shouldn't. "Certainly." He jumped up, years of manners requiring that he stand in the presence of a lady. "Please, have a seat." She did so on the small settee next to his reading chair. He could smell lavender in her hair. Feeling awkward, he abruptly sat back down.

"I brought a peace offering from Mrs. Coats," she said, handing him the bag. "Molasses—one of your favorites."

He opened the sack and inhaled. *Delicious.* "Are they as good as yours?"

"Actually, they are mine. I gave her the recipe." She stopped. Frowned. "How did you know?"

"Kit told me a long time ago. She said you were quite the cook, that I'd been enjoying your creations without even knowing it. Why didn't you tell me?"

Mandy shrugged. "It wasn't important." She looked around the room and noticed the book he'd put down. "What do you think of Mr. Sinclair's answer to the plight of the working man?"

"You've read *The Jungle*?" He couldn't mask the surprise in his voice.

Mandy grinned. "Believe it or not, I can read, yes. And I think perhaps the author went too far to make his point. He said himself, 'I aimed for the public's heart—'"

"'—and by accident I hit it in the stomach.'" Will finished the quote and they both paused, smiling at each other. "I think I'll wait at least a week before eating my next steak," he quipped. "But do I think socialism's the answer to the problems he lays out? Absolutely not. With all its faults, capitalism still has the best record for pulling people out of poverty over time."

"Yes! That's why I think the Chinese immigrants, despite everything that's stacked against them, are going to do all right.

Most of the people I know have that drive to work hard and suc-ceed." She scooted forward in her enthusiasm. "Wu Jade, for instance. She is going to have a baby, yet she is still working hard every day to make sure the school prospers." She waited a beat before solemnly asking the question he could tell was on her mind. "Do you miss her? Tam Shee, I mean?"

He leaned back and closed his eyes briefly. How to answer that without sounding cold? "In the abstract I do. I think about the kind of loving person she was, what a good mother, what a dedicated, loyal wife. I feel for her, a prisoner of the old ways. I wish the ending to her story could have been written differently." He looked directly at Mandy, willing her on some level to under-stand. "But do I pine for her at night? No."

He watched Mandy incorporate that news, watched her nod slightly. There was no smile, no self-centered relief, just an under-standing and acceptance of what the widow had meant to him. The silence between them grew and he moved to fill it.

He pulled out a cookie and took a bite, almost groaning with pleasure as the perfect blend of ginger, molasses, and lemon enveloped his palate. "*Heavenly*. I missed little things like this on my trip," he said. "Missed them a lot."

"But oh, you must have learned so much," she said with a sense of excitement. "What was the most important thing?"

It was a difficult question; there were so many things. "I guess…I guess I learned who I really am, without all the trap-pings. Without all the folderol that comes with being a Firestone."

Mandy smiled softly. "And what kind of man did you dis-cover under all that folderol?"

"Honestly? A smart one, but a stubborn one. I like making something grow from nothing. I prefer doing things my way, and when I want something, I *want* it. I like solving problems, and I have very little patience for people who make mistakes and blame others for it. And I won't begrudge you a little 'I told you so,' because I found out you were right."

Mandy's brow furrowed. "I was right? About what?"

"Do you remember telling me you were glad I was leaving?"

Mandy closed her eyes and shook her head in apparent shame. "I am so sorry."

Will reached out to touch her. "Don't be. I remember being somewhat miffed, until you explained that my leaving was the only way I would come to appreciate all I was leaving behind. And that's exactly what happened. I found out how very much I love my family and how fortunate I am to have one."

As soon as he said the words he wanted to kick himself, because of course, Mandy was not as fortunate as he. But the smile on her face was genuine. He could tell she was truly happy for him. It embarrassed him, so he took the coward's way out and changed the subject. "I take it you think to whup me yet again with a game of Chicken Foot?" He pointed to the box of dominoes she'd brought.

Her smile broadened; she seemed as happy as he to be on safer ground. "If your self-confidence can afford to be taken down a notch, then yes."

Will snorted. "I'll have you know I challenged everyone from ship captains to Oriental potentates to this game, and I came away victorious every time."

"Oh, I'm sure," she said, her lips quirking. "Well, let's see if it made any difference."

They sat across from one another, playing the game she'd taught him years earlier. He listened to the cadence of her voice, simply happy to be in her company. She asked him more questions about his trip, insightful ones, and he found himself telling stories that he hadn't shared with anyone else. He paused at one point to recognize the sensation wending its way throughout his body. Was he attracted to Mandy? God yes. That went without saying. But this was something else. He finally came up with a word that approached what he was feeling.

The word was *home.*

The hour grew late and Will (who had once again lost) insisted on walking Mandy back up to the Great House.

"It's not necessary," she said. "I'm perfectly safe."

"Humor me," he said, and drew her arm through his as they walked up the hill.

They'd reached the front steps of the mansion when it dawned on him. "You said the cookies were a peace offering. Why?"

She hesitated, and he could sense her blushing, even in the moonlight. "I came to see you because I owe you an apology," she said.

"Apology? What for?"

"For accusing you of tattling on me to Gus and Lia. I assumed, wrongly, that you were telling them what a bad girl I was."

Will sighed and turned Mandy toward him by putting his hands on her small waist. "You are the opposite of a bad girl, but what you're doing is…is…"

She put her slender hands on his chest and his lust for her, which had been in abeyance all evening, reared its head. It was all he could do to ignore it.

"I know you don't approve," she said, "but I am serious. If you would only come to watch a session, you would agree it is all just business."

He looked into her eyes, a hair's breath away from kissing her. "It wouldn't be just business for me."

As if time had frozen in place, they stood there, staring at each other. He could feel her move closer, the length of her body brushing his. He could hear her breaths begin to quicken, and her eyes gave him permission to take whatever he wanted from her. Oh, how he wanted to.

After several charged moments, he gently stood back from her. "I don't think it's wise," he murmured, and wasn't sure whether he meant watching her model or kissing her. Both, he supposed.

Disappointment dropped like a veil over her face, but being Mandy, she accepted it. A burst of anger shot through him as he registered how many times she had been disappointed by others or by fate. He didn't want to be one more tally on that side of the ledger. But wouldn't she be better off with someone other than him?

"I hope you change your mind," she said in an even tone before heading into the Great House. "You might be surprised by what you see."

# CHAPTER FORTY-NINE

———————

*What in the hell are you going to do about her?* Will posed the question to the man in his bathroom mirror, pausing halfway through lathering his face with a new mahogany-handled shaving brush. He'd bought the brush the day before in a gentleman's store on Union Square for no other reason than he'd seen it in the window. The dark hue of the wood appealed to him. And why had it appealed to him? Because it reminded him of Mandy's rich, lustrous hair.

A shaving brush, for God's sake!

He was going slowly insane; he was sure of it.

The morning after playing Chicken Foot with Mandy, Will had headed back to the city, determined to put distance between himself and the girl. He was twelve years older than she was. She deserved someone closer to her in age; someone like—he swallowed and almost nicked his Adam's apple—the baby doc. Didn't she?

A business trip to Seattle distracted him somewhat, although one could only read for so long during a lengthy train ride, and thoughts of her kept intruding. *Come and watch…you might be surprised.* My God, she was inviting him to a peep show. It was absurd.

It was all he thought about.

His mother, who had no idea what he was going through, continued to push Beatrice and him together. Citing business commitments, he'd politely declined further one-on-one outings, but Josephine still found ways, even if it meant putting on yet another dinner party, to bring them into each other's orbit. Bea was always congenial; he couldn't read her well enough to know if she welcomed his suit or was just marking time with him until someone better came along. He fervently hoped it was the latter, and he dreaded the time when they'd have to talk frankly about their expectations. Given his addled state of mind, that time would have to come soon. Bea didn't deserve someone who wasn't one hundred percent enthralled.

He finished shaving and dressed for his meeting with Gus down at Fidelio's. Gus spent most of his time at The Grove now, so when he did come into town, his calendar was quickly filled. Yet he always set aside time for the two of them to "chew the fat," as he called it. Some of their best ideas had cropped up over crab-meat sandwiches and beer.

Today, however, he worried that somehow the subject of Mandy would intrude on their conversation. Because the last thing in the world Will needed was for Gus to know how much he wanted the girl, in every way it was possible to have her.

Mandy was at the top of Gus's list. "She'd shoot me if she knew I'd said anything to you, but Mandy needs your help."

Will tensed, his entire being on alert. The last time he'd seen her she looked fine. Infinitely more than fine. "What's wrong? Is she hurt? Did someone hurt her? My God, is she…is she sick?"

"Whoa, there. No, I didn't mean to spook you. She's fine. But this project of hers…"

It took Will a minute to get his heart rate back to normal. "Project?"

Gus grimaced. "I figured you were out of the loop. Look, Mandy came up with a notion to take your School of Needle Arts idea one step further. She wants to line up some sponsors with deep pockets who'll pay for private school for some of these girls. She says they can achieve a lot more with a better education, and I can see her point." He handed Will a folder. "Here's her write-up on it. She's thought of just about everything, and she's damn persuasive. If her interests didn't lie elsewhere, I'd hire her for Pacific Global tomorrow. She'd keep Hansen on his toes, I can tell you that."

Will flipped through the pages. They were clearly organized and written in Mandy's pretty hand. "'The Young Women's Scholarship Society of Chinatown.' Is it connected to the mission?"

"After a fashion. Miss Cameron's all for it, since she gets to oversee the program."

Will sat back in his chair. "Why didn't Mandy mention the project to me?"

"If I were a betting man—and I am—I'd say she's trying to show you that she's all grown up."

"Why would she need to do that?"

Gus rolled his eyes. "Why do you think?"

Will was afraid to venture a guess. Afraid to hope. So he fell back on his usual tactics. "How can I help?"

"Mandy needs someone to talk up an event she's got going for April. She's convinced some artists from The Grove to come into town during one of the Chinese festivals. They're gonna strut their stuff and put on some kind of show where they bring paintings to life on stage. It has a French name, as I recall."

"Tableau vivant?"

"That's it. They're going to show paintings with young women and use girls from the mission in those slots. They've been hard at it the past several weeks—which you'd know about if you'd made much of an appearance at the estate. The idea is to get your people excited about both the artists and the girls."

Will smirked. "'My people'?"

"Hell, you know when it comes right down to it, Lia and I are just tradesmen to these folks." He shot Will a knowing grin. "But you're one of 'em, through and through. You speak their language, don't forget."

"You're never going to let that rest, are you?"

"Nope." Gus launched into his crabmeat on sourdough bread. "Doesn't get much better than this," he said between bites. After washing down his meal with the last of his beer, Gus threw Will a curveball. "I think you should watch her model."

Will stared at Gus in shock. "*What?*"

"You heard me. Listen, that girl puts on a brave front, but she's hurtin' because she thinks you don't respect her. She needs you to consider her point of view on things, and not just reject them out of hand."

"I can't believe you're saying this. You made it crystal clear what you thought of Lia doing something like that. Why would you expect me to feel any different?"

Gus took his time before answering, but when he did, he was direct and unflinching. "Because it's plain as the nose on your face that you love her." He held up his hand to ward off Will's protest. "You do, and I know the gap in your ages bothers you. But the fact there's a decade and change between you doesn't make a damn bit of difference. I've got practically the same on Lia and it's not an issue. Believe me." Gus leaned toward Will, the intensity in his voice increasing.

"But if you're going to win that young woman, you're going to have to meet her on her terms, whatever those terms happen to be. I'll tell you straight: if Lia decided tomorrow she wanted to model in her birthday suit, I'd bluster about it, but in the end, I'd let her do it. Because it was important to *her*. Not to me, to her. That's what love is all about.

"Tell you what. Come up in a few weeks' time. We're puttin' together a surprise party for her eighteenth birthday up at the Great House. Several of her friends from town are coming out on Saturday, but if you come a few days earlier you can catch her Friday modeling session. Taking her seriously would be the best gift you could give her. I guarantee it."

Will didn't bother arguing with Gus about whether or not he loved Mandy. Gus knew him too well for that.

"I'll think about it," he said.

Gus grinned. "I have no doubt you will."

---

Later that night, after punching his pillow for the third time to make it comfortable, Will gave in to his recurrent insomnia and lay on his back, staring at the moonlight as it caught the edges of the plaster medallions on his ceiling. As the light shifted, so did his perception: what seemed like a ridge one moment looked like an indentation the next. Which observation was the right one? He'd only know if he looked at it in the light of day.

Maybe Gus had a point. How could Will condemn what he didn't fully understand and had never even seen?

Gus said Mandy needed him, and not just to help with her project. She needed his acceptance. In the end, that was all that mattered. She needed him.

Tomorrow he would begin making telephone calls. Then he'd stop by Suen Lok Choy's to get a referral for someone who could create the special birthday present he had in mind. And next week...next week it looked like he was headed back to The Grove.

He couldn't wait.

# CHAPTER FIFTY

---

"Something different today, dear colleagues." Sandy stood at the head of the life drawing class holding up a simple chain dominated by a large, multifaceted piece of citrine. "Culpepper's going to model some baubles so we can explore the use of focus within our study."

Mandy stepped forward and turned around so that he could put the jewelry around her neck. She then disrobed and calmly awaited Sandy's instructions. He placed her on the couch, behind which a sofa table featured a vase filled with yellow hothouse narcissus. He adjusted a lamp on a nearby stand so that it emphasized the stone between her breasts, which matched the flowers in hue.

"Outstanding composition, de Kalb," Mr. Edelman said from his easel. "Quite scrumptious, actually." Based on their murmurs, the rest of the class seemed to agree.

During the second half of the session, Sandy brought the focus in even tighter. He removed the citrine necklace and took a small box from his pocket. Inside lay a pair of slender earrings in the shape of crouching tigers, carved from a rich, milky white stone. The cats had eyes made of diamonds that caught the light from the lamp and glittered.

"They're remarkable," Mandy said, touching them with reverence. "It's as if they're watching us."

"They very well could be." Sandy smiled and handed her the earrings. "Here, put them on and lift your hair up so." After placing her in position, he turned to the artists in the room. "Come closer," he said. "You'll want to catch the detail of the cats against Culpepper's flawless skin."

That day's session sparked a competition of sorts among the artists to see who could come up with the most dramatic pose. The following week, the textile artist Gloria Pinyon brought one of her colorful soft-as-butter scarves hand woven from homespun alpaca yarn. She posed Mandy holding the scarf behind her with her breasts thrust forward, as if she were letting go of the last of her inhibitions. To the side of the couch a small fan powered by heated kerosene kept the scarf fluttering, with the added benefit of keeping Mandy warm.

When it was her turn the next week, the glass blower and jewelry designer Frieda Mallock brought in an exquisite Egyptian-style crystal and gold headpiece, along with an equally dramatic jeweled collar. She explained what she was after while Mandy undressed. "You are a consort to a king of Egypt. You are the essence of female power because you control this most powerful of men," she said.

Although she was only slightly over five feet tall and somewhat round, Frieda was quite sensual, which came across clearly in her art. She stood on a small stool so that she could more easily attach the dramatic headdress to Mandy's tresses. She had chosen to leave them flowing to one side of Mandy's body.

"Do I care for this king, or am I only interested in whatever power I can wield?" Mandy loved knowing the story behind the poses so that she could get into character as much as possible.

Frieda grinned, putting the last hairpin in place and stepping down off the stool. "Oh, you love the power," she said, "but it doesn't hurt that your king is a superlative lover."

Mandy giggled. "I am happy to hear that, at least."

Normally Mandy simply walked out from behind the screen naked, but Frieda wanted to impress the class, so she explained in advance the pose she wanted Mandy to take. Then she had her put on a hooded cloak. "I'll announce you and then you reveal yourself. Let's see what kind of a reaction we get," she said.

Mandy nodded, came out from behind the screen, and looked out at the class.

"Oh," she whispered, her heart leaping into her throat.

Because standing at the back of the room was none other than Will Firestone.

---

*She looks like a sacrificial virgin in that hood,* Will thought, disdain masking more than a hint of anticipation. She was standing on the small raised platform at the front of the studio. The stage had no props, just a gold curtain for a backdrop. Next to her stood little Frieda Mallock, beaming like a cat that ate the canary. He saw the moment Mandy noticed him; she seemed to pause even in the act of simply standing there. Her lips formed a small *o*.

"Behold, I give you the pharaoh's prized concubine," Frieda announced with a flourish. She stepped aside as Mandy, who continued to stare at him, slowly removed her cloak.

"Oh, my God," he murmured.

She continued to stare at him, now wearing a slight smile. If she'd felt a momentary discomfort at his presence, it was completely gone now.

The robe fell away to reveal the embodiment of Woman in her most delectable, lust inspiring form. A shimmering gold headpiece served as a sort of crown, while the large, ornate collar gave the appearance that she was owned. *Owned.*

He grew hard. Instantly.

Mesmerized, he watched as she struck a pose, turning to profile, transforming from a mere human to an almost other worldly figure. She stood straight and tall, her chin elevated, her entire being radiating fire and dignity and…and *power*, as if the one who controlled her was in reality controlled by her.

Her body was flawless: her breasts were perfectly sized globes, round and full; her waist was small and her hips flared. Legs, as graceful as her arms, were long and slender and beautifully shaped. And between her legs…

He swallowed, his mouth dry as the Egyptian desert. He glanced around, wondering if anyone had noticed him. Had his tongue been hanging out? He clamped his jaws together firmly just in case.

Marcus Edelman stood in front of his easel, ready to sketch. "Brilliant, Frieda!" he called out. "Now that's what I'm talking about, George," he remarked to George Winterfeld, whose easel stood next to his.

"I must agree," Winterfeld replied, then, louder, "Superb presentation, Culpepper!"

Culpepper?

Mason Tanner, the sculptor, said nothing. He merely began tearing away at the three-foot slab of clay on his pedestal as if to capture her before she disappeared into the mists of time.

Will looked at the other artists in the room; they all began to work in earnest, paying no attention to Mandy except to glance at her once in a while. By their comments, they seemed as enthralled with Frieda's props as they did with the woman wearing them. Were they all blind? Couldn't they see that the image they were trying to create was all about the model and not the costume? He shook his head. *Imagine that getup on Ethel Steubens. Preposterous.* He snorted at the thought.

Part of him—the evil part—wanted to call out to her and at least get her attention. Break her concentration, perhaps. *I'm here,* he wanted to say loudly enough for all to hear. *You wanted me to see you and I see you. All of you.* But she continued to stare off to the side in perfect stillness, maintaining the pose she had adopted several minutes earlier. He was astounded all over again. How did a person keep their body from moving for so long?

After a few more minutes, it dawned on him that it was exactly as Mandy had described: the artists were professionals, and she was, too.

Will left quietly by the same side door he'd entered and headed back to his cottage. Mandy had been telling him since his return that she was no longer a child, that she was all grown up. Was that just about wanting respect, or was she trying to tell him something more? Something about how she felt toward *him*? What would she do if he treated her like the incredibly desirable woman she had obviously become?

If he let her know all that he wanted from her?

His imagination on fire, he immediately headed for the shower in the cottage's small bathroom.

Yes, he was definitely going insane.

---

When Mandy awoke on her eighteenth birthday, she was only slightly disappointed that not much had been planned. The sun was shining and there was a possibility that Will, whom she'd seen only briefly at yesterday's modeling session, might still be at The Grove.

"I thought you and I could go on a picnic to the cove this afternoon, then get dressed up and pretend we're royalty this evening," Lia told her over breakfast.

"Oh, that's not necessary," Mandy had told her. "If it's just the three of us. Unless Will or some of the others…"

"Most everyone's heading back to the city, I'm afraid. You know how it clears out on the weekends around here. But that doesn't mean we can't make a special time of it. Which is why I bought you this."

Lia handed Mandy a beautifully wrapped box from the City of Paris department store. She opened it to reveal a black silk evening gown with an empire waist and low square neckline featuring an inset of sheer black netting. The neckline and hem were trimmed with a delicate floral design in silver metallic thread. Simple yet sophisticated, it was a stunning dress for the right woman. There were even black silk slippers to match. Mandy's eyes welled up.

Lia chuckled and reached for Mandy's hand. "I can't help myself, you know. It's so fun to shop for someone who can carry off a dress like that."

"I feel like Cinderella," she said.

Lia grinned. "Then tonight we'll have our very own ball."

Mandy wiped her tears and smiled. "That's silly. But of course. Why not?"

It turned out to be a delightful afternoon. Mandy and Lia both loved lying on the beach, and although it was brisk, late-March weather, they felt the stirrings of summer yet to come.

Mrs. Coats had prepared a small basket of victuals for the two women. "How is your scholarship venture coming along?" Lia asked as they nibbled on sliced chicken, cheddar cheese, and a sourdough boule.

"The tableaux vivants will be a success, I think. Everyone has been working hard and the five girls I picked from the mission have been so eager to participate. But it's less than two weeks away and I'm not certain we will get the attendance we need—or at least the right kind of people."

"The ones who can help you financially, you mean."

"Yes. At this point we can only hope all our efforts pay off."

"So…speaking of scholarships, it's been a few months since you graduated from the Weems Academy. Have you thought about what worlds you want to conquer next? Gus and I have talked at length about it, and we would be more than happy to support you if you want to go on to a university and further your formal education."

Mandy regarded her dear friend and on impulse, put her head on Lia's shoulder. "Aside from my mama and my pa, you are the best parents I could ever have hoped for. And as Gus would say, 'that's a fact.'" She let out a sigh. "But honestly, I don't know if I could bear to go."

Lia put her arm around Mandy's shoulders. "I can see where you might say that. Just know it's an option."

Mandy sat up, smoothing her skirts along with her emotions. "May I stay on and help you with the retreat in the meantime? I was thinking I could also apply for a writing job someplace to earn some extra money. And…"

"And what?"

"And you know, I've been writing in my journal for a while and I think…I think I'd like to try my hand at writing some short stories."

"That's a wonderful idea, Mandy. We've got enough characters at The Grove to keep you going for quite some time!"

Mandy laughed. "Yes, but I'll make sure the names are changed. I wouldn't want it to be too obvious who my characters represent."

"A wise decision. Sometimes I'll paint secondary characters into my work and they aren't always depicted in a flattering light. I've worried their real-life counterparts will someday come knocking at my door, club in hand. But so far, so good." The two of them chuckled and Lia checked her pendant watch, similar to the one she had given Mandy. "Oh, four o'clock already. Let's head back and get ready for our Cinderella ball. I'll come knock on your door at six so together we can make a grand entrance." She winked. "Gus will be so impressed with us."

They returned to The Grove and Mandy indulged in a long bubbly soak before donning the gorgeous gown Lia had given her. She felt a bit silly dressing up for a quiet dinner at home, but Lia asked so little of her that she was glad to oblige. She wondered if Mrs. Coats would prepare chicken and dumplings, which was Mandy's favorite meal in all the world because it reminded her of when her mama had been alive.

She spent some time trying out the latest style of pinning up some of her hair and letting the rest flow down over one shoulder. And at the last minute she added a bit of shadow to her eyelids and blush to her cheeks. The person who looked back at her through the dressing room mirror looked older, perhaps slightly more like a woman of the world. Mandy smiled at the thought. As if she were any different today than she had been yesterday.

She was ready when Lia arrived and they did indeed walk down the stairs arm in arm. The house was particularly quiet except for a strange whispering sound. "Do you hear that?" Mandy asked.

"Oh just the pipes, I'm sure. I told Gus to meet us in the library. Shall we?"

Then she opened the door.

# CHAPTER FIFTY-ONE

"Happy Birthday!"

They were all there. Every one of her friends. The artists: Sandy and Mr. Edelman and Mr. Winterfeld and Frieda and Gloria and Mason, just all of them. Even Ethel Steubens had come, her pregnancy in full bloom.

And Donaldina was there with Cheung ti Chu, and Wu Jade stood next to Fung Hai, and they must have brought Ling Ma and Ah Fen and the others who would be in the program, because the girls all clustered in a little group, chattering away in Cantonese now that they were allowed to make noise.

Kit had broken away from her busy schedule to come too, and so had Dr. Tom Justice, who stood on the other side of the room from her. Next to Dr. Tom was Anson, and Mandy felt a twinge of embarrassment because obviously he hadn't told anyone how their date had ended. *Maybe I can smooth things over,* she thought. *It's good he came tonight.*

She searched the crowded room, looking for someone in particular and feeling her heart begin to flutter when she found him, standing in the back. He looked directly at her and held her gaze. She trembled and exhaled slowly to stay composed.

It took but a second before she was engulfed in hugs and good wishes.

"Ah, to be eighteen again," Donaldina said when she walked up with Cheung. Her escort was dressed in the formalwear of his country: a long-sleeve red satin jacket embroidered with a fierce-looking dragon. He wore a matching cap.

"I doubt you look any different," Cheung replied. Donaldina shook her head and they laughed at the sentiment, but Mandy knew what lay behind it, and believed they were somehow happy that she understood them.

Gus and Lia took turns embracing her and Lia whispered, "Surprise."

"You fooled me completely," Mandy said, laughing. "I had no idea."

After all the congratulations, and socializing with drinks and canapés, Mrs. Coats announced that dinner would be served in the main dining room.

"Is it—"

"Chicken and dumplings? Of course, my dear. I wouldn't forget a thing like that."

They had never had so many people sitting down at once; it was a good thing Gus had had the table custom made with several extensions. The mission girls were wide-eyed at being allowed to dine with such august company, but the artists took the young ladies under their wing. Mr. Edelman said that after dinner he'd show them pictures of the paintings they'd be posing for, and Mason Tanner suggested they hold an impromptu rehearsal.

There were a few rough spots during the party. Kit, looking so beautiful in a daring gown of emerald green, made it her mission to ignore Dr. Tom all evening. Instead she engaged Anson in intimate conversation, touching him now and again. He happily reciprocated and Mandy reaffirmed her concerns about ever feeling secure with a man like him. During one of their exchanges, she glanced at Will to see him frowning as he watched his sister and Anson interact. He looked at Mandy as if to say *Are you going to put up with that?* She shrugged slightly to let him know it didn't bother her, because it didn't. She only worried that Kit might take Anson too seriously. She looked over at Dr. Tom and watched pain flit across his face. He too had noted the flirtation. It was obvious he was attracted to Kit, but Kit simply couldn't see it—that, or she chose deliberately to cause him anguish. *Oh please,* Mandy thought, *don't let that be the case.*

After dinner, they all migrated to the large gathering room. Mr. Edelman brought out copies of the paintings and the group involved in the fundraiser talked about how to present them while others looked on or began conversations of their own. Mason Tanner had taken a quilt from the sofa and placed it on the floor. "That is the grass by the river," he said. He placed two of the girls on his imaginary lawn to imitate Courbet's *Young Ladies on the Banks of the Seine.* Mandy was offering her input when Anson tapped her on the sleeve.

"May I talk to you outside?" he murmured.

Mandy looked around. "Where's Kit?"

"What does that matter?" His voice sounded strained. "I need to speak with *you*."

He appeared upset, so Mandy rose and took him through the French doors that led out to the mansion's wraparound porch.

"Not here," he said, glancing at the partygoers inside. "Let's walk a bit." They headed down the steps, but at the bottom, Mandy stopped, beginning to feel uncomfortable. "Are you all right, Anson? You seem agitated."

"I *am* agitated," he said. "I can't stop thinking about you… and I don't believe you when you say we aren't meant for each other."

Mandy looked around the by-now darkened grounds, stalling for time while she searched for the right words. "I care for you very much, Anson, but—"

"I knew it," he said, reaching for her. "You want me…" He jerked her roughly to him.

"No, please—" Just as she went to push him away, a hand clamped onto his shoulder and forcibly dragged him backward. He stumbled and fell, looking up to see Will, whose eyes seemed to be glowing with rage.

"I told you that you would have to answer to me."

Anson looked at both of them, cynicism lacing his words. "If it isn't the cradle robber."

"Why, you—" Will cocked his fist back and reached down with his other arm to pull Anson up, but before he could slug him, Mandy forcibly stopped his hand.

"No!" she cried.

Anson scrambled backward and finally got enough purchase to regain his footing. He brushed his trousers off and pulled his jacket down, trying to recapture his dignity. "You want her just as much as the rest of us," he said, "only you don't have the guts to admit it." Then he stalked back toward the light of the house.

Will was still breathing harshly and Mandy reached out to touch him. He angrily brushed her hand away. "So what happened? You tell your young man he'd have to wait for the next modeling session to get an eyeful?"

*What?* The nerve of him—the gall! Without thinking, she swung her hand back and slapped Will directly across the cheek as hard as she could. His head snapped back but then he righted himself and, eyes boring into hers, took her around the waist with one arm and drew her to him just as Anson had done. But there was no one to stop him and he didn't hesitate. He put his other hand behind her head and tilted her face to more easily plunder her delicate mouth. And plunder it he did.

—⋅⋅⋅⋅⋅⋅⋅⋅⋅⋅⋅⋅⋅⋅•◦•⋅⋅⋅⋅⋅⋅⋅⋅⋅⋅⋅—

The dam had finally burst. All of the lust and desire and *love* he felt for Mandy came surging out, manifest in his kiss. He felt her push against him for a heartbeat, and then her slender arms wound their way around his neck, perhaps to hold on while he vented his frustration on her. She whimpered, and rather than check him, the sound egged him on to further transgressions. He angled his head to take the kiss deeper and she opened her mouth to him—what else could she do? Their tongues dueled and he nipped her full lips, marking them. Marking her. He brought a hand down to her backside and brought her even closer, forcing her to feel the hard length of him. He pressed her against the side of the house and began his conquest of her neck and her breasts. She moaned as he cupped one of her globes through the silk and squeezed its fullness. He had to have this woman. Had to. Had to.

"Mandy? Are you out here? It's time to open your gifts." The sound of Lia's voice in the darkness caused both of them to freeze. Mandy looked at him with those innocent, mesmerizing eyes. She seemed to be saying *I thought you cared about me.* And she couldn't know how very much he cared because how had he shown her? By acting no better than that rutting baby doc. In fact he was worse. He was a fucking hypocrite. He nodded slightly and Mandy moistened her lips before calling out, "I'm talking with Will. We'll be in momentarily."

She straightened her dress and looked up at him. "Do I look all right?" she whispered.

He reached up and replaced the pins that he had dislodged, then used his fingers to comb her glorious hair back into some semblance of order. He rubbed his finger along her lip where he had bitten it. "I am so—"

"Don't say it," she hissed, taking two fingers and touching his lips. Then she turned and hurried back up the steps.

He paused, the enormity of what he'd done just beginning to sink in. He had sworn to protect her, but instead, like so many times before, he'd hurt her. And even now, instead of remorse, as he felt his lust retreating to the corner of his consciousness, his only regret was that he hadn't finished what he'd started, that he'd been stopped before he could drive himself so deeply into her that she would know with every fiber of her being that she belonged to him, and only him.

Now and forever.

---

*He kissed me.* The sensations coursing through her body stayed with Mandy for the remainder of her birthday party, and part of her worried they might show, that someone would come up to her and say, "Are you feeling all right? You look so different than you did an hour ago." But another part wanted to shout it from the rooftops: *He kissed me!*

She rejoined her friends, who had demanded she sit in one of the big plaid wingback chairs by the fire and open the presents they had so carefully picked out. The mission girls had each made her a delicately embroidered handkerchief. Wu Jade had sewn a companion quilt to the one Mandy's mother had made. Donaldina gave her a Bible and Cheung offered an official, bound translation of the writings of Confucius. They all laughed at the dichotomy between Donaldina's present and his.

Dr. Tom gave her reading material as well: her very own edition of *Gray's Anatomy: Descriptive and Applied.* The mission girls fell on it immediately and marveled at the amazing illustrations. Anson gave her nothing.

The Grove artists had put together a framed montage of her nude poses, based on their work. None of the studies showed above her neck, so an outsider would never know she was the model. But the assumption seemed to be made by everyone old enough to understand such things, and several guests, including

Dr. Tom and Anson, looked surprised. Cheung ti Chu seemed bemused, but Donaldina looked shocked, a pinched expression marring her pretty face. *It's exactly what you think it is*, Mandy thought with a sense of calm defiance. *I hope you can accept it.* She glanced around to check Will's reaction, but he wasn't in the room. She couldn't worry about it now. She felt no shame and reveled in the lightness within her.

Kit, as always, chose to share her love for Mandy through fashion by gifting her with a peach and cream walking dress that could only be considered *au courant*. Gus and Lia gave her a copy of *The Complete Novels of Jane Austen* as well as Leo Tolstoy's *War and Peace*. "My library is becoming quite impressive," she quipped.

After that, only one box remained. The tag read "From Will." Mandy looked around again. "Has anyone seen Will?"

"He sends his regrets," Gus announced. "Says he's catching an early train from Point Reyes Station and decided to bunk there tonight. What some people will do just to sleep in." Everyone laughed except Mandy. *He can't face me*, she thought. *He thinks he made a mistake.*

She took her time opening the gift, prompting Kit to say "Hurry up, we're growing moss over here."

"It's my last one," Mandy bantered back. "I've got to make it last, don't I?" In truth, she felt sadness slithering inside to lurk beneath her heart.

She opened the box and pulled out a leather briefcase. But not just any briefcase that a man might use. Hers was distinctly feminine, smaller with rounded edges, made from the softest golden brown leather she had ever touched.

Her name was embossed just beneath the handle: *Amanda Marie Culpepper*. And on the front was a vertical column of Chinese calligraphy, discreetly etched. She held it up to Cheung ti Chu. "What does it say?"

He looked at it. "It's a well-known proverb. It says 'the palest ink is better than the best memory.'"

Inside the briefcase was a journal bound in the same leather. It had a leather tie that held the book from casual eyes. Mandy untied the book and opened it. A note slipped out, which read: "Whether it be writer, model, or philanthropist, you are magnificent. Never forget that."

Tears welled up before she could stop them. She quickly folded the note, stuck it back in the journal, and re-tied the string.

"What did the note say?" Frieda called out.

"Oh, just that I should keep writing," she parried. She stood up and looked at the faces of the people she had come to love so much in the last few years. "I am so happy that you all came to celebrate my birthday." The tears were now starting to course down her cheeks. "I will never forget your kindness and your friendship. Truly."

Gus stood up and helped his wife do the same. "Don't know about you all, but I hear tell Mrs. Coats has baked the most delicious birthday cake this side of the Rocky Mountains. She'll tan my hide if we don't all take a piece of it."

Mandy stayed behind while her guests made their way back to the dining room for chocolate cake and homemade strawberry ice cream. Gus touched her shoulder.

"He said he overstepped his bounds," he said quietly. "Did he?"

"No! That is...he didn't do anything I didn't want him to do."

Gus nodded. "I thought as much. He sets pretty high standards for himself, Mandy girl. You going to be able to handle that?"

"I don't know," she whispered. "He may not let me." She let out a shaky sigh and the tears started to flow again. Gus opened his arms and gathered her in, comforting her as her own papa would have done. It was one of the best days of her life, but also the most confusing. She closed her eyes for a moment, wishing she could stay like that for a long time.

"The future always looks better when you're eating cake," Gus said. "Let's go join your guests, all right?"

Mandy nodded, wiped her tears, and put on a smile. It was her birthday celebration, after all.

# CHAPTER FIFTY-TWO

The Qingming Festival always took place on the fifteenth day after the Spring Equinox. This year it was to be held in Chinatown on April fifth.

During one of their planning sessions at the end of March, Cheung ti Chu had told Mandy the name of the festival meant "clear and bright." The Chinese people considered it partly a celebration of spring.

"It is a time for enjoying the outdoors after the cold of winter, for spring plowing…even for young people to begin courting." He paused and caught her eye. "Speaking of which, where is Mr. Firestone? I have not seen him lately."

Mandy felt her cheeks flush. "I…I believe he is out of town on business. At least that is what I've heard." She steered the conversation back on track. "What a lovely reason for a festival. I suppose it's all about rebirth and renewal, somewhat like our Easter?"

The representative shook his head, his voice somber. "No. It is really more about death."

"Death?" Mandy frowned. "How so?"

"In my country we revere our ancestors, I think more than you. We are careful to live a proper life that does not dishonor them. But during Qingming, our forefathers receive special care from us. We sweep off their tombs and pray for them. We give them food and drink and other useful items for the afterlife. It is how we express our gratitude to them. After all, they were the ones who gave us life."

It struck Mandy that whenever she wanted to, she could travel to Little Eden and visit her parents' graves. She'd done it a number of times since her pa's death. Sometimes she just brought flowers, and other times she brought a picnic and sat and talked to them while she ate.

But Cheung ti Chu couldn't do that, nor could any of the Chinese immigrants who had come to "Gold Mountain" to seek their fortune. She remembered how important it was for Tam Shee Low to pay the bone tax and have her husband's remains sent back to China. And how Tam Shee herself, along with Sai-fon, ultimately joined him. She hoped Tam Shee's brother and other family members would honor them during Qingming. Perhaps even take a picnic lunch to their burial place and talk with them.

"I'm sorry you can't be there in person to take care of your family tomb. It must be difficult to be so far away."

Mr. Cheung smiled, a wistful tilt of his lips. "You see things others don't see. I can understand why Mr. Firestone is taken with you."

She could feel the blush spreading once more. "You're mistaken, Mr. Cheung," she said in her best imitation of Donaldina.

"But regardless, it is irrelevant to our business. Now tell me, have you arranged for the stage and the chairs?"

---

The day before the event, Mandy stopped by the Chinatown School of Needle Arts to make sure the costumes for the tableaux vivants were completed. She found Wu Jade attaching a willow branch to the front door of the building. Her friend was now more than six months' pregnant, but still she worked tirelessly.

"We use the willow to ward off evil spirits," Wu explained. "They wander during the time of the festival. If we are not careful, bad things can happen."

"Please don't say that," Mandy cautioned. "It's frightening enough just thinking about all the things that could go wrong with our presentation."

Wu Jade touched Mandy on the shoulder and handed her a small willow branch. "Carry this with you and all will be well." She took Mandy upstairs to show her the clothing for the "living" paintings. Each item was pressed, labeled, and ready to go. Why had she even bothered to worry? Wu Jade had it all in hand.

---

The day of Qingming was indeed clear and bright. As a result of the forced clean-up efforts over the past few years, Chinatown had never looked better. Incidents of plague had all but vanished, and the city's white residents were much more comfortable visiting the mysterious community within their midst.

In the heart of the celebratory atmosphere, Cheung ti Chu had provided the perfect venue for the scholarship fundraiser, complete with custom stage, lighting, dressing rooms, and seating for fifty people. Mandy insisted they keep general ticket prices low, but she set aside the first two rows for more expensive "preferred seating." She'd crossed her fingers that some of those seats would be filled with society matrons—the real audience she was after.

She needn't have worried about that either. The upper crust of San Francisco showed up in droves, filling every seat. Somehow word had gotten around that this was the place to see and be seen, and educating Chinatown's brightest girls was the latest philanthropy to be involved in. Even Will's mother came. Not only that, but Josephine Firestone had brought more than twenty of her nearest and dearest friends. Mandy swallowed her disappointment that she hadn't brought her son as well.

Creating the tableaux vivants proved to be technically difficult, but worth the effort. In addition to Courbet's work, they performed Mary Cassatt's *The Loge* and Edmund Tarbell's *In the Orchard*. Sandy, Mr. Winterfeld, and Mr. Clayton Jones had all contributed original paintings as well. Sandy's, called *Catching Seven Pieces*, depicted three Chinese girls playing a game that looked a lot like jacks in the middle of a Chinatown alley. Mr. Clayton Jones painted two girls eating ice cream cones at the zoo, and Mr. Winterfeld, whose first choice of girls swimming nude had been soundly rejected by the hanging committee, opted instead for a Degas-like scene showing the girls waiting backstage at a theater before dancing. Thanks to Mason Tanner's detailed choreography, the mission girls gracefully moved into place, slowly transforming each painted backdrop into a living recreation of the original work of art. When a painting called for additional models, the girls were joined by The Grove artists themselves. With the help of Frieda's lighting, the effect was mesmerizing and resulted in standing ovations, which caused the girls to giggle and bow too many times at the end of each performance.

Between shows, the city's wealthiest women, who had purchased nearly all the preferred seating, learned about the new scholarship program. Several of them were so impressed, they signed up on the spot.

Those same women, joined by others, also got to know The Grove artists on a more personal level. From the sidelines, Mandy watched with amusement as Mr. Winterfeld and Mr. Edelman competed for the role of "most tortured *artiste*." The ladies seemed to lap it up. Whether the contacts they made would result in commissions down the road remained to be seen, but it was a beginning.

The only person who'd failed to come through was Peter Raines. He hadn't shown up in the morning to take photographs like he'd promised; instead he appeared early in the afternoon, with Lia of all people, to watch the program. Gus, she explained, had been detained at a board meeting and Peter had coincidentally stopped by to see if she needed anything. "Peter can be so helpful at times," Lia said, smiling at the young man and slipping her arm comfortably through his.

*Yes, when it suits him.* Mandy took exactly fifteen seconds to wonder why he'd bothered to come into the city at all, then dropped it in lieu of the hundred other thoughts that took precedent. Fortunately a photographer from *The San Francisco Chronicle* had recorded the entire event and promised to give Mandy copies of his work. She made a mental note: *Don't count on Peter Raines for anything.*

By late that afternoon, Mandy was fairly bursting with pride and her cheeks hurt from smiling so much. She had created something out of nothing and now several girls from the mission would have the chance to go to school. Mr. Winterfeld had pronounced it an earth-shattering achievement, and Mr. Edelman had agreed, albeit in less effusive terms.

She was gathering up her papers when Donaldina came up to hug her with Cheung ti Chu in tow. "Brava, Mandy! You have certainly outdone yourself today."

Mandy gestured to the group cleaning up around her. "Not me—them. Everybody pitched in to make it a success. And you, Mr. Cheung, we couldn't have done it without you."

Mr. Cheung bowed slightly. "A single string cannot make music."

"We must be off," Donaldina said. "Miss King is on the five p.m. ferry and we're collecting her. You will be there tonight, I hope? She's quite an impassioned speaker on the rights of women."

"The Dangui Theater. Yes. I wouldn't miss it. Seven p.m.?"

"A little before. I will save you a seat."

"I too have a guest coming," Cheung added in a light tone. "We will make an evening of it."

Shortly afterward, Mandy left the Six Companies headquarters and caught a taxi back home to Gus and Lia's. She peeled down to her chemise, placing Wu Jade's willow branch carefully on her dresser. She lay on the bed, mulling over all that had happened that day. A certain melancholy wafted over her. It was always a bit of a letdown when a project, even a successful one, ended. And though she hated giving in to it, she couldn't help feeling angry that Will hadn't been there—if not to support her, then at least to support the girls and the mission. He was a major benefactor, for heaven's sake!

The real question was, what next? What did she, Amanda Marie Culpepper, want from her life?

"I want to write," she said out loud to the ceiling. "And I want to make a difference in some small way."

Then she dared to voice that which she selfishly wanted with equal fervor. "I want Will Firestone to love me. I want to make a life with him and create a family all our own."

Mandy's faith had taught her those weren't the kinds of things you prayed for. Strength to face the loss of a loved one, yes. An open mind to new possibilities? Of course. Acceptance of whatever the Lord had planned for your life, certainly. But to pray that someone loves you as much as you love them? With so much hurt in the world, that seemed much too frivolous to ask for.

And so the tears came, winding their way down her cheeks in lazy rivulets. Mandy closed her eyes and let them flow. When she opened them again, she realized she'd nodded off and time was now short. She hopped in the shower and dressed quickly. Since neither Gus nor Lia had returned home, she had just enough time to call a cab to take her to the theater.

In her haste, she left the willow branch on her dresser.

As Mandy was soon to discover, Sieh King King was a tiny young woman with a gigantic heart and mind. She had grown up in Guandong Province, blessed with wealthy and open-minded parents who sent her to missionary school in Shanghai. A few years earlier she had bravely decided to make the journey to America, to learn all she could about western education. She would take what she'd learned back to China, she said, because her country would not survive unless it progressed. It would not prosper until it brought half its population—more than twenty million women—out of the dark ages.

Mandy sat next to Donaldina in the front row of the theater. They had just listened to Cheung ti Chu introduce Sieh King King to a packed house comprised mainly of women. White and Chinese. Young and old. Women in peasant clothing, women in silk. Women whose feet were calloused from working in fields outside the city, and women whose feet were twisted because their culture had told them such deformity was to be desired above all things.

Would Tam Shee have come to this talk? Would she have finally gotten the courage to make it down those stairs and onto the street, if not for herself then for little Sai-fon?

"Today is Qingming and we venerate our ancestors," Sieh began. "We thank them for the life they breathed into us. We honor their memory. But that doesn't mean we must continue to make the mistakes of the past. The world is changing and we must change with it. We can no longer afford a country with so many ignorant citizens who cannot fully participate in the progress of our nation. We must end all practices that keep women from realizing their potential. We must end foot binding. We must end the slavery of the mui tsai. We must end sexual exploitation. We must end polygamy. Then and only then will we begin to fulfill the promise of our ancestors, of a great and prosperous China."

After each of Sieh King King's demands, the audience had responded with shouts of support and cheering. It grew louder and louder in the hall. By the end, she had worked the crowd into a near frenzy. Mandy was so focused on trying to glean all she could from the speaker's Cantonese that it took her a moment to realize the seat next to hers had finally been taken.

By Will.

He leaned over and murmured in her ear, "Such a modern woman...just like you."

Mandy turned to him and saw love shining in his eyes. For her. Her heart sent a joyful surge throughout her body. Will took one of her hands and laced their fingers together. And just like that, she felt at peace. The wisp of an idea floated past before disappearing: *God knows, even if you don't ask.*

She didn't hear much of Sieh King King's remaining words, nor those of the Reform party representative who had sponsored the young woman's speech. She tried once more to concentrate when Cheung stood up to conclude the event.

"We are doing our part here in First City," he said. "Our community leaders have passed new restrictions against those who would keep us all in darkness. The sin and vice and inequality that holds us back shall be no more." Cheung paused and then said a very brave thing. "I support Sun Yat-sen's Three Principles of the People: Nationalism. Democracy. And the Welfare of the People. *All* of the people."

The response to his simple, heartfelt words by the women in the theater was deafening. Mandy leaned forward to make eye contact with Donaldina. The missionary was looking at Cheung, tears rolling down her cheeks, a woman in love.

Mandy looked back at Will and saw that he too was proud of Cheung ti Chu. He gazed at her and raised their joined hands to his lips.

After Cheung came back to his seat Will apologized to the group. "I was stuck at a meeting all afternoon—barely made it here in time."

"So you missed Mandy's triumphant program, then?" Donaldina asked.

"Oh, I saw it, the first performance, at least." He glanced at Mandy and smiled.

"I didn't see you," she protested.

"I didn't want to…distract you. But I was there, and it was astonishing."

Elated, Mandy touched his arm. "It was, wasn't it? And you will never guess. Your mother came later in the day with nearly a dozen friends."

"Did she, now?"

"Yes, she did. And she—" Wait. Of course he would know. He would know because he had told his mother about it. And many others, no doubt. And talked it up in the language he knew so well, the language of those who *have*. That was why so many had shown up. But why had he done it? She looked directly at him and he answered her unspoken question with a look of his own. *For love.* In a rush, she threw her arms around him and buried her face in his neck. "Thank you," she whispered. "Thank you so very much."

Will grasped her lightly by the shoulders so that he could look into her eyes. Then he gently took her face in his hands and kissed her. Sweetly. Lovingly. Thoroughly.

"It looks like we have much to celebrate," Cheung said. "I would like to invite you all to dinner." He glanced at the members of the audience who were slowly exiting the theater. "I've parked in the back. Let's avoid the crowd and go out that way."

Thugs were waiting for them in the alley.

Seven of them. Seven tong highbinders, their pigtails wrapped up inside their high-crowned hats. Within seconds, one man each had grabbed Donaldina and Mandy, ripping their dresses as the women instinctively fought back. Both women screamed at the top of their lungs before large, meaty hands held them silent.

Will caused greater problems, yelling and striking his attackers viciously, finally requiring three men to restrain him.

But Mandy, Will, and Donaldina were merely the sideshow. The animals really wanted Cheung. The two remaining gang members proceeded to tear at him with their fists. Methodically striking. Punching. Pounding. Ripping.

And when his face and body had been pummeled almost beyond recognition, when he could no longer stand, they let him drop and then kicked him. Over and over again.

"You sleep with White Devil, you pay price," the leader of the gang hissed.

Just then Mandy looked over at the entrance to the alley. Three white police officers stood there. Watching. It looked as if one of them wanted to intervene but was being held back by the other two.

Will saw them at the same time. "What are you doing?" he yelled at them. "Help us, goddamn it!" He was rewarded with a cuff to the jaw for his outburst.

The leader of the gang took note of the police. He leaned down and, pulling a large knife out of the back of his waistband, held Cheung's queue in his hand. His move distracted the thug holding Donaldina enough that she wrenched herself away. She reached into her reticule and brought out a small pistol, which she pointed with shaking hands toward the leader.

"Let him go," she said. "Now."

The leader glanced at her, then back down at Cheung. "You no longer Chinese," he spat out, and quickly sliced off Cheung's braid. He signaled to the rest of the gang, who let go of Will and Mandy and darted off down the opposite side of the alley. Will started to run after them but Mandy lurched forward to hold him back.

"Will, no!" she cried. "Let them go!"

Donaldina seemed to be in a daze. She looked down at Cheung and then at the gun in her hand. Turning to face the direction the tong members had fled, she pointed the gun at them, even though they were out of range, and shot until there were no more bullets. Will seemed to realize he might have been shot himself had he run. He calmed down enough to take the empty gun from Donaldina. For an instant she didn't appear to recognize him.

Mandy called out to her. "Donaldina. We must help Mr. Cheung." Only then did Donaldina turn and, eyes brimming, kneel down to help the man she had obviously grown to love so deeply.

———◦⟨⟩◦———

It was nearing midnight. With frustration bubbling just beneath the surface, Will sat with Mandy and Donaldina while they waited for Dr. Justice to patch up Cheung. His injuries were severe, but it looked like he would survive them.

At one point, Mandy got up and used the telephone in the room where they sat. He could tell she was talking to Lia, no doubt letting her know what had transpired.

When the door to the exam room opened, Donaldina rushed forward and put her arm around Cheung. "You'll stay at the mission tonight where we can watch over you."

Will's once cocky friend didn't even raise his head. "No. Please, just take me home now. I need to sleep."

"Then I'll stay with you," she insisted.

Only then did Cheung look directly at her. "No you will not." He turned to Will. "Please, dear friend."

"Of course." They drove the short distance to the mission and dropped Donaldina off.

"I will come to see you first thing in the morning," she said to Cheung.

"Goodbye, Donaldina," he replied, his voice weary. "Thank you for everything."

When they arrived at Cheung's home on Stockton Street, Will got out to help him up the steps.

"We will prosecute the bastards who did this," Will vowed. "And do the same for those cowards in blue who just stood by and did nothing."

Cheung shook his head slightly. His words were slurred because of his swollen lips. "I know which tong did it and why. They are seeing their livelihood melt away and cannot figure out how to replace it yet. As for the police, why should they interfere? It is to their benefit that we kill each other. Less work for them. It is the way of the world." He bowed slightly to Will. "Thank you for all you have done, both for me and my people."

On a whim, Will embraced the man whom he had come to love and respect, despite their differences. "We will do more, I promise you, as soon as you're back on your feet."

Back in the car, Will could hardly bear to look at Mandy. "I'll be taking you home now," he said formally.

"Yes you will," she replied. "To *your* home."

Did she know what she was saying? "I don't think Gus and Lia—"

"They know where I am and where I'll be tomorrow morning. I'll be with you." She looked straight ahead as if that were the end of the matter.

Maybe she was right. They had to talk, and they couldn't do it with her guardians watching over them. Then it occurred to him:

she was eighteen. Technically she was no longer under their wing. He inhaled sharply and let it out. *Remain calm.*

They rode in silence the rest of the way to his place on Russian Hill. When he parked, he walked around to open Mandy's door, but she had already gotten out and was walking resolutely up to the front door.

Once inside, she turned to him, calmly took off his spectacles and laid them on a little table beside the door. Then she looked him in the eyes and said, "Kiss me."

Will hesitated. She couldn't really want him after—

"*Now,*" she said, her voice sharp, "before I—"

Will glared at her and snapped, his mouth imprisoning hers before she could speak another word. *You want me to kiss you? That, at least, I can do well.* The thought careened through his body along with the lust that was always waiting, waiting, to pounce on her. He pushed her against the wall and caught her thick hair in his hands, forcing her to take his thrusting tongue in a crazed attempt to scare her, or prepare her, he didn't know which.

She responded, not like a frightened virgin would, but like a woman who knew exactly what she wanted. She pressed back against him, eager to give as well as take. How could she know? How could she want someone as ineffectual as him? He pushed away from her in disgust, taking in great gulps of air. He watched her breasts heaving beneath her prim shirtwaist.

"What is wrong with you?" he snarled. "Why do you want—"

"Why do I want a man—" she poked him in the chest, her voice somehow strengthened by that brutal kiss "—who tries but doesn't always succeed?"

He stopped short, shocked by her own raw honesty.

"Because you don't, you know. You fall short sometimes. Like the rest of us. You can't predict what's going to happen or control every outcome. You can't fix every problem and right every wrong." Tears began falling down her cheeks, unheeded. "You couldn't save Tam Shee and Sai-fon. Tonight you couldn't help Cheung…and you won't always be able to help me."

She stopped, capturing him with her magical eyes, putting her slim hands on his cheeks. "But you can love me," she whispered. "The way I love you."

He stared at her, searching for the truth in those eyes and finding it, feeling the warmth of her love wash over him, soothing him and exciting him all at once. He wanted to shout to the rooftops how much he adored this woman who, miraculously, loved him back. Unable to contain his joy within words, he poured his love into his kiss, not forced this time, but deep and reverent, an act of worship.

They didn't speak after that. They didn't have to. Will took her by the hand and led her to his room, thankful that Fleming was gone for the night.

He undressed her, piece by piece, and then she stood before him, tall and proud, wearing nothing but her love for him.

Humbled, he paused to cherish the gift she was giving him, but she stepped forward to show him there was no turning back.

She unbuttoned his vest and shirt and took them off. The tattoo on his left bicep caught her eye.

"It looks like the rays of the sun," she said. "Does it have a meaning?"

"It represents those whom I missed most while I was gone." He pointed to each ray as he spoke: "My mother, my father, Kit, Jamie...and you."

She rewarded him with one of her spectacular smiles, then knelt and unbuttoned his trousers. The site of her administering to him, as a willing slave would to her master, nearly undid him. He quickly divested himself of his remaining clothes and stood face to face with her, Adam to her Eve.

He felt the need to give her one more chance. "It's not too late," he offered.

"It was too late for me when I was fifteen years old," she replied. "Even then, although I didn't fully understand it, I knew you were meant for me and I for you."

Will kissed her then, using his lips and mouth and tongue to express what he had been so afraid of for so long. He thought of their ages and Gus's words came to mind... *doesn't make a damn bit of difference.* Gus was right. And suddenly Will felt as light as air.

———◦◦———◦●◦———◦◦———

As a model, Mandy felt comfortable in her nakedness. But she felt even more at ease now, as she lay on Will's bed watching him watch her. The fact that he would soon join his body to hers added layers of delicious anticipation to the joy thrumming through her blood.

He had asked her to lie down and said, "I just want to look at you. Explore you. Just for a moment. You are simply beautiful."

"I'm not. But I am yours," she said. "All yours."

* * *

Sometime later, after he had taken her and their heartbeats had slowed somewhat, they lay entwined, as close as two people could physically be. "I shouldn't have done that," he said lightly.

"Shouldn't have made love to me?" She couldn't help the plaintive tone of her voice.

"No," he said, tucking a stray lock of hair behind her ear. "I shouldn't have spilled my seed in you."

She turned and looked at him, her heart stopping in its tracks. "Do you not want to have children?"

"With you I will want as many children as you're willing to give me," he reassured her. "But I don't want to put the cart before the horse."

Will didn't ask her to marry him, and she would have felt uncomfortable if he had. She couldn't bear the thought of him feeling obligated because of a momentary loss of control. For now, what they had was enough. Or it would be enough once she had made love with him again. She reached between them.

"What do you think you're doing?" he asked with a grin.

"Don't mind me, I'm doing some exploring of my own. Why don't you lie back and close your eyes?"

He did as she suggested, and over the next hour she proceeded to give back the pleasure he had given her, and more.

---

Will and Mandy made love twice more before dawn and fell asleep exhausted in one another's arms. She had never slept naked with someone before. It was heaven to snuggle next to a warm, firm, masculine body.

They awoke mid-morning to the sound of a telephone ringing downstairs. Will did not keep one in his bedroom. After several minutes there was a knock on Will's bedroom door.

"Yes?" he called out.

"It's Donaldina Cameron," Fleming said. "She says it's urgent."

Will put on a robe and planted a quick kiss on Mandy's forehead. "I'll be right back," he said. "Stay put."

He went downstairs but returned in a matter of minutes. The expression on his face told Mandy that something terrible had happened.

"It's Cheung," he said. "He hanged himself last night."

# CHAPTER FIFTY-THREE

*Death never gets easier,* Will thought as he sat with Mandy and Donaldina during the small, impromptu memorial service for Cheung ti Chu. Like Tam Shee Low and her family, Cheung's body was scheduled to be shipped back to his home province for a traditional funeral and burial. But his high standing in San Francisco's Chinese community dictated that a special wake be held in his honor. The new acting President of Six Companies was coordinating the ceremony that would take place the following day, but given the hard feelings between whites and Chinese that had indirectly led to Cheung's death, all parties agreed it would be better for non-Chinese friends to pay their respects separately.

"I should have insisted." Donaldina second-guessed herself to no one in particular. Her eyes remained red and bloodshot, a stark contrast to her too-pale face after three days of mourning. "I should not have left him alone with his thoughts, especially after they cut off his queue."

"Perhaps we all should have realized what that would do to him," Mandy agreed. "He told me once how important it was not to dishonor his ancestors. He must have felt so ashamed that his most visible link to his heritage was gone."

Will took Mandy's hand in his. It was incredible to him how comforting that simple act could be. "He tried very hard to straddle his culture and ours. He felt he was meant to be a bridge. It can't have been easy."

Donaldina said nothing, apparently lost in her grief. When he'd told Mandy about Donaldina's call the morning after the beating, Mandy's first concern had been not for Cheung, but for Donaldina herself.

"She was in love with him," Mandy had told him. "To lose someone you have given your heart to must be the worst pain in all the world." Then she had spontaneously kissed Will with such passion he had reeled from it.

Despite all that had happened, he felt like the luckiest man on earth.

---

Mandy had decided to remain in the city for the next week, until Cheung's body was safely on its way home. She wanted to remain close to Donaldina and provide support wherever she could.

The sadness surrounding their friend's death was palpable, but it didn't diminish Mandy and Will's hunger for one another; on the contrary, it seemed to feed it. *Life is fleeting*, fate seemed to be telling them. *Take what joy you can while you can.*

As much as Will wanted Mandy to stay with him on Russian Hill, they both conceded that discretion was called for, and she moved back to Gus and Lia's estate. Her stay was only temporary, however, because the Wolffs had recently sold the mansion to a developer from Saint Louis.

"We spend ninety percent of our time at The Grove now, so it's a waste of money to maintain two homes," Lia had reasoned. "We love the Palace, so we'll just stay there when we come to town."

Lia had remained in town for a few days after the festival to supervise the packing of the estate's furnishings. She left the bare necessities for Mandy, who would see that the place was completely vacated by the time escrow closed on the fourteenth of the month.

Despite their separate sleeping arrangements, Will found it nearly impossible to stay away from Mandy for long. Fortunately she felt the same. They concocted any number of excuses to be together: lunch in Union Square...a meeting about the scholarship program at the School of Needle Arts...a visit to the de Young Memorial Art Museum to view the latest exhibits.

And whenever they got together, it wasn't long before they got physical. Will simply couldn't keep his hands off her. More than once they nearly broke the rules of public propriety, and on a few occasions—notably an afternoon spent in the Queen Wilhelmina Tulip Garden—they left those rules far behind. They were just damn lucky no one else had chosen to explore the windmill used to bring water to Golden Gate Park.

Practical at his core, Will had purchased a box of rubber condoms, which he kept in his Winton's storage box. Even though the sensations were slightly less intense when he wore the sheaths, he figured he'd have years of pleasure being inside Mandy without the barrier.

Years of pleasure. That of course meant marriage, and if it had been up to Will, he would have whisked her off to a judge immediately and gotten the job done.

But his mother would never have forgiven him, so Will decided to do it right. He would formally ask for Mandy's hand and announce their engagement at a party held at The Grove.

"I want to ask you a question," he said to her over lunch at the Cliff House. That morning at Shreve & Company he had purchased a three-carat diamond engagement ring circled with emeralds and set in platinum filigree. It was spectacular, like she was, and would be ready for him to pick up the following morning. He played with her left hand across the table.

"Ask away," Mandy said.

"No, I want to ask it in a different setting, at The Grove…. in front of Gus and Lia, and my parents." He took her hand and kissed it before gazing back at her. "I guess I just want to know if I'll get the answer I'm looking for."

Mandy smiled at him, her eyes sparkling. He could tell she knew exactly what he was talking about. "What do you think my answer might be?" she teased.

"I hope it would be the same answer I'd give if you were to ask me," he said. "A thousand times yes."

"You would be right," she said, and leaned forward to kiss him. They were lucky to make it back to his car before breaking another one of society's rules.

The day of departure arrived and they met Donaldina, Wu Jade, Fung Hai, and other mission friends at the dock to say farewell to Cheung ti Chu. It was a familiar ritual. They watched his coffin, draped in a black shroud, being loaded onto a cargo ship headed ultimately for Canton. Donaldina was stoic; she seemed to have hidden her grief behind a barrier of firm resolve.

"We will see the new face of China emerge right here in our city," she vowed. "I will make sure it's the face Cheung wanted so much to see." She turned down their offer of lunch in order to return to the mission. "There is much to be done," she said.

Two days later escrow closed on the Wolffs' mansion and Will took Mandy to catch the mid-morning ferry to Sausalito. "I'm going to tie up some loose ends here today and I'll follow you tomorrow," he said. "That way we'll both be there to greet my parents on the sixteenth. Gus and Lia have agreed to host a luncheon and have them stay overnight if they want to. Is that all right with you?"

"It is more than all right with me," she said, "but I'll miss you all the same."

Just the words brought Will intense satisfaction. *I've got it bad...and that's good.* He took Mandy in his arms and lowered his mouth to hers. Their kiss started out chaste but rapidly turned carnal. Only the sound of the ferry's horn broke them apart.

"Until tomorrow," he said.

<hr />

Wanting to surprise both his parents and the Wolffs with the engagement announcement, Will had merely invited his mother and father to tour The Grove, leaving out any word of his romantic intentions. His mother was thrilled by the invitation and excited to see the place he'd mentioned on so many occasions.

"We'll be there with bells on," she told him.

But Josephine had a surprise all her own. When Will arrived at Point Reyes Station to pick them up, she'd brought along some extra guests. One was his sister Kit, but the other three...the other three made him want to howl with rage.

# CHAPTER FIFTY-FOUR

*Mandy's Journal*
*April 16, 1906*

Dearest Pa,

It's funny how I always feel the need to write to you when something that means so much to me is happening. How I wish you could be here on what I do believe will be one of the happiest days of my life. I am almost certain that Will is going to ask me to marry him, in front of Lia and Gus and his parents. They will arrive soon and I should be taking this time to get ready, but I am so excited that I just had to tell you about it.

The past three years have been so life-changing for me, almost like a Cinderella story. I don't like to think that your passing helped bring it about; I'd rather believe that somehow, some way, I would still have met Will Firestone and come to love him as much as I do.

Regardless of how we came to this point, we are here now and I am ready to burst with joy. He loves me, Pa. He will be a good husband, and a wonderful father. I in turn plan on making him as happy as it is possible for anyone to be. So in case you have worried about what will become of me, there is no more need to fret. My future is all that I could have ever wished for.

Mandy closed her journal and set it back on her writing desk. She'd decided not to record *everything* that had happened to her in the last ten days. For instance, the things Will had done to her in the forest yesterday afternoon were nothing short of scandalous and would remain just between them; the memories alone were enough to set her heart pounding and her insides to bubble with delight.

Today she was determined to play the part of a proper young woman, one whom the Firestones would be proud to consider part of the family. She put on a pretty pale-blue shirtwaist with a matching blue-and-white-striped skirt. And instead of trying to do something fancy with all her hair, she merely held it back with a ribbon. An image crossed her mind of what naughty things Will might do with such a ribbon, and she had to bite the inside of her cheek to keep from smiling. It would never do to be fantasizing in the presence of her future parents-in-law!

She glanced at the clock on her dresser and realized Will would be returning with his parents at any moment. She ran down the stairs and glanced at the dining room on her way out the door. Mrs. Coats was putting more settings on the table. "Oh. Are more people coming?"

Mrs. Coats shrugged. "Mrs. Wolff seemed baffled when she told me to add four seats," the housekeeper explained. "Said that Will's mother called and asked if they could bring their daughter and a few more guests. Sounds rather cheeky to me, but there it is. I'm just glad I made plenty for lunch is all."

Who else was coming? Mandy's question was answered a minute later as she saw Will swing the buckboard around in front of the Great House. In the back of the wagon sat Will's parents, Kit, and another older couple. But sitting next to Will with her arm snuggled possessively through his was none other than Beatrice Marshall.

Apparently there'd been a disastrous change of plans.

# CHAPTER FIFTY-FIVE

"Dirty business, that head Chinaman getting roughed up like that." Clarence Marshall offered his opinion during pre-luncheon cocktails in the library. "I heard he died of his injuries, but at least they can't blame it on the whites this time."

Bea's father was a florid, barrel-chested man with graying, ginger-blond hair and a love of both money and drink. The city's rumor mill had it he liked his women, too.

Will made eye contact with Mandy and shook his head slightly. She still looked shell-shocked by Bea's unexpected arrival, but her inclination would be to set Marshall straight. The lout wasn't worthy of her. Will would handle it. "Mr. Cheung was attacked by tong members who were against his efforts to clear his community of excessive vice," he said. "He was a true hero."

"Indeed, he was quite a modern thinker," Will's father added. "He worked hard to do right by his people and he'll be greatly missed."

"Listen, it don't make sense. We got ourselves a gorgeous city, with a junkyard right smack dab in the middle of it called

Chinatown." Marshall downed his second gin and tonic. "If it were up to me, I'd send them all back where they came from."

"Well, I'm sure as hell glad it's not up to you, then." Gus didn't suffer fools nearly as often as Will did; Marshall had better watch his step.

"Poor Mr. Marshall, you do know we've entered the twentieth century, don't you?" Kit asked in a discreetly condescending tone of voice. "Perhaps you ought to brush up on your Emma Lazarus. You'll find her work at the base of the Statue of Liberty."

Will grinned for the first time that day. Kit loved to skewer blowhards with a lethal pin prick rather than a sword. He glanced at Mandy; she too was fighting a smile. Thank God. They would get through this.

They were spared further argument on the topic by Mrs. Coats, who announced that luncheon was served. Bea immediately took Will's arm and insisted on sitting next to him. Mandy hung back, and by the time she entered, the only available seat was next to the blowhard at the far end of the table.

Will's irritation increased tenfold. He began casting alternate plans for the day: after lunch he would make excuses to the others, take Mandy aside and propose to her, then quietly explain the situation to his parents. Once they got rid of the Marshalls, they would all celebrate as a family. He mentally kicked himself for not warning his mother ahead of time about what was going to happen. What had she been thinking to invite the Marshalls?

He stopped himself. He knew damn well what she'd been thinking because he hadn't made it perfectly clear that he and Bea were never going to be a couple. In truth he had no one to blame but himself. He began counting the minutes until he could set everyone straight.

It happened sooner than he thought, and in the most horrific way possible.

They were halfway through the meal and Will was trapped in the verbal miasma of listening to Bea recount an insipid story of an outing with some mutual friends when he noticed a commotion at the other end of the table. Kit was glaring at Marshall, who looked surprised when Mandy stood up abruptly, shot a wide-eyed look at Will, and quickly walked out of the room. Marshall shook his head and finished up yet another drink.

Will interrupted Bea mid-sentence. "What happened to Mandy?" he asked Kit.

"Tell him what you said." Kit stared at Marshall, looking unsure of himself for the first time that day. He glanced at his wife, who gave him a disgusted look.

Kit's subtle sarcasm had disappeared. "Tell him!"

"I was merely making conversation..."

"Tell him or I will," Kit growled.

Marshall looked like he'd been asked to eat rotten fruit. "That girl, that Mandy is a fine lookin' woman. Beautiful, in fact. You all know that, it's as plain as day. Well, I was just telling her that Dr. Cotter told me that he knew for a fact she liked to take her clothes off for people, without even bein' paid for it. So I just asked her—just joking around, mind you—when she might be free to come do that for my poker group. She must be quite the little tart, that one." He laughed half-heartedly and looked around. No one laughed back. "Well, that's what I heard."

"You, sir, are a cretin," Kit said, getting up and leaving the room to find Mandy.

Will looked at Gus, who was steaming and about to bodily throw Marshall out of the house. He stood up, walked to the head of the table, and put his hand on Gus's shoulder. "Please. Everyone. I have something to say.

"First, I want to apologize to our hosts for not being straightforward about the reason for today's visit. I wanted it to be a surprise for everyone, but the surprise was on me. And Bea, I am so very sorry if I have led you on. You deserve someone who...who will appreciate all of your fine qualities. That person is not me."

He turned to Josephine. "Mother, I asked you and Father to come today to share my joy. Because the woman you have just grossly insulted, Marshall, the woman you have dismissed as a 'tart,' is in fact the woman I love more than life itself. I am about to ask her to be my wife."

Bea looked extremely embarrassed, as if she'd been caught in public in her underwear. But Will's mother appeared completely flummoxed; for once Josephine didn't have a handle on the situation.

"Darling," she sputtered, "Mandy is a nice young girl and we all adore her of course, but do you really think she is...do you really feel she's appropriate for you? That she's the best you can do?"

Edward, Will's father, took his wife's hand. "Ill advised, darling."

Will looked at his mother as if she'd grown two heads. "Appropriate for me? *Appropriate?* What does that mean? Does she have the right pedigree? Does she come from good enough *stock*?

"Let me tell you about the woman who just left. Marshall? You're right about one thing: Mandy is beautiful. Exquisite in fact. But what she looks like on the outside is nothing, *nothing* compared to who she is on the inside."

He looked around the table and then back at his mother. He leaned his hands on the table. "Do you see me, Mother? Do you see me standing here? Because I wouldn't be here if it weren't for Mandy. You and Father never knew this, but I...I found myself in a situation where I became very ill, and it was contagious. Kit wanted to care for me but Dr. Justice wouldn't let her. He was afraid you'd lose two of your children. Imagine that. *Two of us*. Kit's still mad at him for doing that, but he was right.

"Yet someone had to step in," Will continued, "and do you know who did?" He pointed in the direction Mandy had gone. "Mandy stepped in. She told them, 'It's all right, I have no one waiting for me.'" Will didn't realize tears had formed. He blinked them away. "No one waiting for her. No father, no mother, no sibling. No one. She was willing to die for me.

"But she vowed she'd keep me alive and she did. I didn't even know it was her, but she bathed me when I was burning with fever, and kept me warm when I thought I was going to freeze. She stayed with me through the worst of it and didn't say a word when I treated her shamefully—even after I was on the mend."

He pointed again. "I cannot begin to tell you all there is to know about that woman, but I can tell you this: she knows me. She *knows* me. And she understood me even before I understood myself.

"And do you know what the most amazing thing of all is? She loves me. Me, who is not nearly the best that *she* can do. Now if you'll excuse me, I'm going to go upstairs, get on my knees, and beg her to marry me before she figures that out."

Will left everyone sitting in stunned silence except for Gus, who called after him, "It took you long enough."

He took the stairs two at a time and knocked on Mandy's bedroom door. Kit answered with a grave expression and ushered him inside. She shut the door quietly on her way out.

Mandy sat on the bed with red-rimmed eyes and a hand-kerchief crumpled in her hand. Will wasted no time. He knelt in front of her and pulled out the ring that had been burning a hole in his pocket all day.

He was about to speak when she held up her hand. "Please don't."

And Will felt the bottom fall out of his heart.

# CHAPTER FIFTY-SIX

"Mandy, I—"

Mandy knelt on the floor so that she was facing Will at his level. How could she give up this wonderful man whom she had loved for so long? But loving him, how could she not? She inhaled deeply. His scent entered her and she tucked it safely away. She would never forget it. "I've thought about it and Mr. Marshall may have done us a favor," she began. Even as Will shook his head, she pressed on. "He gave us a taste of what it would be like being hitched to me." She pressed her small hand against his cheek. "How could I do that to your parents, much less to you?"

Will closed his eyes and covered her hand with his own. And when he opened his eyes he looked at her with such, such *longing* that she wondered if his eyes were a mirror into her own soul.

He began in a calm, controlled voice. "I told you that on my journey I discovered a lot about myself. But there was one thing I didn't tell you. Do you remember what you wrote?"

Mandy's eyes grew wide with trepidation. "What...what I wrote?"

"In your journal. You left it when you went upstairs the morning I left home. I glanced at the last page—and yes, that's all I read. You said…"

She swallowed. "I said you were in search of the key to your own true heart."

He nodded. Gazed at her.

Mandy's entire being began to tumble with emotions like that old roller coaster. "So…so you found the key?"

"I did. But I didn't fully grasp what it was until I returned. Because when I came back, I realized almost immediately that what I wanted, what I *needed*, was you. You were the key to my heart."

Mandy began to shake her head, but he stopped her. "I wanted you, but I told myself you were the wrong thing to want, that you were too young, that you could do better. But you need to understand this: *never* did I feel you weren't good enough for me."

Could she believe him? Assuming what he said was true, it still wouldn't stop the gossips and the haters. Mandy lowered her head, but Will reached over to gently tip her chin up. "When you started to model, it drove me crazy. Bringing up the social consequences was just an excuse. Inside I was too inept to claim you, yet I couldn't bear the thought of others seeing the beauty that I selfishly wanted to keep for myself. Cotter was right about that, at least."

"But don't you see? Even if you weren't thinking about what it meant for my reputation, others were, and are. I am completely disappointed in Anson, but if not him, it would have been someone else. And if not the modeling, then it would be my upbringing. My station in life. It would always be *something*."

"You're right. There always will be Clarence Marshalls. And Anson Cotters. And if we live our lives trying to starve them of the prattle they feed on, we'd only be killing ourselves. Isn't that what happened to Cheung? It took me long enough to realize it, but in the end only one thing really matters, that we love each other." He searched her eyes. "Amanda Marie Culpepper, I love you with all my heart and mind and body and soul. You told me once that you loved me too. Did you mean it?"

She nodded. "Heart and mind and body and soul. So much that it petrifies me. But—"

He held up a finger. "That's all I need to know." He stood up and pulled her gently to her feet. "Given what's happened, I think everyone will be returning to the city on the afternoon train. I'm going with them. Come with me."

Mandy trembled. "Oh, I couldn't. To travel all those hours with the Marshalls would be...excruciating."

Will began to pace, wheels obviously turning in his head. "You're right. That is asking too much." He grinned at her. "They don't deserve the pleasure of your company, anyway." He took a few more steps, absently removing his eyeglasses, pulling out his shirttail, and cleaning the lenses. Then he abruptly stopped in front of her, popping his spectacles back on, a conclusion apparently reached. "Then come in three days. By then Mother, Kit, and I will have planned the party to end all parties. With your permission I'm going to enlist Kit's help to buy you a gown that shows off your natural beauty to perfection and we're going to announce to everyone who'll listen that William Arthur Reginald Firestone is the luckiest man in the world. Why? Because he's going to make the lovely writer, philanthropist, and *model* Amanda Marie Culpepper his bride. Let the tongues wag. Let's revel in it. Believe me, anybody who aspires to be anybody will want to be there to wish us well. And if they don't, the hell with them." He kissed her exuberantly and she couldn't help but respond. He made it sound so…possible.

Her body began to hum and their kiss escalated from joy to need. Will backed her up to her bed, all the while tasting her and unbuttoning her shirtwaist. He laid her down on her back and followed on top of her, raising her skirt and pushing his leg between hers.

"Your parents are downstairs," she gasped even as she reached into his trousers. "Gus and Lia…"

"Not their party," he murmured as he proceeded to make love to her. He hadn't used protection, but she didn't care. No matter what happened between them, she would cherish any child they made together.

Afterward Will spooned her, nibbling her neck and talking nonsense about the different parts of her that he adored, like her ear lobes and the crook of her neck, all the while pointing them out with a stroke of his tongue or a caress of his hand. He told her about all the good things they would do together for people less fortunate than them…the places they'd see…the stories she'd be able to write…the babies he looked forward to making with her. He began kissing her again, but she reminded him of his plan, and he sighed, at last getting up and dressed in order to catch the train.

"Won't you please take it?" he asked, offering her the engagement ring once more.

She shook her head. She would give him time to really be sure. "I haven't said yes," she reminded him.

He took her in his arms a final time and kissed her deeply. "You will." The self-confident, take-charge Will Firestone was back.

After he left, Mandy lay back down amidst her covers. She had given him an out, but he didn't seem to want it. He wanted *her*. Despite who she was. No. *Because* of who she was.

What she had dreamed of for so long had come true. She had someone who loved her. And he was the very best someone she could have prayed for. She hugged herself tightly to keep her happiness from floating away, daring to hope it might finally settle on her for a while.

Sometimes a while can be a very short time indeed. Two days later Mandy's happiness left for parts unknown.

# CHAPTER FIFTY-SEVEN

—⚜— ——⬦•◉•⬦—— —⚜—

"Oh!" The first jolt ripped Mandy from a restless sleep. It was loud and sharp, like the blow from a giant's sledge-hammer. She gripped the edge of the four-poster as it slid side-ways across the room. "Will," she whimpered, even though she knew she was alone.

It was too early for dawn and the near darkness magnified her terror. What was it? What was it?

In seconds, she knew. The Great House began to roar, rock-ing and shaking violently, heavy roof timbers groaning in protest. Mandy scrambled off the bed and screamed as one of the picture windows shattered. She could feel the cold of the sea air below... could hear the frenzied crashing of the waves against the shore. She watched, horrified, as a large landscape painted by Lia fell from the wall, the canvas tearing on one side. Through the murk-iness she saw the contents of her writing desk—her journal, some letters, a nearly full bottle of India ink—skid off the table and spill onto the floor.

"Oh Lord in heaven," she cried, momentarily frozen before common sense kicked in and she scanned the room frantically for a safe haven. The outer door to her bedroom swung crazily back and forth, but the arched passageway to her dressing room offered the protection she sought. *Arches are strong,* she had read once. She crawled off the bed and wedged her body between the two thick walls, bracing herself for the end of the world. Her thoughts centered on one man as she fought an overwhelming sense of panic.

After what seemed an eternity, the chaos stopped. In its wake an eerie silence reigned, as if even the earth itself were shocked by what had just occurred.

A minute passed. And another. Mandy waited, afraid to move. Was that the worst of it? Would there be another?

Her fear for Lia and the other members of The Grove finally compelled her to act. Were they all right? She had to know.

She pushed herself up from the floor and made her way to her closet to find something serviceable to wear. Pulling on a simple day dress, she stepped into sturdy boots to protect her feet before picking her way back across the glass-strewn floor and out the bedroom door.

Fortunately the stairway was still intact, and she paused on the landing. "Lia?" she called upstairs. Two days ago Gus had headed into San Francisco along with Will and his family. Lia would be up there all alone.

In a moment she heard Lia's faint reply. "I'm coming." She waited and several seconds later Lia, dressed in similar fashion, carefully picked her way down the stairs from her third floor suite.

"Gus should be here," Lia said. "Or I should be with him."

Mandy felt the same way about Will, but that wouldn't help matters. "Nonsense. You're where you are for a reason, and so is he."

A smaller aftershock rattled the mansion. "Oh God," Lia cried, clutching the banister.

They hurried down to the ground floor. Just as they crossed the foyer and reached the front door, it was flung open.

"I was just coming for you—are you all right?" Ignoring Mandy, Peter Raines took Lia in his arms and buried his face in her neck.

Lia looked surprised as she gently pushed him away. "Yes, yes, I'm fine," she reassured him.

Mandy gaped at him. *What was that about?* But there was no time to ponder it, not when they had so many other problems to deal with. She reached for her coat in the entry closet and handed one to Lia. "How are the others?" she asked Peter.

"They're all right—at least those I saw on the way over here were. Shaken up, of course, and crying, some of them. But I don't think anyone's been seriously hurt."

"I hope you're right," Lia said. "But we've got to take a head count. Tell everyone to alert whomever they see: we'll meet in the front gathering room in fifteen minutes."

Peter left to spread the word and within minutes, artists and other residents of the retreat began to coalesce in the main parlor of the Great House. Mandy saw Lia heave a sigh of relief as she noted Sander de Kalb standing in a circle with George Winterfeld and Marcus Edelman, who had his arm around Frieda Mallock.

Gloria Pinyon sat on the couch with John Clayton Jones, who was sniffling. Mason Tanner paced the floor.

Eventually nearly two dozen people, both artists and estate workers, filled the room. Lia stood resolutely in front of the group. "Who's missing?" she asked Peter for the third time. He had written down a list of everyone who should be on the property and was checking them off as they appeared.

"It's looking good," he said. "I think everyone is present and accounted for." He hesitated before adding, "Except Mr. Wolff, of course."

Lia paused, her eyes brimming with tears. Peter reached again to comfort her, but Mandy intervened.

"Gus will be fine," Mandy said in a firm voice. "He's very resourceful. Besides, Will is there, too. They will know what to do."

Lia drew her arm through Mandy's and took a deep breath. "You're right. Of course you're right." She turned to the rest of the group. "As many of you know, Gus went into San Francisco two days ago and is no doubt bossing people around as we speak." The group laughed, grateful to ease some of the tension in the room. "So we'll just have to muddle through on our own. Our first order of business is to make sure we all stay safe." She nodded to the two gardeners standing at the back of the room. "Richard and Lee, would you please start in the kitchen here and then go around to each cabin and be sure there are no gas leaks? And please, everyone, no lighting any fires until we have your stoves checked out.

"Peter, I would like you to find a group sleeping space for tonight that looks like it can handle more shaking, possibly the stables or the life drawing studio. I'm not sure we should chance staying here in the Great House. I believe in an earthquake like this, there can be more damage from the aftershocks because buildings have already been weakened." As if in response, another tremor shook the mansion and the Great House began to sway.

"Enough if you please!" Lia called out. The group tittered again.

Peter squeezed Lia's shoulder and left.

"Mrs. Coats, as soon as Richard checks the gas, will you brew some coffee and see what you can rustle up to feed everyone? I think it's going to be a very long day." The housekeeper nodded and hurried off, no doubt grateful for something productive to do.

Lia turned to the head of maintenance, a muscular-looking older man. "Norris, I'd like you to organize two or three volunteers to check on our neighbors, especially the Wheeler family at Puerta del Mar. The fastest way will be to take the deer trail. We should also see if anyone in the town of Little Eden needs our help. Everyone, after breakfast, please take stock of the damage in your area and above all else, stay safe. Let's all plan to meet back here at four p.m. this afternoon."

As the remaining members of the retreat filed out, Lia sat down on one of the sofas. She looked exhausted. Mandy sat down and put her arm around her friend.

"I meant what I said. Gus is going to be fine."

Lia's tears began to flow in earnest. She looked away briefly before turning back to Mandy. "We parted on bad terms. He wanted to see his old friend Caruso perform, and I accused him of wanting to meet up with that warbling blond from the opera company again. He said why didn't I come with him if I didn't trust him, and I said I did trust him and he said it didn't sound like it and that I was being ridiculous."

"Then what happened?"

Lia sniffed. "He kissed me within an inch of my life and told me he'd miss me and couldn't wait to get back home and practice making babies with me. We decided about a month ago to have one of our own. Oh…" Lia's words turned to sobs.

Mandy hugged her former guardian. "That's wonderful, Lia! You know, you might be the last person on earth to realize it, but your husband is madly in love with you."

"Do you think so, Mandy? Because I know I couldn't go on without him. I wouldn't want to."

Mandy took one of Lia's hands between her own. "I *know* so. Just as I know that he and Will are going to survive this terrible event and come back to us."

Lia looked at Mandy closely. "You've accepted Will's proposal, then?"

It was Mandy's turn to look away, a hint of moisture in her eyes. When she turned back, she felt a blush creep over her. "Not officially, no. But he is…determined."

Lia squeezed Mandy's hand. "He's a good man. After you left, he let all of us know in no uncertain terms how much he wants you and why. He absolutely adores you, and with good reason. I have no doubt that you will easily win over any and all skeptics."

"Like his mother?"

Lia smiled. "Josephine is a pistol, but her heart is golden and her love for her children is limitless. Now that she knows how much you mean to her son, she will do everything she can to ease your way into their world."

"If you're right, then I would say we are both pretty darn lucky, wouldn't you?"

Mandy watched as Lia surveyed the room. Vases had fallen, their flowers strewn across the floor. Shelves had lost their contents and chairs had slid from their customary locations. The room looked as though someone had destroyed it in a fit of temper. "Lucky?" Lia chuckled without mirth. "I'm not so sure about that." She stood up and straightened her skirt. "But you're right, there's no time for a pity party. I'm sure that any time now we'll be seeing them, or hearing from them, or—" she waved her hand as if to encompass the whole of the situation they faced "—something."

—————————

But the day wore on and no word came from either Gus or Will. Along with the other members of The Grove, Mandy began the long, laborious process of cleaning up, stopping now and again to calm herself as smaller aftershocks jolted her fear back from where she had stuck it in her mind.

A few of the cabins had been damaged by falling trees, although fortunately no one had been seriously hurt by the toppling giants. The artists and staff members worked together to keep the paths clear and to shore up structures until more substantial repairs could be made. Perhaps for others the time went by quickly, but for Mandy it slowed to a crawl. Finally, in the early evening, Mrs. Coats' brother showed up on horseback to relay the news that the entire city of San Francisco was engulfed in flames.

"They're sayin' the fire chief died in the quake," he explained to everyone who had gathered back at the Great House. "The water mains all broke so they been tryin' everything they know to stop the flames from spreadin'—even usin' dynamite. But some say it's just making it worse. There's whole neighborhoods gone—Nob Hill. Russian Hill. Chinatown. They say it's surely hell on earth."

Mandy listened to the young man and tried to maintain a façade of tranquility when inside she was beginning to succumb to frustration and fear. Why hadn't they sent word? Why weren't they *back*? The various possibilities, all of them bleak, began to play themselves out in her fevered imagination. Russian Hill gone? Could Will be stuck in his home, trying to get out?

And Chinatown—what about Donaldina? Wu Jade and Fung Hai and the school?

Because of that worry she only caught the tail of the man's story as he ended with the words "Palace Hotel."

"Palace Hotel?" Mandy asked. Gus would probably be staying there. "I'm sorry, what were you saying?"

"I'm sayin' the Palace Hotel burned to a crisp," the messenger said. "It ain't no more."

Mandy looked over at Lia, who had turned pale as a sheet.

"Thank you for sharing the news," Lia said, her voice unusually soft. "I'm sure your sister can find you something to eat, and you're welcome to stay the night. Now, if you all will excuse me."

She headed outside, but when Mandy tried to go with her, she waved her off. "See to the others, won't you?" she asked before heading in the direction of the deer path. No doubt she was seeking the healing atmosphere of the cove. Peter scooted by and caught up with Lia. They exchanged words, although Mandy couldn't make them out. He walked with her a bit farther and when they turned the corner, she couldn't see them anymore. Peter was a toadie, for certain, but maybe Lia could use that kind of fawning support right now. She would check in with her later.

The following day dawned and still no word. Their lives turned into a tortuous game of wait and see. Ever since hearing about the loss of the Palace, Lia seemed to be in shock. She kept to her room most of the time, leaving Mandy to organize whatever clean-up or safety efforts needed to be undertaken.

Strangely absent was Peter Raines. In fact, after watching him with Lia the previous day, Mandy hadn't seen hide nor hair of him, nor had anyone else.

"He's simply vanished," Sandy told her. "His cabin's cleaned out and he's gone."

Typical, Mandy thought. I knew he couldn't be counted on.

Mandy went about her business as if in someone else's story. She couldn't, simply couldn't go down the road of thinking Will was gone. Somehow she would know, in her soul, if something had happened to him. Wouldn't she?

On the third afternoon she saddled up Rowena, one of the horses from the stable, and rode down to the village of Little Eden. A number of the buildings had sustained damage, but no one was seriously hurt there either, thank goodness. After stopping by to check on Sarah and Dell and the children, she headed toward the little cemetery on the far edge of town. There she hobbled Rowena and gave the horse an old apple before sitting down on the green grass to eat a bit of lunch in front of her parents' headstones. The earthquake had tumbled several of the monuments onto their sides, but her parents' markers had held upright. Despite the circumstances, she felt at peace.

"I keep having to learn the lesson, don't I, Pa? Our lives can change in a moment. In the falling of a branch, or the cold of a storm…or in a rumble beneath the earth. And what we thought we knew before is nearly wiped away." She thought about it. "But not completely. We have our memories, don't we? We have our chicken and dumplings, and our soft, soft quilt. If we are left with stories, we can write them down to keep them safe." She thought of Lia and touched her own stomach. "And maybe, if we are very lucky, we are given something else to remind us of what we had. So even if the worst should happen, it's possible to find something good."

She lay down on the grass, closed her eyes, and listened to her heart to see if it was telling her something she ought to know. And after several quiet moments, it did.

---

Mandy pushed poor little Rowena to her limits galloping back up that hill. She remembered riding Old Buck the same way the day her pa died. Rowena was all lathered up, that sweet horse, she worked so hard.

She was nearly out of breath herself as she pulled Rowena up at the entrance to the barn. Joey, one of the stable hands, was working nearby and she asked him if he'd give Rowena a good rub down and extra oats. "She's earned it," Mandy said.

She raced back up to the Great House. Lia had taken over a small back parlor as a temporary bedroom in case of a too-strong aftershock. Mandy found her there, curled up like a little girl facing the back wall. When she rolled over at the sound of Mandy's voice, Mandy was shocked to see how distraught Lia was. Her hair was disheveled and her eyes were like black sockets. She appeared to be in some sort of a daze.

"This will never do," Mandy said, gently bringing Lia to a sitting position. "Gus is coming back today and you need to be your best for him."

Lia grabbed her arm, her grip surprisingly strong. "What? Have you heard anything?"

"No, but I know Will and I sense it. I feel it. He's coming back. And so is Gus."

"If you're wrong, it will kill me," she said.

"I am not wrong. Come on, it's time to get ready." She located a basin, a washcloth, and some water, and helped Lia with her ablutions. Then she ran upstairs to find clean dresses for both of them. Within an hour, they were both ready to greet their men.

Who didn't come.

And didn't come.

And still Mandy waited patiently, until her heart told her he was near and she took off, running down the hill to meet the two old plow horses who were heading toward her. And when Will saw her, he spurred his horse on the best he could, pulled back on the reins right in front of her and jumped off, grimacing hard. He took Mandy in his arms, saying nothing, but bringing her down with him as his leg gave out. Mandy looked up as Gus rode by, a man on a mission.

"She's waiting for you," Mandy called.

Gus nodded. "Will smashed his knee pulling someone out of a house. Shouldn't have traveled, but I've never seen a man so bound and determined. Never." With that he dug in his heels and headed up the hill.

Mandy took Will's ravaged face between her hands and said one word:

"Yes."

He smiled, reached into his pocket and pulled out a very small, dirt-covered box. The ring inside was still shiny and innocent, as if it had no idea what monumental tragedy had just occurred. He put the ring on her finger. "Now I'm home," he said, and wrapped her in his weary but loving arms.

**THE END**

# THANK YOU

Thank you for reading *The Depth of Beauty*. I hope you will share your thoughts with others via social media like Twitter, Facebook, Google+, and Pinterest. Reviews on Amazon and Goodreads are amazingly helpful, even vital, to the success of the book, so it would be awesome if you posted one. I'd love to hear from you directly as well. Please visit my website at www.abmichaels.com.

*The Depth of Beauty* is part of my multi-generational series, "Sinner's Grove." The series follows different generations of men and women associated with a world-famous artists' retreat on the northern California coast. Some of the stories, such as *The Art of Love, The Depth of Beauty,* and *The Promise* focus on the generation of the retreat's founders, Gus and Lia Wolff. Others, beginning with *Sinner's Grove* and followed by *The Lair,* take up the story in the present day. Each is a stand-alone novel. *Sinner's Grove* and *The Art of Love* are both available on Amazon, Barnes & Noble, and other online booksellers. *The Lair* is currently available on Amazon as well.

---

## THE ART OF LOVE

With nothing but a strong back and a barrel full of ambition, August Wolff finds wealth beyond measure in the frozen wilderness of the Klondike. Success, however, comes at an unbearably high price. Now Gus walks alone, and all the money in the world can't buy him what he needs.

In the late 1800's, when women are largely seen and not heard, Amelia Starling longs for a life limited only by her imagination. Blessed with abundant artistic talent and an even bigger heart, she dares to defy convention in order to help the ones she loves. Leaving scandal behind, she moves to the boomtown of San Francisco, hoping to make her mark in a man's world, living with the pain of a sacrifice no woman should ever have to make.

Brought together by the city's flourishing art scene, two wounded yet defiant individuals discover a rare connection and long to build a life together after years of loneliness. But society has other plans for them—plans that will tear them apart.

## AN EXCERPT FROM *The Art of Love:*

Gus dressed in formal attire and arrived an hour after the party had begun. No sense in milling around too long and having people think he actually *wanted* to be there. He talked to a few people he recognized and lingered at the back of the ballroom, watching the hoopla unfold. Turns out he'd made it to the Firestones' Pacific Heights mansion just in time.

"And now, may we present *The Family*, a painting by Amelia Starling." Edward and Josephine, Will's parents, jointly pulled a silk cord and the curtain rose, so to speak, on a huge canvas.

The guests erupted in a collective "Oh!" The painting was incredible, unlike any family portrait Gus had ever seen. Instead of everyone in the picture looking straight ahead, they were in the middle of playing croquet on the front lawn of their estate. Will's brother, sister, and Will himself were in it, along with his parents, and Gus got the sense from their particular actions that they loved each other but there was tension too. He started to move through the crowd to see it better, but froze at what, or rather who, he saw next.

"And we are happy to introduce the creator of this brilliant work, Miss Amelia Starling."

The woman who stepped forward, smiling at the crowd, was none other than Ruthie...but not the sweet young girl Gus had met several weeks before. No. This woman was beyond beautiful, her eyes with some kind of color on them that made them seem even larger and more exotic than before, her gorgeous dark hair swept up with some kind of shiny netting woven through it, and glittery diamonds hanging from her delicate ears. And her body. Lord have mercy. Her body was encased in a long, deep-colored dress, a kind of red, he thought, that displayed her breasts and every other curve with elegance and grace. She was magnificent.

Gus was furious.

He strode through the crowd but stopped so that she could see him as she talked to one admirer after another. At one point she saw him and her eyes grew wide. He continued to stare at her and she didn't look away. The man she was talking to—a geezer with money, no doubt—finally had to touch her arm to get her attention. Good.

He waited, patiently, until the crowed had thinned and the Firestones had announced the buffet was open. Then he made his move.

"I take it this is what you meant by 'a little of this and a little of that'," he said.

She smiled awkwardly, looking around the room, probably for someone to come and bail her out.

"No one's going to rescue you this time...Ruthie." He stepped closer and noticed she was breathing rapidly; it was doing wonderful things to her cleavage. "Who is Ruthie, by the way? Did you just make her up on the spot?"

"No. It's my middle name," she explained in a quiet voice. "Look, Mr. Wolff..."

"Oh, so you know *my* name."

"I knew who you were the instant I saw you." Her chin rose. "Your...reputation precedes you."

"Ah. Well, I'll tell you what I tell everybody else: don't believe everything you read." He cocked his head. "Why did you lie about who you were?"

She shrugged her beautiful shoulders. "I don't know. I guess I wanted to hear an honest opinion of my work. You would hardly have been straight with me had you known I painted it."

Gus leaned in to whisper in her ear. She smelled like lavender. "I assure you, Miss Starling, I would be nothing but straight with you."

The young woman stepped back and glared at him. "I'm sure you would be, Mr. Wolff, until the next distraction turned your head." She made a point of looking around the room. "Speaking of which, where is the melodious Miss Lindemann? I don't see her anywhere."

This woman was a pip. Gus wanted more of her. He captured her gaze and answered calmly. "Miss Lindemann and I aren't seeing each other anymore. I haven't been with a woman since before you and I met." He mimicked her perusal of the ballroom, even though most of the guests had migrated to the dining area. "Come to think of it, where is your swain—or swains, as the case may be? Let's see, there's Charles, from the other night, and then there's your *live-in*. What's his name? Sander? My my, how do you keep them all straight?" He smiled wickedly. "Oh dear, there's that word 'straight' again."

Miss Starling's delectable face, which had shown wariness before, now exploded into a storm of outrage. Apparently so mad she didn't care who saw her, she pulled her arm back to slap Gus's face. He caught her arm easily and wrapped it around his waist. Once again he pulled her close and nuzzled her. "I don't give a damn who you're with today, as long as you're with me tomorrow."

"That is never going to happen," she hissed.

"Never say never," he said, letting his breath caress her ear. He let go of her and stepped back, his voice rising to a normal level and his tone serious and heartfelt. "I am giving it to you straight, Miss Starling. I don't know a lot about art, but I do know how something makes me feel. Your work is astonishing. You know how to capture the...what shall I call it? The *truth* of a given moment. That is rare and something to be very, very proud of."

The siren opened her mouth but no words came out. As they stared at each other, Will walked up. "Ah, I see you've finally met Lia," he said. "Isn't she spectacular?"

Keeping his eyes on her, Gus concurred with a murmured, "Yes indeed. Spectacular." *That's not the half of it* careened through his head. He had to have this woman. Had to. He smiled and added, "If you would be a good sport and escort Miss Starling to the dining room, I'm afraid I have to leave. Business, you know."

Will rolled his eyes. "Come on, Gus. It's New Year's. You can take a least *one* day off."

"No rest for the weary," Gus said, heading over to the cloak-room. He stopped halfway and turned around. "Miss Starling. Amelia *Ruth*. It was a pleasure to make your acquaintance. I love your work and want to talk to you more about it. I'll be in touch. You can count on it." He smiled at the frown he put on her face, turned around again, and left before she threw something at him.

---

## THE PROMISE

April 18, 1906. A massive earthquake has decimated much of San Francisco, leaving thousands without food, water or shelter.

Patrolling the streets to help those in need, Army corporal Ben Tilson meets a young woman named Charlotte who touches his heart, making him think of a future with her in it. In the heat of the moment he makes a promise to her family that even he realizes will be almost impossible to keep. Because on the heels of the earthquake, a much worse disaster looms: a fire that threatens to consume everything and everyone in its path.

It will take everything Ben's got to make it back to the woman he lovesand even that may not be enough.

*The Promise*, a stand-alone historical novella, is part of A.B. Michaels' "Sinner's Grove" saga.

## SINNER'S GROVE

A startling discovery when she was fourteen left San Francisco artist Jenna Bergstrom estranged from her family; unforeseen tragedy only sharpened her loneliness. But now her ailing grandfather needs her expertise to re-open the family's once-famous artists' retreat on the California coast. The problem? She'll have to face architect Brit Maguire, the ex-love of her life.

Seven years ago, Maguire spent a magical time with the girl of his dreams, only to have her disappear from his life completely. Now she's back, helping with the biggest historic renovation of Brit's career. No matter how deep his feelings still run, Brit can't afford the distraction of Jenna Bergstrom, because something is going terribly wrong with the project at Sinner's Grove.

**AN EXCERPT FROM** *Sinner's Grove:*

"What the hell?!" Brit turned around when a second explosion followed on the heels of the first. He immediately wrapped his arms protectively around Jenna.

"My God, was that a bomb?" she cried. She couldn't believe what was happening. She quickly dropped her leg and straightened her dress, fear turning her passion into panic.

"I don't know," Brit said grimly. "Let's find out."

They ran out of the building, passing several workers and a few investors rushing in different directions with terror-stricken faces. The street lights had not gone out, and Jenna saw her brother across the lawn.

"Jason! Do you know what happened?"

"It looks like the equipment barn blew up!" he called as he ran in that direction. "I just called 911."

"Anybody hurt?" Brit yelled.

"Don't know yet!"

Brit took Jenna by the shoulders. "Go back to the Great House. I'll check it out."

"Not in your life," she shot back. "I'm staying with you."

Brit nodded curtly and started running toward the maintenance area. Thankful she'd worn flats to the presentation, Jenna easily kept up with him. As they crested the hill, Brit stopped short and stuck out his arm to keep Jenna from running past him. "Too dangerous!" he yelled.

She grabbed onto his arm to stop her momentum. *Oh my God— this is hell on earth.* The front two-thirds of the huge barn was a fireball shooting flames a hundred feet into the sky. And the heat was so intense, she felt as if even her blood was boiling. Smoke was everywhere, sucking the oxygen from the air. Men were shouting and running back and forth, trying to be heard over the roar of the inferno. *Please keep Jason and Da away from this,* Jenna prayed, her breathing harsh and labored.

"How's it looking, Jack?" Brit called out to the man he'd pegged to help manage the crew.

"Not good." Jack, looking disgusted, tossed a hose on the ground where it joined several others coiled haphazardly in the gloom like somnolent snakes. "Whoever did this cut the hoses. We can't get any pressure, so we're down to a bucket brigade until the fire trucks get here."

"Everybody accounted for?"

"I think so, but it's pretty crazy right now. Maybe we oughta do a head count."

Brit looked around in frustration. In the distance sirens could be heard. "Good idea," he said. "Maybe—"

"Mr. Maguire! Mr. Maguire!" Parker Bishop and Kyle Summers ran up to the group.

"What's wrong?" Jenna cried.

"I think...I think—" Parker seemed to be particularly anxious.

"Spit it out, man," Brit barked.

Jenna glared at Brit. "Give him a chance to calm down!"

"We think…we think maybe that guy Lester's still in the building!" Kyle said.

"How do you know?" Brit asked sharply.

"We were on litter patrol down around the lower bungalows. Parker said he saw him go inside."

"How could you see in the dark?" Jenna asked.

"I think it was him, but I don't know for sure." Parker hedged.

"The light wasn't that good, but we saw *somebody* go inside and close the slider. You can tell when that big sucker closes," Kyle explained. "I didn't think much of it and kept working."

"Me too," Parker said.

"No, you were on the phone, dude, remember?"

Parker nodded. "Yeah, that's right. My dad called. And then, *Kablam*! So we started running back here."

Brit didn't waste a second. "Anybody seen Lester?" he yelled to the members of the makeshift fire crew.

A chorus of "no's" came back.

"Jack, you got a master key on you?" he called out.

The man shook his head.

"Get one!" Brit yelled. He then headed toward the back of the barn.

"Where do you think you're going?" Jenna cried, grabbing his arm.

"If he's in there, there's a chance he's in the back and can't get out," Brit said. "He may not be able to get to the side door. We've got to get it open and help him out."

"But you're not going in after him, right?"

Brit paused and looked at Jenna, running his fingertip down the side of her cheek. "Don't worry." With that he took off, glancing back once before he turned the corner of the building.

Speechless, Jenna watched his retreating figure as if in slow motion. She noticed vaguely that Kyle and Parker had walked up on either side of her. Kyle put his arm around her shoulders.

"It's all right," he said soothingly. "We're here."

Jenna turned and looked up at the large, muscular young man. He had the same glittery look he'd had the last day of school. Then she looked at Parker. He was staring at Kyle and his eyes burned fiercely, just as they had that same day. Fear, slippery and cold, slid over her.

"We need to help Brit," she said neutrally, hoping her voice wouldn't betray the anxiety threatening to overtake her.

By the time she worked her way safely around to the side of the burning barn, several burly workmen were in the process of battering the side door with what looked like a large fence post. The door was already starting to buckle from the heat. When it finally gave way, smoke billowed out and Jenna watched in horror as Brit tore off his jacket, tie and shirt, soaking the latter in a nearby bucket and wrapping it around his nose and mouth.

"Don't go in there—please!" Jenna cried.

Brit looked at her briefly, his eyes communicating what words could not. Then he disappeared inside the carnage. Moments later another deafening explosion ripped apart the air.

"Nooooo!" Jenna screamed. Tears streaming down her face, arms wrapped around herself to keep from falling apart, Jenna stared in shock at the burning, crumbling building, her only words a mantra-like "please God, please God, please God."

She felt someone—Parker, perhaps—urge her back from the heat of the fire, but she couldn't seem to move. Her entire focus was on the jagged hole into which Brit had run. She couldn't believe he was gone. Wouldn't believe it. He was going to walk out again. Any second now. Any second. Any second.

---

## THE LAIR

After her father dies in a boating incident, innkeeper Daniela Dunn must travel from Northern California's Sinner's Grove back to Verona, Italy and her childhood home, an estate called the Panther's Lair. It's a mansion full of frightful memories and deeply buried secrets, where appearances are deceiving and the price of honesty is death. As Dani is drawn further into her family's intrigues, she has an unlikely ally in handsome Marin County investigator Gabriele de la Torre. He says he's come along merely to support her, but his actions show he has an agenda all his own.

Gabe de la Torre needs to settle old family debts before starting fresh with the woman he feels could be The One. But once Dani finds out whom he's beholden to, all bets might be off. When a mystery woman reveals that Dani's father may have been murdered, the stakes rise dramatically and Gabe realizes they're now players in a dangerous game. Protecting Dani becomes his top priority, even as she strives to figure out whom she can trust: her relatives, Gabe, or even herself.

**AN EXCERPT FROM** *The Lair*

"Nothing like a wide awake drunk," Gabe muttered an hour later. They'd gotten back to La Tana and as usual Fausta had grudgingly let them in. "Hey, you can always give us a key," he'd joked, but his aunt had simply turned around and gone back to her room.

Once in their suite, Dani had been asleep on her feet, which were a little unsteady at best, so he'd pointed her in the direction of her bedroom and reluctantly bid her good night. *God she was beautiful.* So elegant, so feminine, even though she didn't put on airs *at all*. He'd spent the entire evening fighting the impulse to touch her everywhere, even in places that demanded privacy at the very least. He'd known instinctively that she'd get along great with Marco and Gina, and she hadn't disappointed him. Man, she was driving him crazy. He heaved a sigh. Both tired and wired, he couldn't tell which was more to blame, the alcohol or the stress of keeping his desire in check.

He reflexively reached into the small refrigerator for a beer before he realized he was already half pickled, so he opted for water instead. Unscrewing the cap, he drank half the bottle while pulling his shirt out of his slacks. To keep his libido in check he decided to focus on something decidedly unsexy. Reaching for the jacket he'd tossed on the back of the sofa, he pulled out the report that Marco had given him earlier that evening.

"I think we're on to something," Marco had told him quietly. "We found a match."

He was just beginning to scan the document when the bedroom door opened and Dani appeared. Her hair was tousled and she walked a bit uncertainly, as if she were slogging through mud in high heels, even though she was barefoot. She wore an ivory-colored cover-up of some kind and she looked nervous.

"I'm ready," she said.

He looked at her quizzically. "Ready for what, bella?"

"For us…you know." He didn't have a chance to reply before she tottered up to him and threw her slender arms around his neck, locking her lips with his.

After his initial shock, Gabe took a moment to enjoy the feel of Dani's curves against him. Jesus, after all that booze his body still reacted immediately, hardening in response to her softness. She felt so damn good—like falling into the most luxurious bed when you've been sleeping on the floor all your life. He smiled inwardly at her inexperienced but earnest attempt at seduction, and cursed his inner cop—the prig who wouldn't let him take advantage of her while she was intoxicated. Reluctantly he took her by the upper arms and peeled her away from his body. "Uh, sweetheart, I don't think this is a good thing to be doing…"

"What?" she asked softly but defensively. "Don't I measure up to your other women friends? Don't I? Just a little?" She stepped back and before he could stop her she dropped the cover-up, revealing a perfect—and perfectly naked—female form encased in a 5 foot two inch frame. Her breasts were full, high, cream-colored mounds with luscious pink nipples. Her waist was small and her hips slightly flared. She was biting her full lower lip, practically screaming for his approval.

An image flashed before him of Dani pregnant. She was ripe and luscious—the epitome of Woman. Instead of cooling him off, the thought of her big with child—*his* child—only made him hotter, and made what he had to do all the more difficult. He looked at her a long time, so long that he could see uncertainty, followed by embarrassment, overtake her. He reached down and picked up the wrap, putting it around her shoulders.

"I...I'm sorry," she mumbled. "I thought ..." She turned to go, but Gabe took her shoulders and turned her back toward him.

"If you think for one second that I don't want to bury myself in you right now, you are sadly mistaken," he said roughly. "When you and I make love, I am going to be all over you. You are going to feel me everywhere and know when I've taken you higher than you've ever been before." He tore himself away and covered her back up. "And the next morning, you're going to remember everything I did to you and want me to do it all over again. Count on it. Now go to bed."

"But—"

"Please," he said firmly, turning her around and practically pushing her back into the bedroom. It took several minutes after her door shut for Gabe's upper brain to start functioning again. "Keep your eye on the prize," he repeated like a mantra. "Keep your eye on the prize." The prize, in this case, was a Dani who felt no regrets about whatever physical gymnastics they might partake in together. He'd waited this long for the timing to be right; he could wait a little longer, even though it was damn near going to kill him.

# ABOUT THE AUTHOR

A native of California, A.B. Michaels holds masters' degrees in history (UCLA) and broadcasting (San Francisco State University). After working for many years as a promotional writer and editor, she turned to writing fiction. She lives with her husband in Boise, Idaho.

CPSIA information can be obtained
at www.ICGtesting.com
Printed in the USA
LVOW11s1711310517
536449LV00002B/415/P

9 780991 508969